HIDDEN PASSIONS

Keso forced himself to step away from Wannie, knowing he had no right even to think what he was thinking. All these years, he'd cherished and protected her as she turned from annoying brat to gangly girl-child to grown-up beauty. In a few months, she would belong to another man.

Maybe if he finally told her how he felt about her, she'd change her mind about marrying Cleve. "Wannie, I . . . I want you to know that, well, I love you."

"I love you, too, Keso," she said absently and looked toward the window where the fireworks flashed. "You've truly been like a brother to me."

He almost cursed aloud at that. "No, what I meant to say was . . ."

She looked up at him expectantly and he felt like an idiot. He'd told her he loved her and she'd brushed it off. There was no need to say more. Wannie—sweet, sweet Wannie. He would die for her, or kill for her, but he would never have her.

Keso wished for a fleeting moment that he was back among the Cheyenne, attacking Wannie's train or stage-coach and taking her captive. As a savage brave, Keso would fight any man who tried to claim her, and Wannie would belong to the victor as a warrior's prize.

If only life were that simple.

ALSO BY GEORGINA GENTRY

WARRIOR'S PRIZE

GEORGINA GENTRY

Zebra Books
Kensington Publishing Corp.

http://www.zebrabooks.com

ZEBRA BOOKS are published by

Kensington Publishing Corp.
850 Third Avenue
New York, NY 10022

First Printing: February, 1997
10 9 8 7 6 5 4 3 2 1

Printed in the United States of America

Two women with the same first name have had a lasting impact on my life. This novel is dedicated with love and gratitude to:

My grandmother, **Sarah Jane Crooks Rushing**, whose passing left a hole in a little girl's life that no one else ever filled,

and

Sara Orwig the best-selling romance author who found me in her university writing class and changed my life forever.

PROLOGUE

It would go down in American history as the last great Indian uprising—that brief time when the Ute Indians of northwestern Colorado rose up against oppression and fought the whites who coveted the Utes' land.

Unaware of the bloodshed about to explode across the rugged mountains, three people rode into this untamed wilderness: a dark-haired beauty accompanied by two very different men. One of this pair was a light-haired, back-East gentleman, the other an Indian brave. The only thing the two men had in common was that both desired the woman as did some of the Ute warriors. She would become a prize to be fought for and won . . .

ONE

Late June, 1879

He had loved her all his life; he realized that now as he stared out the window of the moving train. Did she feel the same or was he about to make a fool of himself?

He would soon find out, Keso thought with a shiver of apprehension. He shifted his tall, muscular frame in the red plush seat even as the engine whistled, shuddered, and began to slow.

"Boston!" yelled the conductor, working his way down the aisle. "Coming into Boston!"

So many people and such big buildings visible through the dirty window! Even Denver, where he seldom ventured, had nothing like this. Wannie had said she would meet the train, knowing he had never been out of Colorado. Keso looked around, aware that other passengers were staring at him. Was it the new suit that fit his big frame so badly? His shoulder-length black hair? Or maybe his bronze, high-cheekboned face?

As the train slowed coming into the station, Keso reached into his pocket to reread the graduation announcement: *The Class of 1879 invites you to the commencement ceremonies of Miss Priddy's Female Academy . . .*

How the time had flown! He stared at her card: *Miss Wannie Evans*. She hadn't been home at all these past four years. He wished now he had written her about how his affection had gradually changed into something much deeper, but he wasn't good with words on paper. His answers had been brief and casual.

He took his little gift from his vest to reassure himself. The antique silver ring gleamed in the sunlight, highlighting the flowers entwined around the band and the old French words: *Pour toujours*. The shopkeeper said it meant *For always*. Keso couldn't read French, but the well-educated Wannie could. When he asked her to marry him, surely she'd say yes. Maybe he was taking too much for granted, even though they'd grown up together.

The brakes screamed as the train ground to a halt. Keso put the ring back in his pocket and looked out the window again. He felt uneasy and bewildered by the sprawling array of buildings, carriages, and crowds of people waiting on the platform in the summer heat.

Eagerly, his gaze searched the crowd. Ah, there she was, beautiful, black-haired Wannie in a stylish sunshine-yellow dress complete with a bustle and an elegant flowered hat. Oh, how she did love clothes and pretty things . . . maybe too much.

He waved frantically, but she didn't seem to see him, even though her brown eyes were searching the length of the train. Grabbing up his carpetbag, he pushed through the crowd and stepped off onto the bustling platform. "Wannie! Wannie! Here I am!"

"Keso!" She came toward him, arms outstretched, flinging herself into his embrace. "Oh, Keso! I'm so glad to see you! I was afraid you'd make a wrong connection and get lost!" She kissed his cheek and hugged him.

She felt so good in his arms. He stifled the urge to kiss her, really kiss her the way he'd been dreaming of. However, the throngs of people were turning to look at the couple and anyway, just to have her in his arms was enough for the moment. She felt so warm and smelled like wildflowers. Reluctantly, he gave her just a quick peck on the cheek. "Wannie, you've turned into a grown-up lady!"

"Spoken like a brother." She laughed, kissed his cheek again, and pulled out of his arms. Then she turned toward the pretty blond girl standing next to her. "I'm forgetting my manners—this is my roommate, Alexandra Griswold. Alexa, meet my big brother, Keso."

Keso made a slight bow to the tall, blond beauty in the expensive peppermint striped dress. One did not need to know much about fashion to know a wealthy, stylish aristocrat when he saw one. "How do you do, Miss Griswold."

"Very well. So you're this Keso I keep hearing about." Alexa Griswold assessed him with a bold gaze, put out her hand, and shook his rather than curtsying. "Such an unusual name. Tell me, what does it mean?"

"Keso? It's actually *Poh Keso*," he said. "It's Cheyenne for 'Fox.' "

Alexa held onto his hand, staring up into his dark eyes as he disengaged his fingers. "Your sister talks about you all the time."

"Good things, I hope." His gaze returned to the dark beauty, wondering how much time would pass before he could be alone with Wannie.

"I've always wanted to meet a real Indian," Alexa said, her blue eyes bright with curiosity. "Have you ever scalped anyone?"

"Alexa!" Wannie gasped. "You're impossible!"

For a moment, Keso was taken aback, unused to such rude behavior. "Well, I haven't tomahawked anyone lately," he said, "but you do have a lovely head of hair."

Alexa threw back her head and laughed boldly. "I suppose I deserved that."

"Alexa, Miss Priddy's doesn't seem to have taught you anything," Wannie sighed.

"I wouldn't say that. You should have met me before my aunt threw up her hands and sent me to the academy."

Alexa Griswold was evidently both spoiled and rich, Keso thought, and such a physical contrast to his petite foster sister. The way Alexa was looking at him in fascination and amusement made him feel like a country bumpkin.

Wannie took his arm. "Come on, Keso, you must be tired. There are rooms on campus for relatives arriving for the ceremonies." She studied him a moment, smiling gently. "We really should get you a new suit while you're here."

Did he look so bad? "This *is* a new suit."

"Oh." Wannie bit her lip. "I—I'm sorry, I forget fashion is always several years late getting to Denver."

"He just has such wide shoulders and a big frame," Alexa said, her blue eyes sweeping over him in unabashed admiration. "He needs custom tailoring. I'm not sure what my family's going to think when they see him."

He started to tell Alexa that he didn't care much what her snooty family thought, but decided it wasn't polite.

"Hush, Alexa," Wannie said. "You'll ruin my surprise."

Surprise? What surprise? Maybe she suspected about the ring, although Keso hadn't even told their foster parents.

"I am tired. It was a long trip." He smiled down into her beautiful, olive-skinned face, loving the feel of her arm linked with his. For the hundredth time, he rehearsed in his mind what he would say to Wannie when they were finally alone.

"Is that all the luggage you brought?" Alexa's eyes widened as she stared at the little carpet bag.

He nodded, feeling like a backwoods hick again.

"Now, Alexa, maybe Cleve could take him shopping and—"

"Who's Cleve?" Keso asked.

"My cousin," Alexa said, "and quite a stylish dandy— his tailor is the best. Come along then," she gestured. "We've got Uncle's carriage."

They started across the platform, Keso keeping his stride short so that the petite Wannie could keep up with him. "Your family's in town for your graduation, Miss Griswold?"

"Actually, my parents are dead. I've been reared by my aunt and uncle. Aunt Bertha's a Griswold. They're coming because they're so delighted I'm graduating, but I wouldn't have without your sister's help."

"Oh, the brat's not really my sister," Keso corrected with a smile. "We're both orphans taken in and raised by Silver and Cherokee Evans."

"They couldn't have been more loving if they were really our parents," Wannie said as they walked. "I'm so disappointed they couldn't come."

"So were they," Keso said with a shrug, "but as the telegram told you, Silver's been down with the grippe and didn't feel up to traveling, and, of course, Cherokee wouldn't leave her. They've missed you terribly."

As I have, he thought, threading his way through the noisy crowds. Well, he could stand this smelly, confusing place a couple of days, knowing that he'd soon be on a train returning to the Colorado wilderness with his beloved Wannie. In his mind, he was already picturing the log cabin he would build for her in the Valley of the Singing Winds with a view of snow-capped mountains.

They paused on the curb and Keso smiled down into Wannie's lovely face, thinking that the first time he had ever seen her, she was a little girl of about four while he was a street kid of ten or twelve. He really didn't know his true age or much about his background.

"Here's the carriage," Alexa said and gestured toward a fine coach and four matched gray horses in silver-studded harness.

"Fine horses," Keso nodded with approval as a coach-man in gray livery climbed down, bowed, and opened the door while taking Keso's bag.

"The Brewsters can afford the best—Uncle Cleveland's rich," Alexa yawned.

"Alexa!" Wannie scolded. "Remember, proper young ladies don't discuss money."

"Admit it," Alexa challenged with a toss of yellow curls. "You love fine things, too."

Wannie colored. "I—I suppose I do."

"Brat, Miss Griswold knows you well." Keso laughed as he assisted the ladies up into the coach, then got in himself, "Even when you were little, you were always playing princess in Silver's dresses, and making me play the prince or the servant, whichever you needed at the moment."

"I guess I was a silly child," Wannie admitted. "You were so patient to put up with me."

I raised you to marry you, he thought, but he didn't say it. "If your mother had lived, she would have been proud."

"Oh, yes, the Duchess," Alexa said as the coach pulled away. "The Brewsters are so impressed with royalty."

Duchess? Keso glanced over at Wannie, wondering just what Wannie had told her roommate. He hadn't even been sure Wannie knew about her past. Wannie ignored his inquisitive gaze and looked out the carriage window at the crowded road.

Keso was dreading the next several days, knowing he didn't fit in among the elegant people of Boston. He should have stayed up in the Rockies and waited for

Wannie's return, but it had seemed a shame for her to graduate with no family in the audience. He resigned himself to Alexa Griswold's empty chatter. Wannie seemed pensive, as if she had something on her mind. Later, he consoled himself; later he and Wannie would have time alone together and he would give her the ring.

"So," Alexa said, staring at him in unabashed curiosity, "I'm just eaten up with curiosity about the details of your family. Wannie is always so vague."

"Maybe she just thinks some things should be kept private," Keso said. He was a very private person and he didn't know quite what to make of this brittle beauty.

"Well," Alexa said, seeming quite unabashed, "I just think it must be a really romantic story about how the Evanses became your foster parents."

"Why?" Keso blinked.

"Keso, I just told her how the Evanses found us both," Wannie blurted. "I know it's not very interesting to you to dredge all this up."

Alexa looked from one to the other. "Of course it's interesting! I can see them befriending an Indian boy in Colorado, but what are the chances of a Spanish duchess dying and leaving her little girl for them to raise?"

Spanish royalty? Keso took a deep breath. "Very small chance, I reckon," he said wryly as he looked past Alexa into Wannie's dark eyes. "My little sister is a very unusual person." He must get this inquisitive girl off the subject until he found out exactly what Wannie had told her. "Do tell me about yourself, Miss Griswold."

Alexa beamed at him and began a long monologue about her uncle, a wealthy manufacturer, and how she had always wanted to see the untamed West.

Keso hardly heard any of it; he was looking into Wannie's troubled eyes. Maybe she didn't know the truth about her heritage—or maybe she didn't want to face it. The truth was ugly. He knew and he didn't care, nor did the Evanses. In the West, a person's actions and character were what counted; nobody gave a damn about your ancestors or your wealth.

Alexa chattered on. Keso nodded at the right times and shifted so he could watch Wannie. He was already envisioning being alone with her. They'd been raised as brother and sister, but somewhere along the line, his feelings for her had gradually changed.

When Alexa finally took a breath, Wannie said, "Keso, there's a party tonight for graduates and their visiting relatives."

"I had thought we'd have dinner alone and catch up on old times, brat," Keso grinned.

"There's plenty of time for that later," Wannie said and shrugged him off. "I've got a gorgeous new dress that goes perfectly with my pearls and rubies."

"Clothes and jewelry," Keso said and grinned, "I thought you'd outgrow that."

Wannie ignored that. "I've also spent the last several years learning the proper etiquette for a ball."

"That's not something you'll have much use for back in the mountains," Keso reminded her.

"There's something I need to tell you—"

"So, Mr. Evans," Alexa interrupted, "with so much gold from that mine, why do the Evanses live in a log cabin in the mountains? Sounds as if they could afford to build a mansion in Denver."

"Why would anyone want a mansion anywhere?" Keso said, trying not to be annoyed. Wannie's shallow society roommate was evidently having a bad influence on her. "The cabin's comfortable and plenty large."

"For servants, too?" Alexa asked.

"Servants? We don't have any servants."

"Maybe Alexa's right," Wannie said. "The Evanses

have plenty of wealth from the Silver Heels mine; they could build a fine house in Denver. Servants would make life so much easier for Silver. Think of the parties and costume balls she could hostess."

Keso laughed. "Brat, you're the one who wants to dress up in fine clothes and jewels. Silver wouldn't care about costume balls."

Alexa continued to stare boldly at Keso. "Did anyone ever tell you that white scar across your eyebrow makes you look terribly interesting? I'll wager you got that in a fight."

Wannie laughed. "I should be embarrassed to admit this, but I hit him with a doll many years ago."

He felt himself color. "I was tired of sitting and having imaginary tea with her toys and wanted to go hunting."

Alexa stared at him. "You must have the patience of Job."

"Where the Brat's concerned, I reckon." He watched Wannie, drinking her in, remembering her as a little girl and thinking his wait had been worth it.

"Keso, I wish you wouldn't call me that childish nickname in front of people," Wannie complained.

"I'm sorry; it's an old habit."

Alexa smiled at him. "I'll be delighted to save you a dance tonight."

"I don't know how to dance," Keso replied. "As Wannie's said, there's not much call for it up in the mountains." The last thing Keso wanted to do was dance with Wannie's snooty roommate. He was already imagining that moment when he would finally get Wannie alone, maybe out on a balcony in the summer night, and give her the ring.

"Really? Then I'll teach you," Alexa answered promptly. "I'm quite weary of these foppish young blades from Princeton and Harvard."

He wasn't sure what she expected him to say. The girl

was flirting with him. Couldn't she see he had eyes only for Wannie?

The carriage stopped and the driver came around to open the door.

Wannie leaned over and kissed his cheek. Her lips were warm and he smelled the faint fragrance on her dusky skin. "Here's your lodgings, brother. I'm really looking forward to introducing you around tonight. There's someone special I want you to meet."

Keso nodded absently as he got out and took his luggage, still lost in her smile. A teacher, maybe, or some classmate she hoped to interest him in. No chance of that; did she have even the slightest clue how Keso felt about her? She certainly didn't act like it.

"Until tonight then," he said "Nice to make your acquaintance, Miss Griswold."

"Yours, too. See you tonight," she cooed at him.

Keso stood holding his carpetbag and staring after the carriage as it pulled away. Wannie had changed. She had always been obsessed with clothes and jewels, even as a small child; why, he didn't know. These years in Boston seemed to have turned her into a back East sophisticated lady, making Keso feel like an ill-dressed, uncouth bumpkin.

Don't be stupid, he told himself as he went into the building, she's still the same old Wannie. He ought to know—he'd helped raise her. Spanish duchess, indeed! Well, Keso wouldn't be the one to tell; he loved Wannie too much to do anything to hurt her, and such things were probably very important to people like Alexandra Griswold.

On the other hand, maybe Wannie hadn't deliberately lied. She had been so very young the night of the big fire, almost fifteen years ago—perhaps she had honestly forgotten much of it. It wasn't that Silver and

Cherokee tried to keep it secret; they just never talked about those days.

In his room, Keso studied himself in the mirror. Was the suit out of fashion? He stared at it, feeling glum. True, it didn't fit all that well because he was so tall and broad-shouldered, and it probably was out of style. However, even a stylish suit wouldn't make him look less Indian with his black, uncut hair, high cheekbones, and that small white scar across one eyebrow. No one would think him unusual in a raw frontier town like Denver, but he'd been well aware of the curious stares on the train and even more so in the Boston station. Was Wannie ashamed of her backwoods foster brother?

Keso was somewhere between twenty-five and twenty-seven winters old, by his own calculations. As an abandoned child, he'd survived on the mean streets of Denver until Cherokee had befriended him. In the ensuing years, he'd fought rough miners in Saturday night brawls and had killed two panthers and a grizzly. He could handle a miner's pick as well as a knife or rifle. Nothing scared him—except the thought that Wannie might be embarrassed by him. He sat down on the bed, wishing now he had not come.

No, he said to himself and shook his head, Silver and Cherokee were depending on him to represent the family at this important event. Keso's education was the simple reading, writing, and arithmetic skills his foster parents had taught him at the table after supper in their cabin.

"If I can deal with a grizzly bear, I can get through this," he muttered to himself. "After all, tomorrow night this will all be over and we'll be packing to return to the Rockies."

When should he give her the ring? It appeared she was going to be too busy with this graduation event to allot Keso much time. He sighed as he took off his coat

and began to wash up, dreading this party tonight. He
was used to a quiet, solitary life and simple pleasures
in the mountains. His usual outfit was buckskin and
boots. He had not changed but Wannie had changed
from the pretty little child he remembered to an elegant, sophisticated beauty. Keso surveyed his suit.
Maybe it would look better if he had it pressed.

It was almost dark when Keso asked directions and
walked across the campus to the redbrick building
where the party was being held. The faint sounds of an
orchestra and laughter drifted from the open French
doors. He hoped that her roommate wasn't sticking
closer than a cockleburr tonight.

He hesitated out front, watching the elegant white
people going up the steps. Then he saw Wannie crossing the entry, and nothing else mattered. He almost
ran up the steps. Her crisp mauve-and-creme taffeta rustled as she crossed the marble floor. Deep pink and
creme cabbage roses cascaded down the front of her
dress, accented by pearls and rubies. There were mauve
roses in her black hair, too, and a string of rubies intertwined with pearls around her graceful throat.

"Keso," Wannie said and paused, taking both his
hands in hers and looking up at him. "I'm so glad
you're here. I'm sorry we haven't had much of a chance
to talk."

"It's okay." He smiled down at her, liking the feel of
her small, soft hands. "I understand you have responsibilities until this weekend is over. We'll have plenty of
time to talk later and catch up."

The rest of our lives, he thought, drinking her beauty
in, forcing himself not to take her in his arms. He had
forgotten just how beautiful she was with her exotic

dark features and the swell of her breasts visible in the
low-cut, exquisite ball gown.

She stood on tiptoe and kissed his cheek. "Thanks
for being so understanding, brother."

"Sure, brat. Aren't I always there for you?" He felt
like anyone but her brother. He had a sudden urge to
sweep her up in his strong arms and with a rustle of
taffeta and lace petticoats, carry her into the shadows
and kiss her until they were both breathless. "You look
beautiful tonight."

"That's what Cleve said." Wannie reached up self-
consciously to touch her necklace.

He was only half-listening to her words, thinking how
he envied the precious pearls resting against the curve
of her breasts. "The Duchess's gems look good on you,
Wannie."

"Think so?" she smiled like a pleased child. "I'm glad
Silver saved some of Mother's jewels for me."

Keso grinned. "Even when you were a little girl, you
liked to play dress-up and wear Silver's dancing shoes."

"To listen to you, you'd think you were old enough
to be my father when the difference is only seven or
eight years."

He must not kiss those full pink lips. This wasn't the
time or place to propose to her. "True."

She laughed. "I know you must have been bored silly
having a little girl tagging after you."

"Oh, I know I pretended to be. What half-grown boy
looks after a little girl?" He held onto her hand, thinking how warm it was, wanting to pull her to him and
hold her very tight. Almost in a whisper, he said, "I've
missed you."

"I've missed you, too, you and Silver and Cherokee."
Her tone was bright and casual. "Sometimes I got so
homesick, I almost got on the train and came home,
but it's such a long way."

"I didn't realize how accustomed I was to having that pretty child around until her laughter no longer echoed through the cabin," Keso admitted.

She looked surprised. "You never showed it. Anyway, I stuck it out and got a wonderful education. I speak French, you know, and I can play the flute and the cello."

"That's good, I reckon." The ring with the French sentiment seemed to burn in his pocket. He almost reached for it, then decided this wasn't the time or place. In the glow of the lights through the windows of the ballroom, she was breathtaking. The orchestra began to play.

Wannie whirled. "Oh, we're missing the party and there are so many people I want you to meet."

He almost said he wouldn't care if they stayed out here on the veranda, but she was already linking her arm with his, pulling him toward the ballroom. "Okay, Wannie, don't drag me, I'm coming."

She looked up at him, her dark eyes shining with enthusiasm. "Alexa was quite taken with you. She's not used to a man who doesn't cower before her."

Keso laughed. "I've faced down a female mountain lion—your snippy blond friend is almost as formidable."

"Don't you think she's pretty? Everyone talks about how pretty she is."

"Not nearly as pretty as you," he said and meant it.

"Spoken like a loyal older brother," Wannie said as she led him into the ballroom.

Keso looked around at the other men, realizing that his suit was different. "Wannie, I know I'm not dressed in the latest style—I hope you're not ashamed of me."

Her chin came up. "Of course not. I love you anyway."

As they entered, Keso ignored the curious stares, wishing he'd come several days earlier and let her choose a suit for him. He was very conscious of people

turning to look. "I suppose they've never seen a Cheyenne brave before."

She squared her small shoulders proudly. "Well, just
let them stare."

An orchestra played softly in the background as cou-
ples danced or gathered in little groups to visit. People
were craning their necks to look at the pair. Keso kept
his head high. But for the fact that he might humiliate
Wannie, he didn't give a damn what these fancy city
folk thought of him. A trio over in the corner turned
toward them and Keso recognized Alexa Griswold,
wearing a magnificent pale blue ball gown with a priceless strand of sapphires around her pale throat.

She beckoned, smiling. "Wannie, do bring your
brother to meet the family."

Looking at that elegant trio, it was the last thing Keso
wanted to do, but Wannie was already pulling him toward the little group. "Mr. and Mrs. Brewster, may I
present my brother?"

"Sir?" Keso nodded and shook hands with the stern,
hatchet-faced older man whose thinning yellow-gray
hair had been combed to cover his pink, balding scalp.

The dumpy Mrs. Brewster's glasses slid down her nose
as she peered at them. Her frown didn't improve her
homely face, nor did the expensive green moire dress.
"You say you're her brother?"

The older couple looked so disconcerted that Keso
replied, "Foster brother."

They both seemed to draw great sighs of relief.

A blond, sophisticated man, perhaps several years
younger than Keso, joined them at that moment. He
was so handsome, with a deep cleft in his chin, that
women were turning to take a second look. "Hello, all."

Wannie's face glowed. "And this is Alexa's cousin,
Cleve Brewster. Cleve, this is my brother, Keso."

The dapper young dandy wore a coat that even to

Keso's eye was of a rich fabric and expertly tailored. Cleve offered his well-manicured hand. "Wannie's often talked about you."

"Good things, I hope." Keso was acutely aware that the other man was looking him over with dismay . . . or maybe Keso was imagining that.

The plump matron smiled with pride at her son, then turned her curious stare back at Keso. "I—I didn't realize that you both weren't of Spanish royalty."

What on earth had Wannie told these snobs?

Wannie's dark eyes appealed to him again.

Keso made a gesture of dismissal. "It's a long story. Mr. Evans was a kind benefactor to an Indian boy he found on the streets."

"Indian?" Mrs. Brewster gasped, her homely face turning almost as green as her dress.

He must not lose his temper or embarrass Wannie. Her eyes were pleading with him and he'd do anything for her. "Ah, no, I'm sort of a stray—not from the fine background of my adopted sister."

For a split second, Wannie half-opened her lips as if to speak, but Mrs. Brewster blurted, "How kind of the Evanses! I didn't mean to pry into personal things."

Alexa smirked. "Of course you did, Aunt Bertha."

The older man frowned. "Alexa, your behavior is quite unseemly for a girl of your family and background."

Cleve looked over at Wannie. "In contrast, your roommate is not only proper, but very lovely tonight."

Wannie colored prettily.

It annoyed Keso that she seemed so pleased.

Cleve smiled and the cleft in his chin deepened. "Miss Wannie, I offer your brother my services in any way I can be of assistance while he's in town."

"How kind," Wannie gushed. "Keso, didn't I tell you this was a wonderful family?"

"Umm," Keso said. There was something about this

family he didn't like, but it was certainly wrong to judge them on such short acquaintance. Not that it mattered—he and Wannie would never see them again after tomorrow's graduation.

Cleve favored Wannie with a warm look. "I thought it my duty to do your brother some favors since we're all practically related."

"Related?" Keso stared at him, dumbfounded. If this elegant young dandy thought he was going to marry off that prissy cousin of his to Keso, he was certainly jumping the gun. Alexa was pretty, but he'd chosen his woman.

"Oh, Cleve," Wannie said, putting her hand on the other man's arm. "Now you've spoiled the surprise. I haven't had a chance to tell my brother yet."

Keso blinked. "Tell me what?"

This time, his beloved Wannie was gazing up into Cleve Brewster's blue eyes. "I can hardly believe it myself."

Cleve favored Keso with a smug, superior look. "We've gotten to know each other well over the months I came to visit my cousin. I proposed and Wannie's accepted."

A chill began to build in Keso's belly and the ring in his pocket, the ring he had chosen so carefully, seemed to burn through the cloth and into his flesh. "You don't mean . . . ?"

Wannie laughed with delight. "Isn't it wonderful, Keso? Cleve and I are engaged to be married!"

TWO

Wannie had never felt so happy, looking from one man to the other, awaiting congratulations from her foster brother. Instead, Keso's dark, handsome face had gone suddenly pale. He took a deep breath and the color came back as he squared his shoulders and held out his hand. "I reckon this calls for congratulations."

Was that big, calloused hand trembling? No, of course she had imagined that. "Are you all right, brother?"

"Of course he is, sweet," Cleve said, shaking Keso's hand. "Perhaps you shouldn't have surprised him with it."

"I—it is indeed a shock," Keso said. He was staring at her as if looking for an explanation.

"I hope you're not upset because you found it out from Cleve," Wannie explained, "but we really haven't had time to have a personal conversation since you got here."

Cleve gave her a melting smile. He was certainly much more handsome than his father, and so dashing, Wannie thought proudly.

Mrs. Brewster was radiant. "We have wealth and social position, but we've never had royal blood marry into the family before. My dear, sometime you must give us every detail about how a duchess happened to be stranded in the wilds of Colorado. My friends are going to be so envious!"

Wannie's mouth suddenly went dry. She didn't remember much about her childhood, except that her mother was a cold woman who didn't love her. The only time little Wannie ever seemed to meet with her approval was when she showed an interest in fine clothes and her mother's jewels. "I—I'm afraid there's not much to tell, actually. My mother was in some sort of political exile and we were living at a fine Denver hotel. There was a terrible fire one night. My mother died in the fire and my governess, Silver Jones, rescued me and later married Cherokee Evans."

Wasn't that the way it had happened? She looked at Keso and his dark eyes widened, but he said nothing.

"You poor thing!" the plump dowager gushed as she peered over her spectacles.

Mr. Brewster hooked his fingers in his vest, proud as a peacock. "Cleve, son, you've made a good choice. Let those Vanderbilts and Astors top that!"

Keso appeared speechless. Why? Wasn't she the daughter of a duchess? She had only been about four or five years old when it happened. Silver and Cherokee seemed loath to discuss the past, so Wannie's imagination had filled in the blanks.

"Brother," she said, "why don't we have the first dance?"

Keso hesitated. "Wannie, you know I don't know how—"

"Oh, come on, this is just a slow waltz—you can do it." She pulled him out on the floor and he took her in his arms, a bit hesitant and rigid. She had forgotten how big he was, how wide-shouldered. He was several inches taller than Cleve and certainly more muscular. "Keso, what's wrong?"

"Wrong? I don't know what you mean." He pushed

her across the floor with a grim expression as if he were counting steps. His big hand seemed to completely enclose hers and he was holding it too tightly.

"You don't seem to like the Brewsters."

He hesitated, stumbling over her foot and she saw an amused smile on several dancers' faces. She loved Keso dearly, but he seemed so clumsy and inept in this civilized crowd. "Wannie, if you like him, I'm sure Cleve is a fine fellow. It—it's just such a surprise. I wish you had just given me some clue in your letters that you were serious about someone."

"He only proposed a few days ago. I meant to break it to you when we were alone. Cleve's wonderful when you get to know him—so debonair, good family, and so handsome."

"Hmm." Keso didn't smile as he danced woodenly.

"He knows all the right people and has exquisite taste." She was both hurt and annoyed at Keso's lukewarm response.

"In some ways, little Wannie, you haven't changed." He didn't look at her as they danced. "Jewels and fancy clothes always dazzled you."

"I don't see that that's wrong," Wannie complained. "It's positively silly the way our family only digs enough gold and silver out of the ground to live a simple life."

"To turn it into a giant mining operation might pollute the land and bring a lot of greedy people into our area. That would create problems for the tribes and we've always been friends of the Indians. Besides, you know Silver and Cherokee prefer a simple life."

"Well, I don't!" Wannie snapped. She was crushed and angry that her brother didn't approve of her choice.

"How would you know?" he reminded her. "You haven't been home in four years."

"It's so dull out there in the mountains, rarely even

going to Denver, and Lord knows they don't have any *real* society."

"Maybe now you can educate all us poor yokels so we can think about really important things like stylish cravats."

"Oh, you don't understand at all! I suppose what you're really upset about is that I didn't ask your opinion. I'm not your kid sister anymore, Keso; I don't have to ask for my big brother's permission." Wannie pulled away from him and walked off the dance floor. She was filled with disappointment that her beloved Keso disapproved of Cleve; she had thought he would be glad for her. At least she had finally done something that would have met with her mother's approval. The Brewsters were rich and prominent—that would have impressed the duchess. More important, this prominent family approved of Wannie and were ready to welcome her into their midst.

What difference did it make if her foster brother liked her future husband or not? After all, she wasn't going to be living out on the raw Colorado frontier anymore. As Mrs. Cleveland Brewster, Jr., she would live the good life at the family estate in upstate New York and perhaps vacation at Newport or the British seashore. She'd bring her foster parents back East to visit and dazzle them with the fine things they didn't even seem to know about. If only her real mother were alive to know her disappointing little daughter had finally made the grade.

She flounced toward the doorway, but Cleve caught up with her. "What's the matter? You and your brother seem to be having a disagreement."

She felt herself flush. "He's—he'll just take some time to get used to my engagement, Cleve, dear. You could probably win him over by asking him to be your best man."

Cleve frowned and ran one hand through his luxuriant yellow hair. "Everyone will expect me to ask one of my Harvard friends. Besides, the way he's glaring at me, don't count on him even showing up at the wedding."

"I don't know what's the matter with him." Wannie blinked back tears. "I was so looking forward to his meeting you and your family."

"Don't fret, my darling," he said and took her hand. "I'm sure it can all be smoothed over."

"Thank you for being so understanding; I'm sorry my brother is so rude." She watched Keso as Alexa came up to him quite boldly and pulled him out on the dance floor. He was holding her roommate very close and Alexa was looking up into his face, not even seeming to care that he didn't know the steps. He glanced back over his shoulder at Wannie and held Alexa even closer. Somehow, that annoyed Wannie.

At her elbow, Cleve said, "It appears your brother is quite taken with my snooty cousin. I don't know whether to doubt his taste or his intelligence."

"Oh, don't be glib," Wannie said, dabbing at her eyes. "Alexa is beautiful."

"I'd say the way he's looking at her, he certainly thinks so, even if he is stepping all over her feet. Would you like to dance, Wannie?"

She nodded and he whirled her out on the floor. Cleve Brewster was an excellent dancer. He guided Wannie around the floor so expertly that others made way for them, the other ladies giving him admiring looks. When the music ended, they were the only ones left on the floor and the crowd applauded. Keso looked miserable and embarrassed, even with Alexa clinging to his arm.

Wannie's heart went out to him. "Cleve, he's not having a good time. He doesn't fit in well and he's probably uncomfortable about mixing with all these elegant people."

Cleve stifled a yawn. "Cousin Alexa seems entranced."

Somehow, that rankled Wannie. "He's never been out of Colorado before; I do so want him to enjoy his trip."

Cleve bent over her hand. "My dear, your wish is my command. I have an idea."

"Yes?"

"Mother would be greatly relieved to marry off my sharp-tongued cousin, even to a—"

"A what?" Why did she have such a sinking, uneasy feeling?

He took both her hands and kissed her fingertips. "A—a brother of the girl I adore. Let me tell you my idea."

People around them were amused as poor Keso stumbled over Alexa's feet again. Wannie ached for him. "Cleve, he's making such a fool of himself, poor thing! What's your plan?"

"Nothing compared to what I think my sly cousin might have in mind. Just notice how she stares into his eyes as they dance."

Wannie looked, knowing she ought to be glad the two were attracted to each other. Still, she felt troubled. Alexa might be a beauty, but she was brittle and shallow with a sharp tongue. "She doesn't seem his type. I don't know if she could make him happy."

"Happy? You're so naive and innocent, my darling. Most upper class marriages don't make that a priority."

"Don't be cynical." Wannie tapped him lightly with her lace fan. For some reason, it annoyed her that Keso was staring raptly at the beautiful blonde.

Abruptly, Wannie was ashamed to be so selfish, but she had always thought of Keso as her possession— swinging her up in his arms, letting her ride behind him on his horse, trying to comb her long, dark hair and put it up in pigtails She ought to be glad for him if he fell in love as she had done.

"Look, Wannie, I'm sorry," Cleve was contrite and charming. "We're tired from all the events and excitement. But I'll have to admit I'm disappointed your brother doesn't seem to like me."

Disappointed? Wannie was heartbroken. "If he only knew you as well as I do—"

"Egad, that's my plan!" Cleve crowed. "We'll invite him to the estate."

"What?"

"Weren't we talking of you coming home with my family for a few weeks after graduation so you could look everything over and make wedding plans?"

"I hadn't mentioned that to my family yet."

"Well, my dear," he smiled, "this is the perfect answer. It will be very proper as long as we have your brother along as a chaperon."

"I can't imagine he'd want to go—he can probably hardly wait to get back to the mountains." She turned and looked toward the dance floor. Keso was staring over Alexa's head at her.

"The way he's clinging to my pretty cousin," Cleve said, "I have a feeling she could get him to agree."

Wannie frowned, annoyed with herself at the thought. "Hmm. If he came to visit, it would give Keso a chance to know your whole family better."

He nodded. "Judging from the way my cousin's hanging onto him, I'd say that's just what Alexa had in mind."

Again, she felt slightly troubled as she watched the pair dance, then felt disloyal to both. Alexa had some shortcomings, but she was beautiful and that meant a lot to a man. "Cleve, I think you're right—it's a wonderful idea!"

"No, you're wonderful and I'm determined to have

you, no matter what I have to do." He danced her out onto the veranda and kissed the tip of her nose, then took her in his arms. "Mother thinks of nothing but society, and this will give her the chance to throw a whirl of parties and teas to introduce you around. There'll be endless shopping and jewelers making trips to the estate to show their wares. Why, I might buy you some pieces every bit as fine as that necklace you've inherited from your mother. I take it she left you quite a collection of jewels?"

"Some." Wannie touched the pearls and rubies entwined around her throat. "My mother loved fine things." Through the French doors, she watched Keso dance with Alexa. They were dancing so close, it could cause gossip—especially since Alexa was in the arms of a stranger.

Cleve said, "When your adopted mother feels better, you can invite the Evanses up to spend some time and get acquainted." He kissed her and she waited for the sky rockets that she'd heard other girls giggle about. It was nice, but not exhilarating. Well, maybe her classmates had exaggerated. What was important was that she and Cleve shared all the same goals and interests.

She heard a sound and whirled out of Cleve's arms. Alexa and Keso stood in the doorway.

Keso glared at Cleve. "I must protest this, Brewster. People will talk."

"Oh, let them talk," Cleve said irritably. "We're going to be married."

"But you're not married yet," Keso snapped.

Wannie was sure she would melt into the porch with humiliation. She resisted the urge to point out how close Keso had been dancing with Alexa. "Please, Keso, don't act like such an outraged older brother."

Alexa tittered. "I'd love to be kissed like that."

Keso ignored the bold invitation and glared at Cleve.

A muscle jerked in his hard jaw. "I'm very protective of Wannie."

Tears came to Wannie's eyes as the memories flooded back. When she was a small child, she had almost worshipped the street-wise boy from the moment she had been lifted to the back of his horse and they had ridden away from the smoldering ruins of the destroyed hotel. From that moment on, she had followed him about like a puppy, madly in love. He patiently endured her hero worship. Yet she was grown up now and realized he only thought of her as a pesty kid sister that he had to tolerate because the Evanses had raised them both. Of course, Keso wanted only the best for her, so if he were overprotective and hostile toward her suitor, perhaps he could be forgiven.

Cleve extended his hand. "I will protect her from now on. Let's shake, Keso. I want you to come up to the estate for a few weeks, look things over, get to know us all."

"When is the wedding?" Keso seemed to be shaking hands reluctantly.

Wannie breathed a sigh of relief; she did want the two to like each other. "We haven't set the date, but a society wedding takes months to plan."

"That's right," Alexa said.

Keso seemed to be considering. "In that case, I suppose I accept."

Alexa laughed with delight and caught Keso's muscular arm. "And that gives us more time together. I'm looking forward to that."

Keso glared at Wannie in the moonlight, then put his big hand over Alexa's small one and smiled at her. "So am I. Now come, Miss Alexa, you promised to teach me some new dance steps."

Wannie watched them stride across the veranda and back into the ballroom, the tall man taking shorter steps so Alexa could keep up with him. Wannie's mind was not on tomorrow's graduation or the trip to the Brewsters' sumptuous estate. For some reason that she couldn't fathom, all she could focus on was the way Alexa had her small hand draped possessively over Keso's muscular arm as they returned to the dance floor.

"Happy, my dear?" Cleve took her hand and kissed her fingertips.

"What? Oh, yes, of course." Frankly, she wasn't sure how she felt at this moment.

"Then I suppose I've delayed giving you this long enough."

He had her undivided attention now and she whirled to face him. "Oh, Cleve, a surprise? I love surprises!"

"I'll bet you do, you little minx. Now close your eyes." He took her in his arms.

Wannie closed her eyes. Cleve smelled of pipe tobacco and expensive hair tonic. His custom-made coat of the finest broadcloth was soft against her face. Maybe she had expected too much.

She felt him reach in his pocket. "It's just a small bauble that's been passed down through my mother's family."

"Oh, Cleve!" She blinked as he slipped the ring on her finger. "What a spectacular stone!"

"A pretty for a pretty." He smiled and the cleft in his chin deepened. "This is a diamond worthy of the daughter of a duchess."

She held her hand up and let the light streaming through the French doors reflect on it. "I can hardly wait to show it off."

He laughed. "I hope it doesn't look skimpy by comparison with the jewels the duchess left you."

"There aren't many jewels left, Cleve; most were sold

to finance the Silver Heels Mine until Cherokee struck it rich."

"Oh?" In the shadows, she wasn't quite sure of his expression. "But of course you own a great many mining claims yourself?"

She shook her head. "No, the mines belong to Cherokee and Silver. Does it matter?"

"Of course not, my darling." He kissed her lightly. "It's just that my family feels easier with people of our own station and background."

"I understand."

Cleve nodded almost apologetically. "I think Father feared I might choose a girl who isn't up to our standards; he's so proud of our aristocratic heritage. Bloodlines count, he says."

Bloodlines. She didn't want to think about hers. The music stopped and Keso and Alexa returned to the veranda. Wannie couldn't contain her excitement. "Look!" She held out her hand.

Alexa grabbed her hand, peering at the sparkling diamond. "Oh, the Griswold diamond from Aunt Bertha's side of the family. That should turn a few heads."

"Very nice," Keso said as he stared at it with a grim face.

He could have been a little more polite, Wannie thought.

Cleve put Wannie's arm over his and patted her hand. "I think we should go make the official announcement from the bandstand."

Wannie smiled. "Let's!"

It was afternoon in Colorado as Cherokee paused in the bedroom door and watched his beloved Silver napping. She stirred and those magnificent aqua eyes blinked open.

"I'm sorry, sweet darlin'," he drawled, "I didn't mean to wake you."

"It's all right," she whispered, "I'm almost well now; Doc said so."

He sat down on the bed and stroked the pale silver hair that had given her her nickname. The Cherokee half-breed had been bitter toward all women until Silver Jones had come into his life. "Well, by now, our Wannie's graduated."

"Drat!" she said, "I really hate it that I got sick and we couldn't go to Boston."

"Can't be helped," he soothed. "Besides, they'll be home in a few days and we'll celebrate then."

She smiled up at him. Once she had been the most celebrated beauty in the Rockies, the dance hall girl called Silver Heels. Now there were tiny lines around her eyes, but Cherokee loved her even more now than he had the day they wed fifteen years ago.

Silver looked at her gold nugget bracelet, then up at him and touched his dark hair, now streaked with gray. He was forty-eight years old and his tanned face was weathered, but Cherokee Evans was the only man she would ever love. "I've been lying here looking at my bracelet, remembering the night you gave it to me."

He smiled as if remembering, too. "And then we married and took in two stray children." He turned her hand over and kissed the palm, folding her fingers over it as if the kiss were a treasure that might be lost. It was a secret sign of love between them.

"The night you gave me the bracelet was when I was still beautiful."

"Silver, you will always be beautiful to me. What you did, nursing the sick during that smallpox epidemic, took a real heroine. You've become a legend, you know that? They've named a mountain for you—Mt. Silver Heels."

"I've still got the silver shoes," she admitted sheepishly. "Once in awhile, I put them on; Wannie always liked to wear them." After she'd been scarred by smallpox, Silver had fled to Denver and taken a job as governess to a rich woman's child.

"Buckskin Joe's almost a ghost town now; the mines have played out. Maybe we should go back sometime and visit the few old-timers who might be left."

She didn't answer, both of them knowing why she did not want to return. Once the most beautiful woman in the Rockies, they had called her Silver Heels because of those dancing shoes. She wanted those who had known her in the days she owned the Nugget Saloon to remember her as she had been. Cherokee seemed blind to her scarred face, but then, he looked with eyes of love.

"I forgot," he said, reaching into his pocket. "A passing trapper brought a telegram while you were asleep."

"You rascal!" She sat up in bed eagerly. "You've got a message from the kids and you're just now mentioning it? Open it."

Cherokee opened it, staring at the words. "Oh, hell, they're not coming right home. They're going to visit Wannie's roommate's family."

"Keso, too? That doesn't sound like him." She took the telegram and reread it.

"As I remember from past letters, Wannie's roommate is a pretty blonde. Maybe he likes pale hair as much as I do."

Silver frowned. "Drat it all. Somehow, I always hoped Wannie and Keso were going to end up together; they seemed like such a perfect match."

"I'd like that, too, but sometimes things just don't work out that way," Cherokee shrugged. "Maybe they think of each other as brother and sister."

Silver considered. "You might be right. He always called her 'brat.' "

Cherokee nodded. "He's a deep one. You never know what Keso's thinking; he keeps his thoughts to himself."

"Have you ever told Keso he's not really Cheyenne?"

"No," Cherokee said and shook his head. "Why borrow trouble?"

Silver sighed, remembering. "I'm not sure Wannie knows about her past either; she was so young at the time."

Cherokee put the paper on the bedside table, pulled her into his arms, and kissed her forehead. "I don't know if we did the right thing, not telling the kids everything we knew, but maybe it won't ever matter if they don't find out. The past is best left buried."

"You're right," she murmured. "Out here, people are judged on their actions, not their ancestors."

"I love you, sweet darlin'," Cherokee whispered and kissed her forehead.

He had to be sensing her thoughts. Silver snuggled down in his arms; two mature people, content to be where they were, content with each other. "We've done the best we could for them since the night the Duchess's Palace burned down and we left Denver."

Cherokee reached for the telegram again. "I'm disappointed they're not on their way home."

"Wannie's too enamored with wealth and appearances," Silver sighed. "I can tell by her letters. Her roommate's family are evidently rich society people, but if they knew about Wannie's background—"

"Oh, don't borrow trouble." He leaned over to pull the blankets up around her small frame. "We'll never have to meet that family, and now that Wannie's graduated, she'll never see them again, either."

"I guess I'm being silly, but I wouldn't want Wannie hurt by anyone uncovering her past."

"Yes, you are being silly, Mrs. Evans. Now go back to sleep." He gave her a reassuring pat. "There's no reason for that scandal about Wannie's past ever to come out!"

THREE

The Brewsters' fine carriage wound its way through the estate grounds up the drive to the palatial Victorian mansion.

"Why, Cleve, it's beautiful!" Wannie gasped as she stared out the window. "Look, Keso, isn't it wonderful?"

Keso merely grunted.

Alexa said, "Steel Manor is about like the other estates in the area; you'll enjoy the visit."

"Just think, Wannie," Cleve said and smiled at her, "someday, you will be mistress here."

His mother nodded. "I'm sure the daughter of a duchess is up to it."

Wannie winced, not wanting to remember her past. There was something shameful back there, she was certain of it, and the little she did know, she wanted to forget. The Brewsters would never accept her into their family if they knew.

The carriage halted before the mansion. The ornate doors opened and an elderly butler and various footmen and maids in drab gray dress with crisp white aprons and caps hurried out to meet, them. Wannie thought they looked like so many harried mice, scurrying about as the coachman opened the door. Before Cleve could assist her, Keso reached to lift Wannie down, looking into her eyes a moment.

As always, she was overwhelmed by the strength and power of her adopted brother. When she was a small child, she had idolized him, followed him around. She had thought he was the most wonderful male in the whole world besides Cherokee Evans. Now, he seemed so awkward and out of place next to the dapper and charming Cleve Brewster.

The elderly butler bowed low to Mr. Brewster. "Welcome home, sir. "We hope you had a pleasant trip."

Mr. Brewster nodded absently. "We've brought guests, Jeeves. Do see to them."

The servants were unloading the luggage as Keso struggled with the elderly butler over his bag. "I'm big enough to carry my own bag, thank you."

Wannie felt her face burn at the smiles of the others. "Keso, you're not supposed to do that. Let him take it."

With seeming reluctance, Keso let go of the bag. "If you say so."

"Tell me," Wannie said as she looked up at the lofty turrets and the imposing brick structure, "just why is it called Steel Manor?"

Mr. Brewster smiled benevolently at her, his bald head gleaming through his thin blond hair. "Made my fortune in steel bayonets and swords during the war. Now its pots and pans, butcher knives, kitchen implements, farm machinery."

His wife wiped her plump face with a lace hankie. "It's so trashy to talk of money."

"You're right, Aunt Bertha," Alexa agreed. "Only low-class people worry about money. Thank God, we have plenty!"

The butler bowed low as he opened the door and the group of travellers went inside.

The interior of the mansion was even finer than the outside, Wannie thought in awe. Everywhere she looked were fine paintings, carved furniture, and crystal chandeliers. There was even a coat of arms in the grand front hall.

Keso broke the silence. "It looks like a castle."

Mrs. Brewster smiled, evidently pleased as she peered at him over her spectacles. "Appropriate, don't you think, since we're to have the daughter of a Spanish duchess in the family? That's the Brewster coat of arms. Some of my husband's family came over on the *Mayflower*. Jeeves," she addressed the old butler, "we'll have tea served in the drawing room at four. All the best families do it."

"Tea. Balderdash!" the older Brewster glowered. "My ancestors helped throw the stuff in Boston Harbor."

"Cleveland, don't be difficult," his wife said.

"And do shut up, Bertha," he snapped, "I get so tired of your constant prattle."

There was a moment of awkward silence before Alexa gestured to Wannie. "Come along, Wannie—there's a lovely guest room next to mine."

Wannie followed her as a footman carried the luggage up the stairs. She paused and looked back at Keso. He appeared ill at ease in the grand foyer—the exact opposite of the debonair Cleve. Of course, the handsome aristocrat had grown up in this elegant atmosphere.

Her fiancé smiled up at her. "I'll take care of him, Wannie."

"Fine." She returned his smile and gave an encouraging nod to her brother. "See you later." Then she turned and followed Alexa. In the sumptuous room, a pretty, red-haired maid busied herself opening windows and hanging up dresses, shaking out wrinkles as she unpacked Wannie's things.

"Maureen," Alexa said, "this is my roommate from

school, Miss Evans. She'll be our house guest for several weeks."

"Very good, ma'am." The maid's accent was Irish and she curtsied slightly.

"Hello, Maureen," Wannie said and smiled warmly at the girl but saw only curiosity in the green eyes. Then the girl returned to unpacking the luggage.

Wannie looked about the expansive bedroom, almost awestruck. It was done in yellows with fine cherry furniture and expensive oil paintings. Crystal and imported glass knickknacks covered every dresser and tabletop. "Alexa, everything is beautiful!"

"Think so?" Alexa sat down in a chair with a yawn. "I suppose I've gotten used to it."

The servant finished hanging up the clothes, then curtsied. "Miss Alexa, I'll go to your room next. Is there anything special you want?"

"Yes, do remember to press my ball gowns. We'll be having several parties to introduce our guests." She made a gesture of dismissal.

The red-haired girl looked Wannie over as she left. "Yes, miss."

Wannie walked about the room, surveying its fine things, then paused to look out the window. "What lovely gardens and stables."

"Auntie's showplace for our success. The finest families come to our events. However, your mother should really be the one to give the big party to announce your engagement."

Wannie thought of the isolated log cabin up in the Rockies. "You don't know how my family lives, Alexa. I'm afraid the kind of people we see wouldn't know what to do at a fancy ball."

She looked at the glittering diamond ring Cleve had given her and felt a flash of annoyance at the Evanses' simple life style. It seemed so dull next to the way the

Brewsters lived. "It isn't as if the Evans' didn't have wealth and couldn't have more," she hastened to say. "I'm afraid they would think it silly."

"Well, soon you'll be a Brewster and you can live our lifestyle," Alexa said.

"I've always thought this would be so wonderful," Wannie said before she thought, "but Cleve's parents don't seem very happy."

Alexa shrugged. "Uncle Cleveland has his successful business and Aunt Bertha has her social position, and they both have Cleve. I suppose they don't expect more."

Wannie thought about the warm affection Silver and Cherokee showed each other. "Maybe I expect too much from marriage."

Alexa laughed. "I think you do. In our social set, a plain girl like Aunt Bertha would never have gotten a husband if her family hadn't been rich and the Brewster fortune almost gone."

"Alexa!" Wannie was shocked at her frankness.

"It's the truth and everyone knows it," Alexa added as she began to take the pins from her yellow hair.

Wannie felt uneasy gossiping about Cleve's parents. "They both seem to dote on Cleve."

Alexa nodded. "He's been spoiled worse than me, if that's possible." She laughed and shook her hair loose. "Uncle Cleveland is immensely proud of Cleve. He sees his only son taking over his kingdom someday, keeping the long, noble line of Brewsters going."

"I'll certainly try to give Cleve a son."

"Then you'll insure your position as Aunt Bertha has done."

"Alexa, Cleve adores me. I don't need to insure my position."

Her schoolmate winked at her. "Love and beauty wouldn't do you any good, my dear, if you didn't have a flawless background and money, even if your adopted parents may seem a bit eccentric."

She was more than a little annoyed. "Silver and Cherokee aren't eccentric."

Alexa got up from her chair. "From this family's standpoint, they'd be thought so. They don't seem to know what to make of your brother. I think he's the most man I've ever met, even if he is a bit uncouth."

Wannie didn't like anyone sneering at him. "Keso just comes from another environment where they have different values."

Alexa yawned. "You don't need to be so defensive; he's like a diamond in the rough, and maybe he just needs the right girl to polish him. By the way, everyone who is anyone in the best social circles will be coming the next several weeks."

Wannie didn't answer, wondering if she would fit in with all the rich aristocrats.

"I'm going to freshen up and take a nap," Alexa said and walked to the door. "Feel free to do the same. Don't forget tea time."

Alexa left and Wannie flopped on the four-poster with a sigh. Somehow, it annoyed Wannie that Alexa had set her sights on Keso. Alexa probably wanted to carry on a minor flirtation, but Wannie didn't want him hurt. He was the sincere type and he wouldn't understand her little coquettish game. Alexa was pretty. If anyone could turn him into a polished gentleman, the elegant blonde could. If Keso married Alexa, the Evanses had plenty of money for a fine mansion in Denver's best section; certainly Alexa wouldn't settle for anything less.

Yet Wannie felt a twinge of longing for the homey log cabin and the pair who had raised her. They, and the tough, street-wise Cheyenne boy were really the only family she had ever known. What would they think of

Cleve when she brought him to visit? More than that, what would Cleve and his family think of them?

Wannie stared at the ceiling and tried to recall the past. The Evanses seemed loath to talk about it in detail, so she hadn't asked much. As Wannie remembered, it was a grand hotel and Wannie's real mother had owned it.

Everyone had called her the Duchess. Wannie remembered almost nothing about her dark, beautiful mother except for her expensive jewels. Wannie had been playing dress-up with some of them and had her pockets full of priceless gems when the fire started.

The Duchess had died in that fire. Wannie might have, too, except that Silver, her governess, risked her life to carry the child outside. The Duchess. Wannie wasn't certain she was royalty, but Alexa had seemed so impressed when Wannie first mentioned it, and she had felt so lonely and intimidated by the snooty girls at Miss Priddy's Female Academy, that perhaps she had embroidered the tale a little. There was no reason the Brewsters should ever learn any more about her past than what Wannie had told them.

Keso was awestruck as he followed Cleve to the guest room on a ground floor wing of the imposing house. "It's all so big."

Cleve lit his pipe and shrugged. The scent of rich, imported tobacco drifted on the warm air. "You'll get used to it. There's whiskey in the desk drawer."

Keso looked around the room. It was furnished in a masculine style with dark, carved furniture and prints of horses and fox hounds. "Cherokee doesn't drink, so I never picked up a taste for it."

Cleve grinned. "I can see I've got a lot to teach you about the good things in life."

There was a knock at the door.

"Yes?" Cleve said.

A pretty redhead in a gray maid's uniform stuck her head in the door, started to speak to Cleve, then paused as she saw Keso. "Oh, sir, I didn't know you weren't alone. I—I've put fresh linens out, sir."

"Fine. Maureen, this is Keso Evans."

Keso nodded. "Hello."

She made a slight curtsy. "If you need anything, don't hesitate to ring, sir."

"You may go, Maureen." Cleve frowned.

She shut the door.

"Pretty girl," Keso said. "All the maids here are pretty."

"In my Harvard days, I used to bring friends home on holidays. Pretty maids can be quite entertaining to a bunch of rich, bored young men. Of course," he hastened to add, "that was before I met Wannie, but I didn't have the heart to fire them. Jobs are hard to come by for the lower classes."

"How kind of you." Be fair to him, Keso admonished himself, you don't really know him at all and damn it, you're jealous because Wannie is going to marry him instead of you.

Cleve reached in the desk and took out the bottle. "If you're not going to use this, I might as well take it with me. We'll be excused from the tea—it's a ladies' thing. Dinner is at eight. By the way, do you ride?"

"Yes." He might not dance well, but if there was one thing Keso could do, it was ride. With his Indian blood, he sat a horse like it was part of him.

"Good—maybe we can get my friends together for some polo."

"Polo?" Keso shook his head, "I'm sorry, I don't know what that is."

Cleve groaned. "I don't suppose you fence or play lawn tennis, either."

Keso gave him a blank look.

"Well, at least I've arranged a fox hunt for all the local gentry tomorrow." Cleve sighed. "You do hunt, don't you?"

Keso nodded. "I'm good with a Winchester."

"I meant a fox hunt. You have the proper clothes?"

Keso felt like a country bumpkin again. "I reckon not by your standards."

Cleve sauntered to the door, still clutching the bottle. "It's not proper, but I suppose you can ride in whatever you've got. Last hunt," he announced proudly, "I was awarded the brush."

"Only the tail? Who got the rest of the fox?"

Cleve looked amused. "The dogs, of course."

Rich white people were indeed a puzzlement. "Perhaps I fail to understand. A great many people go to a lot of trouble chasing after a little fox and if they catch it, they keep only the tail?"

Cleve rolled his eyes in evident exasperation. "With your lack of background, I suppose it's understandable that you miss the point. See you at dinner."

Keso nodded, still puzzled as Cleve left. He had a distinct feeling that Wannie's fiancé intended to show him up tomorrow, make him look stupid. Keso smiled to himself. Young Brewster had his work cut out for him if he thought he could outride a Cheyenne!

A servant had already unpacked his things, so there was nothing for him to do. Later, he would clean up for dinner, but now he sat down in the chair, took the little silver ring from his pocket, and turned it over and over in his big, brown hand. He ought to throw it away, but he couldn't bring himself to do that. What a naive fool he had been to hope that Wannie might think of him in any way except as a brother. Keso was already dreading spending several weeks at Steel Manor and meeting all the Brewsters' high-toned friends.

With a sigh, he put the antique ring back in his

pocket. Compared to the ring Cleve had given her, this looked insignificant and cheap. Keso stood up and walked over to the French doors that led onto a veranda. He opened them and looked out. At least this Hudson River country was beautiful, though not as lovely and cool as the Rockies at this time of the summer. Keso's curiosity was up about the Brewsters' horses. If there was anything he appreciated from living in the West, it was good horses. He went out on the veranda and turned down the gravel path through the formal rose garden. The heavy scent of blooms drifted on the late afternoon breeze—big cabbage roses, heavy with fragrance and as red as blood. He took a deep breath of their perfume. The scent he loved best were the wildflowers that Wannie wore in her hair back home. In the distance, he could see the stables and sauntered down there.

He whistled aloud as he walked into the big white barn and saw the many fine mounts in the stalls. Perhaps a dozen grooms and stable-hands bustled about. "These are some of the finest horses I've ever seen."

An older, blondish man stopped polishing a bridle and grinned. "Ah, I like a man who appreciates a fine horse! I'm Ian O'Hearn, the head groom." His Irish accent was not strong; perhaps he had been in this country many years.

"I'm Keso Evans," he said and reached out to shake hands. The other hesitated, then shook.

"Ain't you one of the swells visiting the nabobs up on the hill? Sorry, governor, I hadn't meant to be so familiar. I know me place." Once this man might have been handsome, with his light-colored hair now turning gray, but a groom's life was not an easy one.

Keso shrugged to put the man at ease. "I'm not anyone important."

"A friend of the young master's, perhaps?"

"No, I'm invited to be a house guest because my sister was Miss Griswold's roommate at school."

The other laughed, a twinkle in his blue eyes. "Aah! We've heard of you through the coachman. T'was kind of you to offer to help with the luggage."

At least here, he wasn't being condemned. "It seemed the only thing to do; there were so many bags."

The other returned to polishing the bridle. "They do say the young master's brought home a future bride. What's she like?"

"Beautiful," Keso said with a sigh, "and kind and sweet, but maybe a little immature."

Ian looked at him a long moment. "I see."

The way he said it made Keso wonder if his love for Wannie was so evident. "Wannie will make a good choice for young Cleve, although he doesn't deserve her. She'll give him fine sons." The thought pained him. Those should be his sons.

"A son is important to a man," Ian said after a long moment and reached for a saddle. "I know it was for the old master. He's spoiled him. I've watched young Cleve grow up here. He's got a wild streak, that one, but no doubt he'll settle down. Someday, he'll be master of all the Brewster lands and fortunes. Yes, a son is a man's immortality."

"You have no family of your own?"

The groom paused a long moment, then shook his head. "None save the horses. I was in love with a woman once, but she was socially above me. Believe me, I know my place."

"Well, the gentry's certainly teaching me mine," Keso said and rubbed the tiny scar above one eye, thinking of Wannie. He also had a burn scar on the back of his right arm, but he'd had that so long, he didn't know how he came by it. Keso looked around at the stable, thinking he was going to have a pleasant hour. "Tell me about the horses."

The other grinned warmly. "Mr. Brewster preaches fine bloodlines among folks and horses—says you can't make a silk purse from a sow's ear, so he buys the best blood."

Keso sighed at the thought. Bloodlines. These Brewsters were such snobs. What would they say if they knew Keso didn't even know who his parents were? He barely remembered a Cheyenne woman who drank too much, nothing else. As for Wannie . . . he wouldn't court trouble by thinking about what he knew of her heritage. Instead, he settled down on a bale of hay to visit with the groom.

Cleve watched out his window as the tall savage walked out on the veranda, looked around, and sauntered down the path toward the stable. Damn him! Cleve was going to have to win Wannie's brother over or risk his wrecking the engagement.

Behind him, the red-haired maid paused while shaking the wrinkles out of his suits as she hung them up. "What do you see out there?"

Cleve turned, grinning. "One of our house guests. I was afraid he might come over to my room, but I think he's gone down to look over the horses." He came up behind her, reaching around to cup her generous breasts with his two hands. "I've missed these."

"And me, too, I hope." She turned in his arms, smiling up at him.

He kissed her hungrily. "You know what I want."

"Aye, it's a maid's duty to please the master," she whispered against his lips.

"You always do." He molded her ripe body against his rigid maleness, enjoying the familiar heat and feel and scent of her. Having the lovely but virginal Wannie in his arms as they danced had only made him need a woman badly. He began to unbutton Maureen's bodice.

She caught his hand. "First tell me who that dark beauty is?"

"Just a house guest, that's all." He slapped her hand away and continued unbuttoning her bodice. "The girl's my cousin's roommate, and the big savage is her brother. Maureen, sweet, you're the one I want, just like always, you know that."

Her green eyes softened and she appeared somewhat mollified. She was standing next to the bed and he took her in his arms and fell with her to the mattress.

"Not wearing any drawers as always?" He grinned, pushing up the full gray skirt of her maid's uniform.

She smiled archly. "I know you like me to make it easy for you."

That was the truth. How many times in the last few months had he used her standing in a dark hallway or thrown quickly across a table? Once it had even been the massive walnut desk in Father's study. The danger of getting caught by that stern patriarch had only heightened the thrill.

He unbuttoned his pants, stroking her breasts and wishing she were Wannie. He lusted for Wannie, but a proper girl wouldn't let him between her silken thighs until the ceremony was over. Not that he intended to give up this wanton Irish slut. This was a man's world—always had been. Even if a woman knew her husband was keeping a mistress, what could she do about it once he had gotten control of all her wealth and property?

"What are you thinking?" she whispered.

"Nothing but how much I want you," he lied, stroking her breasts. Somehow, he was going to have to tell Maureen he was announcing his engagement. Surely this lovely slut could understand that a man of his social position had to marry a girl of impeccable background. Wannie filled that requirement as the daughter of a duchess. Even his humorless father seemed to approve of her. Good! Maybe now the old man would loosen the purse strings a little. If not, it appeared the Evanses had plenty of gold that meant nothing to them, and as a son-in-law, Cleve could surely get his share of it.

Maureen shook her flame-colored hair loose on the coverlet, then pushed up her skirt above her long, slender legs. "See? I told you I was wearing no drawers."

He ran his hand up her hot thigh, wondering what Wannie looked like naked. The image heightened his passion and he rolled over on the maid, thrusting hard into the core of her while she moaned and clawed his back.

Just before he reached that peak of ecstasy, he thought that whoever said you couldn't have your cake and eat it, too, had never met Cleve Brewster!

FOUR

Wannie rested, washed up, and changed into a light yellow cotton dress, then joined Alexa on her way downstairs for tea.

Alexa led the way, talking about the parties they would have. "Wannie, your brother could be a real handsome blade with a bit of social polishing and some decent clothes."

"Keso never cared much about clothes," Wannie admitted with a rueful laugh. "He probably grabbed the only suit in the store that would fit him."

"He does have breathtaking shoulders," Alexa sighed, "and he's so tall!"

"Yes, he is, isn't he?" In fact, Wannie thought, Keso had a much better physique than Cleve. She knew she should be glad her friend was so enamored with Keso, but Wannie was surprised to realize that wasn't quite true. How selfish, she thought with a flush of shame.

They went into the drawing room that was done in rich creme and jade brocades with fine Oriental rugs on the polished wood floors. Mrs. Brewster sat on a damask Victorian sofa, wearing a patterned green silk dress. With her bulk and plain face, she looked somewhat like an oversized frog, Wannie thought, and then chastised herself.

Bertha Brewster favored Wannie with a smile. "My

dear, sit near to me so we can talk. Alexa, please pull
the bell cord for old Jeeves so he'll bring the tea."

Wannie sank into the chair, looking about in wonder.
"It's such a grand house!"

The plump matron beamed at her. "So glad you like
it, since you will be the mistress here someday."

Alexa pulled the bell cord on the silk-papered wall
and came over to join them.

"It's so exciting," Wannie said.

Mrs. Brewster regarded her a long moment. "Give
your husband a son, and your position will be secure."

"Sons!" Alexa snorted. "Don't women count for anything? It isn't fair."

The plain dowager surveyed Alexa over her spectacles. "Life isn't always fair, Alexa," she said calmly. "To
survive in a man's world, you do whatever it takes.
You're luckier than I was because you're pretty."

Wannie shifted uncomfortably. "You have done a
grand job here—Mr. Brewster must be proud."

The older lady made a noncommittal shrug. "He's
proud of his son and therefore, I am mistress of Steel
Manor. I hope, my dear child, you, too, will be realistic
and not be swept away by romantic twaddle."

Twaddle? The relationship between Cherokee and
Silver seemed so warm and vibrant. Wannie decided it
would not be polite to dispute Cleve's mother.

The homely matron looked at Wannie's hand with
satisfaction and nodded. "That's the Griswold diamond, you know—came down through my family. The
Brewsters come from a fine, blue-blooded lineage, but
unfortunately, not much wealth."

"Oh?" Wannie didn't know quite what to say.

"I'm glad to see you appreciate jewels and the finer
things in life." The older woman patted Wannie's hand
and smiled. "The daughter of a duchess! Yes, you will
make a fitting wife for dear Cleve."

The elderly butler entered just then, bearing a heavy silver tray with a gleaming tea service monogrammed with an ornate "B," and set it on a table before the mistress.

Wannie's eyes widened at the beauty of the silver. "It's beautiful."

Bertha Brewster nodded. "Someday, my dear, you, too, will continue the Brewster legacy. You'll sit in this drawing room and pour tea from this service for *your* daughter-in-law."

Wannie stared at the ornate tray of tiny sandwiches, cookies, and the gleaming silver tea pot.

Mrs. Brewster poured. "Lemon or cream?"

"Cream, please," Wannie answered.

The three of them enjoyed their tea and the delicious pastries. Although Wannie didn't want to admit it, she would have felt more at home back in the log cabin with Silver pouring coffee into crockery mugs. But she would learn to love it here, she thought as she nibbled another small pastry.

Finally, Mrs. Brewster had other duties to see about, so Alexa retreated to her room and Wannie decided to tour the house. It was indeed a marvelous mansion— just the kind she'd always dreamed of. She could throw endless parties, wear the latest ball gowns, and own boxes full of jewelry. She looked at the big diamond on her hand. Yes, she could have all that and eventually be mistress of Steel Manor. She should be very happy, yet there was something missing. What was it? Wannie wished she could sit and have a long talk with Keso to see how it looked from a man's point of view. Because of their rocky start in life as orphans, the pair had always been so close. She had missed him terribly all these years she had been away at school. Now they would be separated permanently.

Well, maybe not. Perhaps Cleve would build her a

summer home in Denver; possibly his father's large
company did business there. She wasn't quite sure what
it was Cleve did at Brewster Industries and when she
had asked, her fiancé had brushed her off by shrugging
that he was a vice-president and that was enough for
her to know. Maybe it was. Wannie smiled. She was the
luckiest girl in the world to receive Cleve Brewster's pro-
posal—everyone said so. With a smile, she went upstairs
to get ready for dinner.

Cleve met her at the foot of the stairs as twilight came
on. "That peach-colored silk is ravishing against your
hair, my dear. You are breathtaking, you know that?"
Her heart skipped a beat. Yes, this was the romantic
dream she had once had. He smelled of fine cologne,
tobacco, and bourbon as he kissed her lightly on the
lips. "Oh, Cleve, what will your parents think if they see
us?"
"That you're as proper as both of them." He laughed
and caught her hand. "Which, I suppose, means you'll
make the perfect Brewster wife."
"I hope to be more than that to you." She didn't
want to be like Cleve's mother.
He kissed the tips of her fingers. "I can hardly wait."
She heard footsteps and Alexa came down the stairs
wearing a dark blue silk dress. "Is dinner being served?"
"Not yet, cousin," Cleve said. "We're waiting for everyone to gather."
Keso strode down the hall toward the pair, hesitating
as he reached them. "I—I wasn't sure what to wear, so
I had the maid press my suit."
He really did need an expert tailor, Wannie thought,
but she only said, "You look fine, brother." She gave
his arm a comforting pat.
The front bell rang and old Jeeves hurried to answer

it. "Evening, sir," he said and bowed as Mr. Brewster entered. "How was your ride around the estate?"

"Fine. Ian's just bought us another champion mare—don't know what I'd do without him." Cleveland Brewster came over to join the trio.

Keso said, "I met your head groom today—fine fellow."

The foyer lights gleamed on Cleveland Brewster's balding head. "Yes, Ian O'Hearn's been with me for over a quarter of a century and he knows his place; not many servants like that these days."

Keso frowned. "With that attitude, I'm surprised he stays. There must be other positions open to a top groom."

Mr. Brewster frowned. "Of course there is; matter of fact, a number of my friends have tried to steal him, but he's loyal to this family. I expect he'll be here until he dies."

"He doesn't seem to have any personal life at all," Cleve said and smothered a yawn.

"Ian doesn't have time for any personal life," his father said. "His whole life is serving this family—not a bad thing for servants."

Wannie winced at the selfish, insensitive remark. Keso looked as if he were about to say something. Wannie glared at him and he seemed to reconsider.

"I'll go change and clean up," Mr. Brewster said and left.

Eventually, Mrs. Brewster joined them. She was wearing a dress of a brownish hue that was certainly expensive, but not very becoming. "Good evening, all."

Everyone greeted her, but Wannie noted that she had not come from the master's suite. Evidently, the pair did not share a room. When the older Brewster rejoined them, he gave his wife an absent-minded nod—quite different from the way Silver greeted Cherokee when he returned home.

Old Jeeves entered. "Dinner is served."

Cleve took Wannie's arm. "Do me the honor, my dear."

"And I know," Alexa simpered, "that Keso would like to escort me to dinner?"

"It's your house," Keso said. "Don't you know where the dining room is?"

Wannie wanted to go through the floor with embarrassment as she saw the shock followed by amusement on the other faces. However, Alexa laughed and took Keso's arm. "Besides being handsome and strong, you are so witty! You may escort me."

Wannie struggled to keep annoyance from her features. Surely her brother wouldn't fall for such a silly flirtation, but he glanced at Wannie and then positively beamed at Alexa. "Miss Alexa, my strength is at your service."

Wannie gritted her teeth. Who did Keso think he was, Sir Galahad? Except Keso wouldn't know who Sir Galahad was. They all went into dinner.

The room was huge and the furnishings, china, and silver magnificent. A crystal chandelier hung over the long, polished mahogany table and the monogrammed table linens were of the finest white damask. She paused a moment, drinking it all in.

Keso looked around in awe.

Mr. Brewster paused while seating his wife at the end of the table and smiled with satisfaction. "Someday, Wannie my dear, you will preside over dinners here as Mrs. Cleveland Brewster, Jr."

He went to the opposite end of the table where Cleve was pulling out Wannie's chair next to his father's.

Wannie caught Keso's eye and nodded toward Alexa, indicating he should pull out her chair. He did, but he seemed very uncertain about what was expected next. There was only one other empty chair at the long table and Keso came around and sat down across from Alexa. Wannie's heart almost bled for the big Indian; he was completely out of his element here. On the other hand, Cleve had been born to this life.

Wannie looked down the table and beamed at Mrs. Brewster. "You are to be complimented—your home is so well-managed."

The plump woman nodded. "Women of my class are expected to be able to handle the everyday business of managing servants and merchants. I'm sure you'll do every bit as well, my dear."

The glow from the gleaming chandelier sent a million points of light reflecting off the crystal goblets and the heavy silver.

Across from her, Cleve smiled. "Like the place, my dear?"

"It's beautiful." At that moment, Wannie was glad she had learned proper etiquette from the other girls at Miss Priddy's school. Her heart went out to Keso, who looked very uncomfortable at the formal table and was watching her every move closely so he wouldn't make any embarrassing blunders. Already, servants were scurrying about with great silver-covered dishes and platters.

Old Jeeves poured the deep red wine into the fine crystal goblets.

Old Mr. Brewster stood, holding up his goblet. "I would like to make a toast to the happy couple," he said proudly. "May my only son and his bride live long and prosper here at Steel Manor."

"Hear! Hear!" Everyone said as they sipped the wine.

Then they settled down to polite conversation while Jeeves carried a great platter of roast beef around the table.

Wannie glanced over at Keso, who was eyeing the

spread of silverware next to his place. "Is this all for me?" he asked. "Or shall I pass some of it down the table?"

Wannie winced. She thought she heard even old Jeeves snicker. "Uh, brother, everyone has the same silver—you'll use it all as different courses are served."

"Seems as if we're dirtying a lot of extra forks and spoons for nothing," Keso said.

This time, even Alexa was hiding a smile behind her napkin.

"Look, old man," Cleve said genially, "we've got lots of servants—dealing with dirty tableware is their business."

Keso shrugged and tucked his napkin in his collar, then looked around.

Wannie was torn between being embarrassed and feeling sorry for him. She took her own napkin and made a grand gesture of spreading it on her lap so that Keso would do the same. Then everyone began to eat.

The food was superb, Wannie thought as she ate the steaming vegetables and potatoes. The meat tasted moist and excellent. Jeeves hovered nearby with a basket of delicious breads and refills of the finest imported wines.

Wannie noted that Keso tasted the wine, then pushed it back. "I'd really like a glass of milk."

Everyone at the table blinked. Mr. Brewster signaled the butler and within minutes, Keso had his milk, served in an expensive crystal tumbler.

"So," the host said as he watched him, "you were born in the West?"

Keso nodded.

"Had a nephew in the cavalry in Nebraska in '73—my sister's boy, Lexington B. Radley. He went missing during that Massacre Canyon thing."

Wannie's curiosity was piqued. "What do you mean, *went missing*? Did he desert?"

"Of course not!" Mr. Brewster snapped. "That would be very poor form. He simply went missing during the height of the battle—never even found his body."

"The West can be a dangerous place," Keso agreed, "if you aren't prepared to deal with it."

Cleve paused in cutting up his roast beef. "Dreadful place—needs civilizing as soon as possible."

Keso frowned but didn't say anything as he continued eating.

Wannie breathed a sigh of relief. Keso seemed a little more at ease now that he had the right fork and was engaging both Cleve and Mr. Brewster in a discussion of horses and the hunt to be held in the morning.

"Do you have the proper coat?" Cleve asked.

Keso looked baffled. "I need a coat to go hunting? It isn't cold outside."

"There's a proper outfit," Wannie hastened to say. "Of course you don't own one; we don't ride to the hounds in Colorado."

"Dearie me," Mrs. Brewster said. "What an uncivilized place."

Cleve finished eating and signaled the butler to take his plate. "I don't suppose there's a coat large enough for Wannie's brother in the spare things, and there isn't time to have one made."

Keso shrugged. "It's hot, I'll ride in my shirtsleeves."

Alexa looked aghast. "You can't do that—what would everyone say?"

"I reckon they'll say 'there's a fellow who doesn't own a proper coat.' " Keso smiled and returned to his food.

Wannie was torn by her emotions. She was embarrassed for Keso and upset with herself for being embarrassed. He was so noticeably out of place in this environment and he didn't have the foggiest idea about the rules and traditions of the hunt. During her years at Miss Priddy's, Wannie had not only acquired the proper riding habit but had ridden to the hounds several times at friends' estates.

She turned to Mrs. Brewster as a rich chocolate dessert was being served. "Will you ride tomorrow, Mrs. Brewster?"

"Dear me, no." The lady made a polite gesture of dismissal. "But I'll see to the hunt breakfast and refreshments."

Cleveland Sr. had returned to his talk of bloodlines. "Horses are like people," he said, as he ate his dessert, "blood will tell. Just as Brewsters are superior, so are my horses."

"I would think," Keso said with a slight edge to his voice, "that raising and environment might have a little to do with it."

The older man shook his head. "I disagree—can't make a silk purse from a sow's ear, so to speak. My family can trace their lineage back hundreds of years. He looked proudly at his son, then at Wannie.

Wannie blurted, "Mine can, too."

"Why, of course they can," Mrs. Brewster beamed at Wannie. "Imagine—a duchess. I can hardly wait to introduce you to my friends."

Why had she lied like that? Keso was staring at her wide-eyed and she was ashamed of herself. Wannie was not sure she could handle this move up into a very blue-blooded social set, but she was determined to try. She didn't want to humiliate her fiancée.

Once the dishes had been cleared, Jeeves put delicate fingerbowls before each person. Wannie dipped her fingertips daintily in her bowl and started to wipe them on her napkin. She heard a smothered giggle from Alexa, and looked up in time to see Keso drinking from his. As Wannie watched in horror, he drained it, put it down, and wiped his mouth.

"Thanks," he said to the butler. "I was getting thirsty."

She wished she could just die right there as. Jeeves gasped and the others blinked in shock. Keso looked around, then seemed to realize he'd made another social error. His dark face flushed. "I'm sorry if I did something wrong. At home, we wash up out on the back porch."

He was her brother and she loved him. Wannie gave him her warmest smile, even though she was humiliated before these society folk. "It's all right," she said. "You didn't know."

Cleve merely looked pained and embarrassed, but Alexa smiled. "Keso, you have turned our usually dull supper into an entertaining delight."

"I didn't mean to," he mumbled and got up from the table. "Mrs. Brewster, I'm sorry."

No one knew quite what to say.

Mrs. Brewster looked flustered and turned toward the butler. "Jeeves, I think we'll retire to the drawing room for coffee."

Wannie loved Keso and she suffered for him. She only prayed that he could get through the evening without any more social mishaps.

Keso took one look at the dainty china cups and declined coffee. Wannie guessed the reason was that he was afraid of dropping a cup.

Finally, the older couple retired to their rooms while the younger four went out on the veranda in the summer night.

"What a wonderful evening," Wannie said as Cleve took her hand. "With the slight breeze, I can smell roses."

"The garden's just a few steps away," Cleve said. "Would you like to walk in it?"

"All right."

They left Keso and Alexa standing looking out across the vast expanses of the estate's rolling lands and walked through the roses.

"I'm really looking forward to tomorrow's hunt," Wannie said.

Cleve laughed softly, the light gleaming on his yellow hair. "I am, too. You've made me a very happy man, dear. To be honest with you, I've been a bit of a wastrel, drinking and gambling. Father has been about ready to cut off my inheritance if I didn't mend my ways."

She didn't quite know what he expected her to say. "I'm not concerned about money, Cleve, dear."

"Well, I am. I'm used to living well, but I do weary of having to answer to my father constantly like an errant school boy."

"But if you're planning to change your ways—"

"It's not just that," he admitted, "it's not being my own man, don't you see?"

She nodded, touched and flattered that he was sharing his thoughts with her.

"Perhaps I might even consider going West; everyone says there's a fortune to be made there these days."

She brightened at the thought. "You mean, we might have a second home someplace like Denver?"

"Perhaps," he said. "Do you think there are investment opportunities in Colorado?"

"Oh, I'm sure of it! Cherokee would certainly give you advice and introduce you to some people."

He brushed a curl away from her face with gentle fingers. "Tell me about the Evans' mines."

She thought it an odd question. "Cherokee says they could produce enough gold to make us all very rich, but that would only add to the pollution and confusion in the area, and the Indians wouldn't like it."

"Indians?" Cleve sneered. "Why would anyone care about what they think?"

"My family always has," Wannie said with quiet dignity.

"I'm sorry, my dear, I didn't mean to offend you." He bent his head and kissed her. This time, she didn't expect skyrockets. Mrs. Brewster was right; she should be more realistic.

"We really should be getting back," she murmured against his lips and pulled away from him.

On the veranda, Keso shifted his feet and looked toward the rose garden. "They haven't returned."

"Oh, don't be silly. My brother is probably kissing her—that's why he took her off down there."

"Of course." Keso had to force himself to stand and look about casually when everything in him demanded that he stride out to that garden, pull Wannie from the young blade's embrace, swing her up in his own arms, and carry her back to the veranda. Don't be a fool, he reminded himself. She's engaged to be married to the man. Yet even as the ring seemed to burn a hole in his pocket, he flinched at images of Wannie in another man's arms when he wanted her so badly.

"A penny for your thoughts," Alexa cooed.

"What? oh, I'm sorry, I had allowed my mind to wander." He turned toward her, thinking she was a beauty, but light hair and blue eyes would never speak to his heart as dark eyes and hair did.

"My! I must not be very charming tonight then," she said and fluttered her eyelashes at him.

"Miss Alexa, you are very charming." He felt awkward, not knowing for sure what was expected of him. "I—I was thinking I made a fool of myself tonight; the Evanses don't serve formal dinners like that."

"You know what I like about you, Keso?" She put her hand on his arm. "You're honest and straightforward. I could teach you all that, if you really want to learn."

"Could you?" He looked down at her, thinking how different she was from his beloved Wannie. "I know I'm embarrassing Wannie, and I don't want to do that."

"So thoughtful." She ran her hand up and down his arm. "I know you think I'm bold; I've even toyed with the idea of being a suffragette."

"How—how nice." He didn't know what that was.

Abruptly, she slipped her arms around his neck and kissed him. He was caught completely off guard and for a long moment, he stood stiffly. Miss Alexa must have had plenty of practice, he thought, because she molded her supple body into his so he could feel the soft curve of her breasts and thighs, and the tip of her tongue pushed between his lips in a lustful kiss. Without even thinking, his arms went around her. He pulled her into his embrace, his eyes closed, pretending she was Wannie, yet angry with Wannie for being so blind to his devotion, and unable to control his own need.

But it wasn't the same. He loved Wannie. Reluctantly, he reached up to pull Alexa's arms from around his neck even as he heard a step on the gravel path and turned. Wannie and Cleve stood there and in the moonlight, Wannie looked thunderstruck.

Alexa recovered first. "Oh, hello, you two. Well, I'll see all of you at the hunt early tomorrow." She whirled and hurried inside.

Keso looked at Wannie. He couldn't be quite sure what she was thinking, but he knew no man was supposed to be so familiar with a well-bred girl on such short acquaintance. "Good night, Wannie."

Keso went inside, striding to his room, but once there, he lay on the coverlet, fully dressed, and did not sleep. Was Wannie still out there in the moonlight with

Cleve? He gritted his teeth and told himself she had
chosen her husband and Keso had better mind his own
business. Cleve was probably a fine fellow if Wannie
loved him, yet Keso was struggling even to like the man.

Wannie stared after the pair who had just gone into
the house. She felt a sense of shock at seeing Keso kissing the spoiled beauty. Don't be silly, she scolded herself, you should be happy for them both.

"Hmm," Cleve said, "it appears we have another romance going on here—Alexa's a terrible flirt."

"She's not Keso's type at all," Wannie finally managed.

"I'd say the way he was holding her, she's got something he wants badly." Cleve chuckled.

Wannie had a sudden vision of Keso making love to
the bold blonde, the two of them naked together in a
way she had never been able to picture herself with
Cleve. The thought upset her. "I—I'm getting a headache, Cleve. I'm going to bed."

"All right, my love." He walked her to the foot of the
stairs only a few feet from the French doors that led
out onto the veranda and the nearby garden. He kissed
her and caught her hand as she started up the stairs.
"I'll think of you all night," he whispered.

She nodded, her mind still full of the images of Alexa
in Keso's arms. "See you in the morning." She pulled
away and hurried up the stairs.

Cleve watched her go with a sigh, then turned and
sauntered down the dark hallway toward his room.
Maureen stepped out of the shadows. "You!" she hissed,
"I heard from the other servants about the toast at tonight's dinner party! You led me on, all the time getting
yourself engaged to some prissy friend of your snotty
cousin's."

"Shh!" He put his finger to his lips in warning. "Be
quiet—someone will hear you. Keso's room is close by."

"And what if they do hear?" she raged. "I can fix you good with your fiancée."

Damn all jealous women to hell. "Now, Maureen, dearest," he wheedled in a soft voice, "if you do that, you'll cause me a lot of trouble. And my mother will promptly fire you—you know how she is about preserving the Brewster family image."

"And I'm supposed to continue in the role of the dutiful slut?"

He knew what women liked to hear—he'd had plenty of practice. "I forget how beautiful you are until you get angry."

He pulled her close and kissed her. At first, her mouth was a grim, hard line, but he ran his tongue along her lips, kissing and holding her close, and she melted against him.

Keso had been lying on his bed, and when he thought he heard Wannie go upstairs, he breathed a sigh of relief and closed his eyes. Cleve's footsteps came down the hall and then stopped.

Keso tensed. Be had lived in the wilderness a long time—he had keen hearing that picked up a slight murmur of angry voices. Had Wannie come back downstairs and she and Cleve were having an argument? Quiet as any Indian tracker, he stepped to his door and opened it a crack. Enough light shone through the shadowy hallway to see Cleve exchanging hot words with a woman. Why, wasn't that the pretty red-haired maid from this afternoon? And at that precise moment, Cleve took the girl in his arms, kissing her, running his hands all over her.

Keso blinked, not believing what he was seeing. Cleve was engaged to Wannie and any man lucky enough to be her future husband shouldn't even be tempted by another woman. Now the girl pulled away from Cleve.

"You bastard," she snarled, "I thought you were going to marry me!"

"Shh, Maureen! Keep your voice down," Cleve pleaded. "Neither of us needs a scandal; my old man is finally loosening up the purse strings a little now that he thinks I've straightened up."

"But what about us?"

"Be practical, baby." He tried to take her in his arms again, but she pushed him away. "You know my background; do you think my parents would let me marry a servant, no matter how much I cared about her? And I do, Maureen, believe me, I do!"

Keso gripped the doorknob to keep from striding out in the hall and slamming his fist in Cleve's face. What a rotten cheat and liar!

The Irish servant made a noise that sounded like she might be mollified. "I—I suppose I can see that. So what am I supposed to do now?"

Cleve put his arms around her again, kissing her and running his hands over her ripe body. "Prominent men have always kept mistresses—"

"You expect me to settle for that?"

"It's just the way things have to be, baby. My father has a thing about blood lines. He'd cut me off without a cent and I'd have to go to work."

She pulled out of his arms. "Suppose I tell your fiancée?"

Cleve laughed. "She won't believe you. Wannie's terribly naive; she trusts me completely. Now, just hold your temper, Maureen, and do things my way. A mistress is a very comfortable position—you'll have plenty of fine dresses and your own maid. Think about it."

There was more talk, the clever maid badgering and

arguing, but Keso couldn't hear most of it. It didn't take long before she seemed grudgingly mollified.

Cleve said, "Now you understand how it must be, baby. We'll talk more later."

They parted and Keso quickly closed his door as Cleve passed, then leaned against it, his big fists clenched. He had a terrible urge to follow Cleve to his room and beat the stuffing out of him. No, he thought as he shook his head, struggling to control his temper. If he did that, the noise would bring everyone running.

Should he tell Wannie what he had seen? It would hurt her terribly. Would she even believe him? It was going to be a long night, Keso thought with a sigh as he forced himself to return to his bed where he lay sleepless, torn by indecision. Tomorrow morning was the big fox hunt. Tomorrow, maybe he would know what to do.

FIVE

It was not yet dawn when the baying of hounds awakened Wannie. She hurried from her bed to look out the window in breathless anticipation. The rolling acres of the estate were already alive with horses and red-coated riders, while dozens of hounds scurried about, sniffing the grass and barking in excitement.

Wannie had purchased a proper outfit, but she was afraid that her beloved Keso would make a fool of himself today. Was it because she was worried about Keso or concerned she'd be humiliated? What kind of a person had she become?

She heard a rap at the door. "Miss Evans? It's Maureen."

"Oh, yes, come in please." She'd forgotten that wealthy women had maids to help them dress.

The pretty girl came into her room, a bit tight-lipped and grim, Wannie thought. " 'Tis a nice day for the hunt, miss."

"Yes, isn't it?" Wannie watched the redhead lay out things for her. Maureen seemed hostile and tense, and Wannie could only wonder why. Perhaps Mrs. Brewster had scolded her—the Brewsters didn't seem too popular with their own servants.

The maid took the pins from Wannie's hair and began to brush it. "Are ye really related to a duchess?"

What a strange question, Wannie thought. "My mother," she said.

"And very rich?" The Irish girl asked as she brushed.

"That's not a proper remark," Wannie said as she stared into the mirror and into the girl's hostile eyes.

"Excuse me, miss, I totally forgot meself." Now she was almost fawning in a way that made Wannie very uncomfortable. "We poor Irish are just curious about how the other half lives."

"It's not important," Wannie said. "My adoptive parents have the wealth—some gold mines."

"Ahh!" That seemed to mollify the girl. "I do hope you won't report me to the Brewsters, ma'am. I need this position, at least for awhile longer."

"It's already forgotten," Wannie said and waved her away. "I can finish my own hair, thank you."

The girl curtsied and scurried out of the room.

Wannie pulled her long black hair back and tied it with a ribbon. When she surveyed herself in a full-length mirror, she was pleased with what she saw; she did look like she belonged with the wealthy hunting crowd, in her red jacket, full black skirt, and shiny riding boots. She wouldn't want to embarrass Cleve among his own friends.

A rap came at the door. "Wannie, are you ready?"

"Yes, Alexa," she said and hurried to open it. "This is so exciting! What a July Fourth this is going to be!"

The pair ran lightly down the stairs and into the large entry hall where Cleve and Keso waited. Cleve was fetching in his dapper red coat and riding breeches, but Keso wore only a pair of pants, his shirt, and boots.

Alexa linked her arm with Keso's. "You're so handsome, it doesn't matter what you wear."

Keso smiled at the pert blonde. "Thank you, Miss Alexa. Let's go out to the horses, shall we?"

"Let's!"

The two turned and strode toward the veranda, leaving Wannie and Cleve looking after them. Why had she never noticed how tall and masculine her foster brother was? She could almost see the muscles ripple under his shirt and the way Alexa was clinging to his arm so possessively annoyed Wannie no end.

"He's going to be laughed at, you know." Cleve seemed annoyed.

Wannie shrugged. "He can't help it if he doesn't own the proper outfit."

"That doesn't seem to make any difference to Alexa," he snapped. "I think she's set her cap for him."

"So?"

"It just won't do," Cleve muttered, "having a savage—"

"What?" Wannie's temper flared, but perhaps she hadn't heard him correctly.

"I'm sorry, my dear." He took her hand and kissed it, once again the smooth, polished gentleman. "I'm out of sorts this morning."

"A lot of people seem to be," Wannie answered, feeling a little better with his apology. "Even the maid was snappy."

"Who? Maureen? I'll speak to her," he declared, his blue eyes peering into Wannie's dark ones. "What did she say?"

"Never mind, it's not important, and don't you dare scold her. Poor thing's trying to make a living."

"Oh, Wannie, you're so—so democratic!" Cleve kissed the tip of her nose.

In the first dawn of the warm holiday morning, a bugle blew outside and the dogs set up a clamor.

"We'd better go." Cleve looked Wannie over with evident appreciation. "Egad, but you're lovely in that outfit. Do you ride well?"

"Not bad," Wannie smiled up at him, "but not nearly so well as Keso."

Cleve's lips crinkled at the corners as if he knew a secret joke. "We'll just see how well big brother rides."

"I do hope you two are going to be friends," Wannie said as she took his arm and they walked toward the veranda.

"Of course, my dear. Why, he's the one who's hostile. I've been trying to be nice to him just to make you happy!"

They went outside where they were greeted by a large, boisterous crowd of wealthy local landowners, all mounted, hounds running about, grooms scurrying with last minute chores. Mr. Brewster sat a big gray steed, visiting with the local gentry. Mrs. Brewster was playing the perfect hostess, greeting prominent riders as they arrived while the servants hurried to serve a final bracing stirrup cup of liquor before the chase began. Through the French doors, Wannie could see servants setting up tables for the lavish after-hunt breakfast that would be served when the riders returned.

An older, blond man led a dainty bay mare forward. "Be you, Miss Wannie? I'm Ian O'Hearn, the head groom. Here's your mount."

"Oh, what a beautiful mare!" Wannie reached to pat the velvet muzzle even as Keso and Cleve both seemed to jostle each other for the privilege of offering a hand up to the sidesaddle. Then Keso seemed to remember his place and stepped back reluctantly to help the now pouting Alexa to her chestnut mount.

Cleve swing up on a fine sorrel stallion. "Ian, did you saddle up Black Prince for our other guest as I instructed?"

"Mr. Cleve . . ." The hesitation showed in the groom's blue eyes, and when he frowned, the cleft in his chin deepened. "That's an awful spirited stallion, he is—"

"I said Black Prince, Ian," Cleve's eyes were as cold as his voice. "Mr. Evans says he can ride, so we'd all like to see if he's telling the truth."

A murmur and nervous laughter ran through the crowd as the Irish groom turned away, shaking his head. "One of you boys bring him up, then."

Wannie caught her breath as two boys brought the big, black horse down the path. It was not quite as big as Spirit, Keso's stallion back home. This thoroughbred had two grooms hanging onto the bridle as it snorted, trying to rear and paw the air.

Mr. Brewster frowned at his son. "Cleve, you aren't serious!"

"Cleve," Alexa protested, "that horse—"

"Will be a great mount for an accomplished rider," Cleve said and he smiled at Keso. "Of course, if he's too much horse for Keso, we have several old geldings that the ladies aren't using today."

The crowd grew quiet except for a slight, excited murmur. Wannie's breath caught in her throat; Keso's manhood was being challenged. She looked toward Mrs. Brewster for help, but that plump matron had returned inside to oversee the setting up of the hunt table. Keso was a good rider, but this horse looked like a killer.

Even as she started to protest, Keso strode forward. "This mount looks fine to me," he announced to the crowd, "I'll take him. Hold his head, Ian, please."

The cleft in the Irishman's chin deepened as he frowned. Then he sighed and stepped forward to take the bridle. When Keso attempted to mount, the big black whinnied in protest and reared, lifting the groom off the ground while the hunt crowd murmured and laughed.

"I like a horse with spirit," Keso said in a loud voice, "since I intend to be in the front of the pack."

"Governor," Ian murmured, "you'll be a lucky bloke if you're not under it!"

The crowd laughed and Keso laughed with them as he swung into the saddle.

The big stallion snorted and tried to rear again.

"Let him go, Ian," Keso said. "I can handle him from here."

Wannie watched with admiration as Keso sat the horse. The unruly stallion danced about, but Keso sat the saddle as if he'd been born to it, looking masculine and magnificent even without a red coat. She heard a murmur of appreciation run through the crowd and the women riders were all looking at him with soft eyes. Wannie heard the whispers: *Who is that handsome, tall rider who isn't properly dressed? A relative of young Cleve's intended, I hear. Doesn't he know that horse has killed a man?*

Wannie felt her blood run cold. She glanced over at Alexa with a question in her eyes, and the blonde nodded—yes, it was true.

Wannie opened her mouth to protest, to shame Cleve for his cruel joke, but Keso had evidently read her intention because he signaled her to keep silent. The big stallion pranced about, yet Keso handled him easily. "I hope I'm not holding up the hunt," he said and smiled a challenge at Cleve.

"Not at all," Cleve said. "Father, are we ready?"

Mr. Brewster looked over the black horse as if he thought he should say something. "If our guests are." He signaled the master of the hounds, who blew his horn again. The hounds bounded away across the rolling pasture, baying loudly. Immediately, the well-trained horses set off at a trot after the hounds. Keso handled the spirited black horse well, Wannie thought with relief as he rode to the front of the crowd and fell in next to Cleve.

Alexa rode next to her as their horses began to trot.

"I guess I can forget riding next to your brother; it seems there's going to be a little contest."

"I'm seeing a side to Cleve I've never seen before." Wannie reached to spread her long skirt across her saddle so that it swept almost to the ground.

Alexa laughed and turned an admiring eye on Keso's broad back. "And I'm seeing a side to your brother I've not seen before. Cleve's very competitive and the best rider in the county—everyone knows that."

"He's never ridden against Keso," Wannie said with confidence as she settled herself into a slow canter. The horses left the vast lawn of the estate and started across the rolling pasture. "My brother may not know anything about fox hunting, but no one can beat him as a rider."

Alexa stared after the broad back as the riders topped a hill and started down the other side. "It really was a dirty trick to give your brother that stallion. Black Prince has stomped a groom to death and nearly killed the last rider foolish enough to take him on the hunt."

Wannie felt a chill run through her, yet she was confident of Keso's ability in the saddle. It dawned on her that she was pulling for him to win and she felt a bit guilty, thinking she ought to root for her fiancé.

About that time, the hounds picked up the scent and set up a howling chorus as they dashed madly across the meadows. The horses took off at a gallop, too, and Wannie had no more time to think about anything except keeping her own seat. She was an expert rider, but back in Colorado, she always rode astride wearing Keso's old pants and shirts; it was difficult to sit a side-saddle.

Her heart beating hard in the cool morning, Wannie stayed in the middle of the pack, enjoying the ride and the exhilaration of the chase. They took a low hedge, then a brook, her little bay mare running easily. She glanced over at Alexa. "Great horse!"

"It's the bloodlines!" Alexa shouted back as they galloped on. "Nothing quite so important!"

They crossed the pasture and leaped a low fence, the hounds' baying echoing through the warm morning. Alexa yelled to get her attention, then pointed up ahead.

Wannie looked. Sure enough, Keso was handling the black stallion with a superb hand as he rode neck and neck with Cleve, the other young blades strung out behind them as hounds and horses raced after the prey.

Over the brooks and fences they went, her heart seeming to stop each instant her mare left the ground, then starting again as the dainty mount landed on the other side and kept running. Around them, horses stumbled or riders fell as a mount refused a jump. Others, the horses tiring and lathered or the rider less skilled or enthused, dropped out to watch the merry chase from the sidelines.

Across the rolling meadows the hunt thundered, spotted hounds baying, the pack thinning as horses fell or refused a jump. Yet in the lead, Cleve and Keso still rode neck and neck.

Up ahead, Wannie saw a big stone wall and she felt a sinking feeling. Most of the horses would never clear that. She glanced over at Alexa, who signaled her that most would swing through the open gate only a few yards down the fence. With a sigh of relief, she reined her mare to do so. Even as she did, she looked toward the wall. In front of the pack, many of the young dandies were reining their mounts away but Keso and Cleve were headed straight for it.

Her breath seemed to catch in her throat as she watched. The wall was high and solid stone; a horse and rider could be killed if they failed that jump. At the last possible moment, she saw Cleve hesitate, then rein his big sorrel toward the open gate. Keso, instead, leaned forward in the saddle and urged Black Prince on.

No! She almost screamed it out, but her voice caught in her throat as Keso urged the big horse into the jump and it left the ground. For a heart-stopping moment, man and horse seemed to hang in mid-air and she heard the moan go up in throats around her.

Oh, Keso, I don't want you to be hurt! I don't—and then the stallion cleared the wall with inches to spare and landed on the other side, still running.

A cheer went up from the crowd that had reined in to watch and Keso turned the lathered horse and swung it back around at a slow trot, acknowledging the cheers with a modest nod of his head.

Only Cleve did not cheer. "The hunt's not over yet!" he shouted, and lashed his horse savagely, taking off again after the disappearing hounds. The rest of the hunt group took up the chase again, but at a slower pace.

"Wannie, your brother is superb!" Alexa sighed, staring after Keso as she trotted her horse through the open gate in pursuit of the others.

Yes, isn't he? Wannie thought with quiet pride, then felt a twinge of guilt. She should have been cheering for Cleve; after all, he was going to be her husband. She pushed the guilt to the back of her mind as she nudged the little mare forward and joined in the hunt.

Up ahead, Cleve and Keso were once again side by side and in hot pursuit of the hounds, who seemed to have cornered their prey up in the rocks of a hill ahead. The first rider there would be awarded the brush if they caught the fox, but she sensed the intense rivalry between those two had nothing to do with a fox. It puzzled Wannie.

A low wall lay ahead. She saw some horses clearing it, others refusing. She might have turned her own horse aside if she had kept her mind on her riding, but she was concentrating on the pair of men galloping toward the hunt finish where the dogs barked and bayed around that rock pile.

"Look out, Wannie!" She heard Alexa scream a warning, but even as she felt her little mare refuse the jump, it was already too late. Wannie tried to regain her seat, but she'd lost her balance. In that split-second as she flew from the saddle, Wannie saw both men look back over their shoulders. Then the ground rushed up to meet her and she landed hard.

Wannie lay there in a tumble of skirts, her eyes closed. She knew she ought to get up, but the confusion and neighing horses seemed very far away and she was not sure she could stand. Surely Cleve would return to carry her back to the house. Nothing would matter to him but her safety; he wouldn't care who won the brush.

"Wannie?" came Alexa's distant voice. "Are you all right?"

She felt scratched and bruised and the grass beneath her face smelled fresh and green in the morning heat. She didn't answer because it seemed to take too much effort even to open her eyes.

She heard the sound of a horse galloping up, then the creak of a saddle as a rider dismounted. Strong arms cradled her, brushing the curls from her forehead. She felt safe now, safe and secure in this muscular embrace. It was so wonderful to have a man who loved her this much.

Cleve? Very slowly, she opened her eyes and looked into Keso's worried face.

"Wannie? Are you all right? Speak to me!"

She reached up to touch his dear, dark face. "Keso? You—you didn't get the brush?"

"To hell with the brush!" he muttered, then he swung

her up in his arms. "I think I'd better get you back to the house."

She saw Cleve gallop up just then. "Is she all right?"

"What do you care?" Keso snapped. "You got the fox, didn't you?"

"As a matter of fact, it got away," Cleve said, seeming quite annoyed. "Here, let me take her."

"No," Keso said, "I'll carry her."

In a daze, Wannie saw the peering, curious faces gathered around as Keso strode across the meadow toward Black Prince. She had forgotten how strong and confident Keso was. Even when she was small, he always looked after her. Cleve had returned, too, she reminded herself.

Only the tiniest part of her mind remembered that Cleve had made sure the fox was gone before he returned to see about her. Well, he knew everyone else had stopped and she was already being cared for, Wannie thought.

Keso swung up on the horse, cradling her gently in his strong arms. She laid her face against his broad chest and looked up at him. "Thank you," she whispered.

"It's that damned sidesaddle," he said. "You aren't used to it. You've always been a great rider, Wannie. Let's get you back to the house."

"I'm fine," she protested.

"No, you're not and I'm taking you back."

"You sound exactly like you did the time I stepped on a fish hook all those years ago."

"Some things never change," he said.

"Well, pretty soon, I'll have a husband and you won't have to worry about me anymore."

He frowned and didn't say anything. Holding her very close against him as he rode, she could hear his heart beating. She felt small and cherished and safe in his embrace. Funny, she had never really thought of him as a man before, only as a big brother who saddled ponies, pushed her swing, and allowed her to tag after him when he went fishing or exploring the wild mountains around their home. However, she was a grown woman now and soon, Keso would find a wife and Wannie could no longer trail after him or expect him to pick stickers out of her toes or help her up in a tree she wasn't big enough to climb. Right now, he looked lost in thought—and grim.

"Keso, what are you thinking?"

"Nothing."

"You have to be thinking something," she insisted. "You look mad."

"I'm not mad."

"You look mad."

"Okay—have it your way, brat."

"I'm getting a little old for you to call me that."

"Don't I know it!" He looked even grimmer.

"Now what's that supposed to mean?"

"Nothing." He looked straight ahead as he rode, his eyes fixed on the horizon.

His hostile attitude puzzled her. "I'm sorry I kept you from getting the fox."

"I said forget about the damned fox! These dandies have to be a little loco to spend all this energy over one ragged old fox when no one needs the fur to keep warm and they can't eat it."

"Then why were you trying to outride Cleve to get it?"

"Making a damned fool out of myself, I reckon."

"The ladies all thought you were wonderful."

"I don't care what the ladies thought." His mouth looked even grimmer.

"I don't know why you're so annoyed. You can put

me down and let me return to Cleve; I'm perfectly all right."

"Let me be the judge of that."

"Why is it you've always got to take charge?"

"Hush, Wannie."

"I will not!"

"If you weren't addled from landing on your head, I'd turn you across my knee and dust your britches like I used to."

"You wouldn't dare!"

"Don't tempt me."

She struggled to sit up and get out of his arms, then realized she wasn't strong enough. With a resigned sigh, she laid her face against his chest.

"That's more like it," he said.

"What about the others?"

He looked back over his shoulder. "They're coming. Cleve looks like he's swallowed a green persimmon."

"Can you blame him? You made him look like a fool."

"He didn't need much help."

"Keso, you're talking about my fiancé."

"No other."

She felt called to defend her choice. "He's really a fine fellow; you just don't know him very well."

"Better than you think."

"Now, what's that supposed to mean?"

Keso stared straight ahead. "Just forget it, okay?"

She was too weary and bruised to try to make any sense of all this conversation. Keso was no doubt angry because Cleve had plotted to give him that unruly horse, but in the West, cowboys often did that to a greenhorn. Otherwise, she couldn't imagine why Keso had taken such a dislike to her fiancé.

Keso reined in before the veranda and the head groom came running. "Lord protect us! What's happened, sir?"

"My sister had an accident, Ian. I'll take her up to her room. The others are on their way in."

He dismounted, swinging her lightly as he carried her up the steps.

"Dearie me," Mrs. Brewster said as she hurried into the hall, wringing her plump hands. "I hope she hasn't hurt anything."

"Her pride, maybe," Keso said laconically. "She'll be all right by tomorrow, I think." He started up the stairs. "Wannie, which room is it?"

"The third door on the right," she said, "but I'm not going to stay in bed 'til tomorrow."

"Yes, you are." His tone sounded final and he kept walking.

"I'll miss all the festivities," she wailed, "the fireworks and all."

"You can watch them out the window—a maid will bring you some food." He kicked the door open, carried her over, and laid her on the bed very gently. For a long moment, he leaned over her. She felt an unaccustomed urge to reach up and touch his face, then reminded herself he'd think she was loco. He had been raised as her brother and he had his eye on pretty blond Alexa.

He pulled away suddenly, looking very uncomfortable. "I—I need to be going."

"Oh, go on downstairs," Wannie grumbled, "I wouldn't want you to miss a moment of all those pretty girls ogling you and dropping their hankies so you can pick them up."

He looked puzzled. "Is that what I'm supposed to do?"

"The way some of them were staring, I imagine they'd drop their drawers for you, too," Wannie snapped.

"That's awfully crude talk for a young lady who just graduated from Miss Priddy's fancy school."

"Stop lecturing me like a big brother," she huffed.

"That's me, all right—your big brother. Now hush and stay in bed!" He looked furious as he started out the door.

"I reckon you intend to go down and party and dance with Alexa and all her pretty friends," she pouted.

"You damn betcha!" He went out the door and slammed it so hard, it echoed.

Now what was he so angry about when she was the one who was stuck up here for the afternoon? She lay there staring at the flowered wallpaper and thinking about defying him. She might just get dressed and go downstairs anyway. On the other hand, she had no doubt he'd make good his threat to dust her britches, probably in front of everyone, and then Cleve would protest and there'd be trouble.

In a few minutes, Alexa came up with a tray. "Keso sent me up. Mother's in a dither and Cleve's making noises about calling a doctor."

She shook her head. "Tell everyone to stop worrying—I'm fine."

Alexa set the tray on the bedside table. "Your brother was wonderful today, so gallant and good-looking. Everyone's talking about him. All the ladies are gathered around him downstairs."

The image of pretty girls cooing and flirting with Keso annoyed Wannie to the point of gritting her teeth. It was only because he was going to be having fun while she lay up here bruised and bored. "Are you going to stay up here and keep me company?"

"Are you kidding?" Alexa snorted. "I'm going to hurry down and see if I can sit by Keso at the hunt breakfast before someone else grabs that seat."

"He's pretty shy," Wannie said. "All those eager girls may scare him."

"Really? When I came up, he was laughing and talking with half a dozen of them. They were clustered around him like hens around a rooster. I'm going to ask him to be my partner at croquet."

Wannie gritted her teeth. "He doesn't know how to play croquet."

Alexa winked at her as she went out the door. "Then think of all the fun I'm going to have teaching him! And maybe he can teach *me* something!"

Damn! How dare Alexa be so bold. Wannie remembered seeing the couple kissing on the veranda last night and gritted her teeth.

Mrs. Brewster came in as Wannie ate. There was a bowl of fresh fruit, the ham was crisp, the biscuits light and fluffy, but Wannie's mind wasn't on food. She assured the lady she was all right and didn't need a doctor, but she did say she'd like to see Cleve.

He came upstairs, leaving the door open behind him. "Wannie, are you all right?"

"Fine, thank you."

"Thank God!" He walked to the bed and gave her a quick peck on the cheek. "I certainly meant to carry you to the house myself, but your brother just shouldered me aside."

Maybe that was how it had been; it was difficult to remember exactly. "You'll have to ignore it, dearest. He's been looking after me so long, he probably hasn't gotten used to the idea of handing me over to someone else."

"And doesn't intend to," Cleve muttered.

"What?"

"Nothing, my dear, forget it. I'm just so relieved you're all right."

Through the door, she could hear the laughter and talk downstairs as the festivities continued.

He looked toward the noise with a wistful sigh. "Really, it's not proper for me to stay up here in a lady's bedroom, even with the door open."

"I wish you'd stay and talk and forget what's proper."

He drew himself up proudly. "Wannie, people of our status never forget what's proper. Besides, some of the fellows have a card game going in the library."

"Run along then." She hoped she sounded more cheerful than she felt.

"Are you sure you'll be all right?"

"Yes, go on. I'll take a nap and watch the fireworks from the window tonight."

"Fine." He was gone before she could reconsider.

Wannie lay there bored and sore, staring at the big diamond on her finger. Someday, she would be mistress of Steel Manor and in charge of all these festivities. Her children would be riding their ponies in the hunt with the other well-bred children. Children. She felt her face flush as she pictured herself naked in Cleve's arms. Somehow, she didn't like the thought. She closed her eyes and smiled, remembering the way Keso's strong arms had cradled her and carried her up to her bed; that split-second when she had touched his face and felt . . . Her eyes flew open in horror. What in God's name was the matter with her? She must have really landed on her head to have such a thought about her own brother!

SIX

Cherokee walked into the kitchen as Silver finished putting away the dinner things.

"Hey, sweet darlin," I'm glad you're feeling better." He kissed the back of her neck, then slipped his arms around her.

Such a comforting feeling, his nuzzling the back of her neck. She let her body relax to fit into the curves of his. "Not much of a Fourth of July. I miss the kids."

"They'll be home in a few days," he comforted. "They're probably in the middle of big doin's at that fancy estate today." He kissed the back of her neck again, moving his hands up to cover her breasts, squeezing gently. "Then they'll marry and have a bunch of babies for us to spoil."

She stared out the window at the mountains in the distance, her hands going up to cover his. "I'm sorry I didn't give you any children of our own."

"What are you talking about?" he said, whirling her around in his arms. "We've got two nice kids; so what if we didn't hatch 'em? I couldn't be happier if they were our own flesh and blood."

"What—what do you suppose Wannie would say if she knew all the horrible scandal about her parents?"

"Maybe she knows already; kids are smarter than you

think. Anyway, I can't rightly think of a good way to tell a kid something that terrible."

"And my part in it." She slipped her arms around his neck and blinked back tears.

"Hush, sweet darlin', you only did what you had to do." He began to kiss her face, trailing kisses along her jaw. "I love you; stop worrying about the past."

His big arms were comforting as always and finally, she stopped crying.

"I know what we can do to celebrate the holiday."

She laughed softly. "We can do that without a reason."

He swung her up in his arms and kissed her again. "Yes, but it is a great idea, don't you think?"

She smiled at him, her pale blond hair hanging across his arm. "We'll make a few fireworks of our own."

"Now, that's more like it." He kissed the tip of her nose, "and the kids aren't around to interrupt about the time the skyrockets go off."

"They'd probably faint to think an old married couple like us still make love." She closed her eyes as he carried her into the bedroom.

He chuckled. "Kids never think of their parents making love at all; if they only knew it's better when you grow older . . . that is, if you really love each other."

Cherokee laid her on the bed and very slowly unbuttoned her bodice. "God, you're beautiful."

"To you, maybe," she said, thinking of her scarred face.

"Does any other guy's opinion matter? I'm the one who's married to you." He lay down next to her, tracing his finger around the pale rosette of her breast.

"Almost fifteen years we've been married, come November," she recalled, closing her eyes as his warm mouth found her nipple. "Don't you ever tire of making love to me?"

"Not in a million years." His breath was warm against her breast and she ran her hands through his gray-streaked hair, thinking he was as handsome as he had been all those years ago when they wed the day after the Duchess's Palace burned down. The night it burned, she and Cherokee had taken the two children and ridden out of Denver, only hours after she killed Wannie's father.

She let Cherokee touch and caress her skin with the slow leisure of an expert, mature lover who was in no hurry to finish until he had explored and tasted every inch of her body while gradually making her want him beyond all reason. Their hurtful pasts were behind them now and they trusted and cherished each other as they never would anyone else.

She let her thighs fall apart as his hand went up to stroke and tease her. "Make it last a long, long time," she whispered.

"It will be my pleasure to amuse you, lady," he promised, "and if you aren't pleased, I'll start all over again." He returned to kissing each breast into pink, turgid peaks.

She settled into the curve of his arm, pulled his dear, weathered face down to hers, and sucked his tongue deep into her mouth, feeling his breath quicken with desire. She let him play with her and stroke her, knowing it was raising his ardor. Finally, when neither of them could stand the waiting one second more, he probed her wetness with his throbbing hardness, waiting for her to lock her long, slim legs around him, dig her nails into his broad shoulders, and pull him deep into her.

They made love in a slow, satisfying rhythm that each knew so well after all these years. Then they settled against each other and drifted off to sleep in the warm afternoon. "I love you, Mrs. Evans," he murmured, "and I think it's been a great holiday."

She smiled sleepily at him. "A great holiday," she agreed as she settled into the big half-breed's arms to sleep, safe and secure against anything that might hurt her.

I hope Wannie finds this kind of fulfillment, she thought. *Waanibe;* it was Arapaho for Singing Wind. Perhaps the girl need never know the scandal of her past.

The celebrating crowd had scattered about the house, resting in the hot afternoon as Cleve went down the hall to his father's study. He was more than a little annoyed. Wannie was upstairs in her room, resting. Maureen was somewhere in the house and he hoped to find her and wheedle a few minutes' entertainment out of her lush body since he was losing heavily in the card game in the library. Now Father had sent for him. Had the stern old goat found out Cleve had broken his promise and returned to his excessive drinking and gambling?

He knocked at the door. "Father?"

"Come in."

It was like facing God, Cleve thought with distaste as he came in and closed the door. Seeing his father sitting at his desk, it was like approaching Jehovah's throne.

Cleveland glowered at his son, thinking perhaps that the boy's wayward habits had resulted from spoiling him so. He had waited a long time for a son, and finally, the plain Bertha had conceived about the time Cleveland was ready to brave the fire of criticism and divorce her. By then, he controlled Bertha's wealth and his acquaintances would have understood his leaving her if she hadn't produced an heir.

"You sent for me, Father?"

Cleveland gestured him to be seated and fixed his gaze on his son, who lounged indulgently in the chair across the fine mahogany desk. "You acted like a damn fool on the hunt this morning."

"Well, the savage said he could ride—I wanted to see if he could."

"He made you look stupid, which, if I may say so, usually takes little effort."

"So you constantly tell me." Cleve shifted restlessly.

"Wannie Evans is a lovely girl—just the type I have always hoped you would marry."

"And I will, Father." Cleve smiled and leaned forward in his chair.

"Not if you get too cross-ways with her foster brother."

His son made a gesture of dismissal. "He'll return to the wild West and be out of the picture soon. I promise you a houseful of wonderful, blue-blooded grandchildren."

Cleveland nodded. "She really has royal bloodlines?"

"So it seems; Mother's quite impressed and can hardly wait to lord it over all her friends." Cleve began to fill his pipe. "Wannie's pretty, too. I was afraid I was going to get stuck with one of those ugly society cows Mother was pushing at me."

Cleveland watched his son light the pipe and thought about his own arranged marriage. "Men do what they must. Love is silly, sentimental nonsense poor poets sing about. Marry for money and social position, my father told me, and he was right. You can buy love in any whorehouse."

Cleve's blue eyes widened in surprise. "Father, you surprise me."

"Unfortunately, you don't surprise me. People are gossiping about your wild ways again."

Cleve started to say something, then looked out the window instead, smoking his pipe.

He was handsome, Cleveland thought with enormous pride, and his hair wasn't thinning like his own was. His pride and joy in his only son made up for living with a plain, dumb thing like Bertha. "Son, I'm glad to see you're taking a wife. I hope this means you're going to throw yourself into helping to build our fortune, not just spending it."

"I don't know what you mean," Cleve said and blew a cloud of sweet-scented smoke. "I work in the office—"

"Balderdash! You collect a paycheck and pinch the girls who work there." Cleveland leaned back in his chair and glared at his heir. "It's time you behaved like a Brewster and took some interest in expanding the business."

"Like what?" Cleve looked petulant and bored.

"Oh, I don't know—like maybe exploring new markets," Cleveland said. "With all those settlers moving West, there's going to be a big market for Brewster kitchenware and farm equipment."

"I suppose." Cleve yawned.

God, how he had spoiled his son and even his niece. Of course, no one expected Alexa to do anything but marry well. Cleve was shallow, vain, and a spendthrift.

"I have worked hard and made many sacrifices to build this company into something grand for you, my son. I've dreamed of you running for governor or senator."

"Now, Father," Cleve said and took the pipe from his mouth and made a soothing gesture, "I don't know what you've heard, but whatever it is, it's a lie—"

"I doubt it, more's the pity."

Cleve knocked the ashes from his pipe into a crystal ashtray. "Look, Father, may I go now? There's a card game in the library and I was trying to make up my losses—"

"Shut up, sit still, and listen to me!" Cleveland commanded, his voice rising like thunder. "Or would you rather talk about being disinherited?"

Cleve sank back in his chair, glowering like a tiger on a circus stool. "I didn't mean to offend you, Father. What is it you want?"

"I want you to be more circumspect; your wild ways are being talked about among my business associates."

"If you're talking about Maureen—"

"I am. I'll take care of that for you as I've always cleaned up your scandals, but you must change."

"What's the point of being rich if you can't enjoy it?"

"A gentleman enjoys himself discreetly," Cleveland said and reached into the humidor on his desk for a fine imported cigar. "Most of all, he thinks about his heritage and his son's future."

"I don't understand—"

"Balderdash! Shut up and listen to me. You are engaged to a lovely young woman, whom I understand is of a highborn family; she will be perfect as the mother of my grandchildren."

"Wannie is beautiful," Cleve agreed with a grin, causing the cleft in his chin to deepen. It was one of his most attractive features. Cleveland tried to remember who among his forebearers had had that distinctive feature. Maybe it had come from Bertha's side of the family.

"Father?"

"What?" Cleveland came out of his thoughts with a start. Abruptly, he realized his son was staring at him. "I—I was merely thinking," he said crisply and stood, then paced up and down. "Now, my boy, here is what you will do. You will be more discreet with your wenching and everything else you've been doing, lest the young lady break the engagement. After you're legally married, I don't care whether it's happy or not, as long as you maintain appearances."

As your mother and I have done, he thought. He despised Bertha, but he persevered to build an empire for his son.

Cleve ducked his head. "Whatever you say, Father."

"Good. Now that we understand each other, you may return to your card game, but cut back on your gambling."

"Yes, Father." Cleve left the library, closing the door behind him.

Cleveland tossed his cigar into the brass spittoon and sat back down at his desk, listening to the holiday crowd out on the lawn and in the house. He had ledgers to look at—no matter it was a holiday. Business and his son were the only interests he had. Once, he had had a taste for expensive whores, but that passion had burned out with advancing age. At least he had been discreet and Bertha never suspected a thing. They had not shared a bed since she had become pregnant with Cleve and Cleveland neither knew nor cared what Bertha thought or felt about anything.

He stared at the row of portraits of his ancestors on his library wall. Blue-blooded aristocrats dating back to the *Mayflower*, he thought with satisfaction. Blood counts in both men and horses, so eventually, young Cleve would reach his potential, fulfill his heritage. His son's existence made this loveless marriage worth the price Cleveland had paid for it.

It was growing dark when Keso went up the mansion's stairs and knocked on Wannie's door. "Wannie, it's me."

"Go away! With all the laughter and noise out on the lawn, I expect the dancing and fireworks are about to start."

Instead, he came in. "They are. I thought maybe I could carry you downstairs so you could watch."

"Watch you having a great time dancing and flirting? Must you rub it in?"

She wore a sheer pink nightdress as she sat in bed propped up by pillows, her long, black hair hanging loose over her shoulders. She had never looked so desirable to him. Once, when she was about fourteen or fifteen, he had accidently seen her swimming nude in a mountain brook and had been ashamed at how his body had reacted to the sight.

"Wannie, you ought to put on some kind of a wrap if you're going to entertain company."

"Oh, for heaven's sake!" She waved him in to sit on her bed. "You're not company, you're just my brother."

He didn't feel like her brother, but he couldn't resist the invitation to cross the room and sit on the edge of her bed. Through the sheer, pale, pink fabric, he could see her breasts. He kept his hands clenched on the coverlet to keep them from coming up to cover those dark-tipped mounds.

"Is everyone outside?" She sighed and the lace of the gown slid off one shoulder. Keso stared at that bare flesh. He wanted to kiss along that shoulder until he reached the swell of that breast, then pull it down so he could taste that nipple. He took several deep breaths, trying to control his body's urgent throbbing.

"What's wrong with you, Keso? Are you choking on something?"

"No, I-I'm just hot, that's all; it's a hot night."

"It certainly is." She fanned herself with her hand, looking absently toward the window. When she moved her arm, her breast moved beneath the sheer fabric.

The throb in him became an agonizing ache and Keso had to grit his teeth to contain a sound. Innocent that she was, she had no idea how she was affecting him. In his mind, he tumbled her into the covers, kissing her passionately, possessing her, protecting her. He felt sweat break out on his forehead. Underneath that sheer fabric, no doubt her body was shimmering with heat. He imagined the feel of it naked against him as he embraced her, slipped the silver ring on her finger, made her his in every sense of the word.

Laughter and music drifted through the open window.

Wannie frowned. "Alexa will come looking for you soon."

"I know—I just thought I'd see how you were." He found himself staring at her mouth. Wannie's lips were full and soft, he thought.

She absently ran her pink tongue along those lips and it was all he could do to keep from taking her in his arms and kissing her deeply, thoroughly.

Sounds of firecrackers and cheers echoed through the darkness, lit only by a single lamp.

Wannie craned her neck toward the window, and when she did, her face almost brushed his. "Sounds like the fireworks are starting."

"Would you like me to carry you over to the window so you can watch?"

"I could walk—I'm okay."

In answer, he swept her up in his big arms, marveling at how light she was. Her arms went around his neck and when he breathed, she smelled like wildflowers. He swallowed hard, carried her to the window, and stood where she could see out.

"Keso, I'm heavy—you could put me in a chair."

"I could lift you with one arm, and you know it. Besides, brat, you can't see as well from that chair." The light reflected on her shining black locks and he wanted to stroke them, tangle his fingers in them. He could feel the heat of her breast through his shirt and her long, pretty legs were draped over his arm. He wondered if she could feel the pulse pounding through his aroused body.

She looked up at him and abruptly seemed upset and troubled.

Oh, damn—he was sure she sensed he wanted her past all reason. "Wannie, what's the matter?"

"N-Nothing. Keso, put me back in bed, please." She trembled in his arms. Wannie must have realized how he was reacting to her.

With a sigh, he carried her over and put her gently in the bed. She pulled the cover up over her breasts and he saw that her small fingers were clenched in the sheet tightly. He had unnerved her, he thought with regret. He took her small shoulders in his hands and kissed her forehead. "I love you, brat."

"Thanks for what you did for me this morning; I suppose I acted badly."

Keso shrugged, thinking how warm and silky her flesh was under his fingers. He wanted to pull her up to his mouth and kiss her thoroughly. She'd be horrified. "Part of a big brother's job, I reckon."

He forced himself to let go of her and step back, knowing he had no right even to think what he was thinking. All these years, Keso had cherished and protected her as she turned from annoying brat to gangly girl-child to grown-up beauty. In a few months, young Cleve would take the virginity Keso had guarded so carefully all these years. Cleve, the rich, rotten heir who would cheat on Keso's beloved, break her heart, and make her cry if she discovered the truth. "I'll always be there for you, Wannie, if you need me. Remember that."

"I know."

Maybe if he finally told her how he felt about her, she'd change her mind about marrying Cleve. "Wannie, I—I want you to know that, well, I love you."

"I love you, too, Keso," she said absently and looked toward the window where the fireworks flashed. "You've been the best kind of brother a girl could want."

He almost cursed aloud at that, realizing now that she had misunderstood his meaning. She loved him like a brother, nothing more, and thought he was saying the same. "No, what I meant to say was . . ."

She looked up at him expectantly and he felt like an idiot. He'd told her he loved her and she'd brushed it off. There was no need to say more—he'd only make a fool of himself and make her uncomfortable with his groveling. Her heart belonged to Cleve Brewster. Well, Keso had tried. He had to get out of here now before he reached out and took her in his embrace, whispered soft words of endearment. Wannie—sweet, sweet Wannie. He would die for her, or kill for her, but he would never have her. Tears came to his eyes and Keso blinked rapidly.

"What's the matter, Keso?"

"Uh, smoke from the lamp chimney." He forced himself to stride to the door. Maybe if he could get her back to Colorado, he could buy some time to decide what to do about that rotten Cleve; maybe he could even change Wannie's mind. How could he? Cleve was handsome, sophisticated, polished—everything Keso was not. Keso was rough and ill-mannered, and knew nothing of the life she aspired to. Against an elegant gentleman like Cleve Brewster, Keso couldn't compete. He wished for a fleeting moment that he was back among the Cheyenne, attacking her train or stagecoach and taking her captive. As a savage brave, Keso would fight any man who tried to claim her, and Wannie would belong to the victor as a warrior's prize.

"Keso, Cleve said he might consider asking you to be his best man."

"What?" He'd been lost in the image of fighting the

snooty heir with lance and knife, then claiming his bride, sweeping Wannie up in his arms and carrying her into his tipi to warm his blankets. If only it were that simple. "I'm not sure that's a good idea, brat. Besides, he'd probably really rather have one of his college friends."

She seemed to relax now that he had moved away from the bed. "We've got lots of time to talk about it—fancy society weddings take a lot of planning."

"Remember when Silver and Cherokee got married in that country preacher's kitchen? I was the best man and you were the maid of honor."

She laughed. "I remember. We were just children and it wasn't much of a wedding."

"Good enough—they're still married."

"Sweet memories." She smiled, thinking. "Remember how I was such a silly kid who said I was going to marry you when I grew up and you could hardly stand me?"

He nodded. "I even remember little things you've forgotten, like how you played dress-up in Silver's things. Looks like you'll have all the jewels and clothes you want now."

"I guess that's a weakness of mine." She looked down at her big diamond. "Once you made me a necklace, remember?"

He colored. "A daisy chain. I reckon it was a stupid thing to do."

"I thought it was sweet."

"Well, yeah, I reckon it's the sort of thing a rough country bumpkin would do. I know I've embarrassed you in front of your fine friends, Wannie, and I'm truly sorry."

Her eyes misted. "You can't help it if you weren't born to his life, Keso. I love you anyway."

But not in the way I want. He choked back an impulse

to scream the words at her, grab her and shake some sense into her. "We are planning on leaving in a few days, aren't we? Back to Colorado?"

She nodded. "Good night. Have fun dancing with Alexa."

"I'll have a great time," he lied. " 'Night, Brat." He left her room, but he didn't go down to the dance. Instead, he went to his room and to bed, but he didn't sleep. He lay there picturing Cleve Brewster stripping Wannie's nightgown off on their wedding night and taking her.

Keso clenched and unclenched his fists, wanting to pound the young heir senseless. What should he do with his knowledge of Cleve's unfaithfulness? Should he tell her what he had seen? Should he step back and let her marry the spoiled young dandy? Could he stop Wannie even if he tried? All Keso knew was that he loved her beyond all reason. It wasn't enough; God help him, it wasn't enough!

SEVEN

Cherokee untied his horse and looked anxiously toward Silver standing on the cabin steps in the mid-July heat. More than anything, he hated to leave her out here all alone. "You're sure you'll be all right 'til I get back?"

She nodded reassurance. "Drat it all, Cherokee, you worry about me like I was a child. It isn't that many miles to the Ute Agency; you won't be gone more than a few days."

"Long enough," he said. "I've half a mind not to go."

"You'd never forgive yourself if you didn't, dearest. If someone doesn't do something to ease the tension, there's liable to be another Indian war."

"You're right, as always, sweet darlin'." He reached to hug her one more time. "I may not be on the best of terms with the Utes because of my friendship with the Cheyenne, but I reckon they respect me, so maybe I can cool things down."

Silver stepped back. "I think it's that agent, Meeker, who needs to learn some sense."

He swung up on his horse. "You're right about that. I don't know why whites always think they're right and the Indians are wrong. I won't be gone but a few days."

"Don't worry about me; I've got a gun and I know

how to use it." She leaned against the porch railing. "The kids should be back by the time you return."

"I've missed them," he admitted with a grin. "Maybe now they'll get married and raise some grandchildren for us."

A shadow of worry crossed her beautiful, scarred face. "I wonder about that. After years in a big city, a cabin in the Rockies may seem pretty dull to Wannie."

"I reckon we shouldn't have given in and let her go off. There was a good enough school in Denver. Anything she wanted, Keso always talked us into letting her do—he spoiled her worse than we did. You reckon he's serious about her?"

Silver nodded. "I think he is. Who knows? He's such a private person. Never says much—the Indian in him, I guess."

Cherokee reined his horse away from the hitching rail. "I'll be looking forward to seeing them both. Now, you take care of yourself, sweet darlin', while I'm gone."

"I'll be fine, Cherokee. You concentrate on keeping an Indian war from breaking out in northwestern Colorado."

"I'll do my best." He waved and nudged his horse into a lope, leaving his beloved on the porch waving good-bye.

However, days later, seated in the Indian agent's office across from the spare, elderly man, Cherokee wasn't so sure. "You just don't understand Indians, Meeker."

The man's piercing blue eyes glared back. "What's to understand? I'm going to make a success of this agency. Everyone else has failed, but I don't intend to."

"What you don't understand is that the Utes are like the Cheyenne—they aren't farmers, they're hunters.

They consider plowing woman's work, not jobs for proud warriors."

"Proud warriors!" The man brushed back his iron-gray hair and stood up. "They're on the public dole and taxpayers are tired of supporting them while they laze around, go on an occasional hunt, and mostly race ponies. They who will not work shall not eat."

He must not lose his temper with this self-righteous government employee. "May I remind you that the Utes own millions of acres and have survived on their hunting skills all this time without farming?"

"Those times are no more!" Meeker thundered. "There isn't enough game to support them, they must learn to farm!"

"There was plenty of game before the whites began to trespass on Ute land."

Meeker looked as annoyed as Cherokee felt. "Northwestern Colorado has rich minerals, vast forests, and good farmland. All that is presently going to waste."

"The Utes don't think so—they roam it all."

"That's precisely the point!" Meeker snapped. "They roam like Gypsies without putting a plow to the millions of acres Congress gave them—"

"Congress didn't give them anything," Cherokee said, trying to keep his voice level. If he lost his temper, he would never be able to reason with Nathan Meeker. "This is their land and has been for many generations."

"Be that as it may," this latest agent shrugged him off, "they aren't putting it to good use. White taxpayers who are also voters are asking why they shouldn't be given this wasted soil to farm, cut timber on, or mine all those minerals. They're tired of supporting loafing redskins."

"The immediate problem is white trespassers killing and driving off all the game the Utes need to survive."

"They must change," Meeker said, his blue eyes

gleaming with determination. "The Cheyenne and the Sioux have had to change as the buffalo were killed off. Now it's the Utes' turn. I will teach them to farm."

"Even if you could teach them and they were willing, which I doubt, much of northwestern Colorado is too arid."

"That's what everyone said about the area around Greeley, which I founded, but I showed them it could be done." He got up from his desk and walked up and down the room.

"At what cost?" Cherokee rolled a cigarette. "I've heard you've put yourself in a lot of debt with that town you created."

Meeker's face turned a ruddy flush. "It—it's true I've had financial difficulties and I have a family to support." He came back to the desk and leaned on it with both hands, looking earnestly into Cherokee's face. "I'll be honest with you, Evans. I need this position and this income. I've worked for a newspaper and I write poetry, but that doesn't buy food. The previous Indian agents here all failed and were fired. Don't you see? If I can make the Utes farm successfully, I can keep this job and pay off those debts. I'm not a young man anymore."

Cherokee was touched by the older man's earnest plea, remembering that Greeley, the publishing mogul, flattered at having a town named for him, had used his influence to help Meeker get this job. "I can understand your viewpoint, Meeker, but you don't understand Indians. You'll never turn Utes into peaceful farmers."

"We'll see." Meeker went to the window and stared out. "My wife and daughter are working with the women and children and soon we'll dig some irrigation ditches. There's a fertile place out there in this valley that would be great for crops."

Cherokee got up, came to the window, stared out,

and saw the mid-July heat shimmering over the land. "That valley? Surely you can't be serious!"

"I certainly am."

"But that's where the Utes race their horses. They've used it as a racetrack for years. They'll never let you plow that up."

Meeker made a gesture of dismissal. "I don't need their permission. I'm in charge here, and Washington tells me they'll back me up as needed."

"It'll be needed," Cherokee promised as he shook his head with disgust, "believe me. The Utes have lived at peace with whites for generations, but when you try to make them stop racing their beloved horses, you go too far."

"Mr. Evans, you exaggerate the possible danger," Meeker sniffed. "I'm sure the Utes will eventually see that I'm right about this. I've got Chief Ouray coming in today to talk this over and calm things down."

With a sigh, Cherokee went to the door. "Ouray is a great man," he said, "he's of a different clan farther south. I don't know how much influence he'll have on these northern Utes."

Meeker shrugged. "The Utes must learn to live like white men. The time of the roaming, uncivilized savage is over. This past year the Cheyenne, the Bannock, and the Ponca have had to face that harsh reality, and the Nez Perce the year before that."

There was no use talking to this man, Cherokee realized. "What you say may be true, Meeker, but change has to come gradually. Believe me, if you plow up that valley where they race their ponies, you're going to have trouble."

The agent snorted in derision. "I think you exaggerate and overestimate these simple savages. Besides, Washington says I can count on help from Fort Steele."

"You'll need help," Cherokee promised him, "but by

the time you realize it and those troops get here from Wyoming, it may be too late. Fort Steele is almost two hundred miles north of here."

"I don't need you to teach me geography. I know this agency is isolated, but the Utes are docile, except for sneaky things like setting fire to forests."

"Be sensible," Cherokee said as he pushed his hat back. "The Utes are getting the blame for those forest fires, but my guess is they're being started by drunken timber men or would-be settlers trying to stir up trouble."

Meeker pulled out his watch. "I've wasted a lot of time this morning, Mr. Evans. I do appreciate your concerns, but I'm capable of dealing with a handful of Indians."

He was being dismissed, and the man had not listened to a word he said. Cherokee gritted his teeth to control his anger. "At least my conscience is clear. Who is the officer in charge at Fort Steele?"

"Major Thornburgh, I believe."

"Oh, yes, one of those officers sent to try to corral the Cheyenne in that trouble a year ago. As I remember, that was an embarrassment for him."

"So he'll be trying twice as hard to clear that off his record." Meeker's blue eyes gleamed triumphantly. "Thornburgh will deal with the Utes if I need him."

"Two hundred miles across rough, desolate country to get him here," Cherokee reminded him. "At least, Meeker, think of the safety of the others at this agency."

"Are you saying my wife and daughter, Mrs. Price and her two little children, and all my workmen might be in danger?"

"Only if you persist in pushing the Utes beyond endurance."

"Good day, Mr. Evans," the agent dismissed him. "It was kind of you to come."

"Damn it, man, I didn't come out of kindness," Cherokee roared. "I'm trying to stop an Indian war!"

He stalked out the door and slammed it behind him. He had wasted his time, Cherokee thought as he walked toward his horse. Maybe the man would think it over and take his advice. There was nothing to do now but go home.

He mounted up and tipped his hat to the elderly Mrs. Meeker and her pretty grown daughter, Josie, as he rode out. There was an attractive woman hoeing a garden with two young children playing around her feet, as well as perhaps a dozen white men doing chores around the place that Meeker had been unable to force the Utes to do.

As he rode away from the agency, he met a dignified Ute riding in on a dapple pony. The man was not yet fifty, but he looked older. Everyone had heard the leader was not in good health. Yet, "the Arrow" was an apt description. Cherokee paused and held up his hand. "How, Ouray."

The chief reined in his pony. "Ah, long time, my half-breed friend."

Cherokee nodded. "Will you sit and smoke *pora?*" He touched the sack of tobacco in his shirt.

The bronze face registered regret. "Not this day. The *maricat'z* agent expects me and white men are slaves to the ticking thing in their pockets." He laughed.

Cherokee laughed, too. "The great chief Ouray is right and the agent is upset enough already. I try to talk sense to him."

"They are taking our land little by little. They took those mountains to the south they call the San Juans and now they want the rest of it." The dark face saddened. "For many generations, we have been friends of the *maricat'z*. This is how they repay us."

"I know. I feel shame for my white blood this day."
Cherokee sighed.

Ouray looked around as if thinking. "Much of this
land is too dry for farming. The white man will water
it with our blood unless I can calm the *nunt'z*, my people."

"I have a son," Cherokee said. "I do not want him
to die fighting in a useless war."

"Once I had a son, but no more." Ouray's dark eyes
grew sad. "A son makes a man's life worthwhile and
gives him grandsons to honor his old age."

"You speak true." No doubt the chief's son had died
early, Cherokee thought, and his heart swelled with
pride at the thought of Keso. He could not love the boy
more or take any more pride in him had Keso been his
own flesh and blood. "Well, good-bye then, and try to
humor the agent. The Shining Mountains must not be
soaked in blood."

Ouray nodded. "I will do my best. Already, my *piwan*,
Chipeta, lives in a house and she buys rugs and forks
and the other trappings of white wives."

"Good-bye, friend." Cherokee nudged his horse and
rode away. He had done everything he could to avert
trouble. Now it was up to the Ute chief.

Ouray watched the big half-breed riding away. Cherokee Evans was a friend to the Cheyenne, but still, the
Ute had a grudging admiration for him. As *tawacz viem*,
chief, Ouray would try to avert trouble so that all could
live in peace. He wished he had a fine son to bring him
pride and put meat on his fire now that he was slowly
dying. The Cheyenne had carried his little son off in a
raid. No doubt the child was long dead. He tried not
to think about that anymore. It had been so long ago
that he doubted he could recognize his own son should
he ever find him again, but there was always that telltale
scar on the back of the child's right arm. An older boy,

Yorowit'z, the Coyote, had said Ouray's son had fallen into the campfire, but Ouray had always doubted that story.

What difference did that make now? With a sigh, Ouray nudged his horse and rode toward the agency, hoping against hope he could reason with this stubborn *maricat'z*, Meeker.

"It's been a wonderful visit," Wannie assured Cleve and Alexa as she and Keso boarded the train in the July heat. For just a moment, she wondered if Cleve would kiss her, but then Keso grabbed her arm. "Come on, the train is leaving."

Alexa smiled at Keso. "Oh, don't worry, there's lots of time yet."

Keso pulled Wannie's arm more insistently. "I think we'd better find a seat." To the couple on the platform, he said, "It was nice. We're much obliged for your hospitality."

Alexa batted her long lashes. "With your sister marrying my brother, surely we'll see more of each other."

"Hmm," Keso murmured with apparent lack of enthusiasm.

How could he be so rude! Wannie thought and held her hand out to Cleve. "I'll be expecting you in a few weeks."

"Yes, I'll come out to meet your parents sometime late next month or early September." He leaned forward as if he were going to kiss Wannie good-bye.

At that precise moment, Keso pulled her away. "We'd better find our seats—the train is pulling out soon."

How could Keso be so thoughtless! He seemed oblivious to everything except propelling her up the steps and into the car. They took seats and waved out the window at the pair on the platform as the engine issued a warning whistle. Wannie blew kisses as the train pulled away.

Once the train was out of the station, she turned on Keso. "You were terrible! Didn't you understand that Cleve was wanting to kiss me good-bye?"

He shrugged and didn't meet her gaze. "Oh, really? Well, he can kiss you after you're married."

How could he be so oblivious to her feelings? "Matter of fact, during our whole time as house guests at Steel Manor, I hardly ever got to be alone with Cleve. Every time, you showed up."

"I was protecting my sister's reputation." He didn't look at her as be settled his big frame into the seat.

"Hah! Spoken like a prissy old maid aunt!" Wannie fumed. "Honestly, Keso, I don't need a chaperon."

"I'm just looking out for you, brat, that's all." He fixed his dark gaze on the buildings and landscape moving past the window.

"What is it with you, Keso?" She was genuinely puzzled. "My future husband is going to look out for me. Why don't you look out for Alexa? Anyone with half an eye can see she's smitten with you."

"Alexa's not my responsibility."

"Well, neither am I anymore. Don't you understand, Keso? I'm not a little girl now."

"Wannie," he said and looked at her as if he was struggling for words, swallowing hard. "Doesn't it matter that I—I love you?"

"Of course it does, dear." She patted his arm absently, her mind on a dozen things. "I love you, too, Keso, and I know it's hard to stop playing big brother after all these years, but Cleve will look after me now."

He opened his mouth as if to say something, shrugged, and slid down in his seat, staring out the window.

What was it with Keso? He'd been acting so strangely

ever since he'd arrived in Boston. Maybe he just wasn't willing to accept the fact that she was grown up. Frankly, she had been uneasy about her own feelings for Keso the last few days. In the years she had been away at school, she had remembered him as a lean youth with legs too long and hands too big. What had greeted her stepping off that train from Colorado had been a grown man—a virile, muscled, adult male. Her own reactions had startled and dismayed her.

"Keso," she said and put her hand on his arm, "let's not fuss anymore. We love each other, remember?"

"I'm not fussing, brat." He covered her hand with his. "You are."

His hand seemed huge, completely covering her small one. She found herself staring up at him, thinking how sensual his mouth looked and how strong he was. She wondered suddenly if Keso had ever made love to a woman on one of his rare trips to Denver. She tried to imagine him taking some faceless woman in his arms, kissing her, unbuttoning her bodice . . .

"What's the matter, Wannie? You look sick."

"Matter? Nothing's the matter," She jerked her hand out from under his, annoyed that the image upset her. Wannie had a sweetheart—it was selfish of her not to want her brother to be happy, too.

"What is it?" He was looking into her eyes intently.

He could read her like a book, he'd known her so long. She felt like a fool for being upset over the thought of him with a woman in his bed. "I—I'm not thinking of anything," she lied and fanned herself. "I'm just hot, that's all. Open that window and let some wind blow through."

He opened the window and she leaned closer, relishing the breeze across her damp face even if cinders did blow into the car.

The silence hung so heavy, she felt she had to break it. "Do you think Cherokee and Silver will like Cleve?"

"No."

"That was blunt."

He shrugged. "You asked me."

"You never gave him a chance," she accused. "You decided not to like him the minute you met him."

He hesitated as if he might say something, then decided against it. "He's not the right choice for you."

She began a slow burn. "I'm a grown woman—why don't you let me make up my own mind?"

Cleve Brewster's a spoiled snob, Wannie. You must be blind not to see that."

She felt a mixture of sadness and anger. "You're just jealous because he's sophisticated and well dressed and knows how to act in proper society. He's welcome in the best of homes."

His eyes grew sad and pensive. "And that's important to you, isn't it?"

She nodded, remembering her cold, distant mother. Money, clothes, and jewels had been important to the Duchess. Wannie had never found her favor, but the Duchess would have approved of the prestigious Brewster clan.

"Look, Wannie," he sighed heavily, "let's stop this wrangling. If you like him, that's all that matters. You're the one who has to live with him."

She swallowed back a sob. "How can I marry a man that my brother hates?"

"Look, Wannie, please don't cry. I'm sorry about what I said." He reached out and put his hands on her small shoulders and pulled her to him.

She laid her face against the broadcloth of his coat and sobbed while he stroked her hair. Somehow, it felt very comforting to be in Keso's arms while he patted her with those big calloused hands. "I—I do so want my family to like my husband."

"I'm sorry," he whispered, "I don't know what got into me. I didn't mean to make you cry." He took out his handkerchief and wiped her eyes. "Now, here, blow."

She took his handkerchief and blew her nose, remembering how many times over the years he had wiped her face and handed her his handkerchief. Dependable Keso. He was always there. "I guess I'm just tired. I want Cleve's visit to go well and everyone to like him."

"Your opinion is the only one that really counts, Wannie," he said gently. "You'll be living in New York, with all the clothes and jewels you want."

"Yes, that's right, isn't it?" She pictured balls, the opera, and all the other glittering events of her future life. "I don't suppose we'll be returning home often."

A deep sigh. "I don't reckon you will, either. I doubt Cleve will like Colorado," Keso said. "It's tough, primitive, and uncivilized."

Just like Keso, she thought, but she didn't say anything. She stared at his profile as he looked out the window. She kept remembering that moment just now in his embrace, the strength and power of his arms as he held her against his chest, the gentleness of his brown fingers as he stroked her hair. She had had the same sensations when he had scooped her up and carried her after she had fallen during the fox hunt and that evening when he had sat on her bed and she was so scantily clad.

Oh, my! Wannie was horrified and shocked at her feelings. Keso would be, too, if he knew. Was she depraved? She would not think about it—she would think about Cleve and the elegant wedding they would have, the clothes and the jewels and the social whirl.

The rest of the trip was uneventful—she and Keso kept up a strained, polite conversation. To Wannie, it seemed like forever before the train finally pulled into the Denver station.

"My heavens, the town has grown! It was a village when I left."

"Almost 35,000 people, I hear—railroad, mining, and a chance that the Ute land will bring them flooding in here."

"Look, Keso, there's Cherokee and Silver waiting for us on the platform!" She waved, feeling a mounting excitement at the sight of her beloved foster parents. She hadn't realized how much she had missed them and this wild and wonderfully untamed frontier state.

The train slowed and shuddered as it pulled into the station. Keso reached for their bags. "Come on, brat."

"I wish you wouldn't call me that!" Wannie snapped as they started up the aisle to the exit. "That's a childish nickname."

"I'm sorry, I keep forgetting. You used to like it."

"I did, didn't I?" It had seemed like an affectionate, possessive special name when he called her that.

Finally, they were off the train and she was hugging Cherokee and Silver. "Oh, I missed you so much and there's so much to tell you, I'm getting married!"

Cherokee's weathered face registered surprise and then pleasure. "Wonderful! Congratulations to you both! Isn't it wonderful, sweet darlin'?" He was pumping Keso's hand.

"We knew it was only a matter of time," Silver gushed, before you and Keso—"

"No," Wannie shook her head. "Oh no, you didn't think Keso and I? Why, he's like my brother."

"What?" Silver looked as if she'd been struck. There was a moment of awkward silence.

Cherokee cleared his throat, looking embarrassed. "We just always thought—well, never mind."

"I know when I was a silly little girl, I said I was going to marry Keso, but I'm grown up now and I've met the most wonderful man!"

Silver said, "Let's not stand here in the station talking, dear. You can tell us all about it on the way home."

"There's so much to tell." Wannie gushed with excitement as she held out her hand to display the sparkling diamond. "My roommate's cousin."

The men gathered up the luggage and pushed through the crowds toward the buggy.

"Good Lord," Cherokee said, "we haven't got enough wardrobes to hold all this."

Keso frowned. "She put most of her stuff in storage."

"Now, Wannie," Silver said, "this might be a schoolgirl crush. You ought to think about this a long time."

"Oh, I have," Wannie said as they got into the buggy. "Cleve is suave and sophisticated, and—"

"And knows which fork to use at dinner," Keso finished.

The other three looked at him.

"Well, he does," Keso said.

Wannie was more than a little annoyed. "That's not a crime, Keso."

"I know—I'm sorry." He got in the buggy.

Abruptly, Wannie's heart went out to him. It must have been humiliating for this man from the wilderness to come East where he felt so out of place. She could teach Keso etiquette if he wanted to learn, but what use would he have for knowing how to deal with a ten-course dinner or the latest dance steps when he already knew what he needed to survive in the Rockies?

Cherokee slapped the reins and the buggy started down the street, dust whirling around the horse's hooves in the late July afternoon. "So tell us about this wonderful man."

"Well," Wannie said, "he's my roommate's cousin, Cleveland Brewster, Jr., heir to *the* Brewster Industries."

"How nice," Silver said without enthusiasm. "Are you sure you aren't just swept up by the fancy social whirl?"

"It will be wonderful to have all the jewels and gowns I want," Wannie admitted.

"As I remember," Cherokee said over his shoulder, "those things were important to you when you were little, but I thought you'd outgrow it."

Wannie felt crushed. "Somehow, I expected a lot more enthusiasm from my own family."

"We just need time to get used to the idea, dear," Silver said and reached back to pat her hand.

"I'm sure we're all going to like him very much," Cherokee said. "When do we get to meet this Prince Charming?"

"Soon," Wannie promised as the buggy clopped along. "He's coming out in a few weeks to meet everyone and see about setting up an office in Denver to expand his father's business. He might bring his cousin—she was quite taken with Keso."

"Tell him not to bring her," Keso said promptly. "I wasn't taken with her."

"Oh, you're just being modest," Wannie dismissed him with a sniff. "She's very pretty."

"Uh-huh!" Cherokee turned around and winked at Keso over his shoulder.

"Uh-huh, nothing," Keso grumbled. "She was silly and empty-headed. Besides, she'd hate Colorado and I really hated New York society."

"We'll try to show your fiancé a good time," Silver said, "although I'm afraid he'll find our simple lifestyle pretty dull."

"It's not dull," Cherokee objected, "it's peaceful."

Wannie had to agree with that. She took a deep breath and looked at the Rockies in the distance. Even in the heat of late summer, the mountains were snow-capped. She had forgotten how much she loved this wild country.

Silver asked, "What kind of wedding plans have you made, dear?"

"Well," Wannie said, warming to the subject, "the Brewsters want to have it at their estate because they have so many friends and business acquaintances, if that's all right with the Evanses, Mrs. Brewster said."

Silver hesitated. "I'm afraid we'd feel out of place in such fine company."

"I certainly did," Keso said.

"Wannie," Cherokee drawled, "couldn't you just get married in a simple little ceremony like Silver and I did?"

"In a family like the Brewsters? Why, they'd be horrified. They're very socially elite."

"Is that another name for snob?" Cherokee asked.

"Oh," Keso said, "you've already met them?"

"I can't believe my family." Wannie felt wounded. "I thought you'd be happy for me."

"Oh, we are, we are!" Silver assured her. "We can hardly wait to meet young Cleve."

"Why, sure," Cherokee said. "Maybe after we get to know this young man, he'll be just like part of the family."

"I don't think so," Keso said.

The silence seemed louder than the clip-clop of the horse's hooves as they headed out of town.

Wannie wanted conversation, any kind of conversation to break this awkward silence. "So what's been happening the last few weeks?"

"A lot of it's not good, I'm afraid." Cherokee shook

his head and slapped the horse with the reins. "Whites are pressuring the Utes and there might be trouble."

"Oh, dear," Wannie said. "Cleve already thinks Colorado is wild and uncivilized—if he hears there's about to be an Indian uprising, he won't want to come."

"Now wouldn't that be too bad?" Keso said.

"Keso, you're the most impossible brother anyone ever had!" Wannie whacked him on the arm.

Cherokee said, "The new Indian agent's trying to get them to farm and that will never happen."

"Cleve thinks it's inevitable," Wannie said. "Brewster Industries has an order for plows and things for Mr. Meeker. They also expect to sell a lot of kitchenware to all these settlers flooding West."

Cherokee shook his head. "It may be inevitable, but the Utes have a treaty and they expect the government to keep its word."

"They've never kept it before—not to my people or any of the other tribes," Keso said.

"I know," Cherokee sighed.

"Can we talk about something else?" Wannie complained. "I want to hear about how things are around the place. Have there been any changes?"

"No," Silver said and shook her head. "Everything's about like it always was."

"That's comforting," Keso said.

"Cleve says change is good," Wannie said. "He says you could take a lot more gold and silver out of the mine if you'd use more modern methods."

Cherokee shrugged. "We take just enough to meet our needs."

"That's what I told him you'd say." Wannie felt a bit annoyed with her adopted father. Cleve was right; the Evanses were old-fashioned and out-of-date when it came to business.

No one said very much on the rest of the long drive

up to the cabin. As they ascended, the air grew cooler and the scent of wildflowers permeated the breeze. Along the narrow road, tall pines and blue spruce towered and eagles and hawks circled and landed in the leafy giants. She felt at peace for the first time in a long, long time.

Glancing over at Keso, she saw contentment etched on his handsome, dark features. He was as at home here as the proud eagles that screamed from the trees as they dived and soared through the crisp, clean air. If he'd been born fifty years earlier, he would have been a Cheyenne dog soldier, galloping across this land half-naked, war paint smearing his muscular body as he raided against the Cheyenne's old enemy, the Utes.

"What are you thinking, Wannie?" he asked.

"Nothing," she shrugged, not wanting to admit how much she loved this land. She had truly forgotten how much the mountains and these people meant to her.

She had also forgotten how attached she was to home. Her eyes misted over as they drove up into the yard and stopped. "It hasn't changed at all."

Once when she was small, she had talked of getting an education, returning to teach both the Indians and the backwoods white children scattered through the mountains. Of course, Mrs. Cleveland Brewster, Jr., could not live in a log cabin up in the Colorado Rockies or teach school. Cleve would never hear of it. Besides, she'd have social obligations and elegant balls to attend. Wasn't that what she'd always hungered for?

Keso got out and held up his hands to assist Wannie. His big hands almost spanned her waist as he lifted her and stood her on the ground. He didn't take his hands away, looking down at her.

Their faces were only inches apart. Why had she never noticed the sensual line of his mouth, the masculinity of his high-cheek-boned face, that tiny scar over one eyebrow? His lips were so close to hers, she couldn't seem to concentrate on anything else but the heat of him and the feel of his brown hands on her waist. She had a sudden feeling that he was going to pull her against him hard and kiss her. And abruptly, she wasn't sure if she had the inner strength to stop him . . . or if she wanted to!

EIGHT

For a split second, she stared up into his eyes.

Then Cherokee said, "Keso, would you put away the horse?"

"What? Sure."

The spell was broken. He let go of her and turned to take the horse away, leaving Wannie looking after him, shaken at the encounter. He'd be shocked if he knew what she'd been feeling. She was horrified herself.

Cherokee patted her shoulder. "Wannie, we've sure missed you."

She hugged him. "I've missed you, too, you and Silver."

"Let's go in," Silver said gently. "I'll make some lemonade and you can tell us about your school and all."

Wannie found herself staring after Keso's broad back as he led the horse away, watching his muscles ripple beneath his shirt, his long-legged stride. "Keso didn't have a very good time, I'm afraid. He didn't fit in."

"You've adapted because you've spent four years back East," Cherokee drawled. "Keso's never been out of Colorado before. You think your intended will like it here?"

"I guess young Cleve won't be staying but a few days," Silver said, "so it won't matter."

"Of course," Wannie smiled. She had just made a

decision. When Cleve came, she would make sure her family saw him in the very best light. When they realized how clever and sophisticated he was, what a fine family he had, they would be delighted she was marrying into the Brewster clan.

Cherokee shook his head as he picked up a suitcase.

"These are only a few of my things," Wannie apologized. "I knew I wouldn't have anyplace to wear it outside New York, so I put some of it in storage."

The three of them went into the cabin, Wannie glancing back over her shoulder at Keso heading toward the barn with the horse and buggy. "I just don't know what's the matter with Keso," she grumbled. "He behaved badly and embarrassed me no end."

Cherokee looked as if he might say something, then hesitated. "I'll just put your bags in your room." He disappeared.

"Silver, I brought you some presents," Wannie said. "You should see the beautiful gowns and jewelry I've accumulated back East."

"You've still got a lot of your mother's jewelry," Silver reminded her. "Besides, not many places out here to wear stuff like that." Silver walked over to the cabinet and got out a pitcher. "About Keso—maybe all this was a big surprise to him. And he can't help it if he doesn't have the skills to fit into high society. Cleve Brewster would have an equally difficult time fitting into life here in the Rockies. Have you given this marriage a lot of thought, Wannie?"

"Of course! I mean, Cleve Brewster is the kind of man every uppity girl at Miss Priddy's wanted."

"Other girls wanted him, so you set your cap for him?" Silver didn't look at her as she sliced the lemon.

"Well, I suppose I did. You'll think he's a good catch, too, Silver. I just don't understand why Keso took such a dislike to him."

Silver hesitated. "We—I mean we probably just took it for granted you'd marry Keso. When you were little, you always said—"

"I was such a child," Wannie scoffed with a toss of her dark curls, "and besides, you remember how he treated me like one big nuisance trailing around after him?"

"Sometimes men feel it isn't manly to show affection," Silver said. "He was probably afraid everyone would laugh at him if he cared too much about a bratty little girl."

"He'd never think of me seriously," Wannie dismissed the thought. "He's so much older—"

"Only seven or eight years."

"That's a lot. I always felt like I had three parents," Wannie complained. "He seemed ancient at times."

"He's quiet and responsible," Silver said, "with emotions as deep and dark as Black Canyon. No one really knows him, I guess. He made it his personal responsibility to look after you."

"Too much!" Wannie snorted. "Why, at the Brewsters' estate, he hung over me like a mother hen. Every time Cleve even acted as if he might kiss me, Keso would be there."

Silver seemed to be stifling a smile. "Looking out for a kid is probably a hard habit to break."

"But I'm not a kid anymore," Wannie said, "and he's just going to have to stop it."

"Old habits die hard," Silver said as she mixed some sugar into the lemonade, "and Keso is a man's man—there's not much going to change him."

"He's hard-headed." Wannie took the glass Silver poured her and sipped it—tart, cold, and sugary. "Umm. Good." Nothing she had drunk in the past four years had tasted so fine.

"Out here, we call that 'grit,' and it's admired in a

man, but I'll ask Cherokee to have a talk with him," Silver said softly.

"It won't do any good. He's stubborn, pig-headed, and takes charge without so much as a by-your-leave."

"The kind it takes to survive out here in the wilderness," Silver suggested, "the kind who can look out for a woman and provide for her."

"I suppose. He won't be pushed around, although for a while, I thought my roommate, Alexa, had his head in a whirl."

Silver started to say something, then seemed to think better of it. Cherokee came out of the bedroom. "How about a glass of lemonade and a few kisses for a thirsty man?"

He slipped his arms around Silver, kissed her twice, and took the glass. Such a different marriage than Cleve's parents—Wannie couldn't help making the comparison.

Cherokee looked around. "Where's Keso?"

"Hasn't come in yet," Silver said.

"I'll go help him put the rig away," Cherokee said and drained his glass, then set it on the cabinet. He paused in the doorway and smiled at Wannie. "Wannie, it's good to have you home. I wish you'd never leave again."

"I'll come back often to visit," Wannie said, but somehow, she knew it wasn't true. Cleve would think this place too primitive and dull.

"You can build a new cabin anyplace on our land you choose. We're going to leave it all to you and Keso anyway."

"Leave it to Keso—he belongs here like the eagles and the bighorn sheep and the grizzlies."

"You're right about that." Cherokee went out the door and they heard his boots cross the porch and go down the steps.

Out in the barn, Keso had just finished unharnessing the horse. He heard a noise and looked up.

Cherokee came into the barn. "Got some lemonade in the house."

"Not thirsty." He hung up the harness.

"Want to talk about it?"

"No." The pain he'd felt ever since Wannie told him she was engaged wasn't letting up any. He still had the ring safely tucked in his vest. He knew he ought to throw it away.

"Okay. I don't want to push."

"Then don't." Keso opened the stall door and slapped the old horse on the rump, closing the gate behind it.

Cherokee seemed ill at ease. He reached to get a bucket of feed for the horse. "It's Wannie, isn't it? Is this Cleve that bad a choice?"

"Worse." He hesitated, wondering if he should tell Cherokee about what he'd seen in the mansion's hall that night.

"We go back a long way, Keso. I'd do anything for you—you know that."

Keso clenched his fists, thinking about Wannie. He'd almost kissed her out there just now when he'd helped her out of the buggy—he'd almost lost control, swept her up in his arms, and kissed her like he'd dreamed of kissing her all these years. She not only would have been horrified, she'd have probably slapped him, humiliating him in front of the older couple. "I know, Cherokee," he said softly. "You took me in when I didn't know where my next meal was coming from and gave me a home. I'll be forever grateful."

Cherokee clapped him on the back awkwardly, then cleared his throat. "Hey, I needed a ready-made family and there you were and there was that orphaned little girl with no place to go."

Keso smiled, remembering. "I never will forget how you put her up behind me on that horse and the way she clung to me." He remembered every detail. She was so small then and needed his protection. Now she didn't. He shrugged Cherokee's hand off. "I'll be all right."

"Will you?"

There was no sound but the breeze making the old barn creak a little and the horses stamping their feet contentedly and chewing hay. "I was a street kid for years, surviving on my wits until you found me. I can survive anything." He thought about that rich bastard with that red-haired slut in his arms and then he pictured Cleve Brewster taking Wannie, his sweet Wannie, to bed. At that moment, emotions overpowered him so that he slammed his fist against the wall, hardly feeling the injury to his hand.

"Keso, damn it, why don't you tell her how you feel?"

"I did. She patted me like a stray pup and shrugged me off."

"Oh. I reckon there's nothing else to say then."

"No. I've made a big enough damned fool of myself. She's made her choice."

"I'm so sorry. We never should have let her go away to school."

"Funny," Keso said ruefully, "all those early years, she was just a little girl, a brat who got into my things and tagged around after me. I don't know when she went from being a nuisance to becoming a beautiful woman."

"I could talk to her—"

"Don't you dare!" Keso whirled on him. "I've told her how I feel and she didn't give a damn. Your begging on my behalf only makes me look like I'm groveling. I don't want her pity."

"Then we're all just going to stand by and watch this big city dude waltz in and take her?"

Keso had never felt so helplessly frustrated. He slumped down on a bale of hay, surveying his bruised fists. "If I could fight him for her, I would, but that won't win her. She's dazzled by fine clothes and fancy manners. A backwoods hick—no, worse yet, a savage—that's how she looks at me."

Cherokee sighed heavily. "I don't know what to tell you, boy."

He stood up. "I know you mean well, Cherokee, but there's nothing anyone can do. But I don't have to hang around and watch her marry that prissy bastard."

"So what are you going to do?"

"I—I don't know." Keso scuffed the toe of his boot in the dirt. "I'm thinking of going back to the Cheyenne."

Cherokee made a sound of dismay. "Why don't you just stay here, boy? You're like a son to us."

Keso shook his head. "Every inch of this place speaks of her—the old tree where her swing hung, that wide place in the brook where I used to make her little leaf boats. Maybe I could find peace among my own people again."

"Keso, there's only a handful of Cheyenne still running free up in the north country now after that tragedy last year. Besides, you haven't lived that life since you were a small boy—you're used to living like a white man."

"But I'm not a white man," Keso said and his soul was as bitter as his voice. "If I was a white man with a good pedigree and all the social graces, Wannie would want me."

"She's naive and unsophisticated," Cherokee argued, "and maybe a little vain. Once she sees young Brewster in her own environment, he may not look so special to her."

"And I'm supposed to just sit here and watch this snooty gent invade my territory, watch him kiss her and touch her?" He shook his head. "It was a struggle to keep from knocking him down every time he got close to her. No, Cherokee, I appreciate everything you've done for me, but if I can't have her, I'm not going to watch Cleve marry her. I'll return to the Cheyenne instead."

"Keso, you aren't serious about that." He patted the horse's head, avoiding Keso's gaze.

"I've never been more serious."

"Have you ever thought about why you were on the streets of Denver?"

Keso shrugged. "I don't remember much except that there was some kind of trouble. My Cheyenne mother and I left the tribe. She began to drink. She died and I ended up roaming the streets just trying to survive."

"Keso, you can't go back to the Cheyenne. You wouldn't fit in."

"I could try." He could see by the expression on the older man's weathered face that he was struggling for the right words.

"Keso, there's something I suppose I should have told you a long time ago . . ." His voice trailed off.

"Yes?"

"Just forget it," Cherokee said, avoiding his eyes. "You wouldn't want to know."

"I couldn't feel any worse than I do now," Keso snapped. "Tell me."

"You've been raised as my son. Would it matter so much if you weren't really Cheyenne?"

"Hell, yes! What are you talking about? Of course I'm Cheyenne. I figure maybe my father was a dog soldier, the best of the best. Maybe he was killed, so my mother left the tribe."

Cherokee didn't say anything. Outside the barn, a bird called in the hot afternoon.

Keso strode over and caught the older man by the shoulder. "You're trying to tell me something. What is it?"

"No, I'm not." Cherokee looked away. "The ladies will be looking for us."

"Cherokee, if you don't tell me what you're hiding, I swear I'll—"

"Are you going to hit me, son?" His voice was as soft as his expression.

At that moment, it was all Keso could do to keep from bursting into sobs. Whatever it was in Cherokee's eyes, it was something almost as terrible as losing his beloved Wannie. No, nothing was as bad as that. "You know I'm not. I'd die for any of the three of you." He turned away so Cherokee wouldn't see his face, then paced up and down the barn. "Tell me, Cherokee, I'd rather know."

"Maybe we should have told you before—we've known almost from the first. My friend, Iron Knife, told me."

"Iron Knife? The Cheyenne dog soldier?"

Cherokee nodded. "Keso, who your blood parents are doesn't really matter—"

"All the Brewsters talked about was bloodlines and who their ancestors were. It must matter a helluva lot!"

"All right, then. You—you were kidnapped by the Cheyenne when you were a very young child with the thought of holding you for ransom. Something went wrong, I reckon, and the Cheyenne girl who looked after you insisted on keeping you for her own, so they ran her out of the tribe."

The words didn't seem to make any sense. "I don't understand—"

"None of this matters," Cherokee said, "as far as Silver and I are concerned, you're Keso Evans, our son."

He looked Cherokee straight in the eye. "Tell me the rest, Cherokee. I can take it."

"All right." He sighed, hesitated, then plunged ahead. "I only know you're Ute—Iron Knife said so."

Ute. The hated enemies of his people. No, they weren't his people after all. In his eyes, the Utes were an inferior tribe—the Cheyenne said so.

For a long moment, the only sound was the breeze making the barn creak and the sound of horses munching contentedly.

"Keso?" Cherokee said, his voice anxious, "are you all right?"

He swayed, feeling as if he'd just been shot in the gut with a 'big fifty,' buffalo gun. "Does Wannie know this?"

"I don't think so. What would it matter to her?"

No woman would choose a Ute—they were white man's Indians who hung around trading posts. He had always taken a lot of pride in his heritage. In his daydreams, his father was the best of the best: a Cheyenne dog soldier, fierce and proud.

"I'm sorry I told you, Keso," Cherokee said and patted his shoulder, but Keso brushed his hand away, his inner pain so intense it almost blinded him. He'd lost his woman and his heritage.

"Ute? I'm really a Ute?"

"Now you see why you can't return to the Cheyenne. They'd kill you for the same reason they ran you and your adopted mother out of the tribe."

"I keep thinking this is a nightmare and I'm about to wake up," Keso said.

"Keso, you're the same man you've always been, what you've made of yourself. Who cares who sired you?"

"Utes!" he sneered. "The Cheyenne think they're cowards."

"Believe me, they're honorable and brave—I've met some of them. None of this should make any difference!"

It would make a difference to Wannie, he thought, so it made a difference to him. Without answering, he turned and strode blindly out of the barn, his throat and eyes burning with unshed tears. He had lost the woman he wanted and now he had lost his history. Worse yet, he was a child of a hated enemy tribe. It was more than he could bear. Keso turned and ran into the woods.

Wannie looked toward the barn. "What could be keeping that pair?"

"I don't know—why don't you go see? I'll start dinner."

Wannie went out the door and to the barn. Inside, she heard voices raised in anguish and fury. What on earth—?

She caught just a few anguished words, something about Keso not being Cheyenne, but Ute.

What? That couldn't be, yet Cherokee had no reason to lie. Poor Keso, Wannie thought—he'd always been so proud of his Cheyenne heritage.

Just then, he burst past her out the barn door, running toward the woods as if he didn't even see her.

"Keso!" she called, but he kept running, not even looking back.

Cherokee walked out of the barn. "Wannie? How long have you been standing there?"

"Just a minute." She turned and stared after the lithe figure disappearing over the rise into the woods. "I caught just a few words about his not being Cheyenne. That isn't true, is it?"

Cherokee nodded. "Afraid so. That's all you heard?"

"Yes. Why?"

"Uh—no reason."

She wondered what he was getting at. "Do you suppose he'll be all right? He didn't even see me, he was so upset."

"He's upset about a lot of things. I don't know where he'll run to."

"I know," Wannie said confidently. "There's a special place—only the two of us know about it. I'll go see about him."

Cherokee grabbed her arm as if to stop her, then seemed to reconsider. "Okay, go on. You're the only one who might be able to comfort him."

She lifted her blue calico skirts and took off running without looking back. There was a private place up in the cliffs with a wonderful view of the valley and snow-capped peaks where a breeze sang through the tall trees. *Waanibe's place, the Valley of the Singing Winds,* Keso called it. When she was little, she had told him solemnly that when she grew up, she would marry him and they would build a cabin on the site. It was always a peaceful refuge for both of them.

Keso ran blindly through the woods, not knowing and not caring where he was going. He had thought nothing could be worse than losing Wannie to another man. He'd almost been right. The second worst thing was being told he was a child of an enemy tribe he had always thought of as inferior slaves to the white men.

Maybe he could leave all this pain behind him. He ran a long time, not even looking where he was going. Finally, he slowed, panting, and looked around—then smiled without mirth. His legs had carried him to Waanibe's secret place. This was her favorite hiding spot as a child. He would come up here to sit with her and spin grandiose dreams of the future. There was a level area near the cliff among towering pines and spruce. In the autumn, golden aspen turned the mountain bright as any treasure. Constant breezes whispered and sang through the branches. It was the perfect place for a home, the home he had dreamed of building for Wannie.

Dreams—what a waste of time. He flopped down under a tall tree, staring out at the beautiful view and remembering. Now that home would never be built nor would she ever wear his ring. He took it from his vest and stared at it. He wanted to fling it over the cliff. He hesitated, then couldn't throw his dream away. Reluctantly, he put the ring back in his pocket, thinking what a laugh his fantasies had been.

All those daydreams of enduring the Sun Dance ceremony, painting his face, and riding wild and free with the Cheyenne dog soldiers faded into oblivion. Now he knew why he had been thrown out to survive on the mean streets of frontier Denver. He was truly as worthless as Cleve and the arrogant Brewsters had made him feel. All he knew of the docile Utes was what his Cheyenne mother had drummed into him before she died.

He leaned against the tree trunk, relishing the feel of its rough bark against his back. He heard the chattering of squirrels overhead, the wind rustling through the leaves like Wannie's high, sweet voice. It brought him peace now as he sat thinking and stared at the sun in the clear blue sky.

Twice in the last few weeks, he'd confessed his love and Wannie had brushed his words aside. It crossed his mind now that the only way he would ever possess Wannie was to kidnap her and carry her off.

Cheyenne dog soldiers. He smiled at the thought, imagining himself riding half-naked and in war paint on a galloping, spirited stallion. He would have sun dance scars on his chest and lead a war party of fierce braves. He imagined Cleve arriving on the train and Wannie meeting him at the Denver station with the buggy. On the way to the Evanses' cabin, Keso and his war party would come charging out of the woods and surround them.

Keso's fine black stallion reared before the startled old horse and the buggy stopped.

Fear shone in Wannie's dark eyes. She had never looked so vulnerable as she did at that moment in her favorite blue calico dress with ribbons in her hair.

Sweat broke out on Cleve's pale face. Even with his golden hair and cleft chin, he wasn't so handsome now. "What—what is it you want? I—I have money—"

"I don't want money," Keso glared back, "I come for the woman."

"Keso?" Wannie seemed to recognize him for the first time. "Is that you?"

"I am Fox, leader of the dog soldiers," he said coldly. "I raid the settlements to add scalps to my lodge pole and marks to my coup stick. All I need now is a woman to warm my blankets and give me sons!" He swung down off the horse.

Cleve looked so scared, he was shaking. "Take her then and let me go."

"You're not a man fit to breed a woman!" Keso sneered as he strode to Cleve's side of the buggy. "A man should be willing to die to protect his woman!"

With that challenge, he reached out and jerked Cleve off the buggy seat.

Fear seemed to make Cleve strike out, but Keso blocked his weak blow. Keso put all his fury into his punch and caught the young dandy in the chin, knocking him backward. Cleve came up fighting in sheer panic, begging for his life. Wannie screamed in the background as Keso grabbed Cleve, slammed him up against the red buggy wheel, hitting him again and again.

The superior sneer melted from the pale white face as Cleve slid down the wheel and groveled on the ground. "Take her! She means nothing to me—take her! Just don't hurt me!"

With that, Keso stepped over the quivering, begging coward and strode around to Wannie's side of the buggy. "You heard your man—he gives you to me."

Wannie looked at him with disbelief, the old fire returning to her dark eyes. "But I always thought of you as my brother—"

"After tonight, you will think of me as your lover." He reached up and swung her down from the buggy, cradling her slender body easily in his strong arms.

"You can't do this," she protested.

"Hush! No woman tells the warrior Fox what he may or may not do. In this wild country, I command!" He carried her toward his stallion.

She struggled in his arms, craning her neck to look back at the sobbing man crawling in the dirt. "Cleve, do you see what he's doing? Cleve, stop him!"

Keso whirled, Wannie still in his arms. "White man!" he challenged, "are you willing to trade your life for hers? If so, stand up!"

Instead, Cleve groveled in the dust, his stylish clothes torn and soiled. "No, don't hurt me anymore! You want her, take her. Just let me go!"

Keso shrugged and swung up on the spirited black horse with Wannie. "You see, woman, his own life means more to him than you do."

She blushed scarlet. "I—I had no idea he was such a coward or that you cared for me."

Keso grunted as he cradled her close and urged his stallion into a lope. "You look but you do not see. He doesn't deserve a beauty like you. You were meant to be a warrior's prize!"

"How could I have been such a blind fool?" Wannie wept, soft and warm against his naked chest as they rode away.

Keso threw back his head and laughed with triumph. "Now you see what you should have known—he's not worth your love."

"Oh, Keso, you're right." She clung to him, kissed his bare chest as they rode and the warm moisture of her lips on his skin sent chills up his back in anticipation.

"You're mine, Wannie—my captive. I've always loved you and tonight, I'll make you truly mine."

It was late by the time they rode back to the Cheyenne village, cooking fires blazing in the darkness and dogs barking. Women ran to meet the victors, trilling the high sweet victory songs. Old warriors lined up as he rode in front of his men, nodding their heads with respect and approval.

Keso dismounted in front of his tipi, then threw his reins to a boy. He reached up and Wannie slid down into his arms. Her long black hair had come loose and fell in a tumble over her bare shoulders as he swung her small body up in his powerful arms and carried her inside to lay her gently on a buffalo robe.

"Keso, what do you intend to do with me?" Her calico dress had fallen from one shoulder and he could see the dusky smoothness of her skin and the swell of her breasts.

"I'm finally going to show you how much I love you," he whispered.

"Suppose I say no?" She looked up at him, her full, ripe lips slightly parted.

He fell to his knees and took her shoulders in his big hands. "Let me kiss you and see what you say."

She bent her head so he could kiss her forehead as he had always done, or maybe the tip of her nose. Instead, he took her in his arms, tilted her face up with his hand and kissed her lips, slipping his tongue deep to caress the velvet of her mouth. She gasped and then reached her arms around his neck, urging him to kiss her even deeper.

He had never in all these years kissed her like that and it was more wonderful than he could have imagined. Her mouth tasted

*like hot, sweet silk and he explored there, his pulse pounding
like the war drums outside in the darkness. Her dress had fallen
down so that her full, warm breasts were pressed hard against
his bare chest. Even as he kissed her, he brought one big hand
up to cover a breast and ran his thumb across her nipple.*

*She moaned deep in her throat and pressed against him,
covering his hand with her own, urging him to caress her
breast. "How could I have been so stupid?" she whispered, "I
was meant to be your woman, to let you love me and give me
sons—your sons."*

*She was so small. He wrapped one arm around her and
lifted her so he could taste her breast, kiss around the pink
circle of her nipple while she writhed and moaned. His manhood felt so hard, it was throbbing.*

*"I've waited a long time for this, Wannie," he whispered,
"I'm going to make it last all night as I take your virginity."
His hand slid up under her long skirt to grasp her bare thigh.
"Tonight, after a million dreams of it, I'm going to make you
mine completely."*

*"Then do it," she urged him, "I can think of nothing to
make a woman more proud than giving her virginity to a fierce
Cheyenne dog soldier."*

Cheyenne dog soldier. Keso's eyes opened abruptly and
he slammed his fist against the ground in fury as cold
reality returned. He was no Cheyenne warrior, he was
Ute. Snide Cleve Brewster would marry Wannie without
ever having to fight Keso to possess her. She was blind
to everything but the fact that the civilized dandy
dressed in the latest styles and knew which fork to use.
Keso had never known such despair—not even when
he was a starving kid on the streets of Denver.

He didn't know what to do or where to go. He
couldn't stay with the Evanses and watch his beloved
Wannie marry that arrogant white snob. He wasn't wel-

come among the Cheyenne and the Utes would think of him as an enemy. Although he'd been raised as a white, he wasn't. He belonged nowhere.

"Keso?" A faint, sweet voice called his name and it echoed through the mountains.

Oh damn, he should have remembered Wannie would know where to find him.

"Keso? Are you out here?"

He tensed, thinking he would run even farther—far away from the sound of her voice, far away from her memory. They'd shared so many dreams in this spot. Maybe if he didn't answer, she would give up and go back to the cabin.

"Keso?"

He could hide, but she'd always been able to find him when he humored her by playing hide and seek all those long years ago. Then he saw her running through the woods toward him, lithe as a doe, and it was too late to hide.

NINE

"There you are!" She raced into the clearing, breathless but smiling with triumph. "Are you all right?"

"Of course, brat," he said, once again her faithful older brother. "Why? What did you think?"

"I—came out to the barn just as Cherokee told you about being Ute."

He stiffened, remembering rushing past her in his blind anguish. "That's all you heard?"

"Yes. Why?"

He couldn't bear to have her brush him aside absently again, or worse yet, laugh. "Nothing."

She plopped down next to him, breathing hard. "I'm sorry."

"Sorry because I turned out to be Ute?" His lip curled with sarcasm.

"No." She shook her head and the pins loosened, letting curls cascade down her neck. "Sorry because it's so important to you."

"It doesn't matter." He looked out at the view so he wouldn't have to look at her. How many times had he dreamed of tangling his fingers in those black locks, pulling her to him to kiss that soft mouth and the nape of her neck where those curls clung?

"It matters to me." She patted his knee. "I care about you—you know that."

But not enough, he thought, and not in the way I want. He must not reach out and touch her. If he did, he might not be able to stop himself from kissing her. He hungered to kiss her, passionately, deeply. "I'm okay—being Ute's not important."

"I doubt Alexa would care. Does her opinion matter?" She looked up at him with eyes deep enough for a man to drown in. "You know, she could come out with Cleve when he comes to visit."

Cleve. Cleve. Cleve. He felt the muscles in his jaw tighten. He was tempted to tell her about how faithless Cleve was, about the shoddy tryst with the red-haired maid. But that would hurt Wannie and no one or nothing would ever hurt Keso's beloved as long as he could raise a hand to stop it. In his mind, he slammed his fist into Cleve's patrician face again and again. "I don't think Alexa would fit in out here and I sure as hell didn't fit in back East."

She frowned. I know that was a miserable trip for you, Keso, and I'm sorry."

He shrugged.

"Maybe when you come to visit me after I'm married, I can help you choose a tailor and teach you proper manners so you won't feel so uncomfortable."

"I doubt I'll be making many trips back East. I don't like it—too crowded and noisy."

"Maybe Cleve will build us a fine home in Denver. You don't mind coming to Denver, do you?"

"If it will make you happy, brat." He forced himself to smile as he leaned over and did what was expected of him—he kissed the tip of Wannie's nose. "It's getting late. Let's get back to the cabin."

She caught his hand and pulled him to his feet. He held on to her for a split second, fighting an urge to jerk her into his arms and kiss her as he had always imagined kissing her, as he kissed her in his dreams.

She would laugh, he thought, and think he was joking or worse yet, be horrified that her brother was kissing her with such passion.

She let go of his hand and the spell was broken. "Silver's probably cooking something special for my homecoming—maybe spice cake. Wouldn't warm cake be good with a glass of milk?"

"Sure." The silver ring he still carried in his vest seemed to burn through the fabric and into his flesh. *Pour toujours.* For always.

She might marry and forget him, but for Keso, she was for always. There would never be any other woman for him. Now that snooty rich blue-blood would be taking her away and there was no way Keso could stop him because she was dazzled by Cleve Brewster. Keso would just have to endure the pain. "Want to race back, brat?"

"I can outrun you!" she boasted. Lifting her skirts, she took off like a flash.

"No fair—you didn't say ready, set, go!" he called after her, enjoying watching her run, her hair streaming out behind her like a wild filly's mane, her long, slender legs moving gracefully.

She turned and yelled back at him. "Anything's fair in love and war!"

"It sure is!" He yelled and took off after her, caught her, and swung her up in his arms.

"No fair, big brother," she protested, "your legs are longer than mine!"

"But you just said anything's fair!" he chuckled as he carried her toward the house. Anything's fair in love and war, he thought with sudden resolve. Wannie was worth fighting for.

Keso was distant and said little as the hot summer days passed. Wannie decided she had to win him over before Cleve arrived. Otherwise, the visit was going to be awkward and tense. She valued her adopted brother's approval and felt wounded that he didn't like Cleve. Finally, one afternoon in mid-August, she caught him in the barn where he labored in the heat, stripped to the waist.

"Keso, can we talk?"

"Talk?" He kept forking hay and pitching it into a horse stall. "Sure, brat."

"I've had a feeling you've been avoiding me."

"I'm busy, that's all." He didn't look at her, still pitching hay. "We've talked lots of times."

"No, we haven't," she insisted, "we exchange pleasantries, but we don't really talk like we used to when we'd daydream up at Waanibe."

He grimaced. "Do me a favor and don't mention that place to me again."

She'd never really noticed how he looked half-naked. He'd always been a lanky boy, but now he was a full-fledged man. She watched his dark, muscular body gleam with perspiration. His sinewy muscles rippled as he moved. There was no mistaking he was all male with those broad shoulders. Besides the mark where she'd hit him with a doll, the only other blemish on his body was a livid mark on the back of his right arm. Watching his sleek muscles ripple aroused a feeling that made her uncomfortable. "You—you never did tell me how you got that."

He paused, craning his neck to look at the scar. Then he shrugged and returned to work. "Frankly, I don't know. It's always been there. Look, Wannie, I'm busy. Don't you have things to do with Cleve arriving in a couple of weeks?"

"That's what I wanted to talk to you about."

He grunted and kept working.

"Will you stop and look at me?" She was exasperated as she caught his arm and whirled him around.

"All right, I'm looking. What is it you want?" His dark eyes were as cold as his tone.

As close as they were standing, she could feel the heat from his big, muscular frame. She had a sudden image of him throwing her down in that soft hay, pinning her with his sweating body. Why, that wasn't a decent way to think about her brother. Her thoughts unnerved her and she turned his arm loose and backed away, thinking he'd be appalled and shocked if he knew what she'd been thinking.

"I—I want you and Cleve to be friends, that's all."

He stared at her in a way that made her nerves come alive and scream a warning. No, of course he was her brother—it was only her imagination. "I'll be polite to him, Wannie, that's the best I can do."

"You haven't changed your opinion then? I was hoping—"

"Look, brat, as your big brother, I'm asking you not to rush into anything. Get to know him better before you set the date, okay?"

"But I feel I know him pretty well," Wannie protested. "I saw a lot of him when he came to school to visit Alexa."

"He was probably on his best behavior then." Keso turned and strode away.

"What's that supposed to mean?" she yelled after him.

Keso didn't answer but just kept walking, every line of his wide shoulders stiff and hostile. Well, Cleve didn't seem to like him, either. Maybe they were just two such different personalities that they'd never like each other. Or maybe when Keso had flirted with Alexa, Cleve had been angry and they had had words over it. The aristocratic Brewster family might not think an Indian was good enough to marry into their fancy family. No, Cleve wasn't like that at all—he was a wonderful man. "I said: what's that supposed to mean?"

"Nothing, except maybe he's not what you think he is." Keso turned on her, eyes blazing like banked fires. "He's not worthy of you, Wannie."

"You hate him because you didn't choose him for me. If you're about to tell me lies about him, forget it!" She ran at him and struck him hard across the face. He grabbed her wrist and they struggled, then went down on the hay with him half on top of her. She could feel the heat of his naked torso through the pink dimity of her dress.

"Wannie, if you were a man, I'd kill you for that."

She looked up, suddenly afraid at the terrible emotion in his eyes and the dark red mark she'd inflicted across his high-cheek-boned face. But she was too furious to be cautious. "Then hit me back! Hit me back, you big liar!"

"Wannie you've pushed me too far!" He jumped to his feet, grabbed her, sat down on a bale of hay, and turned her over his knee. "This is what I used to do when you were little!"

Before she could react, he had jerked up her skirt and was paddling her bottom. She could feel the heat of his big hand across the seat of her drawers. "How dare you! I'll tell Cherokee!"

Whack! Whack! Whack!

"Will you also tell him you slapped me cock-eyed?"

"Ohh, You're hurting me! I'll tell Cleve when he gets here."

"I'm so scared!" He stopped paddling even as she twisted her slender body and sank her teeth into his leg. "Damn! You bite like a wolf bitch! I hope you don't have hydrophobia!"

"If I do, I hope you get it!" She sank her teeth in his leg again.

"Stop that!" He smacked her bottom again. "You're spoiled rotten, Wannie! It's time you stopped acting like a baby!"

"Then stop treating me like one." She couldn't hold back the tears any longer and broke into sobs. "You're not only a liar, you're beating me up just because you're bigger than I am!"

He stopped immediately. She had known he would, knowing he could never bear to see her cry. She sobbed for effect. Once he turned her loose, she was going to grab that pitchfork or a bridle rein or anything she could get her hands on and attack him for daring to hint that Cleve didn't love her.

"Wannie, I'm sorry, I didn't mean to hurt you." He stood up and helped her to her feet. He reached out to wipe a tear off her cheek but she slapped his hand away.

"You hurt me, all right! Why do you keep trying to turn me against Cleve?"

He sighed. "I just wish you'd stop looking at him so starry-eyed and see what he's really like."

"What is it you keep hinting at?"

He hesitated. "I—I don't reckon you'd believe me anyhow. Listen, Wannie, I would never do anything to hurt you, but I'm afraid he will."

Her anger was so strong that if she could reach that bridle, she would whip him like a dog. "You hate him so you're trying to make me hate him, too—"

"Wannie, believe me, he's not a nice guy."

"Can you offer anything but your word for that?"

"My word used to be good enough for you." He took a handkerchief out of his back pocket and gently wiped her tear-streaked face.

She slapped his hand away. "I'll ask Cleve when he gets here."

Keso shrugged. "He'll deny it."

"So it's your word against his?"

"I reckon it is, Wannie. You'll just have to decide which one of us you trust. I'm sorry I told you." His handsome face was sullen; a soul as dark and deep as Black Canyon where the fast-flowing Gunnison River snaked between steep, narrow walls that never allowed sunlight to touch the bottom.

"Perhaps I never really knew you at all," she whispered, sad and weary. "I won't forget you did this, Keso, not until you apologize." She turned on her heel and marched out of the barn, glad that soon she would be marrying and leaving this place where she wouldn't have to deal with this lying, arrogant male. In the meantime, she would be as cool and distant as Keso had been ever since they'd returned from Boston. If the older couple asked, she didn't intend to discuss it; let that rotten brother tell them. Yes, the next several weeks were going to be very strained indeed.

Silver, Cherokee, and Keso were seated around the table having a cup of coffee.

"Drat," Silver muttered, "this guy of Wannie's is due to arrive tomorrow?"

Keso nodded glumly. "I told her I'd drive her to the train to meet him."

"Maybe we're not giving him a fair shake," Cherokee drawled. "If she loves him, he must be a nice guy."

Nobody said anything for a long moment.

"What I'm afraid of," Keso said, "is that she's dazzled by his social position and he thinks he's getting a Spanish duchess."

There was a long pause.

"What?" Silver blinked

Keso looked around. "Where is Wannie, anyway?"

"Down at the barn gathering eggs," Cherokee answered. "What is this about a duchess?"

Keso sighed. "I don't know whether she really doesn't remember or doesn't want to recall her true past."

"Oh my," Silver said and put her hands to her mouth, "this could lead to real trouble if he finds out—"

"She was so little the night her mother's place burned," Cherokee defended, "maybe Wannie doesn't remember her mother ran a . . . well, you know."

The three of them exchanged looks.

"And what's this about Spanish?" Silver asked. "Her mother was Arapaho and her father—"

"Yes, tell me about my father!" Wannie walked in suddenly from the porch, dark eyes blazing.

Cherokee said, "Wannie, how long have you been listening?"

"Long enough!" Wannie was so distressed, she wanted to scream. "Why didn't you tell me all this before?"

"Wannie," Keso said as he got up and came over to her. She backed away from him. "Go ahead and finish it! What was my father?"

The three exchanged looks as Wannie sobbed.

"Wannie," Keso whispered, "we're sorry, we didn't mean to hurt you."

"You were gossiping about me, about secrets. I want to know the truth."

"Well," Silver shrugged, "I guess there's nothing to do but tell you. Maybe we should have told you years ago. Your mother ran a bordello called the Duchess' Palace."

"Oh, my God—worse than I even imagined." Wannie buried her face in her hands.

"Look, Wannie," Cherokee tried to soothe her,

"none of that affects you. You're still the same person you always were—"

"No, I'm not!" Wannie screamed at him. "The Brewsters say blood will tell. They talk all the time about inheriting traits from their fancy ancestors."

Keso tried to put his arm around her, but she was in too much anguish and slapped his hand away.

"Wannie," he said, "it's not who your ancestors are— it's what you make of yourself. That's all that counts."

"Blood will tell—Mr. Brewster said so," she wept. "How can I face Cleve tomorrow, knowing all this?"

"Drat it all, Wannie," Silver said, "he doesn't have to know any of this."

"Maybe," Cherokee suggested, "we should contact young Brewster and get him to postpone his trip."

"Don't you understand?" Wannie paced up and down in an agony of indecision. "He's already on his way. He won't want me when he learns this."

"Brat, if he doesn't want you because of who your parents were," Keso said, "he's not much of a man."

He tried to put his arm around her shoulders but she brushed him off. "You don't understand. The Brewsters are nobility—they set a lot of store on pedigree."

"Look, Wannie," Silver said, "you aren't responsible for your parents and we can't change history."

"And what about my father?" Wannie confronted her. "What were you about to say when I walked in?"

Silver hesitated, her pale aqua eyes full of agony.

Cherokee stood up. "Wannie, this has gone far enough—"

"Don't try to protect me, Cherokee," Silver said and held up her hand. "Maybe we should have told her before."

In that moment of silence, Wannie had a terrible, sinking feeling that she was opening a Pandora's box that she was going to regret, but it was too late now to close it. "Tell me what?"

"Wannie," Silver took a deep breath and faced her, "your father was a Georgia cracker who had been in prison."

"Prison?" Wannie swallowed hard. In that long moment, she looked around at the three of them, waiting for someone to deny it, but no one did.

Silver nodded. "His—his name was Dallinger. He was trying to kill Cherokee and I—"

"Silver, don't," Cherokee said.

"You what?" Wannie had to know, even though she wished now she had never asked.

"I—I killed him to save Cherokee's life."

She felt as if she'd been stabbed in the heart. With a strangled cry, Wannie turned and ran out the door.

"Wannie! Wannie! Come back here!" Behind her as she ran, she heard Keso's voice as she fled to the woods. How could she live with this? Worse yet, how could she face the aristocratic Cleve Brewster with the terrible scandal of her past?

"Wannie!" Keso ran after her, caught up with her, whirled her around. "It doesn't matter!"

She lashed out at him with both fists. "It matters to me! You knew and didn't tell me!"

He caught her wrists and pulled her to him, wanting so badly to kiss her, but she was in love with another man. "How could I? Besides, it's like my being Ute. It isn't something I can change."

She began to cry and he held her close and stroked her hair.

She collapsed against him, weeping. "It hurts so much."

"I know, brat," he whispered and forced himself not to do any more than kiss her forehead, "but Cherokee was right. It doesn't matter who your ancestors were—

it's how you're raised, what you make of yourself that counts."

"What am I going to do? What if Cleve finds out?"

If the young aristocrat knew, he wouldn't want Wannie, and then Keso could have her, but he loved her too much to do anything to hurt her. "He won't find out, Wannie, if it means so much to you. We'll all be very careful—I'll talk to Silver and Cherokee about it."

"My mother was a whore," she wept. "How can I live with that?"

"Crying your eyes out won't change it, honey," he reasoned. "Believe me, if I could change it for you, I would, but like me, you'll pull yourself together and decide it's not the end of the world."

She looked up at him, big eyes bright with tears. "Once we're married, we'll be living far away and he'll never know. That's right, isn't it?"

He loved her more than life itself but all she could think of was the dashing Cleve Brewster. "Yes, Wannie, you can keep your secret. He need never know!"

TEN

It had been a long, uneasy night. Wannie got up early and splashed cold water on her face. Her eyes were swollen, but maybe she'd look better by the time Cleve's train arrived. The only good news was that it was the first week of September and there'd been no real Indian trouble. Cherokee had decided from all reports that the Ute trouble had faded away.

Wannie knew that the other three had talked long and late and were going to try to keep Cleve from finding out about the scandal. She could only hope it worked.

Silver finished clearing off the breakfast dishes and looked around as her children hurried back and forth through the cabin. "Keso, are you and Wannie about ready to go?"

"I am," Keso said and came into the room, his black hair damp and neatly combed back. "You know Wannie, she's still trying to decide which dress to wear."

"Clothes and jewelry mean too much to her," Silver sighed, looking down the hall toward Wannie's closed door, "but it was important to her mother, too. Certainly more so than Wannie was. I suppose it gave the poor child a false sense of values."

Cherokee came through the front door. "Keso, you and Wannie about ready? I've got the buggy hitched up."

A frown furrowed Keso's handsome face. Drat it all, he looked miserable, Silver thought. A hundred times she had wanted to speak to Wannie, but Keso was such a deeply private person, he wouldn't appreciate her meddling. Anyway, according to him, he'd already told Wannie he cared about her and it hadn't made any difference to her. No, Silver's interference could only make things worse. He was already in a state of melancholy over the truth that Cherokee had told him.

She wanted to hug the boy and tell him that everything would be all right, but of course, he was a man now and that would embarrass him. "Keso, we could drive her in to pick up young Cleve—you don't have to go."

"It may be the last time I ever get to be alone with her," he answered softly.

"Oh, Keso." The expression in his dark eyes tore at her heart. "Do you want to talk about it?" She kept her voice low.

"What's the point?" Keso shrugged and looked from one to the other. "I can't seem to change her mind. She's stubborn and spoiled, but then, maybe I helped make her that way."

"We all did," Cherokee assured him, "feeling so badly about the terrible tragedy."

The three exchanged glances.

"It's been many years," Silver said. "We may be the only ones around who remember the scandal and we'll keep young Brewster from finding out."

"Anyway," Keso kept his voice low, "young Brewster will be shocked enough when he sees wild and rowdy Denver and there's no telling what he'll think of you two."

Cherokee leaned against the mantel and looked around the room. "You sayin' we'll disappoint him?"

"Cherokee," Keso said, "you'd have to see how these snobs live. All they think of is money and social position. Young Cleve is no doubt already figuring out what the Silver Heels mining interests are worth and how to get his hands on them."

"No chance of that," Cherokee said.

"Young Cleve's ambitious," Keso warned, "and it takes a lot of money to keep up his grand life style. Frankly, I think the only reason his family approves of Wannie is that they think she's rich royalty."

Cherokee looked as if he might laugh, then he realized that Keso was not joking and his weathered face turned serious.

Keso glanced toward Wannie's door again and put his finger against his lips. "She'll learn to live with the truth."

"But can she hide it from her fiancé forever?" Cherokee asked.

"Hush, dearest," Silver warned, "she might hear you."

The truth was so terrible and tawdry. For a long moment, Silver closed her eyes, seeing the blazing fire as the fancy Denver bordello had been burned down by a drunken mob. The Arapaho slut known as the Duchess had died in the inferno while attempting to save the gold from her safe, heedless of her screaming child. Silver, who was working as Wannie's governess, had risked her own life to rescue the terrified little girl.

"Maybe we did wrong," Cherokee admitted as he slipped his arm around Silver, "but our intentions were good."

Silver laid her face against his broad chest and he patted her hair. Silver had killed that ex-convict, Jake Dallinger, to save Cherokee's life as the two men battled to the death. "Maybe we can keep anyone else from ever finding out."

No one said anything for a long moment, all nodding in silent agreement.

Keso looked toward Wannie's door. "Hey, brat!" he yelled, "if you don't stop primping and come on, your fancy fiancé's going to be cooling his heels at the Denver station. He might get on the train and go back to New York!"

A long moment passed and then Wannie came out, wearing a beautiful pink flowered print dress and some fine dainty gold jewelry along with the big diamond ring. "Oh, I think he'll wait. Silver, have you seen my cashmere shawl?"

Silver pulled out of Cherokee's arms. "Hanging on a peg by the back door, Wannie. Hurry up, Keso's ready to go."

Wannie disappeared a long moment, then returned, wearing the shawl. "How do I look?" She smiled and whirled around.

"Why, Wannie," Silver said, "you're trembling. Are you cold?"

"No, just nervous." Wannie walked to the small mirror on the wall and checked her hair again. "I can't believe after all these weeks, he's finally about to arrive."

"And we aren't going to be there to meet him, brat, if you don't get a move on," Keso grumbled.

Wannie took a deep breath and stuck her chin out. "Cleve just loves this dress. Remember I wore it at one of the afternoon teas his mother gave?"

Silver forced herself to smile. "What's his mother like, Wannie?"

"Very high class—they all are. Did you know some of the Brewster's kin came over on the *Mayflower*?"

"That's nothing," Cherokee scoffed, "I think some

of mine were there to meet them. Too bad we didn't have stricter immigration laws two hundred years ago."

Wannie laughed, but her eyes didn't show it. "Now, Cherokee," she warned, "don't you be teasing Cleve. He's very proud of their position in society."

Oh God, Silver thought, so many secrets. The snooty Brewsters would break the engagement if they found out Wannie was the half-breed daughter of an Arapaho madam. If Wannie married into that family, she would be living thousands of miles away and the Brewsters would never learn the truth. Maybe the Evanses could keep him from finding out. After all, he was only going to be in Colorado a couple of weeks.

Keso opened the door. "I'll try to treat him nicer than he treated me. How's that?"

He followed her out the front door, looking back at the older couple in silent appeal.

Cherokee shrugged at him. Keso sighed and went out.

Silver went to the door and watched the young couple get into the buggy and drive away. "It's sad because it's so important to her. Oh, dearest, what are we going to do?"

He came up behind her and kissed the top of her head gently. "Sweet darlin', I don't know. Her values are skewed, but that's something she'll have to deal with herself."

"Cherokee, I don't know if she's up to it." She leaned back against him, drawing strength from his big body. "This marriage is so important to Wannie."

"Damn it, she belongs with Keso."

"I know that and you know that and Keso knows that, but she's dazzled by this high society dude."

Cherokee turned her loose and began to pace. "It would serve the little priss right if the Brewsters did find out her mother was a whore and he dumped her."

"I don't want her hurt." She walked over and slipped her arms around his neck. "Young Cleve will only be here a couple of weeks and when they marry, Wannie will be in New York, a long way from her sordid beginnings. Her secrets will be safe."

Cherokee kissed her forehead. "If young Cleve's that kind of shallow bastard, Keso could break that engagement up by telling him what he knows."

She leaned into him, loving the feeling of his arms around her, his lips nuzzling her hair. "I'm sure that's crossed Keso's mind, but he's got character—he wouldn't want to win that way. It would hurt Wannie too much. If he can't win her fair and square, he'd rather bow out."

The buggy moved at a brisk pace down the winding mountain road. Wannie clutched the seat to keep her hands from trembling and stared straight ahead without seeing.

"Brat, I know what you're worried about."

"I don't want to talk about it," she snapped. Maybe if she didn't discuss it, it would all go away.

"All right, have it your way." His voice was casual and cool, now that she had dismissed his empathy.

Wannie thought and bit her lip. No, none of it could be true. Her beautiful mother had been a Spanish duchess who had died nobly in a Denver hotel fire while attempting to save her precious child. Her father had died in Europe in a grand duel with some duke or baron. Yes, that was the way it was, Wannie assured herself over and over. After an hour or two, she gradually began to believe it again and stopped trembling.

Cleve was coming. Wannie could hardly contain her excitement as Keso drove toward Denver. She was certain that when she saw Cleve again, her old feelings for him would be rekindled and the uncertainty she had felt these last few weeks would be dissipated.

They drove into Denver, past wagons crowding the roads and bustling crowds on the streets. "It's certainly grown while I've been away all these years," she said. "Once it was just a mining camp and now it's becoming a city. Maybe Cleve won't think it's such a rough frontier community after all."

"Compared to New York and Boston, Denver still won't look like much to that city boy."

"Now, Keso," she said as she put her hand on his arm, "remember you promised you would be polite to Cleve."

"If it'll make you happy, brat, I'd do anything, you know that."

She had forgotten the virile strength of the man. His arm felt like bunched steel under her fingertips. She was abruptly so aware of his masculinity, she took her hand away in haste. "Thank you, Keso."

He glanced over at her as they drove down the dusty road. "Wannie, I want you to know that no matter what or where you are or how much time passes, if you ever need me, I'll be there."

His earnestness touched her heart. "Thanks, Keso, but of course my husband will take over those responsibilities. I realize I've been a real bother."

"No," he admitted with a sheepish grin. "I know I gripe a lot, but I've gotten used to having you around. I'm not sure what I'll do when you're gone—the cabin will seem so empty."

"But you and Silver and Cherokee will come to New York to visit me," she insisted. "I couldn't survive without seeing you all often."

"I don't know what Cleve would think of that." He slapped the horse with the reins to hurry it a little.

"Or," she suggested, "you could marry Alexa and all four of us would be together a lot."

"Now wouldn't that just be wonderful!"

"Don't be so snide. You know you thought she was pretty."

"She certainly was."

He had only agreed with her; then why did Wannie feel such a sinking sensation?

In the distance, a curl of smoke drifted across the sky. The train is already in. Hurry, Keso, Cleve will be wondering where we are!"

Keso slapped the reins and the old gelding broke into a trot. They drove through the crowded, bustling streets with the September sun beating down on them.

The train was already in the station. Wannie's heart beat faster as they reined in before the red brick building and Keso got out, tied the horse to the hitching rail, and came around to help her down. She had already scrambled out of the buggy, not wanting Keso to put his hands on her waist. It always brought her such unexpected emotions, and she was an engaged, respectable girl.

"Here, you'll get your dress dusty." He caught her and lifted her up to the board sidewalk. His hands felt hot as molten steel, she thought, then felt unnerved by her emotions. Maybe she wasn't respectable; maybe she was no better than her mother. "Wannie, are you all right? You're trembling."

She pulled out of his grasp and whirled away. "Like I said before, I'm excited and nervous about Cleve's arrival."

"Yeah, I can hardly wait," Keso said.

Ignoring his sarcasm, Wannie hurried across the platform through the throngs toward the big, hissing locomotive standing in the station. She could hear Keso's long stride on the platform behind her. She put her hand up to shield her eyes from the glare of the sun, looking around for that familiar face. She saw the magnificent yellow hair first. "Cleve! Cleve! Here I am!"

She waved, thinking he looked so handsome and stylish standing there on the platform with his luggage.

He brightened when he saw her and waved back, coming toward her. "Wannie! I was beginning to think you'd forgotten to meet me!"

"Oh, never!" She almost threw herself into his arms, then remembered it wasn't proper, and besides, Keso was watching. Instead she offered Cleve both her hands.

He squeezed them and kissed her fingertips, looking down at her. "Oh, sweet, I've missed you!"

"I've missed you, too. Silver and Cherokee are so eager to meet you!"

Keso came up. "Hello, Cleve."

"Hello, nice to see you again."

The two shook hands warily in a way that made Wannie think of opponents shaking hands just before a boxing match.

Wannie was annoyed but she didn't want to make an issue of it. She linked her arm in Cleve's. "You must be tired, dearest."

"I certainly am. You have a carriage?"

"A buggy," Keso said. "A carriage is a bit too fine for hicks like us."

She glared at Keso. "Get the luggage, Keso."

"I can remember when you used to say 'please.' " He grinned at her.

"Egad," Cleve said, "people of our class don't carry luggage." He looked around. "Where's your coachman?"

"I'm it," Keso said, looking askance at the pile of luggage. "Good God, is this all yours?"

Wannie took a long look at all the bags and trunks and Keso's incredulous face. "Cleve, dear, we live a pretty simple lifestyle. I doubt you'll need all those clothes."

"It's not all clothes," Cleve said. "Actually, I caught an earlier train. I've already been to Governor Pitkin's office this morning to show him merchandise samples—Father arranged it. The governor's excited to think Brewster Industries might open an office here."

"Oh, Cleve," Wannie said, "aren't you clever! What did he say?"

Cleve ran his hand through his hair, evidently pleased with himself. "I told him of Father's friendship with Senator Teller and he said he could envision all of us working together to open up Western Colorado."

Keso frowned. "Did anyone bother to ask the Utes what they think of these plans for their land?"

"The savages? Surely you jest." Cleve smiled and picked up a smaller bag with his free hand. "I hope there's some kind of social life in Denver."

"I wouldn't bet on it," Keso said.

Cleve protested, "But I understand that with all the gold and silver here, there are many rich families."

"Maybe," Keso snapped, lifting a big trunk to one shoulder, "but the Evanses don't hang around with any of them."

Wannie felt her face burn at Keso's rudeness. "We'll have all that in New York," she reminded Cleve as they walked toward the buggy.

"I'm already missing civilization," Cleve said, "but I suppose it'll be good sport to rough it awhile."

Keso made a rude noise as he strode along behind them, loaded down with Cleve's luggage. Wannie was weary and upset over what she'd learned about her parents and now Keso was behaving like a hostile hick. She hoped Cleve wouldn't be too bored and disappointed. There certainly weren't any social events here like he was used to back East.

Cleve looked at the mountains in the distance with distaste. "Is the house really a long way from Denver?"

"I'm afraid it is," she said.

"Well, then, I'll just think of it as a big adventure." Cleve put his one small bag in the back and turned to Wannie. He bent his head and kissed her lightly on the lips. She no longer expected skyrockets; that was romantic foolishness.

"Cleve," Keso said, "I could use some help with your luggage."

He had paused and was glaring at Cleve as if he'd like to throw him over the buggy. Keso wasn't used to being treated like a servant, Wannie thought.

"I can't imagine a station without porters," Cleve said a bit huffily as he went to help Keso.

There was some jostling as they both tried to help her into the buggy. "I'd like my fiancé to assist me," she said.

Cleve put his hands on her waist and helped her up into the back seat of the buggy, climbing up beside her. "I brought you a small gift." He handed her a jewelry box.

"Oh, Cleve, you shouldn't have!" She was thrilled as she opened it. "Look, Keso, a ruby pin with clusters of pearls! Oh, it's gorgeous!"

"A bit gaudy," Keso said as he climbed up on the front seat and picked up the reins.

She ignored him, oohing and aahing over the piece. "It is spectacular, Cleve, dear—help pin it on."

"I'd be delighted." His fingers seemed to brush against her bosom as he pinned it to her collar.

When she looked up, Keso was watching him as if he intended to break both of Cleve's arms.

"Ahh!" Cleve surveyed the pin with satisfaction. "I knew it would be the right piece. When we're married, my dear, I intend to give you tons of fine things."

When we are married, Wannie thought. Would he want her if he ever heard the truth about her mother?

"Keso," she said, "are you going to drive or just sit there all day staring at us?"

For a moment, she thought he was going to say something. Instead, he gave Cleve another black look, slapped the old horse with the reins, and the buggy started down the crowded street away from the station.

He had promised and yet he was being cool and rude to Cleve.

"Dearest," she said, "we'll give you a little tour of the town before we head back."

On the seat in front of them, Keso's shoulders were squared in a hostile stance. "I told Cherokee we'd stop at the general store and pick up some supplies."

The horse clopped slowly along the dusty street filled with settlers, miners, and soldiers. In the heat of the day, many windows were open and music drifted from saloons.

Cleve looked around. "This really is a growing town and bound to get bigger if half of what Governor Pitkin told me is true. Brewster Industries could sell a lot of plows and kitchenware here. Why are there so many soldiers?"

"Because of all those settlers and miners," Keso said over his shoulder. "It looked for a while like we might have trouble with the Utes, so the army beefed up its forces."

"Utes?" Cleve looked blank.

"Savages—you know, like you see in the back-East dime novels," Keso grinned.

Sweat broke out on Cleve's patrician forehead. "Are we—are we going to be in any danger once we leave town?"

"Of course not," Wannie snapped.

"Don't believe her," Keso said. "Why, we might run into a war party on our way back to the cabin."

How dare Keso act this way. "You'll have to excuse my brother," she said and glared at Keso's back, her cold tone leaving nothing to the imagination. "He's always joking."

Cleve laughed a little too heartily. "I'm a good sport—I can take a joke as well as the next fellow."

Wannie heaved a sigh of relief as the buggy creaked down the dusty road and Keso reined in before the general store. Everything was going to be all right now. Cleve helped her from the buggy. "Now, dearest," she said, "you just go along with my brother. There's a shop down the street that's supposed to have some new fashions and I want to take a quick peek while we're in town."

Keso groaned aloud.

"I said just a quick peek!"

"Brat," Keso grumbled, "you've already got more clothes and jewelry than you can wear."

"In her new station in life, she'll need lots of fine things," Cleve said in her defense and she gave him a warm smile.

"The kind of people who are impressed with possessions aren't people to bother with," Keso said.

"You just don't understand the way the civilized world works." Cleve's tone was smug and lofty.

"I reckon not. We judge a man by actions up here, not by what he can buy or who his ancestors were."

Wannie gave him a murderous look. "You two go on into the general store—I won't be gone long." She turned and hurried away.

Inside the exclusive little shop, women from some of Denver's wealthiest families were picking up baubles and examining them. Wannie sighed with pleasure as she looked around. Clothes and jewels were more than mere possessions to her. She barely remembered the dark beauty of her mother, but she remembered that clothes and jewels had been important to the duchess. In fact, the only time the woman ever noticed Wannie was when her governess dressed the child up so exquisitely that the duchess would smile with approval. She had been an indifferent mother at best.

The oily little man bowed respectfully. "Ah, Miss Evans, what may I show you today? We have some lovely frocks to go with that stunning pin you're wearing."

"It is beautiful, isn't it?" Wannie smiled. "Just let me look around a bit—I haven't time for any serious shopping, but I'll come back and bring my fiancé."

The clerk rubbed his hands together greedily. "We can hardly wait to meet him. If you see anything you want, we can put it on your father's bill."

Wannie nodded and began to browse through the shop. So many fine things. All the best families in Denver shopped here. After a few moments, she looked at the clock on the wall. "Oh, the time has gotten away from me—I'll return another time."

The clerk nodded and Wannie hurried out the door. No sign of Cleve and Keso yet. The general store was about a half block away. She'd walk down there and let them know she was ready. As she started along the wooden sidewalk, a soldier stumbled past her and she shrank back from the sour smell of liquor, but he caught her arm.

"Hey, girlie, let ol' Clem buy you a drink."

"Let go of me—you're drunk." She tried to pull away from him, but he held onto her arm, weaving a little.

"Don't get uppity with me, baby. Now we'll just go down the street and have one little drink." He was a big man, she realized with sudden consternation, and very drunk. She looked around, but only women and old men brushed past them on the wooden sidewalk, none of them noticing her predicament. It was a hundred yards down the sidewalk to the general store and Keso and Cleve were not in sight. "Please let me go, soldier—"

"Sweetie, you ain't goin' nowhere but with me to have a drink. How about a little kiss?" He grabbed her, lifting her off the ground, and when she tried to cry out in protest, his wet mouth covered hers as he swung her up in his arms and started down the sidewalk.

She struggled, protesting, but he kept walking. For the first time since the night the duchess had died, Wannie was scared!

ELEVEN

Keso sighed as he came out of the store with Cleve. What a pompous ass! What could Wannie possibly see in this dandy?

Some confusion farther down the wooden sidewalk caught his eye. Then he heard an unmistakable sweet voice shrieking with terror and indignation.

"Wannie?"

A big, drunken soldier had his arms around her and she was fighting him off, hitting him with her reticule.

"Egad," Cleve gasped, "How dare he! I'll get the law."

"Law, hell!" Keso took off at a run.

She was as angry as she was frightened. "Let go!" She hit the man with her purse again, even as he grabbed her. "Help! Help me!"

"You feisty little filly! Ow! Stop hitting me!" The burly soldier picked her up off the sidewalk.

Around her, women watched helplessly while men were melting into doorways and hurrying off down the street to keep from getting involved. Clem was so drunk, he swayed on his feet. She flinched from the cheap whiskey on his breath as he tried to kiss her. "Here, gal, stop this fuss."

"You bastard! Let her go." Keso whirled him around, adding, "Don't you know how to treat a decent woman?"

"Keso!" She breathed a sigh of relief as the man

turned her loose. She stepped away even as Keso's fist flew like a hammer and caught the soldier in the mouth, sending him staggering backward into the hitching rail.

"Get back, Wannie, I'll handle this."

Her relief was short-lived as the man bellowed like a bull and charged at him. Keso side-stepped easily, brought a muscled arm down in a steel blow across the man's neck and the soldier stumbled and fell.

A crowd began to gather, mostly men eager to watch a fight. However, the fight was all but gone from the ugly drunk. He staggered to his feet one more time, blood and curses streaming from his mouth as he charged at Keso.

The Indian ought him under the chin with a hard blow that lifted the man up off the wooden sidewalk. The soldier came down like a sodden blue bag, sprawling across the walk.

A crowd had ringed them and now they congratulated Keso on the fight and more than one lady favored him with a flutter of eyelashes.

"Oh, Keso, you're hurt." Wannie rushed to him, pulling out a dainty hankie to wipe the blood from his lip.

He looked her over anxiously. "Are you all right?"

"I'm fine." She looked around. "Where's Cleve?"

Keso's lip curled in disdain. "He went for the law."

She felt herself blush red with humiliation for her fiancé. "He—he—, well, back in a civilized place like he's from, that's what a man would do."

Keso laughed. "Out here, a man had better learn to protect himself and what's his or someone will take it."

Cleve ran up just then, followed by two policemen. "I'm here. I got help."

"You're a little late," Keso said wryly, picking up his western hat and dusting it off.

Wannie felt the amused glances of the people witnessing the event and was even more embarrassed. "It's okay, Cleve, I'm fine."

The policeman looked down at the sprawled soldier, then at Keso with respect in his pale blue eyes. "That's a pretty big hombre."

"Not big enough, I reckon," Keso shrugged. "He'll be all right once he sobers up and sleeps it off ."

The officer pushed his hat back and nodded. "He'll spend the night in jail before I turn him loose. Been a lot of soldiers in town because of the rumor of Ute trouble. I reckon that's all over."

"Let's hope so." Keso took Wannie's arm. "Come on, brat, we've shown the Easterner enough excitement for one day."

The onlookers snickered, which both angered and embarrassed Wannie. She whirled on them. "Don't you folks have anything to do but gawk?"

"Hey," the officer motioned, "a couple of you fellas help me get this drunk to jail, 'til the army can claim him."

The excitement over, the crowd began to melt away as the law dragged the soldier off the sidewalk.

"Wannie," Cleve explained as the three strolled toward the buggy, "I wouldn't want you to think I was afraid. I really thought it would be better to go for the law."

Keso snorted. "This isn't New York, Cleve. Out here, a man has to defend himself and what's his."

"Oh hush, Keso." Wannie was more than a little annoyed with his arrogance and Cleve's humiliation as Keso's strong arm on her elbow propelled her along the sidewalk to the buggy. "You did exactly right, Cleve," she comforted him, "that brute probably would have hurt you."

"He was certainly hurting *you*," Keso pointed out. "If

I hadn't stopped in, no telling what would have happened."

"I was perfectly capable of defending myself," Wannie snapped, brushing his hand off her arm.

"Uh-huh—I saw that. Next time then, I'll just stand back and watch." Keso's sardonic smile infuriated her. She was angry, embarrassed, and humiliated for Cleve.

"There won't be a next time," Cleve snapped. "Wannie will be moving to New York just as soon as we're wed. Father is right—the sooner we pen up all the Indians and civilize this wild country, the better."

"Attempting to pen up all those Indians is what's brought all these soldiers into Colorado in the first place," Keso said as he shrugged Cleve off and lifted Wannie onto the buggy's front seat.

Now that the excitement was ended Wannie felt a giddy feeling sweep over her. "I—I think I'm going to faint."

"Quick, smelling salts!" Cleve said. "Do we have any smelling salts?"

"Not hardly!" Keso reached out and pushed her head down between her knees. "Sit there a minute, Wannie, and take some deep breaths."

What an embarrassing position. She wanted to argue, but it was difficult with her head down between her legs.

"Smelling salts," Cleve said again. "Are you sure she doesn't need smelling salts?"

Keso ignored him and when she attempted to answer, it was only a mutter with her head pushed down the way it was. She finally managed to slap Keso's hand away and raised her head to take a deep breath.

Cleve's face was paper white. "Are you all right, my dear?"

"Here, brat," Keso said and poured water from a canteen onto his handkerchief and mopped her face with it. "Okay now?"

She managed to nod and held the cool, wet hankie against her hot face. In the background, Cleve sounded almost silly asking again about smelling salts. She reached out and gave Cleve a reassuring pat on the arm. "I'm okay now. I'm not going to swoon and fall off the seat."

"Well, I should hope not," Cleve said peevishly. "What a spectacle that would make."

Keso's grim mouth twitched as he climbed up on the seat next to her and took the reins. "You coming, Cleve?"

Cleve looked from one to the other as if he might say something, then finally climbed up in the back seat by himself. She started to protest and move to the back seat beside her fiancé, but as she started to rise, Keso slapped the horse with the reins. "Giddy-up."

She plopped back down and turned to look at Cleve rather helplessly. "It's only a few hours up the mountain, dear."

As the buggy moved away from the sidewalk, Wannie heard a man in the crowd say, "Did you see that fight?"

"Sure did. Wouldn't catch me gettin' crossways with Keso Evans."

"Who's the dude?"

"Some fella from back East. Pretty, ain't he?"

Keso stared straight ahead, but he chuckled.

Wannie, her face burning, turned and yelled back at the crowd, "Don't you folks have something to do?"

"I went for help," Cleve explained again as the buggy moved away. "It didn't seem quite civilized to get into a fist fight."

"You did the right thing, dearest." Wannie reached back and patted his hand in reassurance. Such fine white gentleman's hands, she thought. She glanced over at Keso's hands. They were big and dark-skinned. Keso had callouses on his strong, capable hands.

She felt vaguely disloyal to her fiancé for the unfavorable comparison. "Cleve, I'm sorry your visit has gotten off to a bad start. Denver isn't always this lawless."

"No," Keso said, "usually it's worse."

Here she was trying to comfort Cleve and her brother had to be a smart-aleck. She reached across the seat and pinched his leg hard enough to take a piece out of it.

"Ow!" Keso exclaimed. "Since when does a lady pinch a man?"

"When he needs it," she said and smiled a little too sweetly.

"In the excitement, I nearly forgot," Cleve said and reached into his coat pocket. "I saw you come out of that shop, so I went in there while I was waiting for the police and asked what you'd been looking at." He handed her a small box.

She took the box, breathless with anticipation. "Cleve, you shouldn't have!"

"I can afford it," he said with a careless wave as the horse clopped along. "It isn't nearly so fine as what I could get back East, but it's probably the best Denver has."

She opened it, revealing several magnificent gold bracelets. "They're beautiful! Look, brother, aren't they grand?"

Keso grunted. "Yeah, grand. Let's hope Daddy can afford it."

"Keso—" she started to reprimand him for his rudeness, but was interrupted by Cleve.

"I'll have you know it came out of my allowance at the company."

"Hmm," Keso said. "Now, brat, where would you wear all this fancy jewelry out here?"

"In case you've forgotten," Cleve reminded him in a

cool tone, "we intend to live in New York where Wannie
will have plenty of opportunities to dress up."

"New York," she said and held the bracelets up and
watched the sunlight sparkle on them as the buggy
moved along the road. "All my dreams of excitement,
fancy parties, clothes."

Cleve beamed at her. "You'll have all that and more,"
he promised. "Brewster Industries foresees a lot of business here in Colorado just as soon as the Indians are
corralled. We're shipping boxcars of kitchenware and
a bunch of plows have already been sent to that Meeker
fellow."

Keso made a rude noise and kept his eyes on the road
ahead. "He'll never turn the Utes into farmers, no matter how many plows Brewster Industries ships in."

"Oh, hush, Keso." She smiled back at Cleve, admiring
the polished, well-dressed gentleman. He was the man
of the future from a civilized place where there was no
need to be able to handle a gun or defend oneself with
fists. Her marriage was going to be full of excitement
and costume balls. Beside Cleve, Keso looked like a
rough, uncouth frontiersman.

Keso glanced over at Wannie as they drove, watching
her pretty face as she admired the expensive bracelets
and put them on. How could he compete with Cleve
Brewster? His spirit sank to his boots, knowing he didn't
stand a chance by comparison. Wannie was dazzled by
the big city boy and she'd never believe that Cleve was
such a cheating scoundrel.

Cleve smiled to himself as he watched Wannie ooh
and ah over the jewelry while Keso sat watching her.
She must be blind not to realize the lout was in love

with her; or maybe since Keso had been reared as her brother, the thought never occurred to that pretty, naive miss. As long as Wannie was so dazzled by style and fine possessions, she'd never notice that big masculine ox who was so awkward on a dance floor and looked as if he'd dressed from a missionary basket. Still, Cleve was afraid to count Keso out. He wouldn't draw an easy breath until he got her away from Colorado and Keso.

The buggy clipped along through the streets of Denver, heading out of town.

"Tell me," Cleve said, "is it true there's still lots of gold and silver that no one has laid claim to?"

Wannie laughed. "Sure, over in the San Juans and maybe throughout the Ute country, but why would you care? The Brewsters certainly have plenty."

"My dear," Cleve said, "one of the first things I learned was that no one ever has enough money." His stipend at Brewster Industries was not enough to cover his women and his gambling debts. He wanted his own wealth that his strict father didn't control.

Keso grunted. "A man can only eat three meals a day and live in one house."

"Very simplistic," Cleve said. "What will power the great American dream is to get the public wanting more of everything: two buggies when they now only have one, more clothes than they can wear, and a bigger house than their neighbor's."

"Yes, Keso," Wannie agreed, "didn't you see the Brewster estate? Someday I'll be mistress of all that."

"You certainly will, my dear," Cleve agreed, "and the queen of back-East society. Other women will envy you."

Wannie sighed. "My mother would have been so proud."

Keso frowned and didn't say anything. *I can't compete with that,* he thought as he drove toward the Evanses' cabin. He would lay down his life for Wannie, fight to protect her, do anything in the world to please her, but he couldn't give her the kind of lifestyle Cleve Brewster could give her—and that meant so much to Wannie. "Won't you miss Silver and Cherokee?"

"Yes, I will," Wannie said, sounding regretful. "Cleve, maybe we could build a summer home in Denver and then my family could come visit us anytime they wanted."

"Uh, of course," Cleve said but the thought appalled him. He didn't want that big savage hanging around where Cleve would have to introduce him to society people. The Injun lout probably didn't even own a silk cravat or a proper formal coat. "However, my dear, I doubt we'd be spending much time in Denver—and anyway, in our social set, you'll have so much to do with charity balls, luncheons for society ladies, the opera. You'll hardly have a minute to call your own."

Keso snorted. "That's the way rich people live? Sounds pretty grim."

"Wannie will love it," Cleve said. What did he care if Wannie was happy or not? It wasn't her job to be happy—she would do what was expected of her as his mother did. Cleve expected to breed her every year, so she would be busy. Father would be so pleased if Cleve presented him with a bunch of grandchildren that the old man might loosen the purse strings a little. His mother was certainly proud that he was marrying into royalty and could hardly wait to introduce everyone she knew to her new daughter-in-law. In the meantime, there was Maureen and business was expanding here on the frontier, which might mean a raise for Cleve.

He wondered if he might be able to get his hands on some of the Evanses' gold and silver claims? If they were as simple and unsophisticated as Wannie's brother, it shouldn't be that difficult.

"Penny for your thoughts?" Wannie said.

If you only knew, Cleve thought, if you only knew. He

reached over to take her small hand and kiss it. The huge diamond that he had charged to Father's account at the best store in New York sparkled in the sun. "Just thinking how pleased I am that you're going to be my bride."

"You say the sweetest things," Wannie cooed and he thought how naive and beautiful she was—the perfect society wife. Wannie was so trusting, he could probably get her to believe anything. It was that foster brother of hers who was going to be the stumbling block.

The trip home was rather strained, Wannie thought with annoyance, and Keso certainly didn't do anything to ease the tension. It was with relief that they rounded the bend of the trail and she saw the cabin in the clearing ahead as dusk settled in. "Here we are. Oh, Cleve, you'll just love Silver and Cherokee."

"This is it?" His tone made her turn around and look back at him. His handsome face mirrored dismay.

"It may not be as grand as you're used to, dear," Wannie found herself apologizing for the log cabin that she'd always thought so warm and cozy, "but it suits Silver and Cherokee."

"They must be a bit eccentric to live up here if they can afford a fine place in Denver," Cleve said.

Keso looked annoyed. "We like it up here, don't we, Wannie?"

She didn't want to be disloyal to her adopted family, but she didn't want Cleve to think she was a hick not worthy of his bloodline. "Perhaps later they'll consider moving to town."

"I doubt that," Keso snorted.

Wannie strained her eyes, peering into the growing twilight. "Oh, look, they're coming out to meet us."

Several mongrel dogs bounded across the porch,

barking a welcome. Then Cherokee and Silver came out, waving.

Keso topped the rise and pulled in before the cabin. "Here we are."

"Hello there!" Cherokee strode down the steps. "What kept you?"

"There was a little trouble in town," Keso said.

"Oh?" Cherokee looked concerned. "You didn't get our guest into anything, did you?"

Wannie's face burned as Keso hesitated, then said, "No, Cleve wasn't in any danger at all."

She felt a sense of relief. Well, at least the ruffian hadn't told them what happened. Cherokee was just like Keso—he would have waded in swinging both fists.

Cleve got down and helped her out as the older couple came to the buggy. "Silver, Cherokee, this is my fiancé, Cleve Brewster, Jr."

For a moment, their faces seemed to mirror dismay as they looked her fiancé over, or maybe she only imagined it. Then they seemed to recover. "We're right proud to know you, young fellow." Cherokee pumped his hand enthusiastically.

Anxiety made her hold her breath as she watched Cleve's handsome face. For a split second, she thought she saw shock in his pale blue eyes. "I'm delighted to meet you two," he said, bowing to Silver, "Wannie's told me so much about you."

"And she's told us so much about you," Silver said.

"Matter of fact," Keso said laconically, "she's hardly talked about anything else."

"How wonderful," Cleve said, obviously deciding to ignore his sarcasm.

"I've got dinner in the warming oven, just waiting," Silver said. "Cherokee shot a couple of rabbits."

"Oh, good," Wannie said and turned to Cleve, "you'll love what she does with rabbit."

"Rabbit?" Cleve looked a little disconcerted.

"With wild turnips," Cherokee said.

"My favorite," Keso said, "let's eat!"

At least the introductions were over, Wannie thought with relief as they started up the steps.

"Hey, Cleve," Keso called after them, "you forgot your luggage."

Cleve stopped and looked at the older couple. "I'm used to servants handling that."

"I'm sorry," Cherokee said, "we don't have any, but Keso will bring your bags, won't you, son?"

"Did you see how much stuff be brought?" Keso complained. "Kitchenware samples and tons of clothes. I don't know where he thinks he's going to wear all this."

"Well, bring it in anyway," Silver said and they trooped into the house, leaving Keso with the luggage.

Inside, Cleve looked around. "It's so—so quaint."

"There's only the four of us, so it's big enough for our needs," Cherokee said as Silver began setting the table.

Wannie took a good look around as Cleve Brewster must see the home. She'd always thought of the place as comfy and warm, but Cleve appeared to be inspecting the place as if he were looking at the inside of a dog kennel. She was instantly embarrassed by the simple cabin and then angry with herself for being so disloyal. "Actually, we'd been thinking of building something much grander, but this is so cozy, we thought, why bother?"

Silver paused in setting the table and stared at her in a way that made Wannie ashamed of herself.

Keso entered just then, wrestling with three big carpet bags. "You can share my room, Brewster."

"Uh, that'll be fine," Cleve said, but his blue eyes registered dismay. "Mrs. Evans, your dinner smells delicious! My favorite is really lamb, but rabbit will be, er, unusual."

"Lamb?" Keso and Cherokee said in unison. "We raise a few cattle, but we don't eat lamb."

"Egad, you've missed something," Cleve said with smug superiority. "What kind of wine are we having with dinner?"

"We don't drink," Cherokee said. "You can have a cup of coffee or a glass of milk—we keep a cow."

"Everyone wash up," Silver said, "supper's on the table."

Cleve looked around. "Where's the bathroom?"

Keso barely contained his amusement. "There's a pump and a washpan out on the back porch and the, well, you know, is up the path."

Wannie's face burned as Cleve looked shocked. "It's—it's all outside?"

"Except when you really want to take a bath," Cherokee nodded, "then we bring a washtub in by the cast iron stove."

"How—how interesting," Cleve said, but his voice sounded strained.

Wannie was already beginning to wish she had not invited Cleve up here. She loved this place, but she saw it now as wealthy Cleve Brewster must see it and felt both disloyal and embarrassed.

The men trooped outside to wash and Wannie rushed to help Silver dish up the food. Silver patted her shoulder. "We'll try not to embarrass you, honey."

She didn't know whether to laugh or cry. "It's already off to a bad start. Keso took on some big galoot of a soldier who tried to paw me. Cleve thinks the whole town's a bunch of barbarians."

"It takes rugged men to tame this frontier," Silver shrugged. "Where was Cleve when this fight was going on?"

Now she was even more embarrassed. "He—he went to get the law."

"Very civilized thing to do," Silver said and Wannie couldn't tell whether she was merely commenting or if there was the tiniest bit of condemnation in her voice.

Everyone sat down to dinner under the hanging coal oil lamp. Wannie felt very conspicuous as Cleve insisted on pulling out her chair and Silver's. The dishes were plain, heavy crockery, but Silver had put a cloth on the rough table. They passed the big bowls of food around, along with a steaming basket of hot biscuits.

"Eat all you want, boy," Cherokee said, "there's always plenty."

"Yes," Keso said, helping himself, "otherwise, we'll just have to throw it out to the chickens."

Cleve took a few spoonfuls. "I want to save some room for the next course," he said.

The others looked at him blankly and Wannie felt her face burn again. "Cleve," she said softly, "we don't eat in courses—this is what there is."

"And you won't get a dozen forks, either," Keso cautioned, "so don't drop that one on the floor. Oww!"

Wannie had kicked him under the table. She'd teach him not to embarrass her in front of company.

Cleve stuck his fork into the steaming stew hesitantly, then put it in his mouth. "Hmm, quite good. Mrs. Evans, our French chef could take lessons from you."

The others relaxed a little and Wannie finally let out her breath.

Silver got up and went for the coffee pot. "Coffee, Mr. Brewster?"

"Yes, please, and do call me Cleve, since you'll soon be my mother-in-law."

Keso made a noise that sounded as if he were choking on a bone.

Cherokee looked over at him. "You all right, boy?"

Keso only nodded and returned to wolfing down his food.

Silver poured Cleve a cup of coffee. He looked a little askance.

"What's the matter?" Wannie asked.

"It's a little stronger than I'm used to," Cleve said.

"Westerners like it strong enough to melt the spoon," Cherokee grinned.

Wannie sipped her glass of milk and watched Cleve squirm as he ate and sipped the strong coffee. Why had she thought the Brewster heir should come to visit? This had really been a bad idea.

They finally began to make small talk as they ate bowls of Silver's hot berry cobbler.

"Excellent!" Cleve proclaimed, "nothing better at Delmonico's."

Silver smiled at him. At least he appeared to be winning her over, Wannie thought. Otherwise, the family seemed to be having a difficult time finding any common ground for conversation with Cleve, but at least, they were trying. That is, Wannie thought with annoyance, Cherokee and Silver were trying. Keso said not a word as he ate three helpings of pie.

"Silver, that was great." Keso patted his stomach as he finally pushed back his plate. "I was so hungry, my belly thought my throat had been cut."

"Keso," Wannie said, "must you be so crude?"

She saw Silver and Cherokee exchange amused glances, then Silver said, "She's right, Keso. With company in the house, all our manners could use a little sprucing."

Cleve didn't say anything for a long moment. "The food was excellent, Mrs. Evans."

Silver looked over at Wannie. "Where'd you get that gorgeous pin and those bracelets? They look like the sort of thing H.A.W. Tabor would buy."

"Who's that?" Cleve paused with his cup halfway to his lips.

"One of our old friends," Cherokee said, "who was just a poor general store owner until he staked a few prospectors. Now he's very rich and is the lieutenant governor of this state."

Cleve's face brightened. He was clearly impressed. "You know people like that?"

"Of course," Wannie said, "we know lots of people who've grown rich in mining." She was so glad that something had finally impressed her haughty fiancé.

I'd like to meet some of these people," Cleve said.

"You wouldn't like them," Keso shrugged, "they're mostly rough hicks—money hasn't changed them much."

She kicked him under the table, but at least, he didn't cry out.

Cleve looked around. "Now what do we do?"

"Do?" Cherokee said. "It's dark—we usually go to bed."

"So early?" Cleve looked startled.

"Long days," Keso said, "and lots of work around a place like this. You'll be tired yourself tomorrow night."

Cleve moved uncomfortably in his chair. "Is there no hired help at all?"

"A few over at the mine," Cherokee said, "but mostly, we do it all ourselves."

Wannie patted Cleve's hand, thinking again how soft and white his hands were. He'd probably never done any real work in his whole life. "They're just joking, Cleve, dear."

Silver shook her head. "We don't expect a guest to work, Cleve. You two can go riding tomorrow and see the sights."

"Is there anything to see?" Cleve asked.

"Why, miles of snow-capped mountains and beautiful

valleys," Wannie said, puzzled. Of course there was a lot to see. As long as she'd been here in the Rockies, she'd never seen it all and she never got tired of the breathtaking view.

"I'd better go along," Keso glowered at Cleve, "just in case you run into a bear or a panther."

Cleve looked absolutely stunned. "Those are roaming around up here?"

"Just a few," Cherokee admitted, "mostly they don't bother you if you don't bother them."

His admission didn't seem to be any comfort to Cleve. The young man shifted uncomfortably. "I hope someone told the animals."

Wannie hadn't had a moment alone with Cleve since he'd stepped off the train. "Cleve, there's a swing out on the front porch—we could take the night air and talk."

He brightened immediately. "Of course." He got up and came around to pull her chair back.

"Come to think of it, it's a hot night," Keso said, "the porch does sound good."

Oh, he wouldn't dare! She sent Silver an agonized silent plea with her eyes.

Silver said, "Keso, Cherokee and I are working on the accounts. Why don't you stay and help us?" She reached out and caught his wrist as he started to get up from his chair.

"Sure," he said, but he didn't look too happy about it.

At last. She led the way out to the porch and she and Cleve sat down in the creaking swing. "I've missed you," she said.

The swing creaked rhythmically for several seconds as he put his arm along the back of the swing. "And I've missed you, my dearest. I've dreamed of nothing all these weeks but your kisses."

Inside the cabin, Keso listened to the swing creaking rhythmically. Abruptly, it stopped its squeak and he came up out of his chair and headed for the porch. That slimy, smooth bastard had better not be compromising his Wannie!

TWELVE

Cleve's lips were only an inch away from her own when the screen door slammed and they both jumped.

"Keso!" She pulled away from Cleve. "What are you doing out here? I thought you were helping with the accounts."

He sauntered over and perched on the porch railing, eyeing Cleve. "I decided I needed a smoke."

"But you don't smoke," she protested.

"Well, I started lately." He reached in his shirt pocket for a little bag of tobacco.

She had never been so annoyed with her foster brother. He was rolling a cigarette so slowly, it looked as if he planned to make a career out of that one cigarette. Couldn't he see that she and Cleve wanted to be alone?

"Wannie," Cleve said as he started to get up, "why don't we take a walk across the yard?"

"Wouldn't if I were you," Keso said as he licked the paper shut, "mountain rattlers out in the cool of the night looking for mice."

"Oh, Cleve, he's just joking," Wannie said, but Cleve had already stopped halfway out of the swing.

"Is there any chance at all, Wannie, that there's a snake out there?"

"Well, maybe one in a million," she admitted.

Cleve promptly plopped back down in the swing. The three of them sat in awkward silence broken only by a cricket and the creak of the old swing. Keso stuck the cigarette between his lips and began a maddeningly slow search through his pockets for a match. Somewhere in the distance, a coyote sang its lonely tune and its wail echoed and re-echoed through the mountains.

Cleve's eyes widened. "What in the name of God was that?"

"Wolf," Keso said somberly, "but they probably aren't hungry enough to attack people . . . yet."

"Keso Evans!" She was truly angry with him. "That's only a scrawny old coyote—it wouldn't attack anyone."

Keso looked at Cleve and shrugged. "She's just a girl—what does she know?"

Keso sat balanced on the porch railing, still searching for that elusive match. In that split second, before he realized what she was up to, she jumped to her feet and smacked him. He lost his balance and went over backwards, landing on the grass below.

"Oh my God, I've killed him!" She was off the porch in a whirl of petticoats, running to kneel by his side. He lay there sprawled on his back, tobacco scattered everywhere. "Keso? Are you all right?"

He lay motionless in the moonlight. She gathered his head into her lap, stroking the dark hair from his forehead. "Answer me. Are you all right?"

Cleve came to the railing and looked over. "Oh, of course he is. That wasn't far to fall."

She paused in her stroking and glared at her fiancé. "You're certainly not being very sympathetic. Maybe he hit his head on a rock, or something. Keso, can you hear me?"

He moaned softly.

"Oh, I've hurt him. Cleve, run inside and get Silver." She kept stroking his face and hugging him to her as

Cleve gave her a cranky frown and went inside, the screen slamming behind him. "Keso, I'm sorry. I didn't mean to hurt you."

His eyes flickered open. "What—what happened? Everything just went dark."

She felt beneath his head. "I don't know what happened. I don't feel a rock or anything."

"Just keep stroking," he murmured, "otherwise, things seem to fade in and out."

"Keso, I'm so sorry. Maybe I should get Silver's medicine box—"

"No," he reached out and caught her hand. "Just keep holding me and talking to me," he said, "so I won't lose consciousness."

"I'm here, I'm here," she assured him and stroked his face.

The screen door slammed again and now there were three faces peering over the railing.

"Is he hurt?" Cherokee asked.

"Drat!" Silver scolded, "Wannie, what did you do?"

"I—I pushed him, horsing around like we always do."

"Where I come from, young ladies don't hit people." Cleve's voice was chilly.

"Oh, shut up, Cleve," she said before she thought.

"Well, excuse me! Perhaps I'd better say good night." He slammed back into the house.

Was that the slightest grin pulling at the corners of Keso's mouth? "I—I think I'll be all right if I just stay out here in the fresh air awhile." He struggled to sit up.

"Here," Wannie said, "let me help you. It's the least I can do after I knocked you off the porch."

Cherokee came halfway down the steps. "Keso, can I help you—?"

"Cherokee, I think he'll be all right," Silver said and

caught his arm. "Wannie will look after him—let's go on to bed."

"Bed?" Cherokee protested, "but if he's hurt—"

"I think Wannie can manage," Silver said and pulled him back up on the porch. "Let's call it a night."

"But I'm not sure I can," Wannie protested. "He's awfully big—"

"Let us know if he doesn't get better soon," Silver said and the older couple went back inside.

Keso moaned. "I—I think I'll try to sit up. Can I lean on you?"

"Sure." She made soft, sympathetic sounds in her throat as he draped his arm around her shoulders and pulled himself to a sitting position. "Do you think you can stand?"

"I'm afraid to try until my head clears. Let's just sit here a minute."

"Okay." She had forgotten how brawny he was. Somehow, with his arm around her shoulders, she was nestled against his chest rather than him leaning on her. "Are you sure you're all right?"

He nodded. "Just hit the back of my head, that's all."

"I shouldn't have whacked you—I'm sorry."

"I think you shocked Cleve. He's not used to prim young ladies from Miss Priddy's getting so physical."

"Oh my!" She put her hand to her mouth in horror. "What's wrong?"

"I distinctly remember telling him to shut up!"

"No wonder he went to bed in a huff."

"And things had been going so well," Wannie wailed. She stiffened suddenly as a thought crossed her mind. "Just why did you come outside anyway?"

"I told you I wanted to smoke a cigarette."

"Liar! You came out here to spy on us," she accused. "You could have smoked a cigarette on the back porch."

"Ohh, Wannie, my head aches," he moaned. "It really hurts my feelings that you think I'd do something sneaky like that. Help me stand up, will you?"

She forgot her suspicions in her concern for his pain. "Do you think you can?"

"I'll try—help me."

He was a big man and he seemed to be all over her as she helped him to his feet. "Watch out, Keso, are you about to faint?"

He put his arms around her and held on tight for a long moment. "I—I think I'm okay."

She could feel his hard body pressed against hers. It had been a long time since she'd been this close to Keso. The memory returned of the time in New York when the horse had thrown her and he'd carried her home and then sat on her bed. Her face flamed at the emotions his body was arousing in hers. He was staring down into her face. She held her breath, looking up at him in the moonlight. For a long moment, she got the craziest feeling that he was about to kiss her and was horrified to realize she wasn't sure how she would react if he did.

Had she lost her mind? This man had been raised as her brother and she had a handsome fiancé sleeping in a bedroom only a few yards away. Wannie took a deep breath and pulled out of Keso's arms. "There! See? You can stand all right."

"Yes, I can, can't I? Wannie . . . ?"

"Yes?"

"Nothing. Let's go in." He started toward the porch.

"Are you sure you're all right?"

He nodded. "You two are going riding tomorrow?"

"Yes." She smiled, already imagining stopping in some shaded dell to share a stolen kiss with Cleve.

"You don't know the woods as well as I do and Cleve

doesn't know them at all," Keso said. "Maybe I should go along."

"Oh, I'm not worried about getting lost." What they didn't need, Wannie thought, was her big brother right at their heels playing chaperon all day.

He put his hand to his head and swayed slightly.

"What's the matter?" She was alarmed.

"I—I don't feel as well as I thought I did."

"Here, let me help you into the house" She slipped his arm over her shoulder and helped him. Damn the ornery galoot—he night be faking, but there was no way to know.

He leaned on her as they went up the steps, then paused in the doorway. "If you don't mind, you might help me to my room. I'd hate to fall in the hallway."

"Sure. I feel terrible about this—I shouldn't have hit you."

"It isn't as if it were the first time," he reminded her. "Remember I've got a scar over one eye because of you."

"Are you going to make me feel guilty over that?" she snapped at him. "I was a little girl then."

He staggered as she helped him inside. "Don't worry about me falling—I wouldn't want you to feel obligated."

"Oh, shut up! I'll help you to your room."

They limped down the hall and paused at the closed door.

Keso sighed loudly. "Maybe you're right, Wannie—about tomorrow, I mean. I don't think I'm going to feel like riding. I'll just stay at the house and pray I don't have a skull fracture."

"Oh God, I feel so guilty!"

They were standing next to the closed door and she was looking up at him again. His dark eyes were intense and smoldering as he stared down at her; their faces nly inches apart. Her pulse quickened. She got the raziest feeling that he was about to . . . no, of course hat would be the farthest thought from his mind. She ad to be crazy even to have that thought.

The bedroom door opened so abruptly that both she nd Keso almost fell.

Cleve stood there. "I thought I heard a sound."

She pulled out of Keso's grasp with a guilty flush. I—Keso felt faint, so I had to help him down the hall."

Cleve looked from one to the other, skepticism in his ale eyes. "Really? He looks strong enough to fell an x to me."

"Cleve, how can you be so unfeeling?" She was more han a little annoyed with her fiancé. "He really needed elp."

"Thanks, brat," Keso said, "I might have fainted try-ng to get here alone."

"Wannie," Cleve bristled, "I think we need to talk—"

"It's late," Keso said. "Why don't you talk tomorrow?" He pushed Cleve back into the room as he went hrough the door. "Good night, Wannie." Keso closed he door with Cleve still protesting that he wanted to alk to Wannie privately.

What a day. With a sigh, she went down the hall to er own room, still seeming to feel Keso's strong arm round her, the heat of his hard-muscled body against er own. It took her a long time to drop off to sleep nd when she did, she had erotic dreams of a man hold-ng her close, caressing and kissing her, and she remem-ered only that the man had black hair, not blond.

The next morning, she was almost embarrassed to ace Keso as she joined the family at breakfast. Don't e silly, she admonished herself. Keso can't possibly know what you dreamed, although he'd probably be as shocked as she was if he knew about its erotic content.

The four of them sat down for breakfast.

Cherokee looked around. "Where's young Brewster?"

"Still snoozing like a baby." Keso's expression was glib as he propped his chair back on two legs.

Wannie felt embarrassed and offered an explanation. "He's used to sleeping 'til nine or ten, I think, unless there's a fox hunt. A servant usually brings him his first cup of tea."

"Ten o'clock?" Cherokee said as he cut up his steak and eggs. "Why, the day's half gone by then."

"Society people do things differently," Wannie said. She looked around at the amused faces and realized Cleve's habits made him seem as out of place in this environment as Keso had looked in New York.

"I guess so," Silver said, "but then, they're used to other people doing their work, aren't they?"

"They can afford to pay people." Wannie felt as if she were apologizing for Cleve.

They were just finishing breakfast as Cleve came out of the bedroom looking rumpled. "Is everyone already up?"

"And have been for hours," Keso said as he stood.

Cleve sat down at the table. "I'll have tea and a poached egg with smoked kippers," he said and then seemed to realize there was no butler at his elbow.

"I'm afraid we only have coffee," Silver said, "and don't know what kippers are. Would a steak do?"

He nodded. "Sorry to put you to so much trouble, Mrs. Evans." He gave her a smug smile. "After Wannie and I are married, I'll get you a hired girl."

"I wouldn't know what to do with one, but thanks for the thought." Silver smiled back.

Damn, Keso thought, now he's working his charm on

Mom. It wasn't enough that he brought them gifts, now he's going to win them both over. "Somebody's got to do some work around here," he grumbled, "I'll go feed the livestock."

Wannie didn't even seem to hear him as she sat at the table, drinking coffee and visiting with Cleve as he ate. At the same time, the young dandy kept up a lively conversation with Silver, complimenting her on her cooking and the charming way she'd decorated the cabin.

Keso slammed the screen hard on his way out.

"What's his problem?" he heard Cleve say.

"You know he hit his head last night," Wannie shrugged, "he probably still has a headache."

It was young Cleve who was the pain, and it wasn't in the head. He'd hoped to discredit the dude, make him look bad in Wannie's eyes, but so far, it didn't seem to be working.

"I'll go help him." Cherokee walked outside and they went to feed the horses and the milk cow. The other livestock grazed in the pasture.

Wannie watched Cleve sip his coffee and eat his breakfast, proud he was handsome and so elegant. He was taking his time as if the only important thing he had to do all morning was eat his leisurely breakfast. "Isn't there a morning paper? I need to see how the stock market's going."

"Afraid not," Wannie said. "Sometimes a passing scout or trader brings an old one by."

"How quaint and primitive," Cleve said.

Silver began to clean up the kitchen. "Wannie, you might tell the men to cut me up some more firewood."

"I'll go tell Keso in a minute."

"Tell Keso what?" He came in then, his shirt half-buttoned in the morning heat.

"I need some kindling chopped," Silver said.

"All right." He looked at Cleve. "Maybe Cleve would—, no, on second thought, he's probably not in condition for it. I wouldn't want him fainting out there by the woodpile like some giddy girl."

"I'll have you know, Evans," Cleve drew himself up proudly, "I'm in good physical condition. I was a fencing champion in college."

"Fancy that!" Keso raised his eyebrows.

"Keso," Wannie protested, "Cleve's a guest and he's liable to end up with a sprained back if he tries to match you chopping wood."

"I can chop as much as he can," Cleve said and then stopped as if he realized he'd been sucked into a contest.

"Let's see about that. You ready, Cleve?"

"Any time you are."

"Cleve, you don't have to prove anything."

"I think I do, at least to some people." Cleve got up from the table and the pair started out the door toward the woodpile. There was nothing she could do but follow them, protesting all the while.

"It's gonna be a hot day," Keso declared and stripped off his shirt, picking up one of a pair of big broad axes. When he moved, his muscles rippled under his tawny skin. It was like watching Spirit, Keso's black stallion, in motion.

"There's a lady present," Cleve said primly as he picked up the other axe, "I don't think it's proper to take off my shirt."

"Suit yourself," Keso said. "It's going to be a hot one today." As he swung the axe, his muscles rippled with power and the axe reflected the sun as it came down and cut into a big log. She had forgotten what it was like to watch Keso work, his strong, sinewy body straining as he swung.

It was immediately apparent that Cleve had never

used an axe before as he swung it up over his head and brought it down awkwardly. He barely missed his boot.

"Watch out!" Wannie cautioned, "You'll cut your foot off."

"I was just taking a practice swing," Cleve said and swung the axe again.

Keso paused to watch him. "Careful, Brewster, this isn't lawn tennis—that axe can do some damage."

"Oh Cleve, dear, I wish you'd stop," Wannie said as she hovered in the background, "you're going to hurt your back."

Cleve brought the axe down again with considerable effort.

Keso grinned and began to cut wood rhythmically, swinging the axe with strong strokes, wood chips flying.

In five minutes, both men were drenched with sweat and Cleve's face had gone a little pale, but he kept chopping.

"Cleve," Wannie said, "you'll get sun stroke."

"Yeah," Keso said, "Cleve, she's right. Why don't you go in the house with the ladies and I'll get Cherokee to finish your share."

"I can do this," Cleve insisted and kept swinging. Every time the axe came down, Wannie prayed he wasn't going to take his foot off.

Wannie turned and ran into the house. "Silver, do something! Keso's working Cleve into the ground out there."

Silver's lips quivered with a smile. "Men. They can be so stubborn." She picked up a pitcher of milk and a platter of fresh-baked cookies and went out the door with Wannie behind her. "Hey, fellas, knock off awhile. I've got cold milk and sugar cookies."

Keso looked up from his chopping. "We're just getting started."

"Keso," Silver said, "that's an order. Stop and have some cookies. You, too, Cleve."

"Well, I'm game for another rick or so," Cleve gulped, "but I wouldn't want to insult you, Mrs. Evans." He stumbled over and collapsed on the porch step, taking a cookie and a glass.

Silver gave Wannie an encouraging nod and returned to the house. At least, the cookies had taken their mind off their fierce competition.

"When we finish up this rick," Keso gulped his milk with satisfaction, "we can start on next winter's supply."

"Why don't you people just buy wood like we do?" Cleve said as he sagged on the step.

"From where?" Keso said. "There's no stores up here."

Cleve didn't answer. He was staring at his palms in horror. "Look. Oh my God, blisters!"

Wannie sat down beside him, taking his hand in hers. "It'll be all right, dearest—I'll put some liniment on it." She stroked his hand and cooed to him, knowing Keso glared in the background. She couldn't understand why her brother was so determined to show Cleve up. Maybe he wanted revenge for the discomfort he'd felt among Cleve's social set.

"I could certainly use a bath," Cleve sighed.

"Hey, we'll do better than that," Keso promised, "we'll go swimming in the creek."

"Keso," Wannie protested, "that water will be ice cold. I think what sore muscles need is hot water."

Keso shrugged. "Well, if Mr. Brewster's too tired to go swimming—"

"I'd love a good cold swim," Cleve said as he stood and glared back at him.

"See, Wannie? Be a good girl and get us some towels."

She started to protest, then decided she was wasting

her breath arguing with stubborn men and went inside
for towels.

"What are they doing now?" Silver looked up from
her sewing.

"They're going swimming," Wannie sighed.

Silver raised her eyebrows, opened her mouth,
seemed to think better of it, and shook her head.

Wannie carried towels outside and tossed them each
one.

"How cold is the water?" Cleve asked her.

"Cold," Keso assured him with a grin.

"It is, Cleve," Wannie said, "it's melted snow coming
down off the mountain."

"Just—just the way I like it." Cleve stood up, his
mouth grim. "Oh, I forgot. I can't go swimming—I
didn't bring a bathing suit."

Keso grinned. "We can skinny dip. Wannie, you stay
up at the house."

"I will not!" In her mind, she saw this horrible image
of Keso holding Cleve under in the creek.

"Wannie!" Cleve's blue eyes mirrored shock.

"I meant, well, you two have a good time and don't
get cramps in that cold water."

They each took a towel and strode away into the forest. After a long moment, she heard a splash and Keso's
voice, "Hey! Feels good. Come on in, Cleve."

A long pause.

"Well, Cleve, if it's too cold for you, I can understand
if you don't want—"

A loud splash, followed by Cleve's agonized shriek.
"My God, that's ice water!"

"Yeah, doesn't it feel great?"

No answer except a long, agonized gasp.

Oh, God. Wannie had a sudden vision of her brother
holding Cleve's head under the icy stream.

She crept through the brush toward the creek. The

two men really were swimming naked in the cold mountain water. She knew she shouldn't watch, but she
couldn't resist staring and she clapped her hand over
her mouth to keep from exclaiming at what she saw.
The two were such a contrast; Keso's hard-muscled,
dark body and Cleve's slender frame with skin as pale
as a frog's belly. She looked away, her face aflame. Somehow she knew that tonight's dreams would once again
feature a dark-haired lover!

THIRTEEN

It occurred to Wannie that she ought to feel ashamed of herself for watching the two swim naked. Properly brought up young ladies, especially graduates of Miss Priddy's, did not spy on naked men. Worse yet, they might catch her at it.

It was difficult to tear herself away, but she forced herself to creep back through the woods to the cabin. She sat in the porch swing, pretending to do needlework, but in her mind, all she could see was Keso's body. Just remembering him naked made her heartbeat quicken and her face flush.

In a few minutes, the men returned, water still glistening on their skins. At least now they had their pants on. Cleve's pale skin had turned a distinct blue.

"Cleve," she said, "you don't look so well."

"I'm fine," he mumbled and collapsed on the porch steps.

Cherokee came around the corner of the cabin. "You all right, young fellow? I'd say you need a little nap."

"At 10:30 in the morning?" Keso said as he sauntered across the yard to join Wannie in the porch swing. "Why, the day's still young. Hey, Cleve we could cut another cord of wood before dinner."

She gave Keso a murderous glare. How could he deliberately make Cleve's stay so miserable?

Cleve was staring at his hands again. "Blisters," he muttered, "I've got blisters just like common working men, and my ancestors were aristocrats."

"We're very democratic in sharing the work around here," Keso said and leaned back in the porch swing, looking very pleased with himself.

Cherokee started to speak, then shook his head and went into the house.

Cleve wiggled his fingers and winced. "Do you suppose I could have some of that liniment?"

"You aren't tired, are you, Cleve?" Keso asked. "I was thinking we might go on a long hike this afternoon."

"You mean, walk?" Cleve looked askance.

"You do know how, don't you?"

"I think we should play cards or something," Wannie said.

"Maybe we could go into Denver for a few days," Cleve said. "Is anyone giving a ball or a social?"

"I understand the Utes have a ceremonial Bear Dance every spring, but there's not much else," Keso answered.

"Maybe a picnic," Wannie said, wondering just how she was going to entertain this sophisticated gentleman for such a long visit.

Cleve brightened and she smiled at him, already picturing a romantic tryst in the forest.

"Yes," Cleve smiled, "a picnic would be nice."

"I wouldn't go off on a jaunt anywhere in the woods without a gun," Keso said ominously.

"Oh, Keso," Wannie dismissed him, "there's no wild animals this close to the cabin."

"I was just wondering if Packer was still locked up or if he might have escaped."

"What is a Packer?" Cleve asked.

Cherokee came out on the porch just then. "Packer? You all talkin' about the cannibal?"

"Cannibal?" Cleve blinked. "Oh, I get it—it's a joke, isn't it?"

Cherokee shook his head. "Nope. Alferd Packer got stranded in a Colorado snowstorm back in '73—ate four or five of the men with him to survive."

"Good Lord!" Cleve gasped.

"You two stop it," Wannie demanded. "Packer's in jail."

"I reckon," Keso said, "but whenever I'm out in the woods, I stay alert just in case he's escaped."

Cleve swallowed hard. "Maybe a picnic is not a good idea. Does anyone play cards?"

"How about poker?" Keso suggested, "and just to keep it interesting, we'll make a few friendly bets."

"Cleve," Wannie cautioned, "don't play poker with my brother—he's learned from the miners and the trappers."

Cleve drew himself up proudly. "I'm pretty good myself—those Princeton and Harvard lads were regular card sharps."

"Great!" Keso beamed. "After lunch, we'll play a few hands."

By mid-afternoon, Wannie found herself sitting morosely watching the two men attempting to best each other once again. What had happened to her romantic ideas about walks in the woods and kisses in the porch swing? She'd hardly had a minute alone with Cleve since he'd arrived.

As far as she was concerned it was a long day watching the men play poker. Cleve lost hand after hand, his pale face getting grimmer, his blue eyes like ice as the afternoon progressed. Once, she would have sworn she saw him slipping cards from the bottom of the deck, but decided her eyes had been playing tricks on her. An honorable man like Cleve Brewster wouldn't cheat at cards. He lost anyway.

Tomorrow, she vowed, tomorrow I'll find some way for Cleve and me to be alone. Maybe they would pack a picnic or go for a horseback ride—anything to spend some time alone with her fiancé and escape from her watchful chaperon.

However, the next morning, Cleve moved like an old man. After breakfast, they sat around the table drinking coffee.

"So Cleve," Keso said, "what would you like to do today?"

"What is there to do?"

"We could cut some more wood."

"I have plenty," Silver put in. "Maybe Cleve would just like to take it easy today."

"I don't suppose you have a croquet set?" Cleve asked.

"No, and no lawn tennis, either," Keso said. "We could go hunting."

Cleve brightened. "Pheasant or fox would be exciting, if you've got good dogs."

"If you want excitement," Keso said, "we might cross the trail of that old grizzly we see now and then. He's stolen a few chickens."

Wannie glared at Keso. How could he be so infuriating? "I don't think Cleve needs that much excitement."

"Well, it's the best I can do since we don't have a croquet set," Keso said. "What about horseback riding?"

"Egad. That sounds invigorating. As you know, I'm an expert rider."

"Now this will be Colorado style," Keso warned him, "no fancy red coats and English saddles."

"I can do that. Sound like fun, my dear?"

"Uh," Wannie hesitated, wondering if Cleve were up to it after yesterday.

"Wannie," Cleve implored, "let's do go riding. You promised to show me the country."

"All right. I'll change clothes. Keso, saddle our horses, will you please?"

"Sure," Keso said.

Silver went into the kitchen. "I'll pack a picnic," she offered.

"I got chores to tend." Cherokee went outside, leaving the two men staring at each other across the table.

"I just love picnics," Keso said. He wasn't about to let this big city dude get his beloved Wannie off alone somewhere.

Cleve favored him with a cold stare. "I meant a ride and picnic for me and my fiancée."

Keso grinned. "You'll need a guide. Wannie really doesn't know all the trails."

"We weren't planning on riding all that far," Cleve said.

Keso fixed him with a meaningful glare. "I know what you planned, Mister."

Cleve took a deep breath. "I wouldn't dream of—"

"Not unless you got the chance."

Cleve glared back at him. "What is your problem, you big hick?"

Keso grabbed him by the shirtfront and half-dragged him across the table. "No unscrupulous bastard is gonna break Wannie's heart."

Cleve managed to pull out of his grasp. "As a gentleman, I assure you my intentions are honorable."

"Gentleman," Keso snorted, "I saw you cheating at cards yesterday."

Cleve's face blanched. "I ought to challenge you to a duel for besmirching my honor."

"Duel?" Keso blinked. "Did you say duel?"

"I wouldn't expect a ruffian like you to understand

how gentlemen settle grievances, but we stand back to back and then pace off a hundred steps—"

"I know what a duel is," Keso snapped, "but I thought they went out with velvet knee breeches. Go right ahead with your duel," Keso dared him. "I shoot well enough to blow your damned head off."

Cleve's eyes widened. "Don't waste your breath telling Wannie about the cards—she'd never believe you."

"I know that." He snarled at Cleve, remembering that he hadn't told her about Cleve's tryst with the red-haired maid, partly because he didn't think she'd believe Cleve would do something so dishonorable.

Cleve grinned, but his eyes were as cold as blue ice beneath the fine yellow hair. "I'm going to marry her and bed her, and there's nothing you can do to stop me."

"We'll see."

"I'll go change. See you in the barn." Cleve dismissed him as if Keso was a stable boy.

Clenching his fists to keep from slugging the arrogant dandy, Keso turned and strode to the stable to saddle the horses. Killing Cleve or even beating him within an inch of his life wasn't going to help. Somehow, he was going to have to make innocent little Wannie see what a rotten bastard Cleve Brewster really was, but she was blinded by love and glamor. How could a rough Indian with no social graces compete? He couldn't, but he wasn't going to give up yet.

Keso had Wannie's bay filly, Dancer, and Spirit saddled when the young dandy strolled leisurely into the stable, dressed in fine riding clothes, tall boots, and carrying a whip. "Good horses," he commented. "I'll take that black stallion."

"I reckon you won't," Keso said. "That's my horse, Spirit—he doesn't let anyone ride him but me."

"I'll bet with a whip and a good pair of spurs, I—"

"Just try using a whip on my horse," Keso said through clenched teeth.

Cleve blinked and stepped back as Keso led out a gray gelding. "Brewster, old Blue will do for you—Silver usually rides him. There's the saddle." He nodded toward the tack room.

"Saddle my own horse? I don't usually—"

"Then it's time you learned. I'll saddle for ladies, but I'm no Ian O'Hearn, the faithful family servant."

"But we don't need a third horse," Cleve protested.

"I thought I might ride along," Keso grinned at him over old Blue's withers.

"Now, see here, Evans—"

He hushed as they heard Wannie's singing. She came into the barn. "What a lovely morning for a ride."

Cleve had been saddling Blue but now he froze, staring at Wannie's costume. "Good Lord, you aren't going out like that?"

Wannie looked down at herself. It was her typical riding outfit: a shirt and pair of pants that Keso had outgrown. "As a matter of fact, Cleve, this is what I usually wear riding up here in the mountains. It's terribly practical."

"Pants? But what will everyone think?" he protested.

"Everyone? No one's going to see us except maybe a passing trapper or a few deer."

"Here's your horse, Wannie." Keso led the bay filly up.

"Why, that's a regular saddle," Cleve said as if daring anyone to deny it.

"That's why I wear pants," Wannie shrugged. "I do hate a sidesaddle."

"But that's positively scandalous," Cleve protested. "My dear mother would faint if she could see you."

"Well, she'll never know. Don't behave like an old

maid aunt, dearest," Wannie replied, more than a little annoyed over Cleve's fussing.

"Wannie," Cleve drew himself up to his full height, "I forbid you to ride astride like a man."

"Forbid?" Wannie's voice rose as did her anger. "Forbid? Please remember that we are not married yet and you have no right to order me about. Keso, give me a hand up, please."

A slight smile played about the Indian's lips as he offered his hands to her booted foot and lifted her up to her saddle. Then he mounted himself. "Coming, Cleve?"

Cleve made a noise of indignation as he finished saddling the gray gelding. "Wannie, I'm seeing a side to you I never saw before."

"And I'm seeing a side to you I never saw before." She kept her tone icy. "Lead out, Keso."

The three of them rode from the barn and Cherokee and Silver came out to see them off, Silver handing the picnic basket to Keso. "There's lots of good things in there—deviled eggs and fried quail."

"I hope you saved some for me," Cherokee said, slipping his arm around her. He waved to the riders. "Now, you be back before dark, hear?"

"Don't worry, Keso assured him, "I'll see the dude doesn't get lost."

"I won't get lost," Cleve informed him, "I don't intend to get that far from the house with Wannie wearing that ridiculous outfit. Someone might see us."

"You're right," Keso nodded in agreement, "and they might tell Mama."

"Oh, stop it, Keso," Wannie snapped, "let's go." She was angry with both men as the trio rode out. Keso had been a horse's rear ever since young Brewster arrived and Cleve was not being a very good sport about his visit. She was torn between loyalty to her adopted family and the thought that her society fiancé might be laughing secretly at the hicks and their primitive lifestyle.

As they rode along the trail, she began to regret the outfit she wore—she had not meant to offend her fiancé. She knew he was right; back East, no society debutante would have dared to wear men's trousers. Why, just the idea of women wearing bloomers that showed under a shorter hemline had caused scandals in proper circles. She looked down at the big diamond on her hand and decided that she would apologize to Cleve later and promise to conduct herself more modestly in the future, although she loved the relaxed freedom of wearing Keso's old jeans.

The ride turned out to be pleasant enough, except that Keso stuck to the couple like flypaper. She was really annoyed with him as they stopped in a little grassy dell to eat. She spread the picnic Silver had sent. "After we eat, Keso, you might want to scout the area to see if any of our strayed cattle might have wandered here."

"Sure." He flopped down and watched her unpack the crispy fried quail. "Great ride, huh, Cleve?"

Cleve seemed to be having trouble dismounting. When he did, he came down off Blue slowly as if every muscle and bone in his body hurt. "Yes, wonderful ride. After we eat, Wannie, we probably ought to start back."

"So soon?" Keso asked. "Why, I thought we might ride another five or ten miles at least."

Cleve grimaced. "I don't think so. At least, not today."

"Pity," Keso said and grabbed up a piece of juicy quail, wrapping it in a hunk of Silver's crusty homemade bread. "I was really enjoying the trip."

"You're the only one," Wannie said through clenched teeth.

He grinned at her as he stuffed his mouth. "Maybe the next ride will be better."

Cleve merely grunted as he hesitated, looking at the food. "You forgot the plates."

"Plates?" Keso said and dug into the food with gusto. "You don't need plates at a picnic, Cleve."

"We're going to have to eat with our fingers?" He sounded just like a prissy old maid, Wannie thought.

"Oh, Cleve, don't make such a big deal of it—you can wash your hands later," she said.

"But we didn't bring any towels."

She must not be short-tempered with him just because he didn't fit into her world. She must remember that soon, they would be living in his world of china plates and crisp linen napkins. A butler would probably accompany picnickers to serve and clean up. "Wipe your hands on your pants, Cleve."

"You must be joking." He picked up the meat gingerly and began to eat.

Just watching Cleve pick at his food set her teeth on edge.

"Well, I'm through," Keso announced and wiped his hands on the grass. "Reckon I'll go water the horses—there's a creek over the next rise." He stood up and led the horses away.

Cleve looked after him until Keso disappeared. "Wannie, can't we do anything or go anywhere without your brother?"

"I don't see how I can politely tell him he's not wanted."

"Try," he said and gave her a charming smile, reaching over to take her hand. "After all, we've hardly been alone together at all."

"I'm sorry, dearest," she said and patted his face, "I have to apologize for Keso."

He looked wounded and sighed. "He just doesn't like me, I'm afraid, and he seems determined to turn you against me."

Wannie shook her head, remembering. "I realize that and I just don't understand it. Why, he was even mean enough to hint you were less than honorable—"

"Whatever he told you he saw Maureen do—"

"Maureen? What about the maid?"

Cleve's face went white, then red, and he stuttered. "I—I'll tell you why he's out to turn you against me if you promise not to mention it to him." Cleve lowered his voice. "He seemed determined to force his affections on Alexa, and you know, she's really promised to one of my friends from college. Keso was very offended when I cautioned him against pursuing her."

Why did she feel such disappointment? Was it because she'd harbored the tiniest suspicion that Keso was jealous of Cleve on her account? "Early on, I thought that he might be interested in Alexa, but he made it clear I was wrong."

"You see!" Cleve said triumphantly, "I just hope you realize now his motive is revenge—if he can't have Alexa, he's determined to break us up."

Her disappointment was tempered by anger. "Don't worry, Cleve, I won't let him do that."

He smiled at her. "Good. Now, we'll just get through this visit somehow and go ahead with our plans. Remember, a big society wedding takes a lot of planning."

She nodded, her thoughts already full of the balls and parties, the clothes and jewels. "Oh, Cleve, I'm so happy."

"Not as happy is I am, my dear." He looked soulfully into her eyes as he kissed her fingertips. "Perhaps while I'm here in Colorado, we might inspect some property. I'm thinking of buying some mining interests and expanding Brewster Industries throughout the state."

"Of course," she said, pleased that he wanted to share his dreams and ambitions with her, "but I thought your family had plenty of money already."

"Wannie, you're so naive," his tone was smug, "nobody ever has enough money. Besides, don't you see? Right now, I'm beholden to Father for a position in his company. I have to ask for every dime. If I could make some successful business deals on my own, he might stop treating me like an irresponsible boy."

"I'll help you," Wannie promised, "we'll look at any town or any property you want to."

"And about your brother," he lowered his voice, "just discount anything he says. I'm sorry he doesn't like me, but now you know his motives."

She nodded, her heart full of love for this handsome, charming man. She was annoyed and disappointed with her foster brother. She hadn't thought he could be so petty and vengeful.

Keso returned just then, leading the horses. "It's getting late. If you two are through eating, we should head back."

Cleve frowned. "Don't you ever ask anyone else's opinion or do you just take charge?"

He pushed his Western hat back and grinned. "I reckon I just take charge, but then, I feel responsible when I'm herding tenderfoots."

"Keso is right, as much as I hate to admit it," Wannie said as she began to gather up the picnic things. "It's time to head back." She favored Cleve with her warmest smile. "It's been an unforgettable day."

"Made possible by an unforgettable girl," Cleve purred.

Keso made a rude noise and Cleve shot her a knowing look. She nodded to show she understood. Such pettiness wasn't like Keso—she was disappointed in him. There was still tomorrow, Wannie thought, and the day after that and the day after that. Somehow, she and Cleve would steal a little time alone to plan their future.

Cleve hummed to himself as the trio rode back toward the cabin. He still didn't know exactly what Keso had told Wannie about Maureen, but he'd convinced Wannie that Keso was being petty and vindictive. Now she would discount everything the lout said.

This trip to this primitive place to meet Wannie's foster parents was a nightmare; these hicks had no idea how to enjoy life. Cleve yearned to get back down to Denver where he could savor the local bordellos and gambling dens. No, he decided as he rode, it wouldn't be worth the risk of Wannie finding out about it. He'd better be careful until he married her. He watched her back is she rode ahead of him. Such a naive beauty, but Father liked her and she'd be a dutiful wife as soon as Cleve broke her spirit so she would behave herself. Once he was her husband, he could lock her in her room or take his riding whip to her if she did such an outrageous thing as wear men's trousers again. Besides, all those fine grandchildren she was going to produce would soften the old man's heart and make him loosen the purse strings.

In the meantime, Cleve was busily planning how to get his hands on some of the Evanses' mining interests or maybe buy up some mines of his own and expand Brewster Industries in Colorado. Just let that ruffian Injun try to stop Cleve Brewster!

FOURTEEN

The next several days were ghastly, Wannie thought. Cleve seemed bored with the simple pleasures around the cabin and the tension between Cleve and Keso was so bad, it hung in the air like a dark cloud.

One night, as they sat around the table after dinner, Cleve said, "Wannie, I'd like to explore some of the Western slopes. Isn't that where they're making new mineral finds?"

Cherokee frowned. "Yes, but a lot of that area is Ute land, Cleve, so that doesn't seem like a good idea."

"Some of it isn't, and it would be such a coup for me if I could expand Brewster Industries into mining and timber."

Keso snorted. "Looks to me like it's already been expanded enough. Didn't you say your father has shipped a bunch of plows and farm equipment to the White River Agency?"

"Yes, that agent, Meeker, ordered them right before I came. That's what interested Father into expanding still further," Cleve admitted. "Pots, pans, and other kitchen utensils are being shipped to Colorado, too. More settlers mean more business."

It all seemed so logical to Wannie as she sat playing with the expensive pin and gold bracelets Cleve had given her and beamed at him. "Eventually, the Utes are going to have to walk the white man's road."

"I reckon even the Utes have accepted that," Silver said. "Tension seems to have died down lately."

"Good," Cleve said, "in the morning, I'd like to do some exploring for a few days."

Keso looked amused. "Good way for a tenderfoot to get lost and die in the mountains."

"Keso's right," Cherokee drawled, "Wannie says your pa sets a heap of store by you."

Wannie said, "I could go with him—I know the area fairly well."

"Drat, Wannie!" Silver reminded her, "that would hardly be proper, even if you are engaged."

"Mrs. Evans is right," Cleve said sanctimoniously. "As a gentleman, I could hardly besmirch a young lady's reputation."

"Unless you got a chance," she thought she heard Keso mutter.

"Keso," she snapped, "what was that?"

"Nothing."

"I might hire a guide," Cleve said.

Silver frowned. "As a matter of fact, the one person who knows these mountains best is Cherokee, followed by Keso."

As much as Wannie hated to admit it, she knew Silver was right. All of them turned and looked at Keso.

"No," he shook his head, "I'm not gonna mollycoddle a greenhorn on a jaunt around the Western slopes."

"I didn't ask you," Cleve snapped.

"Well," Cherokee said, "he sure can't go alone."

Wannie fixed her big, dark eyes on Keso. "Keso, you could do this."

"N-o, no," Keso shook his head.

She took his hand, looking up at him as she had when she was very young and attempting to cajole him into doing something that she knew he didn't want to do. "Please? For me?"

For a long moment, they stared into each others' eyes. She was abruptly conscious of the warmth of his hand. It felt like a surge of electricity passed between them. She turned his fingers loose is if they had burned her.

"Wannie, I don't think so," Keso said.

Cleve seemed peeved. "I'm sure I could hire a competent guide in Denver. I think I'll go down there, spend a few days and look around."

"Why don't you do that, Cleve?" Keso challenged. "You'll hire an old drunk who'll get you lost in some canyon and you'll never find your way out."

"He's right," Cherokee said, reaching into his shirt for his little sack of tobacco. "Keso's the only one who knows this country like the back of his hand."

Cleve looked at Wannie. "Is he really the best?"

She nodded.

"I suppose I could pay you to take me." Cleve's tone was grudging.

"You don't have enough money to tempt me," Keso said and leaned his chair back on two legs.

"Keso!" Silver and Cherokee said in shocked unison.

"That's no way to treat a guest—especially since he's about to become a member of the family," Silver added.

Wannie turned her most imploring gaze on him again. "Please, Keso, do it for me."

Keso sighed. "Damn, Wannie, why do you do this to me?" There was a long pause, but she knew he was weakening. She had always known how to get her way with Keso. She turned big, wistful eyes on him again.

"All right, Brewster," Keso said as his chair came down on the floor with a resounding bang, "I'll do it, but it's against my better judgment. Let's get our gear together tonight and we'll leave tomorrow."

"You know," Cherokee said as he rolled a cigarette, "I might be tempted to go with you two."

"I think not," Silver said gently, "your arthritis can't take sleeping on cold ground. Let these two young bucks go out there and prowl around in the woods for a while if they want, but you ought to have better sense."

Cherokee grinned at her. "You're right."

"Well," Wannie said as she hopped up, "what time are we leaving in the morning?"

"We?" Cleve said.

"Yes, we," Wannie echoed.

Keso laughed and shook his head. "Uh-uh, brat. This is too rough a trip—you can't go."

"You two are going off and explore and have a wonderful time without me? Nothing doing."

"Wannie," Cleve said, "proper young ladies don't do things like this."

"You expect me just to cool my heels here at the cabin until you get back?"

Silver said, "Wannie, stop it. You know we wouldn't even consider letting you go."

"But they'll be having all the fun."

"Sleeping on the cold ground and cooking over a campfire isn't all that much fun. Besides, you'll slow them down," Silver said.

"Silver's right," Cherokee lit his cigarette. "The Utes may have calmed down, but there's still too many reasons a girl doesn't have any business out in the wilderness."

She was losing this argument. She knew it when she looked into their faces. "It isn't fair. Keso used to take me everywhere with him."

"Wannie," Cleve said, drawing himself up primly, "as your fiancé, I forbid it."

"Forbid? Forbid?" She was very close to losing her temper.

Keso looked amused. "Behave yourself, brat. I say you're not going."

She was as disappointed as she was angry. "I'm not a child anymore."

"Then stop acting like one," Keso said and give her his no-nonsense frown. "You can't go."

"Humph!" She knew it was useless to argue with Keso when his mind was made up.

"Well!" Cleve bristled, "why is it what he says carries more weight with you than what I say?"

"Because I raised her," Keso said, "and I know her better than anyone in this world."

He was looking at her strangely and she wondered what he was thinking.

Cleve's handsome face was set in annoyance. "Wannie, when we are married, I will expect you to obey me."

"As a matter of fact," Wannie snapped, "I was planning to have that 'obey' thing taken out of the ceremony."

Cleve looked scandalized. "That would cause a great deal of gossip in proper circles. The next thing I know, you'll be wanting to join up with those crazy suffragettes."

"Just in case you didn't know," Wannie seethed, "I already—"

"More coffee, anyone?" Silver hopped up and began clearing the dishes.

Wannie glanced around the table. Cleve looked annoyed, while Silver and Cherokee seemed to be holding their breath. Keso seemed slightly amused, a grin tugging at the corners of his mouth.

Slowly, Wannie formed a plan. She couldn't win this fuss head-on—she'd have to be more clever than that. She forced herself to smile and ducked her head. "Of course it's not smart to take me—I realize that. I'll just

stay here then and maybe start on some needlework for
my trousseau."

"Spoken like a proper graduate of Miss Priddy's,"
Cleve said with such smug satisfaction that she wanted
to slap him until his teeth rattled.

Cherokee and Silver breathed sighs of relief.

Keso looked at her with puzzlement. He knew her all
too well, she thought, and he's trying to figure out why
I've suddenly become so agreeable. He smells a rat, and
he's right.

Wannie had no intention of being left behind while
the men had all the fun. She intended to slip away from
the cabin and follow them. If she caught up with them
way out in the middle of the mountains, they would
have to take her along. Wannie didn't intend to miss
this big adventure!

At the White River Agency, Nathan Meeker clasped
his hands behind his back and watched out the window
with satisfaction. Out in the valley, the new plow turned
over furrow after furrow of fresh dirt.

A heavy footstep stomped across the porch, then entered the building. As Meeker turned around, the big
Ute the whites called Johnson strode in, his dark eyes
blazing with anger. "We thought we agree—no plow up
our racetrack."

"Be reasonable," Meeker said and made a placating
gesture. "Surely the Utes realize that farming that land
is more practical than using it for a racetrack."

Johnson stomped over, and glared down at Meeker.
"I got many horses. If I can no race them, what I supposed to do?"

"Well," Meeker smiled, "like all the other Indians,
you have more ponies than you can feed. I suggest you
kill some of them."

"Kill them?" The other's eyes widened in disbelief. "Kill my fine ponies?" He reached out suddenly, grabbed Meeker by the coat, and slammed him backward against the desk. Even as the Indian agent yelled for help, the angry Ute turned and stalked out of the building.

Arvilla ran into the room. "Dear, are you all right?"

He stood up and brushed himself off. "Bruised a little, that's all. I'm going to alert Major Thornburgh that I may need his troops. I'm through trying to be reasonable with these savages!"

A lean rider galloped into Fort Steele and swung down from his lathered horse. "Where's the Major? I've got an urgent message."

The old sergeant on the porch eyed the man with curiosity. "Gone elk hunting up in the mountains with his visiting brother—take a day or so to find him. How urgent?"

"Mighty urgent!" The other man wiped sweat from his weathered face. "You better get lookin' for him. Meeker's expectin' an Indian war may be about to break out!"

At the Evanses' cabin, Keso and Cleve had talked of leaving at dawn, but it was the middle of the morning before they got away because Cleve had so much gear. Keso complained, but Cleve insisted on taking a tent, canned goods, and several changes of clothes.

"I didn't know we were going to need a wagon train to haul all your stuff," Keso grumbled as he looked at the pile.

"Egad, you don't expect me to live like a savage, do you?" Cleve countered.

"We don't need to travel like the Grand Duke of Russia," Keso said. The Grand Duke had been on the plains for a buffalo hunt with Buffalo Bill back in 1872.

Wannie looked at the bundles Cleve was tying to the pack mule. "What is all this stuff, dearest?"

"A few pans and trade goods from Brewster Industries," he answered.

"No wonder your luggage was so heavy," Keso grumbled.

"Who knows? We might run across some trappers and get a chance to barter for some furs or something. I'd love to have a bear rug for my library."

They all gathered out front to see the two off. Cleve rode the old blue gelding, Keso his black stallion, Spirit. They also took a pack mule loaded with the extra luxuries and supplies Cleve insisted on taking. It took all Wannie's patience not to start another fuss over going with them, but she stuck to her plan.

Cleve gave her a prim smack on the lips. "Good-bye, my dear—we'll see you in about a week."

Keso kissed the tip of her nose " 'Bye, brat. Maybe I'll find you a gold nugget. You can make a necklace of it."

She smiled and looked down at the expensive ring and all her other jewelry. "Which way are you two going?"

Keso pointed. "We'll spend the first night up at the spring. We should get there by late afternoon. After that, it depends on what Cleve wants to see."

It was all Wannie could do to stand there docilely and wave to the pair as they mounted up and rode out leading the pack mule. If they thought they were going to leave her behind to miss all the fun, were they ever mistaken! She knew the location of that spring up in the mountains. Tonight, she was going to sneak off and follow them. The Evanses wouldn't know she was gone until morning and by then, she expected to have joined the two men. Surely when she caught up with them, Keso would relent and let her ride along. His other option would be to cancel the trip and bring her back. Of course everyone would be annoyed with her, but after all, she was a modern, liberated woman!

The trio watched the pair disappear over a ridge and then turned back toward the house.

Cherokee said, "I've got some harness to mend." He headed for the barn.

"I suppose I might as well start that needlework," Wannie groaned.

Silver put her arm around her. "I'm glad you realized it was too rough a trip for you. The boys'll be back before you know it."

The day seemed to pass slowly. Without arousing suspicion, Wannie went in to clean up her room, but instead she packed a bedroll with a few personal items and Keso's old shirts and pants. Since her bedroom was farthest down the hall, with any luck she might be able to saddle a horse and ride out tonight without waking Silver and Cherokee. They wouldn't realize she was gone until they found her note tomorrow morning and by then, she'd be with Keso and Cleve.

It was dusk dark. Wannie yawned as she helped clear away the supper dishes. "I didn't realize how weary I was—I think I'll go to bed early."

"So soon?" Silver looked surprised.

"With the men gone, there's nothing much to do," Wannie said. "I might lie in bed and read. Good night all." She hugged them both and went to her room, feeling a little guilty, but determined to join Keso and Cleve.

She blew out her lamp and crawled into bed, still wearing her calico dress and lace petticoats. An hour passed and the house grew quiet and dark. Taking her clothes and bedroll, she climbed out the window and headed toward the barn. She didn't change because if Cherokee caught her, she didn't want to arouse his suspicions like she would if she was dressed for riding in Keso's old jeans. She'd change into pants when she was safely away from the house.

Quietly, she saddled Dancer, tied her blanket roll behind the saddle, and led the bay filly from the stable. Now if she could just sneak across the pasture and into the forest, she couldn't be seen from the house.

So far, so good. Once in the woods, Wannie hiked up her skirts and mounted, reining the horse toward the spring where the men would be camping. An owl hooted somewhere in the forest and she paused, the hair rising on the back of her neck. It dawned on her that it was very dark and she was alone. For a long moment, she was tempted to give this up, put the horse away, and return to her safe, warm bed.

"You big 'fraidy cat," she scolded herself, "there's nothing in these woods that can hurt you. Besides, do you really want to spend the week staring at a piece of silly needlework when the boys are having such a big adventure? In a few hours, you'll be safely in their camp."

Thus cheered, she took off in the direction of the mountain spring. With any luck at all, she should find it in the middle of the night.

Hours passed as she rode through the woods. The night had grown chilly and she shivered, wishing she had worn heavier clothes. Occasionally, the wind rustled through the trees or something scampered past her horse's hooves. Why had she done such a fool thing? Because, she shook her head stubbornly, she would have missed a big adventure.

The moon came out and reflected off the snowcaps on distant peaks. It was so beautiful riding this trail.

She had forgotten how much she loved Colorado. When she married, she wouldn't be coming here anymore. The thought depressed her. The moon slid behind scudding clouds and the trail seemed darker than ever as her horse plodded along. Suppose she reached the spring and the boys weren't there? Suppose they had decided to take another route? Somewhere, a coyote wailed and the call echoed through the mountains. Keso. If she could just find Keso, she'd be all right. He always looked after her.

The night turned colder and she wished she had a canteen of steaming coffee. She didn't feel defiant and clever anymore, she felt uncertain and scared. The wind picked up, carrying the scent of pine trees and wildflowers.

Hours passed and she kept riding. It couldn't be that long until dawn and then she'd be able to see the trail. By her calculations, she should have reached the spring by now.

Smoke—she smelled smoke. There was a camp up ahead, but whose? She didn't want to blunder into a camp of outlaws, rough trappers or worse yet, hostile Indians. *Why didn't you think of that sooner, you idiot?* she scolded herself.

She dismounted, trying to decide how to find out. Abruptly, she heard a horse in the camp whinny as it seemed to scent her mare. Wannie reached and grabbed her mare's muzzle to keep her from nickering back. She wanted to make sure it was Keso's camp before she announced her presence. Wrapping a strip of soft rawhide around the mare's muzzle so she couldn't nicker, Wannie tied the horse to a tree and crept toward the camp through the underbrush. How would she know if it was Keso's camp without alerting the occupants?

She could see a tiny fire and what appeared to be two

men asleep in their blankets. Thank goodness she had found them!

She led her mare around to where the horses were tied. Her relief turned to puzzlement as she stared at the other mounts. These weren't Spirit and old Blue and where was the pack mule? She noted then that the horses had the big U.S. brand on the shoulder. Cavalry horses?

She breathed a sigh of relief, knowing she had stumbled on an army patrol. They'd help her find Keso and Cleve. All she had to do was wake them up, tell them her plight and—

"Gotcha!" A big hand clapped over her mouth even as someone reached out of the darkness and grabbed her. Wannie struggled, her heart pounding with terror. Then the moonlight revealed the arm wore a blue sleeve.

Thank God! She relaxed, waiting for the soldier to let go of her so she could explain what she was doing sneaking about their camp.

He whirled her around, a big figure in blue in the shadowy darkness.

"Look, I can explain," Wannie began, "I was looking—"

"I know. You was lookin' for me again, weren't you, sweetie? We got unfinished business, right?"

She stared up into his face as the moon came out from behind clouds. Oh, no. It was the big soldier who had molested her on the street in Denver. She managed to scream long and loud, even as he slapped her hard and put his hand over her mouth again.

"Shut up, damn you! I won't have you alertin' any army patrols out lookin' for us. Hey, Bill, come here and see what we got!"

She fought him, but he picked her up easily, carrying her back to camp, his hand over her mouth.

The other man rose out of his blankets. "Hey, Clem, what in thunder's goin' on?"

"Lookie here what I got!" The big soldier guffawed. " 'Member me tellin' you 'bout the sweet thang I tried to kiss the other day afore we deserted? She came lookin' for me."

"Oh God, Clem, we don't need that kind of trouble! We're tryin' to clear out of this country, remember?"

She fought but Clem held onto her easily. "We're still goin' Bill, but now we got a little gal who wants to go with us and keep us both happy, right, baby?" He ran one dirty hand up under her coat and pawed her breasts. "Some big Injun stopped me the other day, but now she's mine."

Wannie sank her teeth into his dirty fingers so that he pulled his hand away, cursing. She tried to scream again but he hit her hard, half stunning her. "Shut up, gal!"

Wannie tasted blood from her cut lip as she struggled. What was she going to do now? She shouldn't have been so headstrong, following Keso and Cleve. Now she was going to be raped and held captive by a pair of filthy army deserters!

FIFTEEN

Keso had decided against stopping at the spring in the late afternoon. When they'd ridden near, he'd recognized one of the men already camped in that spot as the drunken soldier he'd whipped in town. He didn't know what those soldiers were doing out here—on a scouting party, maybe—but Keso didn't intend to invite trouble by stopping at their camp. He insisted on skirting that spring and riding on to the next watering place only a few hundred yards above the other. What Keso didn't need was trouble with the army.

Keso lay barely asleep by the smoldering fire, listening. The wind was blowing from the direction of the spring. He came awake at a slight sound; it might have been the faint cry of a rabbit as a night-hunting owl swooped down on it. It might have been the echo of a lonely coyote pup. It might have been a woman's scream. He lay there a long moment, listening, tense as a bobcat. Cleve was in his tent, snoring so loudly it was difficult to hear anything else.

The cry had been so faint, he'd probably imagined it. After a long moment, Keso closed his eyes and tried to return to sleep, but the sound haunted him. Who or what might be out there in the darkness? Keso reached for the rifle next to his blankets and checked the big bowie knife that was always within reach. He got up and crept into the darkness, sniffing the wind and listening. Generations of warrior blood kept his senses keen even though he had been living as a white man.

The sound had come from the direction of the soldiers' camp. Keso hesitated. He didn't need any trouble from an army patrol—many didn't like Indians of whatever variety. He paused, wondering whether to awaken Cleve, then shook his head. Cleve would be worse than useless in case of trouble. Keso dared not take his horse; he couldn't risk a soldier's mount nickering at Spirit's approach. Gripping his rifle and knife, Keso took off running toward the soldiers' camp, his swift stride silent as a shadow. If he was heading into trouble, he might be outnumbered, but he'd have surprise on his side.

Wannie had never been so terrified as she was at this moment, fighting to get out of the big soldier's arms. He only laughed, holding onto her easily. "See, Bill? How eager she is to give us a little sugar?"

"Oh God, Clem, let her go!" The other hovered in the background, pleading. "We got enough trouble with the army lookin' for us—I didn't agree to rape no women."

"Wal, now, she came lookin' for us," Clem grinned through broken teeth, "didn't you, sweetie?"

Wannie tried to bite his hand again but he held onto her and laughed. "See how much she wants me to do it to her?"

"Clem," the other pleaded, "a pretty gal like this means trouble."

"Naw. When she goes missin'," Clem said, "they'll think them red-skinned devils, the Utes, got her."

"Don't be loco, Clem, we can't keep her."

"Sure we can." The deserter ran his hands over her slim body and laughed when she tried to fight him off.

"She can cook for us and pleasure us every night as we cross the country. We get to Utah, we head south. There's still a Comanchero or two who'd pay good money for a pretty gal like this one."

Oh Lord, what was she going to do? Wannie struggled again and tried to strike him with her small fists, but Clem laughed and paid no more attention than if she'd been a pesty mosquito.

"Now, sweet, you just save all that energy for the lovin' I'm gettin' ready to give you." With one dirty paw, he ripped the front of her bodice open and squeezed her breast. "I can hardly wait to get my mouth on these."

In sheer terror, Wannie began to fight and claw but he was pulling at her clothes. He was going to have to kill her before she'd submit.

And at that moment, something stepped out of the shadows behind Clem. She saw only the silhouette of a dark face and the flash of a knife glinting in the moonlight. Oh God!

Even as she watched, a strong brown arm reached out and jerked Clem's head back. She saw the sudden surprise in the deserter's eyes as he turned loose of her and began to fight. At that moment, the mysterious intruder cut the soldier's throat.

She screamed, stumbling backward from the smell of fresh blood, then turned and ran blindly, clutching the front of her shredded dress. She fell, scrambled to her feet, and ran on. Behind her, she heard Bill's terrified shout and then the sound of a horse as he swung up on it and escaped.

Wannie paused, breathing hard. Behind her, she heard a running footstep. Whose? Renegades would treat her no better than Clem had. She'd rather be dead than to lose her virginity to rape. She ran on, stumbling and falling. Her heart pounded with the effort and her legs and arms were skinned and bruised. Her lungs seemed on fire and she was certain her pursuer could hear her agonized breathing. Nothing mattered but escaping as she fled blindly through the woods. Abruptly, a figure stepped out in front of her and she screamed again as she realized her pursuer had outsmarted her, circling to step into her path. There was no way to avoid him as his hands reached out and grabbed her. She fought him as he pulled her against him.

"Hush, Wannie," a familiar voice commanded, "you're safe now."

"Keso?" She collapsed in his embrace, throwing her arms around his neck and sobbing.

"It's all right, honey, it's all right, I've got you. Don't make so much noise." He was holding her, stroking her, soothing her.

"Oh, Keso," she sobbed, clutching him, "I thought it was your camp, and then he reached out and grabbed me—"

"I know, I know," he whispered and kissed her forehead. "You're all right now, I've got you." He swung her up in his arms and began to walk.

"They—they were deserting, Keso," she sobbed, "did you—did you—"

"I killed the big one," he muttered as he walked. "The other one cleared out as if the devil was after him."

"I was so scared," she wept against his neck.

"I know, honey, I know. It's all right—nobody's going to hurt you."

Honey? Was he calling her honey? She looked up at him, but he was intent on his mission. She held onto him, awed at the strength of the man and the way he carried her as if she weighed no more than a flower petal. She realized abruptly that she had her bare breasts pressed against his chest and his shirt was unbuttoned so that her nipples brushed against his warm flesh. The

thought sent a shiver through her, but he had not even
seemed to notice.

"Where are we going?"

"To my camp. Where's your horse?"

She gestured. "Over there. Where's Cleve?"

"Still asleep and snoring, I reckon."

She relaxed in Keso's strong arms and nestled her
face against his brawny chest as he walked toward where
she'd tied Dancer. "What made you come?"

He glanced down at her, then paused as he seemed
to realize she was almost naked from the waist up. His
eyes seemed to darken with intensity. "I heard a faint
sound and decided I'd better investigate."

"Thank goodness you did," she breathed.

He frowned down at her. "Brat, now you tell me what
you were doing out here in the first place?"

"I was following you."

"I might have known," he snorted. He put her up on
the filly and swung up behind her. When he slid his
arms around her, his hand brushed her bare breast and
he jerked back is if touched by a hot ember.

She relaxed in his arms as they rode, breathing a sigh
of relief. She could always count on Keso. She hoped
she could do the same with Cleve, but somehow, she
didn't have much confidence in her fiancé's ability to
cope with hostile surroundings. That thought made her
feel guilty.

Keso reined in at his camp, dismounted, and motioned her to slide off the horse and into his arms. She
slid all the way down his body until her feet touched
the ground. He took a deep, shuddering breath and
ran his tongue along his lips, his eyes dark and intense.

"Keso? What's wrong?" She looked up at him, in-
tensely aware that her nipples were almost brushing his
chest in the unbuttoned shirt.

"Nothing. I—I always forget how small and delicate

you are." He swung her up in his arms and carried her over and stood her by the smoldering fire, but he didn't let go of her shoulders. They paused only inches apart, his shirt open, her bodice torn away. Heat seemed to radiate between them and she had a sudden feeling that he was about to pull her to him so that her bare breasts would be pressing against his chest. If he did, what would she do? The answer came to her then that she wouldn't be strong enough to stop him . . . or that she wouldn't want to.

That thought startled her so much that she crossed her arms across her breasts and stumbled backward. "I—I need something to put on."

He seemed to come out of his spell and appeared as uncomfortable as she was. "I'll get you a shirt."

He got one from his bedroll. Even as he reached to put it around her small shoulders, his chest brushed across her bare breasts again. It felt like fire touching her nipples. She gulped and pulled the shirt around herself, thinking he'd be shocked if he knew what had just crossed her mind.

"Wannie, I want you to know . . ."

"Yes?"

A noise came from inside the tent and Cleve stumbled out, yawning and running his hand through his shiny blond hair. "Wannie? What're you doing here? What happened to your dress? What—?"

"It's a long story, Cleve," Keso snapped, squatting to reach for the coffeepot. "The brat followed us."

Cleve glared at her, anger in his pale eyes. "Wannie, you disobeyed me? What kind of wife are you going to make?"

"You might at least ask me if I'm hurt."

"Why? Did that Injun—?"

"That drunk soldier from town had grabbed her," Keso said, and began to make coffee.

What had Cleve meant by that remark about 'that Injun'? Wannie thought with indignation. Surely he wouldn't suspect her own brother had torn her dress like that?

Cleve's eyes turned anxious as he looked at her shredded bodice. "He didn't—? I mean, you didn't let him touch you—?"

"Her virtue is safe," Keso snapped. "I was more worried about her life. Sit down, brat," he commanded, "we've got some bread and leftover meat."

Wannie stared up at Cleve, shocked as she realized what he'd been concerned about. "You don't care if they almost killed me—you were worried you wouldn't have a virgin bride!"

"Wannie!" Cleve looked thoroughly shocked. "That's no way for a lady to talk!"

"But it's true, isn't it?" she insisted. "You were more afraid of your friends gossiping about you getting used goods than whether they murdered me or not!"

"Well, I must admit it would cause talk if you let some soldier—"

"Let?" she was screaming at him, "Let? Cleve, while you snoozed away, they would have raped me and cut my throat if Keso hadn't come to my rescue."

"Now, my dear," he made a placating gesture, "don't get so upset. If your virtue is safe—"

"Will you stop raving about my virtue?" Wannie shrieked.

"Brat," Keso said softly, "you make more noise than a coyote caught in a trap. Now shut up and drink your coffee." He put a steaming tin cup in her hands.

"Oh Keso, thank you." She took it gratefully, sitting down on a log by the fire.

"Are you warm enough?"

She looked into his dark eyes and saw the concern

there. "You're so kind." *Honey*. he had called her in a tense moment; *honey*. Did he even know he'd done it?

"Let's get back to the subject at hand," Cleve bristled. "Did you or did you not disobey me and endanger yourself by following us?"

"Oh, shut up, Cleve," she snapped as she sipped the strong, hot coffee. "Of course I did. I'm sitting here, aren't I?"

She thought she heard Keso laugh, but he had his head turned away, messing with the coffee pot.

"When we are married," Cleve said frostily, "we are going to have to correct your behavior. Society ladies do not disobey their husbands and most certainly don't tell them to shut up!"

She sighed loudly, beginning to wonder what she had ever seen in Cleve Brewster. He was a handsome, prissy prig.

"Brewster," Keso said, "have some coffee and relax. She's had a tough night—think about that while you're chewing her out."

"You're right," Cleve nodded almost grudgingly. "I'm truly sorry, Wannie, my dear—I was just so upset to think you might have been hurt."

"Tell, me, Cleve," she asked softly, looking up at him, "if they'd have done it, would you still have married me?"

"What?"

"You heard me." She stared hard at him, waiting for his answer.

He stuttered for a long moment. "Egad, what a stupid question—no, stupid and irrelevant. You said they didn't. Were you lying to me?" His tone and expression turned anxious.

"You didn't answer my question," she insisted, although suddenly she knew the answer and it saddened her.

"Wannie," Keso said earnestly, "any man would want you for his wife, no matter what."

"The real question is," Cleve dismissed her briskly as he reached for a cup of coffee, "is what are we to do with you now?"

Keso shrugged as he cut a piece of cold meat, wrapped it in a biscuit, and handed it to her. "We'll have to take her back, of course."

She stuffed the food in her mouth. She was famished and it tasted so good. "Oh, but I want to go with you."

"Wannie," Cleve snipped, "don't talk with your mouth full. I swear, didn't Miss Priddy's teach you anything?"

"Brewster," Keso said, "did anyone ever tell you you were a pain in the—"

"How dare you talk like that in front of a lady," Cleve said. "I knew you were an uncouth bumpkin, but—"

"And how dare you call Keso that after he's just saved my life?" Wannie shouted at him, her mouth still full.

"Hush, both of you," Keso ordered in a tone that left no room to argue. "Tomorrow, we take Wannie back to the cabin."

Cleve looked annoyed. "You see what you've done?" he accused. "You've ruined my expedition. How could you have done that after I forbade you to—"

"Oh, shut up, Brewster," Keso thundered. "I'm tired and I'm sleepy and my patience is wearing thin."

"Do you know who I am?" Cleve's voice rose, thin and high. "I'm Cleveland Brewster, Jr., and my father—"

"We know, Brewster," Keso shrugged, "but your rich daddy won't do you much good out here. Now shut up before I shut you up!"

Cleve's mouth opened as if he were going to say something, then he seemed to think better of it. "Very well. I realize we are all tired and cranky. We'll finish this discussion in the morning." He looked longingly toward his tent and paused.

Keso looked at him. "What is it now?"

"I'm trying to decide if it's proper for Miss Evans to share my tent the rest of the night."

"I don't think so," Keso snapped. "I'll fix her a bed next to the fire. Give her your extra blanket."

"But then I'll only have one."

"Right. And I'll give her one," Keso said with infinite patience as if talking to a child, "and then she'll have two and she'll be warm enough. We're men—we can tough it out."

"Very well."

He went inside the tent, got the extra blanket, and tossed it to Wannie. He looked at Keso. "Where do you intend to sleep?"

"By the fire. Why, would you like me to share your tent?"

"Not hardly!" Cleve snapped and strode inside.

Wannie finished her coffee, grateful for the food and weary now that she was warm and the excitement was over. "Why was Cleve worried about where you were going to sleep? Surely he didn't think my own brother—?"

"It *is* the world's most ridiculous idea, isn't it?" Keso sounded angry and that baffled her. "Here, brat." He tossed her his extra blanket. "Now settle down—there's been enough excitement for one night."

He stared at her in the firelight and she glanced down, realizing the shirt had come open and he could see her bare breasts in her torn dress. Hurriedly, she buttoned it, took her blankets, and lay down by the fire. She couldn't sleep. After a while, she whispered, "Keso, are you asleep?"

"Well, I was," he mumbled. "What is it now?"

She was remembering the way it had felt to have her bare breasts pressed against his naked chest, the way he had held her close and called her "honey"; the way he had looked at her with those smoldering eyes just now. If she told him what she was thinking about, he'd think she was both crazy and depraved, especially since she had a very proper fiancé asleep in a tent just a few feet away. "I—I just wanted to thank you again."

"No need."

"No, I mean, really. All those times you've rescued me. You've fished me out of creeks and even climbed a tall tree one time when I got up there and couldn't get down."

"It came with the job."

"What job?"

"Wannie," he whispered, "don't you remember the night the Duchess's Palace burned down? You were the prettiest little girl I'd ever seen and your folks were both dead. Cherokee lifted you up behind me on that horse and told me to look after you. God knows I've done the best I can, but it's been one helluva ride."

"If you don't stop that swearing, Cleve will be out here telling you what's proper."

"I'm sorry, but you make me crazy, Wannie."

She thought over the past fifteen years. He had always been there, always. "I—I guess I had forgotten about that night we rode out of Denver to start a new life as a family."

"Uh-huh. If I'd known what a challenge the job was going to be, I might have thought twice. Now, go to sleep."

"I'm still cold."

"Wannie," he said with infinite patience, "you've got my extra blanket and my place by the fire. I don't know what else I can do."

"If we curled up together, we could save body heat."

"Good God, no!" He sat straight up in his blankets, his eyes horrified.

What was ailing him?

"Cleve would probably think it socially incorrect, like using the wrong fork, but he need never know—"

"No, Wannie, absolutely not." His voice was cold and angry.

"But there's nothing really wrong with it—you're my brother and—"

"God damn it, shut up and go to sleep!" He flopped back down in his blanket and turned his back to her. His fury both shocked and mystified her. What on earth was he so upset about? Why, he was getting as priggish as Cleve!

Finally, she drifted off to sleep and dreamed that she slept curled up safe and warm in Keso's embrace, that he held her close and kissed her lips. When she realized what she was dreaming, she awakened in horror to a cool gray dawn. Was she out of her mind? She was engaged to a handsome, rich man who was everything she'd ever dreamed of and he was sleeping in a tent only a few feet away. In fact, she could hear him snoring. She hadn't realized Cleve snored.

She sat up and groaned aloud because she was stiff and sore. Looking down at herself, she realized she wore one of Keso's shirts. What on earth? Then last night's events returned with a rush. Worse than that, Keso would take her back to the cabin today and she'd miss all the adventure.

She looked over toward Keso's blankets. He was gone. Knowing him, he was out scouting the landscape while Cleve slept peacefully on. Wannie got up, went out into the brush and relieved herself, then splashed cold water on her face from the little spring. When she returned to camp, Cleve had come out of his tent, all mussed with a shadow of beard. His glorious hair that he was so vain about looked like it needed a good combing. "Good morning."

"I'm not sure what's good about it." He sounded peevish and out of sorts. "Is there any coffee?"

"I don't guess Keso's made any yet."

"And he's let the fire die," Cleve complained. "Where is he, anyway?"

She looked around. "I don't know. Scouting the area, I suppose."

Cleve's eyes widened. "You don't suppose he would abandon us out here, do you?"

"Keso?" The idea shocked her. "Never! He makes his main job in life looking out for me."

"So I've noticed." Cleve bit off his words as he fussed with the fire.

"What's that supposed to mean?"

"Oh, stop it, Wannie, you must be blind."

She stared at him. It was unthinkable that he might be jealous of her brother. "I don't understand—"

"Do you know anything about building a fire?" Cleve was attempting to pile up wood. "I've never done this before."

"Never?"

"Well, now, what do you think servants are for?"

She came over and began to break up small twigs on the smoldering embers. "We'd be helpless, wouldn't we, if something did happen to Keso? Go fill the pot, Cleve, and start the coffee."

"I've never made coffee in my whole life. All I know about it is Jeeves serves it in delicate china cups out of the monogrammed silver pot."

She took a long look at him, thinking that her elegant gentleman was as inept out here as poor Keso had been among the gentry. Somehow, right at this moment, knowing how to build a fire seemed a lot more important than whether red or white wine should be served with fish.

Keso stepped out of the woods. "Don't build that fire."

His sudden appearance startled Wannie. "You step as quietly as any warrior," she complained, "and why not a fire? I thought I'd fry some bacon."

He shook his head as he crossed the circle. "No, we make a cold camp for the next few days, and eat leftover biscuits and dried jerky. No bacon—the scent carries too far."

"See here, Evans," Cleve snapped, "we may be camping out, but we don't have to do without food—"

"And I'd keep my voice low if I were you." Keso came over and kicked out the fire that was just sputtering to life.

"How dare you!" Cleve said. "We were just going to make some coffee—"

"I said keep your voice low," Keso ordered.

He must be in a really foul humor because of all the trouble she'd caused last night, Wannie mused.

"Keso, I'm sorry I've made you mad." She looked up into his set, drawn face. "I won't argue with you if you're determined to take me back home this morning."

He shook his head. "Sorry, we won't be going that direction—we'll be moving West and just hope we run into an army patrol."

"Why, you just make these decisions without so much as a by-your-leave." Cleve snapped. "I'll fire you and get myself another guide."

"You just do that, Brewster, but we're stuck with each other for the time being."

Keso was really tense, Wannie thought. If Cleve didn't hush, Keso was liable to hit him in the nose.

"And another thing," Cleve said, "we aren't going on, we're going back, just like we discussed last night. I'm not taking Wannie into this rough, dangerous country to the west of here."

Keso shook his head, staring off toward the mountains between them and the Evanses' cabin. "We're heading west," he said again, "and the faster, the better. Now, leave that tent and most of the rest of this junk you insisted on dragging along."

Wannie knew Keso too well to argue when he used that no-nonsense tone. She began to roll up the blankets, but Cleve caught Keso by the shoulder.

"You ignorant Injun, I've had all the guff I'm going to take off you. I give the orders—"

Keso hit him. Even as Wannie opened her mouth to caution Cleve that no one argued with her foster brother when he used that tone of voice, Keso hit Cleve in the mouth and her fiancé went down in the dirt.

"Keso, you mean, stubborn fool!" She ran over to Cleve and helped him to sit up. "Are you all right, dearest?"

Cleve wiped his mouth and then looked at his soft, manicured hand with horror. "Blood! You hit me hard enough to cut my lip. And look, I've got blood all over my fine monogrammed shirt."

"And I'm gonna hit you again if you don't get moving," Keso said. "Wannie, get stuff packed. We're heading west now!"

"Keso, have you lost your mind? What is wrong with you?" She was almost screaming at him.

He grabbed her and clapped his hand over her mouth. "I said keep your voice low—sound echoes through the mountains."

Something was very, very wrong. She could sense it looking up into his dark eyes and feeling the tension in his hands. Very slowly, he took his hand away. "Oh, Keso, what is it?"

For an answer, he turned and stared again toward the east. "We've got to head west. They're between us and the cabin."

"Who?" Cleve said.

Keso nodded with his head and Wannie turned to look. In the clear blue of the early dawn, a smoke signal drifted over the mountains and after a long moment, another answered it.

"What—what is that?" Cleve whispered.

"Signal fires." Wannie had never seen them before, but somehow she knew with a sudden chill that something had changed.

Keso nodded. "It's finally happened. The Utes are on the warpath!"

SIXTEEN

"What makes you so sure?" Cleve's face turned pale as he stared at the smoke signals to the east. "Anybody could be making that campfire—"

"And sending signals?" Keso pointed at the puffs drifting across the peaks. "I may not know which fork to use, Brewster, but I know these mountains and I know Indians. Something's happened."

"Keso's right, Cleve." Wannie took a deep breath to steady her nerves. "If he thinks there's danger, there is." She got up and began to roll blankets.

Cleve paused uncertainly. "They can't go on the warpath, they've got a treaty—"

"Which white men have been breaking," Keso reminded them as he kicked dirt over the smoldering fire. "Maybe we can make our way around through the woods on the west slopes until we find a settlement or an army patrol."

Cleve still seemed inclined to argue. "Isn't that out of our way?"

Keso didn't pause as he gathered up things. "Cleve, you can stay here and argue if you want, or even try to go back the way we came, but I'm taking Wannie west."

"A few puffs of smoke may not mean much." Cleve said.

Wannie looked at him and sighed. "Cleve, if Keso

says there's danger, listen to him. He knows this country."

"You have more confidence in him than you have in your own fiancé?"

She thought about it a minute. "Yes, I'm afraid I do."

"Why, Wannie, you disappoint me, I—"

"Brewster," Keso said and his tone was as threatening as a rattler's warning. "Get moving, or we'll ride out and leave you."

"You wouldn't dare! Why, my father—"

"To hell with your father," Keso snarled as he paused in checking his rifle. "Don't you understand? This one mess your daddy's money won't get you out of. Now, get a move on!"

Keso's tone left no room for argument, Wannie realized. He was in command here, but then, Keso was in his element against hostile nature and people. Abruptly, that seemed so much more important than knowing the latest style in gentlemen's waistcoats. "Keso, I've got most of it. What about the tent?"

"Leave the tent. We're going to be moving too fast to use it and the extra weight—"

"I paid good money for that tent." Cleve was almost livid.

"Maybe the Utes will find a use for it." Keso began saddling horses. "You coming, Brewster, or are you going to stay here to greet them?"

For a long moment, she was afraid her fiancé might continue to argue. Instead, he began to gather up things and saddle his horse.

Keso saddled her filly and frowned at the overloaded pack mule. "I wish we didn't have that mule to worry about. It'll slow us down."

"Egad, you aren't going to leave my trade goods," Cleve snarled. "That stuff's worth a lot of money."

"More than your scalp?" Keso said, pausing as he tied his blanket roll behind his saddle.

"Oh, don't be so dramatic," Cleve said. "I'm sure when the Utes see what I've brought to trade, they'll listen to reason."

Keso snorted with laughter. "Tell them who your daddy is, too, Brewster. A lot of them speak English—they used to scout for the whites. Come on, Wannie." He lifted her to her saddle and handed her the reins. She watched him mount up, thinking how lithe and strong he looked leading out on the trail. Still grumbling, Cleve fell in behind her, leading the loaded mule.

They spent the day following a crooked trail that gradually descended down the Western slope. When Cleve argued they could save time by riding the straight trail that ran across miles of treeless prairie rather than keeping to the woods, Keso pointed out they would also be easier to see if there were any Ute war parties in the area.

Late in the afternoon, they stopped to rest and water the horses in a small, clear creek.

"Brewster," Keso said, "tie the horses and that mule out to graze for an hour or two. We'll rest here."

"Don't you think we should ride on while we've got daylight?" Cleve asked.

Wannie shook her head. "Keso knows what he's doing." She had supreme confidence in him.

Keso said, "We'll have to cross that big stretch of prairie ahead before we can get back to the grove. I'd rather do that after dark. Now, let's eat a bite and get some sleep."

Wannie and Keso staked out the horses and Cleve tied the mule out to graze in a little clearing. They had some hardtack, smoked jerky, and a drink of water from the spring.

Cleve was grumbling as he ate. "The only good thing

about this is what a rousing adventure tale it'll make back in the city."

"Cleve," Wannie said, horrified, "don't you realize this is serious?"

Cleve laughed. "If we run into any hostiles, I'll just offer them a few beads or junk out of my trade stuff. They'll let us go."

"I wouldn't count on that," Keso said. "The most valuable thing we've got isn't trade goods."

"Like what?" Cleve said.

Keso looked at Wannie and didn't say anything.

She felt a chill go up her back at the thought. "Oh, Keso, I'm afraid." She ran to him without thinking and he hugged her for a long moment.

"You trust me, Wannie?"

She looked up at him. "You know I do."

"I won't let anything happen to you—I promise."

"What a pretty picture," Cleve said, his tone sarcastic. "Wannie, you could at least show a little confidence in your fiancé."

What had she been thinking? "I'm sorry, Cleve. Of course I have confidence in you."

"Let's all shut up and get some sleep," Keso said. He lay down, put his hat over his eyes, and was asleep in seconds.

Wannie stretched out on the grass near him, wishing they were all three back at the cabin. Cleve lay down on her other side, grumbling about things in general. Keso was right, she thought with a sigh, Cleve might be handsome, but he was spoiled and whiny. She was so very tired.

It was almost dark when Keso shook her awake. "Hey, brat, we've got to be moving on."

"Already? I'm so tired."

His expression turned gentle. "Honey, I'm sorry. I

wish I could let you sleep, but we've got to make time while it's dark."

She sat up and he put his jacket around her shoulders. "Keso, you'll get cold."

"I'll be okay. Besides, we've got a worse problem than that." He walked over and kicked Cleve's boots none too gently. "Wake up, Brewster, we've got trouble."

"What?" Cleve ceased snoring and sat up, running his hands through his hair. "What is it now?"

"It's my fault, I reckon, for not checking behind you," Keso said. "I should have remembered you didn't know about things like that."

Wannie felt apprehension. "Oh, Keso, what is it?"

Keso frowned. "I've been looking over an hour and now it's getting dark, so we may not find it."

The horses. She looked to where she and Keso had staked them out then breathed a sigh of relief as she saw all three still grazing peacefully.

Cleve said, "What are you talking about?"

Keso turned and nodded toward where Cleve had tied the mule. There was no mule. "The mule's come untied and wandered off."

Cleve began to swear. "Have you looked for it?"

"Now, Brewster, what do you think I've been doing this past hour? There's no telling where it is."

"All my trade goods," Cleve said.

"Trade goods, hell," Keso said, "all our supplies except the little bit tied behind each saddle. If you thought we were toughing it before, rich boy, wait 'til you see what it's going to be like the rest of this trip."

Another thought crossed Wannie's mind as she got up. "Cleve, the trade goods—what are they?"

He shrugged, "You know, beads and bright cloth, a few copper pots and kitchen things. Why?"

She looked into Keso's dark eyes and saw them widen

with horror as the point she was making dawned on him.

"Oh God," he whispered, "butcher knives—dozens of big butcher knives."

Even Cleve paled. "You—you don't think the Utes might find that mule—?"

"They're as liable to as anyone," Keso said, "and all our extra ammunition and food's in that pack."

Looking into Keso's grave face, she knew that the trio was in serious trouble.

"Egad," Cleve said as he got up, "I just can't believe this is happening to me. My father has considerable influence in Washington. If we can just find a telegraph station or an army post—"

"Brewster, don't you understand?" Keso said. "We're on our own—just the three of us having to live off the land and dodge Indians while we travel hundreds of miles. No one is coming to help us and your damn pack mule is going to aid the hostiles if they find it."

Wannie took a deep breath and squared her small shoulders. "Keso's right, Cleve, all we can do is stop whining and push ahead. Keso will get us out of this if anyone can."

Keso smiled at her. "Thanks for the vote of confidence, Wannie. Now let's mount up and see how much ground we can cover before daylight."

It was a long, cold night. Wannie had never been so miserable as when she was riding through the darkness. Autumn was turning into early winter at this high altitude and there was a light frost dusting the trees and grass. If she was cold, she figured Keso was more so, since she wore his jacket. She watched his broad back ahead of her on the trail, confident that if anyone could get them out of this predicament, it would be Keso

Evans. She had a feeling he hadn't been named "the Fox" for nothing. Behind her, Cleve grumbled and complained all night about being cold or hungry. Cleveland Brewster, Jr.'s elegant manners weren't of much use out here in the Colorado wilderness—he seemed more like a spoiled college boy than a man.

Maybe she was changing, too. She glanced down at the expensive ring, jeweled pin, and gold bracelets and thought how little they were worth out here. At this moment, she would have traded all her jewels for some hot food and extra clothing. Sometimes when she looked up in the moonlight, she could see her own breath hanging on the frosty air. Her hands were cold since she had no gloves. She took turns putting one hand in her pocket while holding the reins with the other.

She began to think the night would never end. Ahead of her, Keso rode without complaining, even though she knew he had to be cold and miserable. Behind her, Cleve did nothing but complain, although he had the warmest coat of the three.

Toward dawn, they heard a faint, high sound carried on the wind. They reined in.

Cleve asked, "What was that?"

There was no mistaking the terror in his tone. She glanced back it him. The moonlight shone on his pale hair and on the sweat of his pasty face, even though the night was cool.

"Hush," Keso commanded, standing up in his stirrups and listening intently. "I'm not sure—it was so faint. Could have been the wind."

All three of them listened. Her filly stamped its hooves and the sound echoed in the sudden stillness.

"What I want to know," she whispered, "is how far away was it and where?"

Keso shook his head. "No way to tell. What I do know

is I don't want to ride any farther in this direction until I figure out where it came from." He dismounted. "Let's rest here awhile."

"I'm so cold," Wannie whispered.

"I know, honey." He came over and held up his hands to help her dismount. She slid off into his arms and let him hold her against him for a long moment. His big body was so warm, his wool shirt rough against her chilled face. He took her hand in his and rubbed it between callused fingers.

"By God," Cleve grumbled, "I'm cold. I want to build a fire."

"Brewster," Keso said and there was no mistaking his tone, "if you try to build a fire, you might end up roasting over it."

"You better not threaten me with violence," Cleve blustered. "You wouldn't dare—"

"I wasn't talking about me," Keso said.

Oh my God, she thought. "Are we—are we in any immediate danger, Keso?"

He held her close and patted her. "Of course not, brat," he whispered, "I was just scaring your prissy boyfriend. We'll be okay."

Somehow, she knew he was lying so she wouldn't be scared. Keso had never been a good liar. "Can we sit down a little while?"

"Sure," he said and kissed her forehead. "I'm sorry we don't have any coffee."

"You're trying to blame everything on me," Cleve said. "I can't help it if I don't know anything about tying mules—that's the stableboy's work—"

"Oh, shut up, Brewster," Keso snapped, "I'm tired of your constant carping. If there's any major fault, it's mine. I shouldn't have let you talk me into bringing you out into the wilderness—you belong at a cotillion or a croquet match."

They led the horses over and staked them out to graze. Wannie sat down on the ground and drew herself into a small ball, trying to stay warm. As she dosed off, she felt Keso wrap a blanket around her shoulders and murmur something.

She smiled up at him sleepily. "What was it you said?"

"Nothing."

"It sounded like *for always*. What did you mean?"

"Hush, Wannie, and get some sleep. There's no telling what we'll be facing tomorrow."

Whatever it was, she thought as she put her head on her knees and dozed, Keso would take care of it; he always did.

The dawn came cold and gray.

Wannie sighed. "I've never been so cold."

"I'm sorry, Wannie," Keso said gently. "We'll be moving to a lower altitude—maybe it'll get warmer later in the morning."

Cleve was stomping his feet. "Have we got any food?"

Keso walked over and dug around in his blanket roll. "Very little. Most of it was on the pack mule."

"Couldn't we shoot some game?" Cleve said.

Keso considered it. "Maybe later. We don't know who's out there listening and sound carries a long way. How are you with a bowie knife or a snare?"

"Don't be silly—I've never used those."

"Too bad," Keso said, "we may be depending on those for food soon." He handed out a little hardtack and some smoked jerky.

Wannie bit into it gratefully. As hungry as she was, it tasted as good as anything she'd ever had at a fancy dinner party back East. She noticed then that Keso wasn't eating. "Aren't you hungry?"

"I—I already had some."

She didn't think that was true. "You're doing without so there'll be more for me, aren't you?"

"Of course he is," Cleve snapped and kept eating. "That makes him look so damned noble!"

"Cleve, you astound me," she said. "Gentlemen don't swear in front of ladies."

"I didn't think you'd notice," he said peevishly. "Gentlemen don't seem to be making much of an impression on you these days."

"What's that supposed to mean?"

"I mean, big, bulging muscles and the ability to fight like a pit bull impress you more."

She looked at him blankly. "I don't know what you're getting at."

"Yes, you do, my dear, you just won't admit it—maybe not even to yourself."

"Stop it, both of you," Keso commanded. "We've got more important things to worry about right now than a little lover's spat."

Keso was right, she thought. Cleve did seem so petty and eager to bicker. The problem was that as the son of a rich, important man, Cleve was used to having everything his way. He didn't know how to deal with adversity or the wilderness and was ill-equipped to do anything about either. Cleve was almost as helpless as she was in this hostile environment.

"We'll ride on," Keso said, "and keep to the tree line so we won't be easily spotted by any lookouts who might be up in the rocks."

"Who put you in charge?" Cleve grumbled.

"Brewster," Keso said, "you are welcome to go it on your own any time. In fact, I'd like that, but Wannie stays with me."

"Well, she's *my* fiancé—naturally, she'd go with me."

Keso put his hand on the hilt of the big bowie knife in his belt. "She stays with me."

"Stop it, you two." Wannie made a gesture of dismissal. "Cleve, be sensible. Keso can handle all this better than you can, so let him."

"Well, thanks for the vote of no confidence."

She looked at Keso—big, strong and capable—going without food and his coat for her sake. Somehow, she wasn't thinking of him as a brother anymore. That was crazy, she thought. "Keso, what shall we do?"

"First, I'm going to tie my knife to a stick and see if I can spear a fish in the creek."

Cleve snorted. "I thought you said we couldn't build a fire?"

"We might have to eat it raw."

"What?" Cleve said. "I'm not used to eating meat raw. I'm used to choosing a good white wine to go with broiled trout—"

"Oh, shut up, Cleve," she snapped. "Can you do anything besides complain?"

"Wannie, I'm seeing you in a whole different light these days."

"The feeling's mutual, Cleve."

"Wannie, you know what Indian turnips look like?" Keso asked.

She nodded. "I'll look around and maybe I'll find some wild onions, too."

"Just don't get too far away," he cautioned.

She was lucky. She searched diligently and was rewarded with a few berries, Indian turnips, and wild onions.

The men came back within an hour. Keso carried two good-sized trout. Cleve was grumbling about tripping and getting his shirt wet. "Do we dare light a fire?"

Keso considered. "If we build it small and keep it under a rock ledge where the smoke doesn't go straight up."

Cleve pulled matches out of his wet shirt. "Without

matches? I suppose, Evans, you'll do an Indian thing and rub two sticks together to get a fire?"

"I could if I had to," Keso said, "but I'm smart enough to keep my matches in a little metal match safe." He reached in his pocket and pulled them out.

"We haven't got any pans," Cleve noted.

"Thread everything on sharp sticks and roast it," Keso said.

Again, when the food was cooked, he made sure Wannie got most of it, although she argued that he should take more. She noticed Cleve ate his greedily and didn't offer to share. The fish was probably the best she'd ever eaten, she thought as she put each warm, crisp bite in her mouth. The Indian turnips and the wild onions had flavored it. She shared the tart, juicy wild berries with the men and wiped her hands on the grass. "Now what?"

"We move on," Keso said. "I haven't seen any smoke signals since yesterday—maybe that was only one stray warrior up in the cliffs."

"I wonder what happened to that pack mule?" Cleve grumbled, "I was hoping we'd find it—lots of food and supplies in those packs."

"And other things," Keso reminded him. "You'd better hope it's just out there roaming around lost. There's panthers and bears in this area—they might have caught it."

At least the men had their rifles, Wannie thought with relief, although they'd hesitated to use them because of the sound echoing through the mountains. "Do you have any idea where we are?"

Keso nodded. "Probably not more than fifteen or twenty miles from the White River Agency—we might go there."

Cleve swung up on his horse. "If the Utes are really on the warpath, won't they attack that first?"

"Maybe not. There's probably at least a dozen men at the agency and they'll be armed. Besides, if Meeker managed to get a message out, troops will be coming in."

"But the nearest troops are a couple of hundred miles away in Wyoming," Wannie thought aloud.

Keso shrugged. "It's the best I can offer right now, brat. That other deserter might also be lying in wait for us along one of these trails."

"I had forgotten about him." Wannie remembered the way the man had galloped out after he'd seen Keso cut Clem's throat. "As scared as he was, I don't think he'll stop to ambush anyone. I'll bet he's out of the country as fast as he could travel."

They mounted up and rode on, keeping to the timber line as they descended down the Western slope so they wouldn't be spotted if there were hostile sentries on the cliffs. Keso rode ahead, scouting the area.

She was so tired, she dozed in her saddle as her mare walked along the trail. Up ahead, she saw Keso rein in, dismount, squat down. After a long moment, he turned and walked back up the trail, leading Spirit. Keso's face was grim. "Well, the question's been answered about where the pack mule might be."

The look on his face warned her of trouble. "You think maybe that deserter found it?"

Keso shook his head. "You can stop worrying about the deserter, Wannie."

"What?" Cleve rode up beside her and reined in. "You're talking in riddles, Evans."

The breeze picked up suddenly, and Wannie took a deep breath and gagged on the scent. Death. It smelled liked death.

Before Keso seemed aware of what she intended, she dismounted and tried to brush past him but he caught her arm. She jerked out of his grasp and ran toward the scent.

"Wannie, come back, you don't want to see that."

She had to know. If something had killed the strayed mule, they could at least get some food out of the pack.

"Oh, my God!" She put her hands to her mouth to keep from screaming as she came to an abrupt halt. Now she knew what had caused the high, thin scream yesterday. Lying at her feet was a rotting blue bundle that had been a man. He had been scalped and his eyes stared unseeing into the sky. The deserter wouldn't be ambushing anyone.

Keso was right about one thing: there was no question who had ended up with the pack mule. Sticking in Bill's chest was a shiny big butcher knife with the brand name, Brewster Industries, on the bloody handle.

SEVENTEEN

As Cleve joined them, the three of them stared at the tortured body for a long moment.

Then with a low moan, Cleve stumbled into the brush and vomited.

Wannie, who had felt a little weak herself, was both embarrassed and sympathetic as she watched Cleve. Next to her, Keso sighed and rolled his eyes.

"He can't help it," she said in her fiancé's defense, "where he's from, things like this don't happen."

Cleve staggered out of the bushes, his face pale, his blond hair tousled. "I—I want to get out of this damned country."

"Easier said than done," Keso said. "First, we've got a man to bury."

"Couldn't we just leave him?" Cleve argued. "He wasn't anybody important and those savages may be watching us at this very minute."

"Cleve!" Wannie gasped, "I can't believe you said that."

"Remember," Keso reminded him, "he was scalped with one of your family's knives and because of you, dozens of Utes are now better armed. Pity any poor devil who meets up with them."

They didn't have shovels, but they did the best they could scraping a shallow grave out of the rocky terrain.

When they were done, Wannie said a few words over the grave while Cleve watched the cliffs around them with trepidation. "Hurry up! Let's get out of here before they come back."

Keso checked his saddle girth. "Let's take stock first. We've got two rifles, a little ammunition, four blankets, and whatever smoked jerky and hardtack was in our saddlebags. That and a canteen each is going to have to last us for probably a week."

The thought was sobering, Wannie thought. Thank God Keso was here.

"I don't see how things can get any worse," Cleve grumbled, "why doesn't the army do something?"

"They probably will as soon as they know the Utes are on the warpath," Keso said, "but it'll be too late for us. We're strictly on our own now. Here, Wannie, let me help you." He put his hands out for her small foot and boosted her into the saddle. "Come on, Brewster, it won't do any good to whine—let's get moving."

They rode a good part of the morning, stopping now and then to rest the horses. Cleve complained constantly about everything. He was nothing but a spoiled boy, Wannie thought with disgust, not a man.

Along in the afternoon, Wannie's mare began to limp.

"Uh-oh," Keso muttered as he dismounted and picked up the mare's front hoof. "She's gotten a stone lodged." He look his knife and pried it out. "There, girl, is it okay now?"

Wannie encouraged the mare forward but the mare took a few hesitant steps and limped doing it. "Oh Keso, Dancer's lame. Now what?"

Keso sighed and shook his head. "We'll have to unsaddle and leave her, brat. Maybe she'll find her way back to the cabin when the hoof's better."

"I didn't think things could get any worse," Cleve

complained, but he didn't offer to help unsaddle Wannie's mare.

Wannie patted her mare's nose as Keso unsaddled. "Good-bye, girl, you're smart enough to find your way home."

Cleve's pale eyes brightened. "If the nag shows up by herself, won't the Evanses send help?"

Keso shook his head. "By that time, we'll be dead or will have ridden out of this hostile country."

Cleve stared around the perimeter of the boulders and rocks. "Are they out there watching us?"

"Who knows?" Keso looked at the horizon.

Wannie's heart went to her mouth at the thought, but Keso patted her shoulder. "You'll be all right, Wannie. A few Utes aren't about to make a liar out of me."

"What do we do?" Cleve asked. "There's three of us and two horses. Wannie, I guess you can ride behind me—"

"No," Keso said as he finished hiding Wannie's saddle, "old Blue can't carry double—we'd lose him next." He swung up on his big stallion then held out his hand to Wannie. "Come on, brat."

She always marveled at his strength. He lifted her lightly to the leather skirt of the saddle behind him. She put her arms around his waist and leaned against his broad back for a long moment and closed her eyes, relishing the feel of his muscles rippling under the rough shirt. His strength and calm confidence was so reassuring. When she opened her eyes, Cleve was glaring at her. Immediately, she straightened up and allowed space between herself and Keso, hanging onto his waist primly.

Keso reached back and patted her thigh. "You ready?"

"Ready, Keso. What do we do now?"

Keso put one hand to his eyes to shield them from

the sun and studied the horizon. "Stay close to the timber line until dark."

"Suppose they're up there in the rocks?" Cleve's voice rose hysterically. "Suppose they're just playing cat and mouse, waiting to pounce on us?"

"Suppose they are?" Keso said calmly, "I reckon there's not much we can do about it. They can outrun us since we've only got two tired horses between the three of us. And thanks to you," he reminded the other, "they're well armed."

They rode out, leaving the mare grazing peacefully behind them.

Cleve let Keso take the lead. He didn't trust the redskin so he didn't want him behind him and besides, if they ran into a war party, Keso would take the first bullet. As the hours passed and they rode the narrow trail, Cleve had to grit his teeth; he was annoyed at the way Wannie held on to Keso's waist, sometimes resting her face against the muscular back. Damn her, didn't she think Cleve could see what she was doing? Or was she still not aware how that Injun felt about her? One thing was certain, her estimate of Keso was going up with every hour that passed. Keso knew nothing about fashion or proper etiquette, but out here in this wild, hostile country, he could do a better job of looking after a woman than Cleve could. They were reverting back to the law of the jungle, he thought bitterly, where being a hunter and a strong protector was more important to a woman than having an eye for fine jewelry.

All afternoon, Cleve studied the horizon, expecting to see war-painted braves topping the ridge and coming at them any moment. The rest of the time, he was forced to watch Wannie riding intimately with her arms around Keso's waist, her breasts pressed up against that muscular back. Cleve tried to make plans.

Was there any way to rid himself of Keso? After all,

two horses between three people was a distinct disadvantage, but if Cleve could figure out a way to leave that Injun behind and take his stallion, two people could escape just fine.

The problem was killing Keso in a way that Wannie would think the Utes did it, Cleve thought as they rode along in the fading afternoon. They only had the two rifles and Keso was a better shot than Cleve. Was there any way to shoot him in the back and let the Utes take the blame? That was going to be difficult without Wannie seeing what had happened. Cleve would have to do some planning and be very clever over the next several days.

One thing was certain: he'd never get as good a chance to get rid of that savage rival. Cleve could never be certain Wannie would marry him unless he eliminated Keso. Her attitude toward the big Indian seemed to be gradually changing from a sisterly affection to a woman's passion right before Cleve's eyes. Worse yet, he wasn't even certain whether she realized it or not.

Keso kept his keen eyes trained on the ridges around them as they rode, aware both of Cleve's glare and Wannie's soft curves pressed against his back. Just the heat of her ripe body made him think forbidden thoughts when he had more important things to mull over right now.

The trio was in bigger trouble than Keso had let on. He didn't want to scare Wannie and that city dude was liable to puke his guts out if he realized just how desperate their situation was. He'd seen other signs besides smoke signals. The western slopes were alive with Utes and their killing of the deserter showed they had thrown all caution to the winds. Something had finally pushed the Utes into war and there was no turning back for them now.

This trio could easily disappear and never be seen

again. Of course, the war parties wouldn't kill Wannie—
she was too pretty. She would become a prize to be
fought over and soon would be warming some warrior's
blankets and producing sons for him.

The thought angered and upset him. He felt her body
warm against his back, her soft breasts pressed into the
rough fabric of his shirt. He glanced down at her slim
arms around his waist with all the diamonds and jewels.
Wannie would always be a pretty, delicate princess playing dress-up. Without thinking, he reached down to
give her hand a reassuring pat and thought about the
silver ring he still carried. She would never wear it or
even know about it, but as far as he was concerned, his
love was for always. She might love that slick dude and
marry him, but Keso would love her and only her forever. For that reason, he had to save Cleve Brewster's
life and get him out of this rough country in one piece
even though it would be so tempting to abandon the
dude to the mercies of a Ute war party. Whatever made
Wannie happy, Keso would do.

The afternoon passed slowly as they rode the narrow
trail that snaked gradually down the west slopes toward
the flat areas beyond the mountains. Behind them, tall
peaks called the Maroon Bells towered and the wind
blew through the pine and spruce. The September day
was crisp with the coming of autumn. Under different
circumstances, Keso would have enjoyed this ride immensely with Wannie pressed against his back, her slim
arms hanging onto his waist. He could fantasize that
she loved him and that they were riding to a hidden
dell where they would spread a blanket and make love
as the sun gradually set and threw long purple and pink
shadows across the mountains.

It was dusk when he finally reined in. "We'll rest
awhile and give the horses a chance to graze, then we'll

ride on under cover of darkness." He swung down off Spirit.

"Ride on?" Cleve grumbled. "I'm worn out—I can't sit a saddle any more."

"You can and you will," Keso said sternly, "or you'll be left behind. Remember, we've got some bare country to cross and we'll be easy to spot in the daylight." He reached up to help Wannie from the back of the saddle. She tried to stand, but her slim legs buckled under her and he had to catch her and carry her over under a pine tree.

"I—I'm sorry," she apologized, "I don't mean to be so much trouble."

He knelt and brushed her hair out of her face. "It's okay, honey," he whispered, "I know you're tired."

"Damn it, I'm tired, too," Cleve said as he dismounted stiffly. "The only one who isn't is Hiawatha here."

"Cleve!" Wannie rebuked him, "that isn't fair! Why, I'm counting on Keso to get us out of here."

"You don't have any faith in my ability, is that it?"

"Oh, shut up, Brewster," Keso commanded, "things are tough enough without your whimpering." He handed Wannie his canteen.

"It's getting cold," Cleve said. "Can't we build a fire?"

Keso sighed. "If you do, a Ute war party may roast you over it. If you don't care about yourself, Cleve, think about Wannie."

She looked up at him as she handed the canteen back, uneasy about changes in the way she was perceiving Keso. "What are you hinting at?"

Keso hesitated. "Never mind. We're back to smoked jerky and hardtack."

"I'm hungry," Cleve said, "and I want something better than that. You're the big hunter—get us some food."

"Cleve!" Wannie was genuinely shocked. "Don't talk to my brother that way."

"May I remind you he's not really your brother?"

She looked away guiltily, not replying. With every hour that passed, she was thinking of Keso less as her big brother and more as a man—all man.

Keso said, "Maybe by tomorrow, we'll be near some prospector camps or run across an army patrol out looking for that pair of deserters. Then maybe we'll be safe."

Wannie had never felt such exhaustion, but she managed to splash water on her face and go off in the bushes to relieve herself. Then she settled on the blanket Keso spread for her and ate the smoked jerky and hardtack greedily. As she finished up and licked her fingers, she suddenly realized Keso wasn't eating. "Where's yours?"

"I wasn't hungry."

She knew he was lying. Keso could never look her in the face and lie to her. "Oh, Keso, you gave me your share, too, didn't you?"

He hesitated. "What if I did? I'm stronger than you are and can go without food longer."

"I feel terrible about this." She noted Cleve was gobbling up his share without any hesitation.

"It's okay, Wannie," Keso soothed her, "maybe I'll snare a rabbit tonight and we'll reach a place where it'll be safe to roast it. Now settle down—we need to get some rest so we can ride on later."

Cleve wiped his hands on the grass and grinned. "Wannie, since it's cool and we're short on blankets, maybe we should curl up together to conserve body heat."

Keso glared at him. "Sounds like a good idea, Brewster. I'll sleep in the middle."

"But, I—"

"That's a good idea, Keso," Wannie said and began to spread the blankets.

"Never mind," Cleve snapped. He got his blanket and curled up in the brush alone. "Remember, Wannie, you're *my* fiancée."

Wannie stared after him with puzzlement as he lay down in the grass. "Now what do you suppose he's upset about?"

"He just doesn't adjust well to adverse conditions," Keso said and lay down next to her, pulling a blanket over them.

She felt a trifle uncomfortable about curling up with Keso, but after all, they were both fully dressed and he was her brother. "This ground's pretty hard," she muttered.

"Here, put your head on my arm, brat." He pulled her up against him and tucked the blanket over her.

She started to protest that this probably wasn't proper, but in this desperate situation, it seemed almost ludicrous to worry about propriety. Besides, Keso's big body radiated heat and she was cold. Wannie put her head on his arm and let him pull her close. Funny, she thought sleepily, she almost seemed to fit into the curve of his big body. She lay her face against the warm, scratchy wool of his coat and threw her arm across his massive chest. He reached over and gave her a comforting pat, and kissed her cheek.

" 'Night, brat."

" 'Night, Keso. You think we'll make it out okay?"

"Sure," he whispered and patted her again, "don't worry."

Wannie relaxed in his arms and smiled as she dropped off to sleep. Keso seemed so competent. In all these years, she had believed him and he'd always told her the truth. Keso knew everything there was to know about her and he didn't care about her past. A thought crossed her mind. She had lied to Cleve about her background. Should she tell him? And if she did, would Cleve still want her to be his bride? For a man with Cleve's blue-blooded background, it would be a great shock to find out her mother had been the madam of Denver's most notorious bordello. She would have to tell him, she thought sleepily, she couldn't stand the tension of waiting for years to see if her terrible secret would surface.

Keso was content, no matter if they might be in danger tomorrow. He lay with his beloved Wannie in his arms, holding her close. No man could want any more than that. She was safe in the curve of his sinewy arm and he'd fight to the death to protect her. Gently, he brushed the hair out of her eyes. "Wannie?"

No answer. Her gentle breathing told him she was asleep. Keso pulled the blanket up under her chin and held her close. In the moonlight, he could see her lovely face, her soft, full mouth. On impulse, he turned his head and brushed his lips across hers. She moved slightly in her sleep and he lay still, holding his breath. He had dared to kiss her lips, something he had never done in all these fifteen years and they had tasted even better than he had dreamed they might. Always he had kissed her forehead or the tip of her nose. Even now, with her soft breasts against him, he wanted more. He wanted to put his bare hand under her clothes and touch those breasts, stroke that satiny skin. Just the thought of her ripe, virgin body under those rough clothes made him go tense with wanting. It wasn't just the need for a woman; he needed Wannie, only Wannie.

Keso lay there aching and yearning for more, but he dared not betray her trust. All these years he had wanted her and they might not survive tomorrow. Oh, it was so tempting, but even as his body hungered, he knew he could never do it. He loved her and she trusted him. He took a deep, shuddering breath and lay still, acutely aware of her small warm body against him, the satin of her dark hair spread out over his arm. At least he had the memory of that stolen kiss that Wannie would never know he'd taken.

He lay there in the darkness, smiling and remembering the satin of her lips under his as he'd brushed his mouth across hers. What he hungered for was to really taste that pouty mouth, taste and tease along her lips until she opened them and let him put his tongue inside, caressing the inside of her mouth until she moaned aloud and pressed herself against him, urging him to bold exploration of her breasts and body.

His body was tense, his manhood aching with his need. He must stop thinking like this. Keso took a deep breath and tried to think of something, anything other than loving Wannie out under the stars. Their present situation was desperate and it was up to Keso to save them. Of course he and Wannie could travel faster if they didn't have a third person, but deserting Cleve Brewster was unthinkable. Keso was too noble to do that, even to rid himself of his rival. Besides, Wannie loved Cleve so he had to save the prissy coward for her. Keso would do anything to make her happy.

He lay there awhile, but he could not sleep. If he slept, it would be too easy for a Ute war party to creep into the camp. Cleve Brewster slept so heavily, he'd never hear the hostiles and wouldn't know what to do if he did. Besides, snaring a rabbit in the darkness would provide food for tomorrow . . . if there was a tomorrow. Keso wanted to do a little scouting, too.

Stealthily, Keso crawled out of the blankets and carefully covered Wannie up. She was so tired, she didn't move as he paused and looked down at her. On impulse, he leaned over and brushed his lips across hers once more, a light, innocent kiss, not the kind of passionate kiss Keso longed to give her. She smiled ever so slightly in her sleep and murmured something.

Keso frowned. No doubt, she was dreaming of being Mrs. Cleveland Brewster, Jr. Keso would do his damnedest to keep them both alive so she could realize her dream of being the rich, bejeweled princess.

He paused, trying to decide whether to take his rifle, finally shook his head and laid it next to Wannie. If he were going to get a rabbit, he'd have to do it with a snare and his big bowie knife would provide him all the weapon he needed. He dared not fire a gun without the echoing sound bringing every hostile in the mountains down on the trio. However, if the Utes found the camp while Keso was gone, Wannie would need the rifle to defend herself.

Keso said a silent prayer as he looked around, trying to decide his course. Then, silent as the shadows of the giant trees around him, he took off at a lope. He paused now and then to look around, sniffing the air for smoke or the warm scent of horses or roasting meat. The only smells were the scent of pine and wildflowers, the sounds were the night sounds of the forest, mountains, and high plains. He saw no sign of any human. Reassured, he set a snare along a rabbit trail through the grass. With any luck, he'd bag a fat rabbit and tomorrow, they might reach a refuge where he'd feel safe enough to light a fire and cook it. Things would get desperate now that they'd eaten all the smoked jerky and hardtack. He suspected Cleve had been sneaking some of the supplies to eat secretly, but he couldn't prove it and it would anger Wannie to accuse her fiancé.

Within an hour, he circled back on the track and smiled to see a fat rabbit in the snare. At least Wannie wouldn't go hungry tomorrow. Even as Keso took the dead rabbit from the snare, he heard a soft, rhythmic sound like thunder. Only he knew it wasn't thunder. His heart beating hard, he looked around, trying to decide a course of action as the war party appeared abruptly over the ridge. The moon shone brightly on the crimson and black war paint of their grim faces. Then they spotted him and with yelps of delight, reined their brightly painted ponies toward him.

He had a split second to make his choices. If he could make it back to camp, there were two rifles there as well as his stallion. With those two things, Keso had a chance. But he would also be alerting the Utes to the camp if they hadn't seen it.

Wannie. He knew what the war party would do to his beloved and nothing, not even his life, meant as much to him as she did. In that heartbeat, he made his choice and his sacrifice. He turned and ran the opposite direction, leading the war party away from the camp. Even though he was fleet of foot, he knew he couldn't outrun mounted men. What he hoped was that the Utes would raise their guns and fire. Even as they killed him, the gunfire would warn the camp. Maybe, just maybe, Cleve Brewster could save Wannie. With two horses and two rifles, the pair at least had a fighting chance. Keso intended to sacrifice his life to see that they got that chance.

He ran, his heart pounding like a war drum, listening to the triumphant shouts and the echo of hooves behind him. Ironic to think that Cherokee had said he was really a Ute. Well, he intended to die like a Cheyenne dog soldier, the bravest of the brave. His lungs felt on fire as his legs ran swift as a deer. Any moment now, a bullet or a lance would impale him in the back. He wondered momentarily how much it would hurt.

This wasn't the way he wanted to go; he wanted to turn and face his enemies, fight to the death, even if he was armed only with a bowie knife. Yet he ran, not to escape his killers—that was impossible out here in the open country and he knew it. All that mattered was leading this war party as far as possible away from his beloved Wannie. This might be her only chance and he was willing to sacrifice his life to give it to her.

Behind him, he heard the yelping warriors gaining on him and shouting to each other in their language. Strange, he could understand a few words. Cherokee was right—he had lived as a Ute once long ago. Even as he recognized some of the words, vague memories surfaced of a happy time with a father who loved him and a mother who held him close. The words "the Arrow" flashed through his mind and he wondered about them. He was only thinking about how they would kill him, knowing they were gaining on him.

Then a pinto horse galloped past him and whirled, blocking his path. Keso paused, breathing hard, reaching for his big knife. Behind him, the war party blocked his retreat.

The warrior on the pinto horse grinned without mirth, his ugly, war-painted face more of a snarl than a smile. "Halt!" he ordered in broken English, "Stop or I kill you right there!" He had a rifle trained on Keso's heart.

Very slowly, Keso lowered his knife. As brave as he was, he knew a knife was no match for a rifle. All that mattered was keeping them distracted from the camp. This ugly brave would delight in raping a delicate beauty like Wannie and besides, she was half Arapaho. The Arapaho, like their allies, the Cheyenne, were bitter enemies of the Utes. "I am Poh Keso," he boasted, "I fear no Ute dogs."

The others surrounded him, keeping a respectful distance but cutting off any hope of escape.

"Poh Keso?" one muttered. "It's Cheyenne for Fox—we have captured a bitter enemy."

Keso threw back his head and laughed. "I spit at the Utes. Take me back to your village and do what you will. I'll show you how a brave man dies!"

It didn't matter what they did to him. The Utes could make his death last a long, long time with slow torture, but that would hold their attention for hours, giving Wannie and the man she loved a chance to escape.

The ugly one nodded. "We will give you a chance to fulfill that boast, Cheyenne dog!" He reached into his waistband and held up a big knife that gleamed in the moonlight. There was no mistaking a Brewster butcher knife. Keso laughed again at the irony of it.

"Go ahead and laugh, Cheyenne," the other scowled. "We have already killed a bluecoat in these mountains who took a long time to die. We found his pack mule and supplies. Now we will carry you back to our village and take a white man's knife to you. Tonight, your scalp hangs from Coyote's lodge pole!"

EIGHTEEN

Keso knew that the Utes would torture and kill him when they got him back to their camp—the obvious relish on Coyote's ugly face told him that. He considered telling the Utes that he was really of their tribe, then decided against it. He didn't think they would believe him; they would think he was attempting to save his own life. From the time he was a starving street kid, Keso had fought the odds and survived. This time, it appeared his luck had run out.

The war party rode into a temporary camp of tipis. In the bustle, curious women and dark-eyed children came out to see the war party riding in. The people looked thin and hungry. Straggly stray dogs roamed around the ponies' legs, barking with excitement. Keso understood just enough of their language to know Coyote was announcing that they had captured a Cheyenne brave, even though he was dressed in white man's clothing.

Immediately, the expressions on the dark faces turned hostile. The two tribes had been enemies for generations. Coyote laughed and jabbed at Keso with the butt of his lance. "See how welcome you are, Cheyenne? Now instead of a dull day, you will entertain us."

Keso said nothing, knowing that Coyote was eager for a chance to strike him. At least, if he endured the torture stoically and made his death last a long time, Wannie and Cleve would have time to escape.

Another brave motioned for Keso to dismount as they reined into the center of the camp circle, but before Keso could obey, Coyote swung his lance and knocked Keso from his horse into the dirt. Keso forgot that he must not let the ugly Ute taunt him into rage. He came up out of the dust fighting, grabbing the lance end, thus unbalancing Coyote who fell into the dirt and came up snarling as other Utes gathered around to laugh.

"Hey, *Yorowit'z*, the Cheyenne wants you to join him in the dirt!"

Obviously Coyote was not well liked, Keso thought, even as the other hit him hard with his lance. It would be worth dying to slam his fist into the ugly face one time, Keso thought, but even as he came up off the ground to act on that thought, two warriors grabbed him from behind and held him.

Coyote, his dignity shaken, now strode over to Keso and struck him across the face. "No, Cheyenne, you will not goad me into killing you quickly and do me out of the pleasure of torture. Your death will last a long, long time."

Keso tasted blood from his cut lip as he struggled to break free and looked at the silent circle of thin, hostile faces ringing the pair. He noted many of the men, including Coyote, had a fine steel butcher knife stuck in their waistbands. He did not need to look closely to know the handle bore the words "Brewster Industries." Cleve had inadvertently supplied the hostiles with enough knives to scalp dozens of settlers and prospectors in western Colorado.

Coyote turned to the braves and shouted an order. Immediately, the pair dragged the struggling Keso toward a post in the center of the camp and tied him with his face against the post. Coyote stepped up behind

Keso, reached out, tore his shirt down the back and then ripped it away, leaving him standing naked from the waist up. "So, you Cheyenne, eater of dog meat, I will begin by whipping you with a quirt as I would any disobedient horse."

"Lower than a dog Ute," Keso sneered over his shoulder, "why do you not just get on with it? I'll show you how a brave man endures."

"Because we do not want to cut our enjoyment short. Now you can understand that, can't you?" He laughed.

Keso didn't answer. The autumn sun beat down on his muscular back and he looked around at the crowd, wondering how long it would take him to die. Would it be time enough for Wannie to escape? Nothing else mattered to him. Around him, pretty Ute girls looked the captive over with admiring glances.

"You women stop looking at the lowly Cheyenne like that," Coyote demanded. "By the time I finish with him, he will be as useless in a woman's blankets as a gelded stallion is to a mare."

The women giggled and exchanged amused glances. Somewhere in the crowd, Keso heard a girl murmur in broken Spanish and English that it was a shame to waste so handsome a man. What about selling him as a slave to the Comancheros?

Coyote seemed to consider that for a long moment. "You know, Cheyenne dog, she is right. Our people have sometimes sold captured enemies to the Spanish to the south to work their ranches and toil in their mines. My family grew very rich in fine horses and good rifles doing this. How would you like to be a slave?" He caught Keso by the hair and twisted his head around to look into his eyes.

In answer, Keso spat full in the brave's face.

Swearing in Ute and Spanish, the man struck Keso across the face so hard that for a moment, Keso thought he might pass out. "You Cheyenne dog," he snarled, "after what I plan to do to you for this insult, you would beg for me to geld and brand you, sell you to labor in the bottom of a silver mine. Now let the torture begin!"

His quirt struck across Keso's bare back. Keso hadn't been prepared for how much it would hurt. He gasped and bit his own lip bloody to keep from crying out. The lash had felt like a tongue of flame biting across his flesh. No, he would not scream, no matter how great the pain. He wasn't about to give Coyote that satisfaction.

One of the other braves stepped up to Coyote and said something. Keso could understand just enough to know that Ouray, the great chief from the Southern Utes, was due in this camp and would be displeased if anyone did something to cause trouble for the people.

"Trouble!" Coyote sneered. "The whites kill us, starve us, cheat us, then dare us to start an uprising. We are always at war with the Cheyenne and their allies, the Arapaho. If I can't kill a white man, let me at least enjoy taking vengeance on an old enemy!"

He struck Keso again and again across the back with his quirt. Keso bit his lip and tried to think of something else besides the lash of fire chewing across his muscular flesh. Great beads of sweat broke out on his dark forehead as the autumn breeze blew cool across his tortured body. Around him, he saw the grim faces of Ute braves, the covertly admiring glances of pretty maidens. He must not think of his pain—he would think of Wannie. Her lovely face came to his mind and he smiled, imagining that she kissed the hurt from his bare, aching flesh.

"Why do you smile, Cheyenne? Does it feel good? Then we will make you feel even better!"

Keso craned his head and saw Coyote pull the big butcher knife from his waistband. The sun flashed on the steel as the man approached him. "I will notch your ears like white men do steers, then I will geld you and throw your manhood in your face."

That alone made Keso desperate enough to fight his bonds and Coyote, watching his struggle, laughed. "Ah, now we know what the Cheyenne fears. He wants to mount women and breed them and I am about to take that pleasure away."

A horse galloped into the circle and a man shouted harsh words and orders. Keso craned his neck to look. A muscular, older Ute on a dapple pony had arrived at the scene and was questioning Coyote in Spanish. "Young fool, even to torture and kill one of our traditional enemies is to chance the wrath of the whites."

"Oh, great Ouray, what business is it of the whites if we kill one old enemy?"

Ouray dismounted and came over to inspect Keso, who was still tied with his hands above his head. He looked weary and old beyond his years. "Who are you and why do you venture into our country, Cheyenne?"

He must not give away the presence of Wannie and Cleve, no matter what. "I—I am the adopted son of someone you know, great chief. I am raised by Cherokee Evans."

"A likely story," the Ute chief scoffed, "you lie to save your life. You have a Cheyenne name. Are you the one who brought trade goods into this area?"

Keso thought about the pack mule and all the butcher knives the stupid Cleve had placed in the hands of hostiles. "I—I came alone to trade."

Coyote snorted. "He is not only Cheyenne, but a stupid Cheyenne who would ride into our country alone."

"Was he alone?" Ouray asked.

Coyote seemed to consider that for the first time. "We did not think to look for anyone else."

"I was alone," Keso snapped.

Ouray shrugged. "Since he is Cheyenne and does us the insult of riding into our country, you may continue, *Yorowit'z*. We'll see if he dies as bravely."

Coyote nodded with a grin of satisfaction and Keso braced himself. He would endure this torture willingly to save the girl he loved. *For always, Wannie, for always.*

He heard the whip sing through the air again as Coyote brought it back to strike another blow.

"Wait!" Ouray ordered. He stepped close to Keso and ran his hand across the livid scar on the back of Keso's right arm. "How came you by this, Cheyenne?"

Coyote snapped, "Why does that matter? Let me continue this entertainment."

But Ouray held up a hand to halt him. "How came you by this mark, Cheyenne?"

"I—I don't remember," Keso said with a shake of his head, "only that I was very small and an older boy pushed me into a camp fire."

"N-Nothing more?" Ouray's voice shook.

Wondering, Keso shook his head. "Cherokee Evans found me on the streets of Denver and raised me. I thought I was Cheyenne—only lately did he tell me I was not."

"Untie him," Ouray ordered, "I want to see his face."

"Untie him?" Coyote protested. "What is this nonsense?"

However, men rushed to do the great chief's bidding. Keso almost collapsed when they untied his arms from above his head. He would not give them the satisfaction of seeing him lying in the dirt like a bloodied, wounded dog. He staggered, then straightened while Ouray looked at the scar.

"The scar," Ouray said and his face betrayed anxiety.

"What about it?" Keso shrugged, wondering.

"Yes, what about it?" Coyote snapped. "I intend to give him even more scars to remember the Utes by."

But Ouray shook his head and bright tears glistened in his eyes. "Yes, you were pushed into a campfire by an older boy—I would know that scar anywhere and it was *Yorowit'z* who pushed you."

"What?" Coyote's eyes widened and he strode over to examine the livid burn mark. "No, it cannot be him—the Cheyenne kidnapped and killed your son."

Ouray looked into Keso's eyes. "I see my own likeness in your face. Are you Ute?"

Keso shook his head. "My foster father, Cherokee Evans, says I am but I don't believe him. I am Cheyenne."

Ouray's stoic face had gone pale. "Bring him into the lodge," he ordered. "I would talk with him. The Great Spirit has seen fit to return what has been stolen many years ago!"

With Keso still denying he was the missing chief's son, he was dragged inside where he was given food and water while Ouray questioned him. At the end of the hour, even Keso was convinced.

Tears came to the chief's eyes. "The Cheyenne stole my little son not long after he was burned in that campfire. Coyote always claimed it was an accident, but I never believed him."

"I do not want to be Ute," Keso insisted, "my mother was a Cheyenne who was run out of the tribe."

"Do you not see now why they exiled you? You and the woman who sheltered you as her own?"

It was all so logical. Slowly, Keso nodded. "It must be then as you say, even though I know only one father, the man who raised me."

Gently, Ouray put his hand on Keso's shoulder. "Welcome back into the tribe, my son. From this day forward, you will be a Ute warrior."

"I'm sorry, great chief, but I will never think of myself as Ute."

"Perhaps someday you will change your thinking," Ouray's face was grave, "or perhaps we will never regain all these years that have been lost. I must go now back to my own village to the south. Will you go with me?"

Keso considered a moment. He thought of himself as a white man but he was not. He thought of himself as Cheyenne, but he was not. Since he belonged in neither of those worlds and had lost the only woman he could ever love, why not stay among the Utes? Here he would be accepted as one of them and could live out his life as perhaps he would have lived it had not cruel fate interfered.

"No, my father, not now. I need more time to get used to this idea." Keso thought of Wannie and Cleve lost in this wilderness. He had no confidence in Cleve's ability to protect her. If Keso stayed in the area, he would insure that she could make it to safety.

"You will stay with this camp then?"

"There is nothing for me among the whites anymore." He thought of Wannie. Now he wouldn't have to attend her wedding. "I have had a deep hurt. Perhaps I could find happiness among the Utes if they will accept me."

Ouray smiled and nodded. "And someday, when your heart has healed, you might want to take one of our women as wife and raise fine sons of your own."

Keso studied the chief. In the deep lines of the dark face, he saw illness. Perhaps Ouray was not well, but for now, he smiled. If he were ailing, it would make the chief happy to think his son would stay among the Utes. "Perhaps I might."

"Good. I will send some girls to tend to your back. If one of them appeals to you, marriage among our people is a simple thing."

Keso said nothing. A Ute girl. His heart belonged to one who was half Arapaho, but he could not have Wannie. Perhaps he needed to stop torturing himself with her image and find peace among his blood people.

"Until I return then, my son." Ouray patted his shoulder and rose to leave the tipi "You will now be treated as an equal among the Utes, but you will not get superior privileges as my son."

"It is only fair," Keso said.

Ouray nodded and went out. Keso drew a sigh of relief. No warrior had ridden in with news of the death or capture of Wannie and Cleve, so perhaps the pair had managed to escape. Nothing else was important to Keso.

Two pretty, dark girls entered the lodge, both shyly giggling. They made sign language to show he should lie down on the soft buffalo robes. Both of them were looking him over quite boldly and their bodies looked soft and ripe. Keso lay down and let the pair tend to his wounds, gentle hands rubbing healing ointment into the quirt welts. The fire in his back gradually cooled. He sighed and relaxed as the two pretty maidens worked over him, supple fingers kneading and stroking his skin. Why not stay among the Utes, forget the white way of life, and live as a warrior in the wild beauty of Colorado for the rest of his days? He could choose a pretty girl to give him sons, and maybe when he held her in his arms in the darkness, he could pretend she was Wannie.

Cherokee. Tears came to his eyes as he thought of the man who had raised him. Keso could still visit Cherokee and Silver now and then when Wannie was not in town. Keso couldn't bear to see her coming to visit as Mrs. Cleve Brewster, Jr.

At any rate, the Utes would be watching him closely the next several days, so there was nothing Keso could do but stay in this camp and pray that Cleve Brewster had managed to save Wannie and get her out of this hostile country and back safe to the Evans cabin.

In the following two days, the pretty pair of girls who doctored his back returned time and again to see to his welfare and teach him a few more Ute words. They let him know by gesture that they were sisters and would be pleased to sneak into his lodge at night and pleasure him. Like the Cheyenne, Keso knew that a good hunter was allowed more than one wife. His thoughts were of only one woman, but he hushed the pair by saying in halting Ute that perhaps later he might want to choose a wife.

When he finally ventured out on the afternoon of the third day, the camp was friendly but suspicious and curious about the stranger. Only Coyote was hostile. "I should have held you in that fire," he snarled. "I hated the attention you got as the chief's son."

"Coyote, there is no reason for us to be enemies," Keso soothed him. "To survive, we may have to hunt together and share food."

"I see you are already trying to share my women," Coyote snarled. "The girls who tend you are the ones I have chosen for myself."

"They don't seem to have chosen you. Anyway, I have no interest in them," Keso shrugged.

"Know this, you would-be Ute," Coyote said, "you may not remember that if there is a difference between men over a woman, I can challenge you to a fight."

"I wouldn't fight you for either of them," Keso said, "my heart belongs to another." He felt in his pants pocket for the precious silver ring and thought about his beloved Wannie.

Coyote appeared mollified. "Let us go hunting together. I'll see how much of a Ute warrior you are."

"I am a good hunter."

"You are dressed like a white man, not a Ute warrior," the other sneered. "I would not be seen with you."

"I will become a Ute warrior then," Keso announced. "Until my father returns, I must have something to occupy my time."

"Good. I will round up some of the other braves and some weapons," Coyote replied. "When I bring in more meat and show the others I am a better marksmen, they will lose interest in you and I will have more respect."

After Coyote left, Keso stripped down to a loincloth. Some of the older men provided him with medicine objects, weapons, and jewelry. He threw away his tattered white man's clothing, but there was one thing he could not part with even though he knew he should. He took the little silver ring and put it on a strip of rawhide, which he hung around his neck. Let it remind him constantly of why he could never return to the life he had led before. Without Wannie, there was no life.

Keso painted red and black symbols on his face and braided his long black hair. When he finished, he stared at his reflection in a burnished copper pot. The image surprised even him. Whatever thin veneer of civilization Keso had acquired in his years with the Evans family had been stripped away along with the clothing. Staring back at him was a savage brave that was not even recognizable as Keso Evans. Perhaps it was better this way.

He strode from the lodge to face the other braves, and saw approval in their dark eyes as they handed him a lance and bow. Even Coyote looked impressed.

"I would never know by looking that only three suns ago, we captured a brown white man and now you are a Ute!"

The others set up a yelping chorus of agreement at Coyote's words. Keso said a few halting words of approval to the men. An elderly brave led out a fine, spirited palomino stallion, already painted with good medicine symbols.

"Today, you are the son of Ouray," the old man announced. "Today, you are a Ute warrior!"

A chorus of chants went up as the people gathered around to see Keso accept the fine horse. In the background, he saw the pretty sisters giving him bold, admiring glances. He ignored them. If he were to become a Ute, he must keep the peace with Coyote. For Keso, there could only be one woman, though she was lost to him forever. Surely Wannie was now safely on her way to some prospectors' bustling camp.

He mounted up, the fine stallion rearing and pulling at the bridle, eager to run. The others mounted up, too.

Keso held up his hand and said a few words of thanks and reined the fine horse around to lead the hunt. As they galloped out of camp, Keso closed the door on his old life forever. From this time hence, he was a Ute warrior!

NINETEEN

Wannie awakened before dawn, stiff and cold in the early autumn morning even though she was snuggled down under two blankets. Two blankets? What was she doing with Keso's blanket? She sat up and yawned, remembering curling up against him for warmth. Funny, she had dreamed he had kissed her and she had responded, wanting more. The thought shocked her. She was an engaged woman. She looked down at the big diamond on her hand and her gold bracelets for reassurance.

She heard Cleve's snoring over in the grass and sighed. Did she really want to listen to that the rest of her life? Where was Keso? Maybe he was scouting the area or snaring a rabbit so they'd have enough food. What she wouldn't give for a cup of coffee and some bacon and biscuits right now. Keso's rifle lay on the blankets next to her. Why would he leave his rifle? Of course he wouldn't need it if he were setting a snare for rabbits. "Keso?"

Cleve raised up out of his blankets then, tousled and needing a shave. "What's the matter?"

"Keso. He's not here." Worry began to gnaw at her as she got up.

"You think he's deserted us?" Cleve yawned as he brushed his yellow hair back.

"Of course not! Cleve, if you don't beat all. Keso would never leave me on my own." Or would he? Cleve had been awfully rude and she'd been a real trial to Keso's patience lately. A horse nickered and she smiled with relief as she spotted Spirit peacefully munching grass nearby. "See? Keso's in the area, all right."

She was surprised to realize how very relieved she was. She depended on him a lot more than she wanted to admit.

"I'm hungry," Cleve complained. "I hope he finds some food."

"We'd be helpless out here if anything happened to him."

"I resent that!" Cleve bristled. "I'm certainly capable of looking after you."

"Umm." She didn't want to hurt his feelings but she realized that she didn't have much faith in Cleve's ability to survive without Keso in this hostile country. Knowing the latest dance steps and popular songs seemed suddenly unimportant. "Let's go ahead and start packing and saddling. He's bound to return any minute now."

They went about those tasks while Cleve complained about how he'd like some hot food, clean clothes, and a bath.

"So would I, Cleve," she said, her patience wearing thin, "but we can survive until we reach a settlement."

"This is not civilized country," Cleve said. "I hope I never have to return to Colorado again."

"It may not be New York," Wannie retorted, "but it has its own wild charm."

"I fail to see it," Cleve snapped. "Where do you suppose Keso is? We're ready to go and he still hasn't turned up."

A chill of apprehension went down Wannie's back. "He wouldn't desert me."

"You seem awfully sure of that," Cleve said. "Maybe he got scared of the Utes and decided to clear out."

"Without his horse? Besides, he's not afraid of anything."

"I'm tired of hearing what a hero the Injun is."

Sooner or later, she was going to have to tell Cleve the truth about her own background or risk attempting to keep that secret forever. "Don't call my brother an 'Injun.' I know Keso. Even if he doesn't like you, he wouldn't leave you out here among hostile Indians without food and a guide."

"I wish I trusted his good intentions like you do."

"I do trust him," Wannie said, "I'd trust him with my life."

"Well, I'm not that sure he's so noble." Cleve took out his watch and frowned at it, then glanced up at the sun. "It's been more than an hour, Wannie. Something's wrong."

"Maybe he went for help," Wannie said desperately.

"Without a horse? I don't think so."

She felt the hair rise on the back of her neck. Cleve was right. Even if he were out snaring rabbits, Keso should have returned by now. The longer they were camped out here in open country, the greater chance they had of being seen by hostiles.

"Why don't we ride on, Wannie?"

"And leave him out here without a horse or rifle?" She glared at Cleve. "He wouldn't do that to you."

Another hour passed. Cleve paced and studied his watch while Wannie tried not to think of everything that might have happened to Keso.

Finally, he put his watch in his coat. "Wannie, whatever's gone wrong, we can't camp out here forever—we don't have the food."

"We'll search for him," she said in desperation. "He's

out there someplace." She made a sweeping motion with her arm.

"Millions of acres is a lot to search," Cleve said and ran his hand through his pale hair. "If he's within calling distance, he would have yelled to us by now. Maybe he's met with an accident; maybe he's dead."

She whirled on him. "Don't you dare say that!" Wannie had a terrible mental image of Keso lying helpless with a broken leg, unable to walk back. She thought of everything that could have happened from snakebite to attack by a rabid coyote. "We'll look for him."

"And where would you suggest we begin?" Cleve surveyed the giant panorama around them.

"I—I don't know; I just know we can't go off and leave him." Wannie couldn't hold the tears back.

He didn't attempt to comfort her, he just looked uncomfortable. "Maybe he's lost and if we get off this trail, we'll be lost, too."

She shook her head and wiped her eyes. "Keso's an expert woodsman. Cherokee says you could drop Keso down anyplace in the state and he could find his way back blindfolded."

Cleve frowned. "I'm tired of hearing how competent and masculine he is. You think I'm a spoiled dude, don't you?"

"Cleve, dear, I didn't say that."

"But you were thinking it," he accused. "I've got news for you, my dear, I'm not the only one who's immature and spoiled."

She flushed brick red. Cleve was right. Too late, she was realizing that Keso's ability to live off the land, to survive and take care of everyone around him certainly was worth a lot more than the knowledge of the proper use of a finger bowl. At this moment, the fact that Keso couldn't speak French or quote Shakespeare didn't seem important.

Keso's stallion stamped its feet.

Cleve pulled out his watch again. "Look, my dear, if he's dead, we can't help him. If he's hurt, we can't find him. If he were here, what would he tell you to do?"

She pictured the big, dark man who was always so caring, so unselfish. "He—he'd tell us to ride on before we run completely out of food or some hostiles find us."

"Then that's what we'll do. If he does show up at this camp, doesn't he track well enough to follow us?"

She nodded and put her head in her hands, wondering what to do. Cleve was being so logical. She didn't want to leave without finding out what had happened to Keso, but she didn't have any good ideas. "I depend on him so much."

"Just once, I wish you'd depend on me," Cleve snapped, peevish. I'm going to be your husband, Wannie, and you should learn to obey me."

Obey him? Somehow Cleve Brewster lacked that masculine assertiveness that made her automatically follow Keso's lead. This was no time to get into a fuss with her fiancé, yet she realized abruptly that she had no respect and no confidence in the suave society heir. "Cleve, you don't have any more idea than I do what to do next."

"You're very impudent for a well-bred young lady. We will just—we will just keep going the way we were going, that's all."

"Suppose we run into a war party?"

"Suppose we do?" Cleve shrugged. "I'll just explain who my father is. They'd help us get back to civilization for the reward Father would post."

Wannie began to laugh because if she didn't, she might cry. "Aren't we a pair? I'm wearing a fortune in jewelry and it won't buy us a bite of food and your daddy's money and influence is no help, either. What we need to get us out of this is the guy I was ashamed of because he didn't know which wine was served at which course. I wish he was here so I could get on my knees and apologize."

"Now, don't get hysterical," Cleve ordered, but he was hovering on the edge of terror himself. "Maybe if we get to a prospector's camp or run across an army patrol, they'll send out a search party."

That sounded logical. Like Cleve, she was helpless and lost in this wilderness and they were out of food. There was no other solution—they had to keep going.

Cleve had a difficult time with Spirit. The black stallion laid its ears back when Cleve tried to mount and he hit the horse across the muzzle with his quirt.

"Cleve, stop that!" Wannie scolded, angry and horrified at his cruelty. "Keso never uses a quirt on that horse."

"Well, he's not here now, is he? His damned horse is as stubborn and independent as he is."

That was what she liked about Keso the most, Wannie thought, biting back her anger. It wouldn't do to get into an argument with her fiancé. They'd have to cooperate to survive.

Cleve finally managed to mount Spirit. "Let's get out of here. Remember what the Utes did to that soldier."

"And with Brewster butcher knives," she couldn't resist reminding him as she swung up on old Blue in her torn and ragged calico.

"Only in this savage, uncivilized state would that happen," he said. "Remember, Wannie, you've shown you prefer my world."

Maybe she had made the wrong choice. No, of course not. She wanted that glittering world of society balls, elegant fashions, and priceless jewels. She would finally show her mother that the small girl the Duchess thought so little of could shine after all.

They rode out, uncertain which way to go, but knowing that they needed to get out of this hostile area. Wannie was so worried about Keso that she could think of little else. She was torn between hoping they would at least find his body so she'd have a reasonable explanation of his disappearance, and dreading they'd find it and she'd know with certainty that he was really dead. One thing she knew—something terrible had happened to Keso or he would never have left her on her own. She began to cry softly.

"Oh, stop that sniveling, you're making things worse."

She was stung at Cleve's cold hardness. He sounded just like his father talking to poor Bertha Brewster. "I—I can't help it, I was just thinking about Keso."

"Well, stop thinking about him and think about saving our own necks," he grumbled. "Do you think we should turn at that fork in the trail up there?"

She admitted she didn't have the slightest idea. "I've been gone four years and I never really knew the Western slopes."

Cleve paused and ran his hands through his blond locks. Even with his cleft chin, he didn't look handsome, he looked weak and frightened. "Let's not panic. Maybe by now, the Evanses have called out the army or the sheriff. My father would send a reward."

"They know we're with Keso, so they won't worry for awhile."

"Must you constantly remind me how very damned competent he is?"

"Cleve, really, I never heard you swear before." The polished gentleman seemed to be unraveling before her eyes.

"I've never been in such a desperate predicament. I'm from civilization, where a man doesn't need survival skills." He reined in, looking in all directions. "I think maybe we should take this trail."

"Are you sure?" Wannie looked around uncertainly.

"Are you questioning my judgment?"

"I certainly am!"

"A lady does not question her fiancé's judgment."

"Oh, Cleve, shut up! I'm sick and tired of hearing what ladies do."

His pale eyes widened. "I'll excuse that on the grounds that you're frightened—as any mere girl should be in these circumstances."

"I'm not a mere girl."

"Of course you are. Now, come along, my dear, this is no place to give way to hysteria—I don't have any smelling salts."

Cleveland Brewster, Jr., was a pompous ass, Wannie thought, but he was right about one thing—this was no time to get into a fracas. With a sigh, she followed his lead down the trail. "Oh, Cleve, suppose the war party got Keso?"

He looked back over his shoulder at her. "Look, my dear, I understand why you're upset, but there's really nothing the two of us can do. When we find help, I'll send a telegraph and we'll have the army out here combing these mountains for him."

"Thank you, Cleve," she sighed with relief, feeling a lot better and kinder toward her fiancé. He was right, of course.

They ate the last of the smoked jerky when they made camp that night. She noticed Cleve didn't offer her his share as Keso would have. "What are we going to do now that we're out of food?"

"I'll think of something," Cleve said, but he sounded uncertain.

They spread their blankets and lay down. Wannie was more terrified than she wanted to admit. Keso had always looked out for her and she didn't have any confidence in Cleve at all. He might be smooth and polished on a dance floor or hosting a formal dinner, but he didn't know how to built a rabbit snare or figure out the direction they were traveling by checking the moss on trees as Keso would have done. She'd been such a fool and he was probably lying out there somewhere dead. Tears began to run down her cheeks, although she tried to smother her sobs.

"Wannie, are you crying?"

"I—I'm sorry, Cleve, I can't help it." She waited for him to offer soft words of comfort.

"Well, stop it. It gets on my nerves. I'll be lucky if I'm not crazy when this ordeal is over."

"You know, I'm beginning to think I never really knew you at all."

"And maybe I didn't know you very well, either. I certainly didn't know you rode astride and behaved like some headstrong female."

"In this part of the country, men admire headstrong women."

"Why doesn't that surprise me?"

"Cleve, don't be sarcastic. What's really bothering you?"

"All right, since you insist," he said as he rose up on one elbow, "I didn't realize your guardian was a half-breed, your adopted brother was a savage, and the family lives like Daniel Boone. I really don't know much about you at all except that you're beautiful and your mother was some mysterious duchess."

"You ought to be ashamed of yourself. The Evanses are fine people and Keso is kind and gentle."

"To you, **maybe**. He's always wanting to sock me in the mouth."

"Okay, so he's got a few rough edges."

"Rough edges? I swear, I thought my family would die of embarrassment and humiliation the whole time he was at our estate."

Once she had been embarrassed by Keso's social blunders, but now that seemed so shallow and silly. What would Cleve think if he knew Wannie's own questionable past? Wannie thought about it a long moment. Someday, Keso had said, Cleve might find out about her background. In the meantime, she would always worry about his discovering the secret. If he loved her, it wouldn't matter. She needed to be reassured. "Cleve, would it—would it make any difference if I'm not what I told you I was?"

"What are you talking about?" He sounded grumpy and sleepy.

Was she afraid to find out? "I—I mean, if my mother wasn't a duchess, would you care?"

He laughed. "Next, you'll be telling me the Evanses aren't rich."

"Does that matter so much?" She leaned on her elbow and looked at him.

"They are rich, aren't they?" He sounded upset.

"Yes, I guess by your standards they are. They own a lot of mining and timber interests they'll never use because of their simple lifestyle."

Cleve seemed to breathe a sigh of relief. "So what is this about the duchess?"

Her mouth went suddenly dry and she hesitated. Somehow, she knew it was going to matter very, very much to Cleveland Brewster, Jr. "Cleve, do you love me?"

"You know I do." His voice was soothing and he reached over and patted her hand.

"More than anything?"

"Of course, dearest, we're going to be married and have a wonderful, civilized life together."

Wannie breathed a sigh of relief. "Then it wouldn't matter to you if my mother wasn't really a duchess?"

He was staring at her in the darkness. "Then why—why would you tell everyone she was?"

A tiny doubt began to build in her mind at the way he was staring at her. She decided to make light of it since there was no way to take back her words. "Ancestors seemed so important to everyone associated with Miss Priddy's. All the other girls talked about their pedigrees and when I met you, you made so much over your father's relatives coming over on the *Mayflower* and all."

"Father also has an earl and an early governor of the colonies among his ancestors."

She waited for Cleve to tell her it didn't matter what her background was, he'd love her anyway. She'd picked the worst possible time to explain her secret. Maybe it was because she was scared and she wanted Cleve to put his arms around her and tell her that nothing mattered but their love and that everything was going to be all right. "You might as well know it all, dearest—the Duchess's Palace was a fancy saloon and bordello in Denver."

He laughed, then stopped short. "You aren't joking, are you?"

She shook her head. "Keso said if you really loved me, it wouldn't matter."

His handsome face mirrored confusion. "A duchess running a saloon?"

"Dearest, what I'm trying to tell you is that my mother wasn't a duchess, she was just an Arapaho squaw, but she did run the saloon. I was fathered by some white trash cracker who served time in prison."

Cleve stared at her, his blue eyes round with surprise, his handsome face pale, the cleft deepening.

"I told Keso it wouldn't matter to you," she rushed on, desperate for his reassurance, "that you loved me and wanted to marry me, despite the fact that I'm not an aristocrat like the Brewsters."

The color gradually came back to Cleve's face. "I—it is just such a shock, Wannie."

"I know—I'm sorry I lied to you," she wept, "but I'm still the same person you fell in love with. Tell me it won't make any difference in the way you feel about me."

"My parents," he said, "I don't know what my father will say—"

"They don't ever need to know," Wannie said. "If you love me, you'll forget it and never tell anyone."

He took a deep breath. "Of course I still love you. It's just such a shock, that's all."

Wannie smiled with relief. "I knew you really cared about me. You won't be sorry you married me, Cleve—I'll make you proud."

"Proud? Oh, of course." He seemed to dismiss her with a nod. "What's important now is getting out of this predicament. We'll discuss the wedding later." His tone lacked conviction.

"You're sure it doesn't matter?"

He shook his head. "You know, it's getting colder. Maybe we ought to share blankets."

She felt uneasy. "I don't think so."

He snickered. "If you were worried about what people would say, you shouldn't have ventured out with two men without a chaperon—and riding astride yet."

"I'm not worried about what people would say, Cleve—only people back East worry about things like that."

Even in the darkness, she could see him frown as the moonlight reflected off his fine yellow hair. "You're worried that Keso wouldn't like it."

It was true, she thought, and wondered why Keso's opinion always seemed so important to her. "You're all right with what I've told you, Cleve? I was afraid you'd be shocked."

"Egad, what kind of rotter do you think I am, dearest? As you said, you're still the same dear, sweet girl you always were. Now, go to sleep. We've got a long way to travel tomorrow."

She breathed a sigh of relief and lay down, concerned about Keso's safety. All this time, she had worried about what her fiancé would say if he ever found out about her background and Cleve was every bit as warm and understanding as she'd hoped. "Good night, dearest."

"Good night." Cleve wrapped up in his blanket and lay down, swearing silently. She was nothing more than a common slut, a half-breed from the worst kind of parentage. Why, a gentleman of his own distinguished background couldn't marry an Injun whore's daughter! With the Brewster legacy, he needed to marry a girl of as fine a lineage as his own. Mongrels begat mongrels. On the other hand, he wanted Wannie in his bed. Maybe he could seduce her and keep her as a mistress and throw out that bitchy Maureen.

The thought cheered him as he dropped off to sleep on the cold ground. Yes, that was what he would do; somewhere along this trail, he would seduce or maybe even rape her. Now that big Indian wasn't around to protect her. Cleve would tell everyone she'd offered to sleep with him and when her secret came out, everyone would believe the gentleman, not the slut. At least Cleve had something enjoyable to look forward to. He smiled, imagining seducing Wannie as he dropped off to sleep.

It was before dawn that he awakened, hungry and cranky. Wannie still lay asleep in the little dell. Maybe he could find some berries, or at least, some water.

Cleve got up and began to scout the area in the first gray light of dawn. He found some wild berries, paused, then considered taking them back to share with Wannie. Then he remembered what she had told him last night. The slut wasn't worth it. Cleve gobbled the berries and ventured farther out, looking for more. He was several hundred yards from the camp now, but the landscape seemed peaceful enough. Maybe he could find some bird eggs and they could cook them over a low fire, or maybe he could kill a quail with a stick. At least, there might be more berries. Up ahead was a bush full of juicy, ripe berries. Cleve ran over to it and began to pull them by the handfuls, stuffing them in his mouth.

Abruptly, he saw a movement out of the corner of his eye and froze into stillness. He was acutely aware that he was out here alone without a horse or weapons. The movement fluttered the grass ahead of him and his heart beat faster. A quail or something edible? His hunger made him lose caution and he took off running toward the movement. Cleve topped a rise and slammed to a stop.

A group of mounted Indians sat their silent ponies just over the rise. Their dark faces were painted red and black as were their horses. They were all naked save for buckskin leggings, feathers, and ornaments. The first rays of sunlight reflected off the silver ornaments, their lances and the long blades of the new butcher knives in their waistbands.

He was too terrified to cry out. Instead, Cleve made a strangled moan and turned to run toward the camp.

Grinning, the silent band of Indians galloped out to surround him. The big ugly one reached out to poke Cleve with the butt of his lance. "Hey, white man, where is your horse?"

He was too terrified to do anything. Even as he began to sob, he felt the sudden wetness in his pants.

Another warrior said in English, "Maybe horse die. Gringo lost, all alone."

Why did that voice sound familiar? Cleve was too terrified to do anything but wallow on the ground, begging for mercy. "Please, my father is rich. He'll give you much gold to free me!"

Someone among the riders translated and the braves laughed.

The ugly one said, "With us on the warpath, where would we spend gold? Killing you would give us pleasure."

"No, please," Cleve was on his knees before the Ute's paint horse, "Please, let me go. I—I'll tell you where there's a white girl if you do. You'd like a white girl?"

"He lies!" said the familiar voice again. "He tries to buy his life with lies! Take him prisoner and let us leave this place."

But the ugly one held up his hand for silence. "No man worthy of the name would trade his freedom for his woman. You must lie!"

"No," Cleve said and pointed, his hand shaking, "she's over in those bushes asleep. Take her and let me go!"

"We take you both!" The ugly one grinned and shouted an order. As he groveled in the dry grass, Cleve was aware that several of the war party nudged their ponies and took off toward the grove, but he was too terrified to care what happened to Wannie.

Wannie had just awakened and was sitting in her blankets, looking around, wondering where Cleve had gone. Maybe he was out in the bushes relieving himself. She'd better do the same. She walked away from the sparse camp to take care of that necessity. She was on her way back when she was abruptly confronted by four warriors.

The guns—if she could just reach the guns. She tried to rush past the horses and the half-naked brown bodies with garishly painted faces.

Perhaps they had guessed her intent because a big, half-naked warrior on a fine palomino horse leaned from his saddle and scooped her up. She screamed and fought him in the dim dawn light, but be twisted her hands behind her and tied them with a piece of rawhide, then threw her up on his stallion before him. She was spilling out of her torn calico dress and he was almost naked. She winced as if touched with a red-hot poker when his warm, naked flesh touched hers. He put his arms around her, cradling her against him. She was too terrified to fight anymore or even look up into his painted face. All she could think of was the heat of his hard, sinewy body against hers, the prominence of his big manhood under the skimpy loincloth he wore as he held her to him familiarly.

He motioned to the others to gather up the weapons and the two horses and bring them along. Wannie knew what they would do to her when they got her to their camp. Oh, Keso, where are you, she prayed silently. If he were here, no one would touch her—he'd fight to the death to protect her.

They galloped out to meet the others and she saw Cleve on the ground, begging for his life. He was too big a coward even to face death like a man, she thought. A big, ugly brave hit Cleve in the head with the butt of his lance and motioned for another to throw the unconscious white man across Blue's back. "I Coyote," he grinned at her, "your man offer you to us to save his life."

Cleve wouldn't do anything that selfish and cowardly, she thought, but said nothing. This was not the time to show spunk. She'd better try to make some plans in case she got a chance to escape later.

"We go to camp now," Coyote said and grinned at her.

Her big captor held her close against his half-naked body, her breasts spilling out of her torn dress and brushing his chest as he held her against him in a possessive embrace. Then he nudged his palomino into a lope and the war party took off at a gallop across the rolling hills.

TWENTY

Keso wrapped Wannie in a buffalo robe, her face against his bare chest so that she could not see his face, gently cradling her against him. He wasn't certain whether Cleve had recognized him or not, but surely Wannie did. With Coyote and the others riding close, he dared not speak to her. What could he do to save her?

He seethed with venom that the rotten Cleve had offered her to the warriors in exchange for his own safety. Keso had done his best to lead the Utes away from the pair, but that stupid Cleve had evidently gotten lost and made a circle so that the luckless pair was almost right back where they had started.

The thought came to Keso as they galloped away that he could have Wannie for his own now. She was his captive and all he had to do was stay among the Utes and make her his woman, whether she wanted to or not. As a white man, he could never have her; as a Ute, she was his possession.

Cleve? He didn't want that dandy's blood on his hands. Maybe he could convince Coyote and the others to turn the white man loose.

Wannie was too terrified to look up into the painted face in the growing dusk in that split second before the warrior wrapped her in the buffalo robe. Besides, her captor kept her face pressed against his naked chest. A silver ring hung around his sinewy neck on a thong, a woman's ring. She felt both fear and anger that a helpless woman had been killed so this savage could possess it. Had the war party raped the woman before this virile Ute stole that ring? Was that to be Wannie's fate?

She wanted to pound her captor on the chest, claw him bloody, break free and escape. She knew she dared not. She could feel the power and raw masculinity of this big male, and she knew she had no chance of escaping from his arms. If only Keso were here. No doubt he was dead; otherwise, he would never have left her on the prairie. Tears started and made crooked, silty trickles down her face. Her heart felt as if it had been torn from her body at the thought of Keso's death. As much as they often squabbled and engaged in rough horseplay, she could not imagine a world without him.

The ugly leader led Spirit behind his own horse. Cleve had been tied and thrown onto old Blue. In the darkness, Cleve looked terrified and exhausted and he didn't ride very well with his hands tied. The horses thundered away toward a string of low hills and she could see nothing else. She and Cleve both might have starved or died of thirst if this Ute war party hadn't discovered them. As it was, they would probably be tortured to death.

She shivered at the thought and her captor pulled her even closer against his muscular body and patted her with a touch that was almost tender. Tender? No, of course not. It was a touch of hot desire and ownership, Wannie decided. In her mind, she pictured what the war party must have planned for her. Before death, no doubt her virginity was a prize that would be shared by all the warriors.

Oh, Keso, I need you so much, she thought and then

bit her lip, remembering that he was no longer around to protect her as he had always done. Sophisticated, urbane Cleve couldn't even take care of himself. All her fine jewelry glittered in the moonlight as she looked at it, realizing that among hostiles, it was worthless.

They must have ridden a long time, but the way she was being cradled by strong arms soothed her and she dropped off to sleep in spite of herself. Wannie awakened as the horses slowed to a walk, wondering for a split second where she was. She stirred, but the powerful arms still cradled her against his bare chest possessively. Oh God, what would happen now? She didn't need to ask; she knew. That silver ring hanging around this savage's neck told her what she could expect.

Wannie peeked about. They were riding into an Indian encampment with tipis circled. In the center, a large fire burned. Horses and barking dogs, crying children and old people watched with dark, curious eyes as the war party reined in. Women came out of tipis to watch and greet the returning men. Why, these people were thin and ragged, she thought; what had happened to the annuity goods they were supposed to get? She didn't need to ask; their thin, desperate faces told the story.

Nearby, Cleve's face was pasty white as the big, ugly warrior pulled him off old Blue and threw him down in the dirt like a sack of flour. Immediately, the crowd pressed forward to have a look. Cleve groveled and begged for mercy as the silent Utes gathered around.

"I'm rich! I'll give you money!" he babbled. None of the Indians said anything, only staring silently. Perhaps they did not understand what he was saying.

The big ugly one, Coyote, said something and the others all turned and looked toward her captor, still sitting his horse, his arm around her possessively. Wannie felt her heart turn over with fear. She let the buffalo robe fall open and took a deep breath for courage. They were all staring at her and with most of the men, particularly the big ugly one, lust burned hot in their eyes. She glanced down at her jewelry and suddenly it didn't seem to be worth much—not nearly as much is their lives.

"I—I will give all this to free us!" She took off the diamond ring and the gold bracelets and held them out. "Do you understand? These are worth a fortune!"

The ugly one threw back his head and laughed. "Some of them do not understand your words, but no matter. Why do you bargain, white girl, when already we have both you and the jewels?"

"I can give you more, much more!" She was pleading, but the faces remained stoic.

Her captor dismounted, pulled her off the horse, and kept her in his arms. "The woman is mine."

"Keso?" She hardly dared to hope, but the painted face stared down at her in the faint fire light with no sign of recognition. No, she must be losing her senses because of fear, grabbing at any slight similarity.

The ugly leader frowned, then leered. "You do not understand, son of Ouray. You will share this prize with those of us who rode the war trail."

"I will not share her." The voice was too cold and deadly to be Keso's.

"Please!" Cleve babbled, running about the circle, offering up his bound hands in a desperate plea. "Keep the woman, enjoy her, but let me go!"

"Cleve!" she shrieked in disbelief, horrified that he would offer her to save his own neck.

The ugly Ute threw back his head and laughed. "You see, white girl? He would let all of us enjoy you to save his own cowardly skin. He is not worthy to mount any woman. Bind the white man."

Two men rushed to do his bidding, quickly tying

Cleve to a framework of crossed timbers where he writhed and begged in fear. Wannie cowered against her captor as the ugly Ute turned back to grin at her without mirth. "Let us share her among us, son of Ouray. Then you may keep her for your pleasure. Let the whites ransom her or we can sell her to the Comancheros. A pretty girl like that one will bring much gold to buy more guns and knives."

She closed her eyes in horror at the thought of having to submit to the lust of Comancheros, ruthless renegades who frequented the Mexican border. She would be forced to pleasure any cutthroat who had the gold to buy her.

"No," said her captor again and he pulled her even closer, his voice low and deadly. "I will not share her and I will not sell her."

He sounded so much like Keso. She looked up into his dark, stone face, searching for a bit of recognition in the painted features, but saw none in the faint and flickering firelight.

The other strode into the circle, hands on hips. "We have a custom in this camp," he snarled at her captor, "if more than one man wants a woman, they may fight for her."

Her captor let go of Wannie and she fell at his feet in a tumble of torn calico and lace petticoats. She looked up at him as he pulled a big knife from his waistband. "I will take on any man who wants her and challenges me."

She was too terrified to do anything except huddle against his moccasins and look around at the crowd. This couldn't be happening. She, who had spent the last four years in Miss Priddy's Female Academy, was about to be fought over like a wild filly by mustang stallions for the right to breed her.

A long moment passed, the only sound the crackle

of the fire and the whimpering of the terrified Cleve. Wasn't he even going to offer to fight for her? Would they let him if he did? She could tell by his expression that at this moment, Cleve thought only of his own safety.

In that moment, most of the men seemed to regard the glittering knife and the strength of the man who wielded it. With a sigh and a shrug of shoulders, they stepped back, away from the challenge. None of them desired her body enough to fight her captor, she realized. Did that mean that this tall, virile savage was now free to carry her into his lodge and ravish her, she who was the chosen bride of the rich Brewster heir who wasn't even offering a protest to this brave's declaration of ownership?

The ugly one stepped forward, grinning down at her as she cowered against the legs of her captor. He spoke in halting English. "I seem to be the only one who wants to mate your pretty body enough to fight. Tonight, white girl, you will warm the blankets of Coyote and I will put my son in your belly."

"No! She will bear no sons but mine!" She looked up into the dark, stormy face above her. "I will spill your blood, Coyote, and then I will breed the girl myself!"

An old man said words in their language. He must have translated her captor's challenge, because a chorus of yelps and dancing went up around them, the news of the coming combat meeting with evident approval of the village.

Coyote's face twisted with hatred. "It is too bad you didn't die that long ago time. Very well, I will fight you, but it is not the custom to shed another Ute's blood."

"So be it!" Her captor tossed the knife away into the circle.

Immediately, two women came forward, grabbed

Wannie, and pulled her to her feet. They made signs to her that she must come with them, then led her into a tipi on the edge of the circle and tied her to a framework of poles inside. Evidently, they wanted to make sure she didn't escape while the people were distracted by the fight. Wannie had never been so terrified as she was now, watching through the doorway of the lodge. Her captor had his back to her and she marveled at the welts and marks of a whip, the strength and rippling muscles of his back. The challenger crouched on the opposite side of the big fire.

Her jewels lay in the middle of the circle, glittering in the firelight. A king's ransom in gold and precious stones, she thought wearily, and no one even cared enough to pick them up.

On the edge of the circle, Cleve hung tied against a framework of poles, watching the proceedings with no expression save fear. He was only concerned with his own safety, Wannie thought. He didn't care that one of these two big Utes would win her virginity and pleasure himself with her ripe body tonight. At this point, she would be happy to escape with her life—her virginity no longer seemed so precious.

Wannie pulled against the rawhide strips that bound her to the poles, but she could not break them. The faint hope she'd had of freeing herself and sneaking out the rear of the tipi while the Utes watched the fight faded and died. No, there was no chance of escape. She would be waiting here for the victor. Perhaps she could reason with the winner, convince him that the gold the Evanses or the Brewsters would offer for her safe return would be worth his while to forgo the momentary pleasure of her body. Certainly if she and Cleve did get out of this alive, Cleve wouldn't want to marry her if she'd been used for the pleasure of some savage. Oh God, what was she going to do?

Out in the firelit circle, Keso kicked the expensive jewels to one side. To these simple savages, the girl's body was more valuable than any gold. His own bowie knife also lay in the dirt, the firelight gleaming on it.

If only he could get word to Ouray, the elder Ute would ride back and stop these attacks against white men, but Ouray was not here. The Utes had been pushed beyond reason and no longer made calm, rational choices. Their desperation made them too eager to follow hotheads like Coyote.

Coyote grinned at him across the circle. "I have spent a lifetime wrestling, but you have not."

"I make up in skill what I lack in practice," Keso said, but inside, he felt less certain. The other man was taller and a little heavier. Moreover, he was certain Coyote would not hesitate to resort to trickery.

Word must have spread through the camp that the battle over the captive woman was about to begin. People were coming from all directions to watch the pair in the center by the roaring fire.

Cleve moaned and Keso glanced over at the cowardly white man, angry that he had been willing to give Wannie to any man who wanted her to save his own skin. Keso would die to protect Wannie, but Cleve would not; therefore, he did not deserve her. Keso must win this fight. He desired Wannie more than anything on earth, and he was no longer certain he wanted to return to the life of a white man. The wild life of a warrior was in his blood and bone. Perhaps he could find happiness and fulfillment living in the freedom of the Rockies and riding with his own blood, the Utes.

Coyote smirked at him. "Are you ready?"

Keso crouched and nodded. Fear tasted like a copper penny on his tongue. He must not lose even though he was at a disadvantage. The thought of Coyote taking Wannie and forcing himself on her and breeding her while she screamed and fought was more than Keso could bear.

Coyote crossed the circle in three quick steps and Keso knew suddenly where the man had gotten his name; he was cunning. Yet there was a reason the Cheyenne had called him Keso, the Fox. Keso braced to meet his foe even as the bigger man collided with him and they closed and grappled. Keso's muscles bunched and bulged with effort as they struggled for the advantage.

He felt sweat break out on his body even as Coyote put his mouth close to Keso's ear. "Tonight, I will take her virginity and you will stand outside and listen to her scream."

"Never!" That terrible image gave Keso strength and he squatted suddenly—the other man's pushing sent him over Keso's mighty shoulder and into the dirt behind. The circled Utes set up a chorus of shouts of approval.

Quick as a rattlesnake, Coyote reached out and caught Keso's ankle before he could move, jerking him off balance. The pair went down, rolling and fighting in the dust. They were both already drenched with sweat, causing the dust to cling to their straining bodies.

Using his superior weight, Coyote rolled Keso over until they were both on the edge of the campfire. The light reflected in his cruel eyes. "I tried to kill you when you were a boy," he snarled through clenched teeth, "now I'll finish burning you!"

Even as he said that, he caught Keso's arm, trying to force it backward into the flames. Keso gritted his teeth at the heat singeing the hairs of his arm. He must not let his arm go back any farther; he could already feel the heat and had to fight to keep from screaming. He put a superhuman effort into keeping Coyote from forcing his arm down. For a long moment, they posed thus, Keso's muscular arm trembling with mighty effort. He could smell his own flesh starting to burn and the agony was unbelievable. At that same time, Coyote was grinning down at him, eyes alight. "Yes, I will have her, you Cheyenne-raised dog! Perhaps I will put a brand on her hip like the white man puts on a filly. Now surrender and I will let you up!"

Never! No one would ever hurt Wannie as long as there was still breath in Keso's body. The back of his arm was scorching; he could feel the fire. It would be so easy to admit his loss, anything to stop this agony. He closed his eyes, gritting his teeth to hold back a scream of pain. In his mind, he saw Wannie's soft, defenseless face, and he knew he would never surrender, not even if Coyote killed him. With a mighty effort, Keso rolled to one side, throwing Coyote off balance and scrambling out from under him.

Coyote came to his feet, bellowing with rage like a rabid wolf. The crowd shouted with excitement, nodding their approval at these two stallions willing to fight to own the woman. While he swayed on his feet, Keso favored his singed arm, thinking he hadn't felt such pain since he was a child and the jealous older boy, Coyote, pushed him into the fire.

He couldn't out-wrestle this Ute—Coyote was too good, but Keso had brains and cold logic on his side. He would keep a cool head and outsmart this cruel savage. Before Coyote realized his intent, Keso stuck his foot out, caught the back of the other's ankle, and brought him down like a dead buffalo bull.

But Coyote was far from dead. He reached up and caught Keso by the throat, grinning with pleasure as he choked off his opponent's air. Keso began to see bright lights and his head whirled dizzily.

"You'll wish you had given me the woman before I'm through with you!" Coyote hissed.

"You—you'll have to kill me to take her."

"That I am about to do." Coyote squeezed even harder.

Keso struggled, the darkness seeming to close in on him. If he surrendered, he would live; yet without Wannie, his life meant nothing. All these years he had protected and cared for her and he knew he would do so the rest of his life, whether she appreciated it or not.

He must not lose consciousness—he could not let this brute have Wannie. With strength born of desperation, he brought both hands up, breaking Coyote's choke hold. He threw the bigger man to one side and staggered to his feet, exhausted and gasping for air.

Coyote threw his head back and laughed. "You know you are beaten, you coward! Say to all present that you give me the girl and we will stop this fight now!"

Not if you kill me inch by inch, Keso thought as he gulped big breaths into his massive chest. He charged into Coyote and they rolled over and over, struggling for superior position. Keso came out on top, but the other rolled out from under him and grabbed Keso's knife that lay gleaming in the dirt. His eyes glittered with anger and lust. "I will kill you and water this dry ground with your blood!"

Around them a chorus of disapproval went up with shouts that Coyote must not use a knife, that the men must wrestle for the prize, but Coyote seemed past hearing. He ignored the others as he crouched, moving toward Keso, the sharp knife glittering and reflecting the firelight. In fact, Keso could see his own almost naked image reflected in the shiny blade as they circled each other. Coyote seemed to pay no attention to those warriors who were shouting disapproval.

Keso took a step backward, trying to decide what to do. "The jewels," he urged, "the jewels are worth much gold."

Coyote glanced down at the gold and jewels lying at

his feet. That temporary diversion was all Keso needed. He charged in, caught the man's knife arm, and twisted. Coyote shrieked with fury and pain even as Keso caught him across the throat with the hard edge of his hand. Coyote dropped the knife and grabbed his throat, choking and coughing as he staggered.

Keso could smell the sweat from Coyote's unwashed body, feel the dust clinging to his muscles and the sting of his singed arm. Coyote went to his knees and collapsed, choking and gasping. With a sneer of contempt, Keso kicked the knife away from the vanquished loser's hand.

An old warrior cried out: "Ouray's son wins! He is truly Ouray's blood! Take your prize—you have won her fair!"

Keso stood feet wide apart in the circle, swaying a little. "I claim the woman as my own!" he shouted. "Does anyone else challenge me for her?"

There was a long silence, broken only by the gasping Coyote lying in the dirt and the crackle of the fire. Keso looked toward Cleve, waiting for him to protest, but he seemed concerned with nothing but his own life as he hung tied from the framework. No one stepped forward and a cheer began to build among the gathered crowd. "Claim her! Claim your woman!"

Keso started moving across the circle toward the tipi. He was so weary that he swayed a little as he walked, but he would reach Wannie if he had to pull himself forward on his belly. Yet his heart was light and his mind was cheering. He had won her. Wannie was now a warrior's prize!

TWENTY-ONE

Wannie had watched the fight through the tipi doorway. In the dim light of the big center fire, the struggle had raged as she held her breath and awaited the outcome. This couldn't be happening; she had planned to be the bride of the Brewster heir, one of the richest men in the country, but that man was tied to a framework of poles, watching as she watched. He hadn't even offered to do battle for her.

As the fight continued, Wannie knew one of these two warriors would take her virginity as a trophy tonight. The thought of being used to slake Coyote's lust terrified her; but the other warrior . . . Could it be? No, of course not. Keso was surely dead or he would have come back to rescue her and Cleve. A big lump came to her throat as she thought of Keso. She hadn't realized how much he meant to her and how much she depended on him until he was gone.

A mighty cheer brought her back to the present. The handsome combatant had vanquished Coyote, who lay on the ground as the crowed cheered. The fight was over. The big savage looked toward the tipi where she was tied. Oh God, now she would be forced to do anything he wanted. She was no more than a possession to amuse the victor and warm his blankets.

If she could only escape! Desperately, Wannie pulled

at the rawhide strips that bound her wrists but they did
not give. There would be no escape. Even as she
watched, the virile savage strode toward the tipi,
stopped, and spoke to one of the women. Mystified,
Wannie watched as the woman brought him a bowl and
some rags. What was he going to do?

He stooped and came into the tipi. In the dim light
of the outside fire, she could barely make out his silhouette. She was terrified and helpless. Perhaps if she
pretended she was unconscious, he would be discour-
aged and go away. Surely no man could take pleasure
in using an unconscious woman.

She let herself go limp and closed her eyes. He
paused before her. She could hear his breathing as he
began to untie her. She must not scream; she must pretend. Maybe his attention would be temporarily di-
verted and she might yet escape.

He caught her in strong arms as she fell, holding her
close against him. Her torn bodice had come open and
she felt her bare breasts pressed momentarily against
his hot, naked chest. She almost panicked, then remembered that she was pretending to be unconscious. She
kept her eyes closed as he carried her over and laid her
on a soft bed of buffalo furs. Oh God, he was going to
rape her after all. Just as she readied herself to scream
and fight, she heard a splash of water and next, a warm,
wet rag caressed her face gently. What kind of man was
this who wanted his prize to be clean before he ravished
her? She opened her eyes only a crack to peer up at
him. His face was shadowed so that she could not see
his expression as he washed her face.

Then he began to unbutton her torn bodice. Now,
he would strip away her clothing and take her. She lay
very still, wondering if she dared to chance jumping up
and bolting from the tipi, knowing there were hundreds
of Utes out there in the darkness of the camp? He took

the warm, wet rag and began to wash her breasts. She closed her eyes again and sighed. The rag caressed her breasts and her nipples. She had not known she could become so aroused by such gentle stroking. What kind of slut was she to enjoy this touch of a savage?

He was unbuttoning her dress down the front. She tensed, wondering what to do. Maybe he was waiting for her to regain consciousness before he took her. In that case, she could pretend all night long. She forced herself not to move or fight him as he pulled the blue dress off and washed her gently. Her owner was looking at her naked body. The humiliation made her face burn, but she dared not move as he touched her so intimately. Would he rape her now or just continue to touch and stroke her as if she were some kind of small pet for his amusement? Instead, he pulled the warm fur of the buffalo robe up over her naked body. The fur against her bare skin felt erotic.

Wannie opened her eyes just a crack to watch her captor. He stood in silhouette from the outside firelight as he stripped off the loincloth and washed himself. What a magnificent body! His muscles gleamed in the light as he washed the dust from his skin. Naked, his big maleness was enough to make her catch her breath in awe and trepidation.

He put the loincloth back on. A woman came to the tipi entry and said something to him as she handed him a bowl and went away. What now? Wannie took a deep breath and smelled something delicious. Food. Of course he was going to fill his belly and then enjoy his captive at his leisure. He knelt next to her, put his arm under her head, and half lifted her, holding the bowl to her lips.

She was completely naked with only a buffalo robe around her; it slipped down her body, allowing her bare flesh to press against his. She should pretend to be unconscious, Wannie told herself, but she was too hungry and desperate to care anymore. The scent of the hot broth was too much to resist and she took a sip. It was so delicious, she could not stop herself.

Finally she paused.

"Enough?"

She only managed to nod, knowing what would come next. But he laid her down and finished the broth himself, setting the bowl to one side. His hand reached out toward her and in her terror, she opened her mouth to scream. He slapped that big hand over her mouth. "Stop it! Don't you know me?"

She stopped fighting and collapsed, almost sobbing with relief. "Keso? Keso! Is it really you?"

His hand went to stroke the hair from her eyes. "No other. Are you all right?"

She wept softly. "I ought to be mad at you—you scared me half to death!"

"I'm sorry, Wannie, I thought you knew me and if not, I didn't dare let them know I knew you."

She rose up on her elbows, peering anxiously toward the tipi entry. "Is Cleve all right?"

His body stiffened and she saw the sudden hostility in his face. "Hell, yes. The yellow coward was willing to trade you to save his own life."

Wannie began to cry and he took her in his arms, pressing her against his bare chest and gently kissing her forehead. "Hush, honey, you're all right. I'll take care of you."

"What did you call me?" She looked at him, unmindful of the buffalo robe slipping down so that she was naked from the waist up.

"Brat."

"You liar, that's not what you said."

"I—I don't remember."

She stared at the ring hanging on a thong around

his neck, then reached up and took it between her fingers, gently rotating it so that the light gleamed on the inscription. *"Pour toujours. For always.* Where'd you get this?"

"What difference does it make?" He jerked it out of her hand.

"Did you steal it?" Somehow, even as she said it, she knew better. Keso was no thief.

"Hell, no, I bought it."

"Bought it?" She looked up at him, trying to read his rugged face in the shadowy firelight. It didn't make any sense that Keso would buy himself such a delicate silver ring in a size so small it wouldn't even fit on his pinkie. Then she remembered their situation and the ring didn't seem important anymore. "Oh, Keso, I'm so scared! What's going to happen?"

He gathered her into his arms, heedless of her nakedness, holding her close against him. "I reckon I don't rightly know. The Utes are so desperate, they'll follow any lead. Tomorrow, unless Ouray returns, Coyote's liable to convince them to kill us all."

She rested her face against his bare chest, feeling secure and protected. "You fought him for me, didn't you?"

"Did you doubt I would? They'll have to kill me to hurt you, honey."

Honey. She hadn't imagined his tender words. She swallowed hard, wondering. "Can I—can I doctor your back?"

"It's okay—don't bother."

"It's no bother." She took the little pot of ointment and half-turned him so she could put the soothing bear grease on the raised welts.

He sighed at her touch as she ran her fingers across his bare flesh, marveling at the power and strength of the man. As she touched him, she became aware that he was tensing, breathing deeper. Wannie paused with her palms against his bare back, feeling his heart pounding hard. What she had at her fingertips was a big, strong male and the thought electrified her. How could she have thought of him all this time as only her brother? "I—I'm finished."

He turned back toward her, his eyes smoldering with unspoken passion. How could she have been so blind to his devotion? She had always taken him for granted, not even guessing that he might care for her. Abruptly, she knew who that ring was for. Her throat swelled to the point of choking and tears came to her eyes and dripped on his chest. "Oh, Keso."

He put his arms around her, hugging her naked body against his. "Hush, Wannie, you'll be okay, don't be afraid." He wiped her tears with one big finger. "I—I don't know how to tell you this, but since I've won you, according to custom, I'll have to come out of this lodge at dawn with proof that I've taken you."

Blood, she thought. He was expected to come out of the lodge with her virgin blood smeared on his manhood. She looked up into his eyes. "I understand."

"Look, Wannie, I'll use a knife. At dawn, I'll cut my arm and smear a little blood on my, well, you know. That way, they'll be satisfied, and maybe I can figure out a way to get you and Cleve out of here safely."

She leaned into him, staring up into his dark eyes, wondering how she could have been so unaware all these years? "You'll try to save me and Cleve Brewster and get us out of here so I can marry him?"

He hesitated, then nodded. "There's nothing in the world I wouldn't do for you."

He bent his head to kiss the tip of her nose the way he always did, and as he did, Wannie reached up and caught his face between her hands. Very deliberately, she brought his face down to hers and kissed him on the mouth. For a split second, he stiffened in surprise and almost pulled away, but she wouldn't let him. She pressed her bare breasts against his naked chest and deepened the kiss, licking along his lips until he opened them, then slipping her tongue deep inside his mouth.

For a moment, he hesitated, then with a soft groan, his powerful arms went around her and he pulled her against him so hard that she could scarcely breathe. She moved her arms around his neck, holding him tightly as she caressed the inside of his mouth with her tongue.

He was breathing hard, aroused and holding her tightly as he took over the kiss, sucking her tongue into his mouth, running his hands around her shoulders and down her bare back to her hips.

The kiss seemed to last an eternity but not nearly long enough. The only man who had ever kissed her was Cleve Brewster and compared to this, it had been nothing. What had she been missing all these years while Keso kissed the tip of her nose and her forehead?

Keso seemed to be fighting for self control as he took a deep breath and pulled away from her. He caught her arms and looked down at her with horror and she realized his big hands were trembling. "Good God, Wannie, I—I don't know what came over me. I'm sorry! I know you love Cleve—"

"Hush." She reached up and put her small hands on his broad shoulders. "Why didn't you tell me you loved me, Keso?"

He started to say something, then looked away. "I did, but you never seemed to hear me. I wasn't fancy enough for you. It doesn't matter, Wannie, I understand. I'd do anything for you."

"You always would," she whispered. "How could I have been so blind?"

"I'm just a rough woodsman, like Cleve said."

"You were willing to fight to the death for me and he wasn't."

"You don't have to be grateful, honey."

"There, you called me that again." She looked up into his face, then reached out and caught the little silver ring in her fingers. "Who did you buy this for?"

He hesitated. "Please don't laugh."

"Keso, dear, I'm not laughing. Don't you see I'm not laughing?" Tears ran unchecked down her face.

"I—I bought it when I went to Boston for your graduation. I was going to ask you to marry me, but all you could talk of was Cleve."

She wiped her eyes. "I never guessed."

"I know—it's okay. I reckon the thought that I might love you never crossed your mind."

"I was such a fool," she whispered.

"Wannie, I don't know what to make of you." His shoulders slumped. "I've looked after you the best I could all these years and I'm afraid Cleve Brewster isn't up to the job, but if he's your choice—"

She reached up and put her fingers across his lips so he could not finish. "You have just fought a fight to the death to take me and now you're willing to cut your arm to pretend you did."

He kissed her fingertips. "Don't you understand, Wannie?"

"I think I'm just beginning to," she murmured, "and wondering why I didn't know."

"What do you mean?"

"You've won me, Keso, and I'm yours for the night, but God willing, I'd like to be yours for always."

"Honey, you don't know what you're saying. Tomorrow, you'll regret this and be back talking of fancy dresses and jewels and big mansions—"

"I want to be your woman," she whispered, "now and forever."

He took a deep breath and stared into her eyes as if he could not quite believe her words. Whatever he saw there gave him his answer.

Very slowly, he reached up and untied the rawhide thong. As he slipped the ring on the third finger of her left hand, he said, "I had always dreamed of doing this before a preacher."

"And if we get out of this alive, I promise you we will," she murmured, "but for tonight, our vows to each other will have to do." She put her arms around his neck and kissed him deeply. He took her in his arms, probing her mouth with his tongue, caressing her lips with his own.

"Oh, honey, if you only knew how much I've dreamed of this." He laid her back on the buffalo robe and slowly pulled it away from her body.

She lay there, smiling up at him, relishing the approval and desire in his dark eyes as his gaze traveled over her bare flesh. "We have all night," she said. "let's enjoy it as if it were the only time we will ever make love."

"I promise you, honey, you will never, never forget tonight."

They both knew without saying that tomorrow, the Utes might change their minds and kill them both, but they had tonight and each other. It was enough.

She closed her eyes and let Keso kiss her eyelids and her cheeks and comb his rough but gentle hands through her dark hair. "I promise I won't hurt you."

"I never thought you would." She reached up and caught his face in her hands and kissed him again until he groaned aloud.

"All these years," he promised, "I've dreamed of kissing every inch of you and tonight, I will." He kissed her neck and along her collarbone.

Wannie had never felt desire when Cleve kissed her,

yet at this moment, need was a hot whirlpool in her belly that radiated through her whole body. Keso was staring down at her as if he was not sure he dared touch her further. For answer, she arched her back, offering him her breasts.

She heard his quick intake of breath and then his rough, brown hands reached out and covered her white breasts and it felt as good as she knew it would. She smiled and arched her back even more, pressing her breasts against his hands so that he raked his thumbs back and forth across her pink nipples until she felt them swell with desire. She took a quick intake of breath herself and put her hands on top of his. "Take pleasure in these—they belong to you."

In answer, he slipped his arm under her bare back, and brought her into his lap where she felt his manhood hard and throbbing against her. Then he put his open mouth on her breast.

She gasped with delight, never having known that a man's mouth sucking her nipple could feel so exciting. Wannie reached up and caught his dark head, pulling his mouth hard against her breast, urging him to take it all into his mouth, urging him to tease it while she writhed in his arms. He sucked it until she was breathless with the throbbing of her swollen nipple. Then he went to the other one.

The thought crossed her mind that she was only a small, helpless toy made for his pleasure except that his touch and his mouth were giving her pleasure, too. Keso kissed between her breasts and left a hot, wet trail of kisses down her bare belly as his calloused hand kneaded and massaged her breasts.

Her whole body was on fire. "Keso, dearest, oh, don't stop . . . please, I'm begging you, don't stop!"

"Not with a gun at my head," he declared, his breath warm on her belly.

His bare chest was inches from her mouth. She reached out and embraced him, catching his nipple between her teeth. He gasped aloud and pressed her face against him. Encouraged, she nibbled and teased with her small teeth, then went to the other nipple while he urged her on with gasps and moans of pleasure.

"Do you like that?" she asked.

"Oh, Wannie, I could never get enough of you if I made love to you every night for the rest of my life."

"For always?"

"For always!" he promised and kissed her hungrily again and again, running his tongue inside her lips, devouring her mouth for a long time before he returned to kissing her belly, moving lower each time she writhed and moaned at his touch.

Surely he wasn't going to kiss her there! she thought with sudden horror as his mouth moved lower still. For a split second she resisted, keeping her thighs together. He raised his head, looking at her, breathing hard. "Remember you are my captive—I have won you and you must please me—and I intend to please you. Don't resist me."

That was right, wasn't it? She was his to do with as he wished. She let her thighs fall apart and closed her eyes. Then she felt his hot breath on her bud of femininity and took a deep breath, arching her body with pleasure even as his tongue touched and caressed there. At that moment, Wannie forgot propriety, modesty, and everything else but the hot desire that swirled from his greedy mouth. She moaned aloud as she caught his head between her hands and held him against her, wanting him to kiss and suck and probe her with his tongue. For a long moment, she writhed helplessly under his mouth, shaking with the desire he was building in her.

After a long moment, he stood up and silently began to remove his loincloth. She lay there naked on the soft fur, looking up at his magnificent bronzed body in the golden firelight. His manhood was as large and swollen as a stallion's. She felt a need to worship at this font of life and came up on her knees, embracing his lower body and pressing her bare breasts against his muscular thighs. She paid homage to his supreme maleness by kissing him there, taking him in her mouth in ultimate submission.

"Wannie, no . . ." But he didn't tear away. After a moment, he caught the back of her head in his hands, pressing her face against his powerful body, letting her, urging her to taste and kiss him there. She wanted his seed, wanted to taste his life force, but he reached down and swung her up in his arms, her long black hair hanging over his arm like silken strands of the deepest night. His eyes burned with intense desire as she arched her back and he held her dangling from his powerful arms as he pleasured himself with her swollen breasts again. "Oh, Wannie, are you sure?"

She took his rugged face between her hands. "Very, very sure. I am a warrior's prize and you have risked your life for this. I offer you my virginity—go out in tomorrow's dawn with the true stain on your manhood!"

He needed no further urging. His hands shook with his own terrible need as he laid her down on the buffalo robe and knelt between her thighs. "I'm too big for you. I—I'm afraid I'll hurt you."

She felt desire burning like an out-of-control forest fire through her so badly she trembled.

He shook his head. "You're afraid, I won't—"

"That's not why I tremble," she whispered, "I want you, Keso. I want your body deep in mine, I want you to own me. Breed me now—give me your son."

He put one hand on each side of her bare shoulders. "Oh, honey, if you only knew how much I love you."

"Show me," she said, "make me your woman—possess me in a way that only one man can and only one time." She reached up and put her hands on his sinewy back, urging him down.

He hesitated just a split second with the tip of his wet, pulsating manhood against the soft velvet folds of her femininity, then he plunged into her to the hilt, even as he covered her mouth with his own.

For a moment, she thought only of the pain, like a giant steel knife turning deep into her very being, tearing through her maidenhead as the warrior claimed that which he had won. She opened her mouth to scream and his tongue went deep into her throat. She lay helpless under him as he covered and dominated her, her mouth and her body subjugated to his need.

Very gently, be began to ride her dainty form and she was helpless to do anything except meld her curves to his hard body to provide him pleasure. She was his property and he could use her whether she agreed or not; yet she wanted to please him.

His hard strokes into her depths, his caressing the inside of her mouth with his tongue began to build pleasure in her even as his muscular chest rubbed against her sensitive, swollen nipples.

With a moan of submission, Wannie locked her legs around his naked, powerful hips, willing him to thrust even deeper. Her hands caught his powerful shoulders, digging her nails into his flesh as she arched her back, wanting even more of him.

She felt him thrusting deep within her, throbbing with the seed he had to give. He was big, all right, so big she was not sure she could take all of him and yet she wanted more and more. "Please, dearest," she begged, "breed me! Breed me now!"

With a groan, he responded to her pleas, holding her close, thrusting hard, throbbing up under her ribs as he put himself even deeper into her body. She was wild with desire, wanting him as she had never known she could want a man. She kept him prisoner with her thighs, holding him in a frenzied embrace while her small body came up off the robe, bucking under him as they meshed and mated. He was holding back, she was sure of it, waiting for her to reach some kind of pinnacle.

She seemed to be moving toward some dizzying height that she couldn't reach and she wasn't even sure what it was her heart and soul demanded, her body ached for. "Now!" she commanded against his lips, using his big body for her own pleasure as she writhed under him, "Now, dearest!"

He rammed into her depths one more time with all the strength and power of his narrow, muscular hips, then paused deep inside her. She clung to him, feeling him throbbing in her belly even as he claimed her mouth again. She felt she was being swept into a whirling vortex of molten desire as she kept him captive with her arms and thighs, not willing to let him go until he satisfied her desperate need.

She felt him shudder and gasp as he began to give up his seed. It seemed to her she could feel it surging hot inside her waiting womb and she gloried in it, needing it to fulfill her burning emptiness, to make her complete. She was like a wild thing bucking under him, clawing his back and shoulders, biting his lips and pulling him deep inside her as his powerful body went rigid. The feel, of that hot fluid in her depths pushed her over the edge and her body convulsed under him, clutching him hard, determined not to let go until her greedy womb had sucked every drop of life-bearing seed from his body.

She had never known a feeling like this—helpless with this sudden surge of emotion, this reaction that was as old as Time itself. Her body convulsed and locked onto his and she held him against her, demanding everything he had to give. He was putting his son in her belly, she was certain and she was glad. Time seemed to stand still and there was nothing but Keso holding her, shielding her, taking her to a high plateau of emotion she had never known.

After a long moment, Wannie came to gradually, gasping for air, Keso lying on her, both of them covered with a fine sheen of perspiration.

"Oh, God, Wannie," he gasped, "what have I done? I—I lost control. I've wanted you so badly."

She smiled at him and reached up to brush his black hair from his eyes. "I love you," she murmured and the silver ring caught the gleam of the firelight. "I'm your woman now, dearest." She kissed his lips gently, then more passionately.

She felt his manhood began to swell inside her. "I want you again," he said against her mouth, "I'll never get enough of you."

"We've got all night," she said and offered her swollen nipples to his mouth again, "you can take me over and over."

He bent his head and ran his rough, dark hands over her bare skin. "Believe me, I intend to," he promised. "If they change their minds and kill us tomorrow, at least I will have had tonight and it's worth it."

"Yes, it is," she agreed and began to move under him. "Do it again, dearest, and again and again!"

He needed no further urging. As the night deepened, he made love to her over and over. Tonight might be all the time they would ever spend in each other's arms, but the precious memories of this passion would last forever.

TWENTY-TWO

With the dawn, Keso awakened and glanced down at the petite girl asleep in his protective embrace. Oh Lord, what had he done? When Wannie awoke, was she going to regret the night of passion she had spent in his arms? Would she realize what she had thrown away with the wealthy young blade and his fortune? Perhaps if she did, Keso could help her pretend that nothing had happened so that the snooty heir to the Brewster fortune would still want her.

Keso's silver ring gleamed on her left hand. Yet in the cold dawn of a new day, he was certain she would have regrets. Had he taken advantage of her innocence and trust? Perhaps she had been swept away with gratitude for his saving her from Coyote.

She moved in his arms and he leaned to kiss her forehead and pull her more tightly against him. There were other worries. This morning, the Utes might have changed their minds and with Ouray out of the camp, Coyote was still in charge and who knew what he might persuade the others to do?

Through the slit in the tipi, he could see Cleve tied up by the fire. The camp was coming awake and alive with noise and movement. He could hear dogs barking, children laughing, horses neighing as people came and went.

Wannie's eyes flickered open and he marveled for an instant at how big and dark they were with long, smoky lashes. She looked up at him in puzzlement.

He held his breath, afraid of her reaction as she remembered last night. "Wannie, are you all right?"

She was still looking up at him, not moving in his embrace. How he wanted to lean over and kiss her full, soft lips, but instead, he only smiled down at her and held his breath.

Her brow furrowed. "Did I—did I dream last night?"

Oh God, she regretted it and it was too late. Keso hesitated. He who had fought for possession of her body and a night of indescribable passion in her embrace was now shy and awkward at expressing how he felt about her. "It was a dream come true for me—I'm sorry if you regret it."

She seemed to tense, listening to the sounds outside. "We're in the Ute camp, aren't we? What's happened to Cleve?"

Cleve. Always Cleve. Did she never think of Keso and his needs?

"He's okay, tied up and grumbling at everyone who walks past him."

"Oh, Keso, what are we going to do?"

He brushed her tangled long locks away from her face. "We'll muddle through somehow."

"Are you really planning to stay among the Utes?" Her small face mirrored concern.

"I'm not certain—I might." She was his prisoner, he knew that and she must know that. If he wanted to live as a Ute warrior, she would have no choice; she belonged to him in body, at least. What he yearned for was her heart and soul.

She was staring at the ring on her hand. "I can't believe what happened last night."

"Believe it." He tried not to betray any emotion in

his voice. Keso had spent one unforgettable night in her arms, but if she regretted it and didn't love him, he wanted to go back in time and erase that scene.

An old woman stooped outside their lodge, tittered, and called out something in a mixture of broken Spanish and Ute.

Wannie tensed. "What does she want?"

"She says everyone is waiting to see if I enjoyed my warrior's prize."

"You don't mean—?"

"Look, Wannie, I don't want to humiliate you or ruin your chances with young Brewster. I can pretend nothing happened and say I return you to the white man."

She paused. "Will that bring you trouble?"

Keso shrugged. "Who knows? I might have to fight Coyote all over again."

Wannie shuddered. "Coyote."

So he had his answer. She might regret giving herself to Keso, but the other alternative was worse. He was already tying the skimpy bit of breechcloth around his loins. "Put your clothes on and we'll go out and face them."

He watched her dress, wanting to take her in his arms and make love to her all over again. That memory of one unforgettable night would have to last him forever . . . unless he stayed among the Utes and kept her as his captive.

Holding hands, they stooped and went out of the lodge and out into the camp circle. There were dozens of Utes about who now fell silent and waited.

In a mix of Spanish and broken English, Keso boasted the girl was now his in every sense of the word. Men nodded with satisfaction and women giggled and exchanged sly smiles.

Only Coyote and Cleve Brewster scowled.

Cleve twisted where he was tied. "Wannie, you slut!

Are you out of your mind? Do you think I'll want you now if you've let that savage—"

"Shut up, Cleve," Wannie said, "I may have saved your life . . . at least, temporarily. Give that some thought."

Cleve's thoughts seemed to return to his own safety. The morning light gleamed on his beautiful yellow hair as he looked at Keso and begged, "Please, can you get me out of this? Are they going to kill us?"

"Brewster, for once in your life," Keso said through clenched teeth, "try not to panic or show fear. We'll have to play this moment by moment with Ouray gone."

"That's right." Coyote grinned, but there was no humor in his dark, ugly face. "I am in charge here with no chiefs in camp. The Chief's son had better watch his back!"

Keso glared into his eyes. "I will tell my father you said so when he returns."

Coyote shrugged. "Ouray is sick and failing; anyone can see that."

"The people would never let you lead them," Keso said.

"We will see," Coyote promised. "The people are confused and afraid. They will listen to a strong leader in this war against the whites."

"That is exactly what the Utes should not do," Keso bristled. "Hostile action is the excuse whites need to exile our people to the hot, dry Indian Territory."

"We would rather die fighting," Coyote promised. "This is how the Great White Father repays us for sending scouts to aid them against the Lakota and Cheyenne after they wiped out Yellowhair Custer."

"I cannot deny that," Keso sighed and rubbed his chin, "but to fight gives them the reason they need to steal the rich Ute land."

A rider galloped into camp, shouting, "Bluecoats! Soldiers coming from the north!"

Coyote frowned and nodded. "You see? They are already making their plans."

A crowd gathered around the rider as he dismounted, a buzz of angry excitement filling the air.

Keso held Wannie against him protectively as he confronted the rider. "What is this you say? Is this only a rumor or have you seen these soldiers?"

"I have seen them," the man nodded. "I was hunting with Colorow and some of the others. Many soldiers come from the north through Yellowjacket Pass and Coal Creek Canyon."

Major Thornburgh, Keso thought. With the hostility of the Utes growing, Meeker had panicked and sent a message for troops. "Perhaps the soldiers are not marching to fight."

"Then why would they come?" Coyote demanded as he folded his arms and glared at Keso. "There is nothing but the White River Agency."

The messenger said, "The officer says he will leave his troops and bring only five men to parlay."

An angry, frightened murmur ran through the crowd and women hugged their babies closer. "Remember soldiers' surprise attack at Sand Creek. They are never to be trusted."

"Let us not panic," Keso raised his voice to the crowd. "You know the Indian agent—he is an old man of faint heart. If there is no trouble, the soldiers will march back up to the fort."

"Ha!" Coyote sneered. "Suppose they lie and plan to put us in chains and take us away to the Indian Territory where even now, the Nez Perce sicken and die? Will we do better there than Chief Joseph's people who, like us, love the high, cold mountains?"

With a murmur of angry agreement, the stolid faces

frowned at Keso, no longer thinking of him as a beloved chief's missing son. The attitude of these people toward him could change at any moment. He and Cleve and Wannie might be killed by an aroused mob while Ouray was away from the camp. "I, too, am Ute," he said, "and like my father, I want what is best for our people."

"You speak not with a straight tongue!" Coyote shouted. "In your heart, you are white."

Was he? He didn't know anymore; yet he had honor, too. "My father thinks always of his people," Keso said, "and I think I know what he would say if he were here: do not fight the bluecoats—you cannot win."

"Better to be dead on the field of battle than caged like animals," Coyote insisted.

"Perhaps as the soldier chief said, he is only coming to parlay," Keso said, trying desperately to reason with them.

"Let us all go see what the soldiers are up to," Coyote snarled. "Let us see if the soldier chief halts his men outside our land. If he does not, let these whites be the first to die!"

A yell of approval went up from the camp. The Utes were confused and afraid, knowing they had been deceived too many times by greedy whites.

Keso's strong arm went around Wannie's shoulders. He would give his life for her, but he might not be able to protect her against so many angry warriors. "We will go with you," he answered solemnly. "Perhaps I can find out why the soldiers come and persuade them to go back to their fort."

"And this time," Coyote sneered, "Ouray is not here to lick the bluecoats' boots. If they lie and cross our land, we will fight them!"

He barked orders to the braves clustered around and men began to catch horses and saddle up.

Coyote smiled at Keso. "You, your woman, and yes,

the white man who whimpers like a frightened puppy will go with us so there will be no tricks. If the soldiers plan trickery, you three will be the first to die."

"So be it." Keso took a deep breath and squared his shoulders. He had hoped to leave Wannie in the camp and give her a chance to escape, but Coyote had forestalled that. He began to saddle Spirit as a warrior cut Cleve down and threw him up on old Blue. What to do? He must get word to Ouray. The chief had not spent his whole life keeping peace for his people to have it all thrown away by a few hotheads like Coyote. Keso wished he knew Major Thornburgh's plans or the message the panicky Nathan Meeker had sent him. If Keso could get word to Ouray, perhaps the chief might arrive in time to stop the confrontation before it escalated into a bloody battle.

He looked around as he saddled Spirit. With his fast horse, he might mount and escape before the Utes knew what he was up to, but that move would sacrifice Cleve and maybe Wannie to the angry Utes. Besides, these were people of his own blood and he truly wanted to help avert trouble for them if he could.

Keso spotted an old man whom he knew was loyal to Ouray, a man he had seen riding at the chief's side. He crept to him and whispered, "Do you know where the great Chief is?"

The old face looked like bronzed leather as he smiled and nodded.

"Go to Ouray, tell him what is happening—there may be blood spilled if he does not get here in time."

The ancient warrior considered. "It is many hours' ride and I am of many winter counts. It also may take some days to find him if he hunts in the San Juan Mountains or in the canyon of the river whites call the Gunnison."

"You must find him," Keso urged. "He must bring

calm before hotheads like Coyote push our people into war."

"I will do my best," the old man promised, and sneaked away in the confusion.

Keso returned to his task. He didn't know how much Wannie and Cleve had been able to understand or if they understood their peril, but Keso would do what he could to avert bloodshed. If Major Thornburgh were coming, surely he wouldn't be foolish enough to ride onto reservation lands. Perhaps Keso could stall trouble until Ouray arrived. If fighting broke out, Coyote would think the trio was part of the plot and all three of them would die.

He wished he knew what Wannie was thinking about last night. "Wannie, are you ready?"

"Don't I get my own horse?"

"I'd just as soon you rode behind me."

"Why?"

"You ask too many questions—just do as I tell you."

She hesitated, that old stubbornness in her dark eyes telling him she wanted to argue. Perhaps she had not understood just how much danger the trio had been plunged into by the unexpected movement of Major Thornburgh's troops. If fighting broke out, Spirit was the strongest, swiftest mount in the entire Ute camp. If there was any shooting, Wannie's best chance for survival lay in being up behind Keso as he made a break for safety.

"Are we in any danger?" Wannie looked up at him innocently.

"No, brat—just do what I tell you." If it cost him his life, he was going to protect Wannie. Last night might be the only night he would ever spend in her arms, but for him, it had been worth it. The memory of her kisses and the way she had held him close was enough to last a lifetime. The new cabin in the valley of the Singing

Winds with their children running about the house might never be, but he would love her until the end of his days and with his last breath would call her name.

He looked over at Cleve, who was still rubbing his wrists and complaining as he mounted up on old Blue. The damned dude didn't even realize how close to death he might be. Cleve ran his aristocratic hands through his fine hair, still vain about his good looks. Aristocrat. It dawned on Keso suddenly who Cleve resembled with the thick yellow hair, pale blue eyes and cleft chin. Could it be? Why had no one else noticed it?

"Injun, what are you staring at?"

"Nothing. I was just thinking you look like your father."

Cleve blinked. "Of course I do. Blood will tell."

Keso grinned at the irony. "Maybe."

The warriors were mounting now. Coyote rode up beside Keso. "Are you coming, or are you afraid to fight?"

The others were watching. Keso squared his shoulders. "I fear nothing—I proved that last night."

Around them, warriors laughed softly and Coyote frowned. "I have not forgotten how you shamed me. There will be another time."

It was an open threat. Keso knew he must be careful not to turn his back on Coyote. He swung up on his stallion and reached down to Wannie. "Come, woman."

He always marveled at how light she was. He swung her up easily behind him and she fitted her small body against him as if she belonged there, her soft breasts molding into his back. Her arms went around his waist and he reached down and patted her hands, feeling his silver ring as a promise he had made her. He might have to pay with his life, but he was going to get Wannie out of this mess alive.

Wannie held onto Keso tightly and nestled herself

against his muscular back. She wanted time to sort out her feelings about last night. There was some kind of trouble—she could feel the tension in the air after that messenger had ridden in and Coyote and Keso had exchanged angry words. Concern was etched deep on Keso's handsome face. It had something to do with soldiers, but she didn't understand much more than that. She trusted Keso to take care of her.

She felt his big hand reach down and cover hers for a long moment, touching the ring. She had never even imagined such ecstasy as he had given her last night on a soft buffalo fur in a primitive lodge. If he stayed among the Utes, would she want to stay also?

Cleve rode up next to them, frowning. "Wannie, you're going to regret this."

"This isn't the time to discuss this, Cleve. We're lucky to be alive."

"You bought our lives with your body, is that it?"

"Brewster," Keso warned and she felt the muscles of his body tense, "watch what you say or I might have to kill you."

"You wouldn't dare! Why, my father—"

"Isn't here to buy you out of this mess," Keso finished.

Cleve lowered his voice to a whisper as he sneered at Wannie. "When we get back to civilization, the savage won't look so good to you. He still doesn't know what fork to use."

"Would you understand that I don't care?" Wannie answered a little too sweetly and pressed herself even closer to Keso's broad back.

"You needn't think I'll want you now when you change your mind," Cleve sneered, "not after you've let that Injun—"

Keso's big hand reached out and caught Cleve by the throat. "Watch your mouth," he said coldly as if fighting to control his temper, "or I will choke the words from your throat this very moment!"

"Keso, don't kill him," Wannie pleaded.

"For you, Wannie." Very slowly, the brave took his hand away as Cleve choked and coughed.

"You—you almost killed me!"

"Thank the girl for your life," Keso said, "and anyway, we've got all the trouble we can handle right now."

She felt the tension in Keso's body as Cleve stared at him with fear in his pale eyes. She looked around at the mounted Indians. In almost every waistband, a big butcher knife gleamed. She saw Cleve looking at those, too.

Coyote rode past and gave Wannie a knowing smile that said he would yet enjoy her body. She trembled at the thought and held onto Keso a little tighter. Her expensive jewelry still lay by the fire in the center of the camp; no one had even bothered to claim it. As she watched, a toddler picked up the priceless ring and chortled with glee. Another little girl and a thin old woman handled the fine gold bracelets with casual curiosity. How could trinkets like that have meant so much to Wannie? Life was what was important, not clothes, jewels, and other possessions. Life and love. She had both; she might lose both.

Coyote and Keso led out, Spirit snorting as he took off at a gallop. Cleve rode next to them on old Blue, grumbling about everything. If there was any real trouble, Wannie thought, old Blue would be hard-pressed to outrun some of these fine Ute horses.

Abruptly, she realized why Keso had wanted her up behind him on Spirit. Sooner or later, he expected trouble and when it came, he had the best horse in the bunch. He was probably planning to make a run for it and he wanted to make sure she got out, too.

Several times, they stopped to water and rest the

horses as the group rode north. The trees were turning, Wannie noticed; the aspen would soon be golden on the hillsides, the birds heading south as autumn deepened. It would be a glorious time to be building a home and settling in before a cozy fire to make love and dream of children. She thought of Silver and Cherokee, wishing she could let them know everyone was still all right. Tears came to her eyes. How could she ever have thought of leaving these people and this beautiful mountain country that she loved so much?

Once when they stopped to eat some dried meat and rest the horses, she asked Keso, "Is there going to be trouble?" For a moment, she was not sure he would answer her. He looked away. "Keso, you were never very good at lying."

"Okay," he acknowledged with a sigh, "we may be heading toward a terrible confrontation with Major Thornburgh."

"They can't come on the reservation land," she exclaimed. "The Utes haven't attacked Meeker."

Cleve snorted. "Not yet, they haven't. Savages, that's all they are, savages who'll probably cut our throats."

"If they do," Keso said, "everyone will know where they got the knives."

"That's business!" Cleve snapped.

"It doesn't make a lot of sense to arm people our soldiers might have to fight, now does it?"

"It's business," Cleve defended himself. "American business doesn't care whether it's with friend or enemy, just so they make the sales. That will never change."

"Then I'd say there's something wrong with American businessmen if they're willing to do that."

"Keso," she said and looked up at him, wanting to touch him, to say something intimate, but not with people watching, "what happens if the soldiers don't stop at the reservation boundary?"

He didn't answer for a long moment. "Major Thornburgh wouldn't be that reckless."

"And what if he is?" Cleve demanded. "Why don't you quit lying to her and tell her they may kill all of us?"

Keso shook his head. "They may get you and me, Brewster, but I'll save Wannie, no matter what."

"You're so damned noble!" Cleve sneered. "Well, I'm not! I think I'll try to strike some kind of bargain with Coyote. Maybe I can offer him money."

Now even Wannie laughed. "Cleve, don't you understand? The Utes don't see any value in gold. Didn't you see what they did with my fabulous jewelry? Last time I saw it, an old squaw and a couple of children were wearing it."

"They understand trade goods," Cleve said, his face pale under his blond hair. "Maybe I can offer—"

"Some more knives?" Keso interrupted. "Or maybe some rifles or whiskey? Why should you care how many whites or Utes are killed with Brewster trade goods?"

"Damn it, I *don't* care!" Cleve's voice rose hysterically. "I'll do anything to save my neck!"

"Cleve!" Wannie exclaimed, wondering how she could have misread him so. "You're a rotten coward!"

"At least I intend to be a *live* coward," he shot back, "while your big protector here is going to be very dead!"

"Brewster," Keso said, "if we both come out of this alive, I'll whip you 'til you can't stand up just for the pure pleasure of it."

"I'll tell the army how you plotted with these Utes," Cleve threatened, "and you'll be lucky if they don't hang you. And as for this pretty slut—"

Keso hit him then, knocking him back against old Blue, who snorted and moved over to keep from stepping on the white man who groveled in the dirt. "Get up, Brewster, I'm going to kill you now."

"No, Keso," she said and caught his arm, "this isn't the time for fighting among ourselves."

Keso glared at her and started to speak, but Coyote strode up just then. "If you two want to fight over the girl, do it later," he said in slow English, smiling at Wannie as if he was still thinking of the pleasures of her body. "A scout has just ridden in to say the soldiers are still marching toward us. It looks as if they don't intend to stop at the reservation boundary!"

TWENTY-THREE

Major Thomas Tipton Thornburgh, known to his friends as "Tip," rode across the barren areas of northern Colorado ahead of his troops. He thought of his pretty wife and small children waiting behind at Fort Steele, Wyoming. It had been difficult to say good-bye to them.

"Lida," he had said as he kissed her, "don't fret, we'll get this little outbreak calmed and be back before you know it."

"Tip, I'm worried." His tiny blond wife's face showed the strain. "Gossip says there's thousands of Utes about to go on the warpath."

"Dear, you're from military stock—you know I've got a job to do." Lida, he thought, had been the pretty, eighteen-year-old sister of one of his fellow officers. They'd met at an officers' dance. Tip was twenty-six years old, ancient by Lida's standards, but he knew the moment he saw her he wanted her—and he got her. The marriage took place on Tip's twenty-seventh birthday, December 26. It was a society wedding with lots of West Point brass in attendance, including four generals. After all, Lida's father was Major Robert Clarke, a distant cousin to General Sherman.

"I know, Tip, I'm sorry." Lida ducked her head, ashamed of her worry.

He was so much taller than she and now he kissed the top of her blond head. "Besides, you know I'm a good shot." He smiled as he pulled out the beautiful Colt pistol his adoring men had given him at an earlier assignment in Fort Foote, Maryland. His name was engraved in silver on the butt. He was such an expert marksman that General George Crook himself had put Tip up for membership in the prestigious Omaha Gun Club.

"Dear, I'm sorry you had to cut your hunting trip short. Did your brother mind?" Lida smiled up at him.

"Matter of fact, Jake was a little put out. We were having such a good time and he's got a couple of important bankers with him." Tip smiled at the memory of boisterous good times; he idolized his older brother, who was influential, having once been a Congressman. "Jake insisted I leave them my scout, Taylor Pennock, so they could continue their hunt."

"Was that wise?"

Tip shrugged. "I'll hire another scout in Rawlins. Maybe not as good, but it'll be fine. Now, dear, you take care of my bird dogs, hear?"

She laughed and hugged him. "I'll looked out for the Irish setters—you look out for you. Come, children, kiss Daddy good-bye."

He hugged the children, Bobby and Olivia. They had had a Centennial baby born in 1876. Sadly, that little son had not lived. "You children take care of your mother 'til I get back."

"And we'll look out for the dogs, too," seven-year-old Bobby declared.

"Daddy," five-year-old Olivia said as she grabbed him about the legs, "can we have a puppy?"

Lida laughed. "Aren't two big hunting dogs enough for one family?"

"We'll see, sweetheart." Tip patted the top of his

daughter's head and kissed Lida again. An aide had
brought his two red setters around and Tip stooped to
pet them both. Then he swung into the saddle and nodded to Captain Payne and the others to mount the
troops.

Tip rode out on that Sunday morning, September 21,
looking back at his little family while the two Irish setters strained and barked at the end of their leashes,
wanting to go along. "Sorry, old boys, I'm not on a
hunt . . . or maybe I am," he said under his breath and
then squared his shoulders and rode out.

He was possibly the youngest major in the army at
this moment, Tip thought, and that made him a very
lucky man. Washington had cut back the military after
the Civil War. Now his mind was on Custer as he took
his position at the head of his troops and rode away
from dusty old Fort Steele, on the bend of the North
Platte River. Custer had been a victim of military cut-
backs, too; his rank had been cut to Lieutenant Colonel,
his men armed with relics left over from the Civil War.

However, Custer had gotten too cocky and ridden
into more Indians than he could handle that hot June
day of 1876. Custer was only thirty-four. Tip had been
slightly intrigued to learn that Custer had a December
birthday, too. If the boy general had lived, he would
have been thirty-five that December of 1876.

Tip shook his head. If he'd lived, George would probably have been court-martialed, too. No, Tip Thornburgh was both calm and thorough, not like the
hot-headed Custer. Tip would celebrate his ninth wedding anniversary on his thirty-seventh birthday this
coming December and wanted to grow old beside his
Lida with grandchildren and Irish setters playing
around his rocking chair. That hysterical Indian agent,
Meeker, was probably yelling 'wolf' again for no good
reason.

Major Thornburgh and his cavalry rode west first, sixteen miles into the lawless little frontier town of Rawlins where outlaws were known to hang out. In Rawlins, two troops from Fort Russell in Cheyenne had been sent to join him.

What worried Tip Thornburgh now was that no member of this command had ever journeyed between Rawlins and the White River Agency. Even as he asked around town about a suitable scout, Tip wished again that he had not succumbed to his brother Jake's pleas and left his best scout and guide, Taylor Pennock, with the hunting party. Someone recommended a local livery stable owner, Joe Rankin, as scout and Major Thornburgh took him along as the troops turned south through the barren badlands of Wyoming and into Colorado.

As the days passed, he didn't feel any better about this assignment. It was almost 200 miles from Rawlins and its railroad to the White River Agency. He was having to take all his necessities by wagon and a load of supplies Meeker had ordered were being sent at the same time.

Captain Payne fell in beside him. "Not a bad trip so far."

Tip drawled, "Leaves are turned red and gold—good hunting weather. I wish I could have brought my setters—probably some quail or prairie chicken thick in this brush."

"You had to leave a hunt to come, didn't you, sir?"

Tip nodded. "It couldn't be helped. Rotten timing on Meeker's part, but a soldier does what he must."

Captain Payne squinted against the sun and looked at Joe Rankin riding ahead of them. "The new scout seems all right."

Tip felt sheepish. "I suppose I shouldn't have let my brother, Jake, talk me out of my scout, but he didn't see any reason their hunt should be ruined, too. After all, they came quite a ways."

"You've even had the president's son up here hunting, haven't you, Major?"

"And General Crook, too," Tip added. "Colorado has superb hunting. No wonder the Utes, poor devils, might be willing to fight to hang onto the land."

"I know. Two years ago, I was with the command that went after Chief Joseph and his Nez Perce. It was mostly old people and women and children with us shooting at them. All they wanted to do was go to Canada and live in peace. They almost made it."

Captain Payne looked pale and too heavy, Tip thought, and moved as stiffly as an old man, although he was Tip's age. Payne's health had broken and he'd never really recovered from his service in the Nez Perce campaign. "It's a dirty business, this corralling Indians and trying to make them live the way we want, where we want."

Captain Payne hesitated. "They sent the Nez Perce down to the Indian Territory. It's hot and dry down there—they're dying like flies."

Tip stared at the gold and red autumn landscape ahead of him. Like the Nez Perce, the Utes were mountain people, too, used to roaming twelve million acres of rich hunting lands. "I think Ouray knows that could happen to his people if he doesn't keep them at peace."

"Excuse me, sir, but aren't the Utes friendlies? Didn't they provide scouts for us while the army was tracking down the Sioux after Little Big Horn?"

Tip sighed and touched the butt of the fine, engraved pistol in his holster. "How does the poem go: . . . *'Was there a man dismayed? Not though the soldiers knew someone had blundered; theirs not to make reply, theirs but to do and die—'"*

"As I recall, sir, the next lines are: "Into the Valley of Death rode the six hundred.""

Tip laughed. "We don't have six hundred and I'll try not to blunder, and get us trapped like Custer. We'll keep our supply wagons close enough so that we'll have all the ammunition and food we need."

"If you say so, sir." Payne looked behind them. "What is that contraption we're hauling along?"

The major shrugged. "Supplies for Meeker. He's ordered a threshing machine from Brewster Industries."

"I remember seeing plows unloaded from the train months ago," Captain Payne said. "You mean to tell me he actually got Utes to plow and plant and now he's making plans to harvest?"

"Maybe he's just being ambitious and planning future crops," Tip Thornburgh said and grinned. "Thank God we'll get this all solved and things will be peaceful again before the weather turns really bad. You ever shoot over fine-blooded dogs, Captain?"

"Are you inviting me, sir?"

"Certainly! My setters are the best. Maybe we'll hunt quail. Lida's a good cook. We'll sip a little good Kentucky bourbon and eat fried quail and tell tall tales about what an adventure this was, even if it turns out to be dull."

"Thank you, sir. I'll look forward to it."

Tip started to say something else, then paused with his mouth open and looked at the horizon. Captain Payne's gaze followed his own.

A handful of Utes, no doubt a hunting party, was silhouetted against the light of a distant bluff. Major Thornburgh raised his hand and the order went down the line to halt.

"Sir, do you think they see us?"

Tip frowned. "How could they miss several hundred troopers and all these supply wagons strung out for more than a mile? I was hoping to reach the agency before they even realized we were in the area."

Captain Payne's corpulent face turned a little paler. "So we've lost the element of surprise."

"That can't be helped, I'm afraid," Major Thornburgh said and shrugged. "What the devil do these warriors have in their belts that reflects the light so?" He handed his field glasses to the other officer.

Captain Payne leaned forward in his saddle, peering through the glasses at the hunting party. "Looks like they're all carrying big knives."

"Now who would sell the Utes something like that?" Thornburgh frowned.

"Maybe they stole them someplace."

"I hope we don't find some trader lying out here in the brush with his throat cut," Tip muttered. He peered through his field glasses again, watching the Utes turn their ponies and come down the ridge, riding toward them.

"Stay calm, captain," he cautioned, "we're not supposed to start any trouble."

The pudgy officer snorted. "You think the Utes know that? They wouldn't think we're out on a Sunday school stroll with all these troops and equipment."

They sat, waiting until the small group of Utes rode to face them, looking over the units suspiciously. An old warrior asked, "Where soldiers go?"

"We are not here to make war on the Utes," the major assured the suspicious old man. "The agent has sent for us to sit down with him and your people to straighten out our differences."

The stony-faced Indians surveyed the long line of mounted cavalry, infantry, and supply wagons. "Much people and guns just to talk. Not come on reservation land."

Tip hadn't planned to. The Utes would see that as

an act of war. "Suppose when we reach the reservation boundary we halt and meet with your leaders?"

The Utes looked skeptical. "How many soldiers you bring to meeting?"

Thornburgh considered. "To show our good faith, what about only five soldiers?"

He saw the sudden alarm in Captain Payne's pudgy face, but ignored it. "We will ride ahead and confer with agent Meeker and set up some kind of parlay."

The Ute nodded. "It shall be as you say." They turned and galloped back up over the distant ridge.

Payne wiped the sweat from his face. "Begging your pardon, sir, but you don't really intend to meet with them with only five soldiers?"

"I'm not here to start a war, Captain. I'm trying to calm things down."

Payne chewed his lip. "Have you forgotten what happened to General Canby?"

Tip shrugged. The only general to be killed fighting against Western Indians so far, Canby and his officers had sat down unarmed to counsel with the Modocs in 1873, and the Indians had suddenly pulled out weapons and killed the little group. "I'm cautious, Captain—I don't think I'll walk into a peace talk unarmed."

The other officer heaved an audible sigh of relief.

Tip leaned on his horse's neck and watched the hunting party disappear into the hills. "Now that we've been discovered, they'll be watching us to make sure we don't come on reservation land. Call a meeting of all the officers and scouts, Captain Payne. I have decisions to make."

The scout, Joe Rankin, was adamant. "We've got food and ammunition, but we've got to have water. We'll probably have to get it from Milk Creek first and then ride on, but we'll be on Ute reservation land by then."

Major Thornburgh shook his head. "I told them we will bring in only five men to parlay. The Utes will see our trespassing as an act of war and act accordingly."

"Can't help that," grizzly old Joe Rankin said. "If you leave your troops at the reservation boundary, they'll be in Coal Creek Canyon. Bad place to get trapped if the Utes decide to attack, like fish in a barrel."

"Trapped and cut off like Custer," someone muttered.

Major Thornburgh frowned. "No, not like Custer. I'm not about to get my troops stopped and waiting where they're easy targets. Send a messenger to agent Meeker that we're coming and that I've arranged to meet with the Utes with a small group of officers to parlay."

"You think they'll trust you?" Lieutenant Cherry, the officer with the Fort Russell troops, asked.

"Maybe when they see the large force, that will cool them down some," the scout said and scratched himself under his fringed leather jacket.

Captain Payne opened his mouth, started to speak, then paused.

"All right, Captain," Tip said, "out with it."

"You're going to ride in and face all those Utes with a handful of men to parlay?"

"It's part of my job, you know. Ours not to reason why," Tip smiled. "Stop worrying, Captain. I'm cautious."

"You'll also be miles from your troops and supplies, sir," Lieutenant Cherry said.

"I'm more worried about my troops than myself. All these men and hundreds of mules and horses need water and as Rankin says, I won't let them be halted in Coal Creek Canyon."

The scout spat tobacco in the dust. "Past the canyon, there's a little valley that Milk Creek runs through. Water's a little chalky-lookin,' but not bad."

"Isn't that on reservation land?" Major Thornburgh asked and frowned at him.

"Wal, yes sir, but these troops have to have water."

"We can't do that," the Major protested and began to pace up and down. "They'll think I lied."

"This is a big country, Major," the scout said, "so maybe they'll never know exactly where we camped. It ain't very far into Ute land."

"What's the alternative?" Thornburgh asked and looked around at the serious faces of his officers.

"Halt 'em in the trap, but with all this drought, not any water there."

No one said anything. Tip paced up and down. He was the commanding officer; it was his decision to make. Somewhere out in the prairie grass a quail called and the breeze blew the golden aspen on the distant mountains. He wished he were with his brother sitting around that campfire, spinning hunting tales of good dogs and fine bourbon. He longed for his pretty wife. He must remember to order her a nice anniversary gift. Possibly, Lida would give a party. Maybe he would get Bobby and Olivia a setter puppy for Christmas. He wished he were sitting down to dinner with his family right now.

"Major?" Captain Payne cleared his throat politely.

Tip blinked and looked around, once more facing choices involving hundreds of soldiers. *Ours not to reason why . . .*

"Rankin, I suppose you're right," the Major said as his broad shoulders slumped. "I intend to keep my word about a small group parlaying with the Utes, but I can't leave my men deliberately stopped in a trap. We'll ride on to water."

Everyone nodded and looked at each other. It was the only logical choice, really. They could only hope the Utes didn't spot the moving column and misinterpret the army's action. If Major Thornburgh and a small peace party could just sit down with them, everything would be all right.

That decided, they rode on. It was beautiful but desolate country, the Major thought as he looked toward the east and old Sleepy Cat Mountain. It was only a couple of days until October brought autumn to the Western slope. Once winter laid its snows across the mountains, the prospectors would stay out of this country until spring, and that would calm the angry Utes. As to whether idealistic Nathan Meeker and his clanking threshing machine would ever convert these warrior Indians to farming, that was debatable, but it wasn't Tip Thornburgh's problem. He was only here to keep an Indian war from breaking out.

Tip held his breath riding through Coal Creek Canyon, but there was no sign of Indians. His troops had to have water so they did not halt. They were on Ute land now and the Utes had a treaty, so there were no legal grounds for soldiers to be here. Newspaper men would be pouring into the area as word of the Indian trouble spread, Tip thought as he rode, bridles jingling. Lida would be so proud if he stopped an Indian war, won a medal, or was mentioned in the paper.

More than that, it would vindicate Tip's father. A proud Tennessean opposed to slavery, the senior Thornburgh had been called a traitor to the South during the War and thrown into the ghastly Andersonville prison, where he died. No one ever thought about Southerners dying in that hellhole.

Captain Payne gestured. "Major Thornburgh, sir."

Tip looked where Captain Payne pointed. Mounted Utes rode along the rim of the bluff. They were on Ute land and the Utes had seen them. Now there was going to be trouble whether the army liked it or not!

TWENTY-FOUR

Wannie clung to Keso's waist as they galloped along with the Ute war party, still attempting to sort things out in her mind. She looked off to her left. Cleve glared back at her, evidently angry and jealous. She had been too easily dazzled by Cleve's sophistication and charm. What a shallow fool she had been!

When she finally got a moment alone with Keso, she was going to tell him how she had changed. How could she have been so blind to his devotion? She looked down at his ring on her finger. If they came through this alive and returned to Silver and Cherokee, she hoped Keso would build her a home up in their private valley. They would live happily for always with many children for Silver and Cherokee to spoil.

Right now, she had other worries. Around them, the Ute war party looked grim and angry as they galloped toward the northern boundary of the reservation. Would there be a confrontation with the soldiers? In spite of everything that had happened, Wannie couldn't help but feel sorry for the Indians. They seemed desperate, harried, and many of them looked ragged and hungry.

The riders topped a crest and reined in. Strung out in the valley between the buttes was a long blue line of cavalry and their supply wagons.

Next to her, Coyote reined in sharply. He looked over at Keso and shouted in English. "I told you white men lie! They promised to stop at our boundary!"

"This is an act of war!" another shouted. "Remember what happened to the Cheyenne at Sand Creek!"

Around her, Utes were stopping, swinging down from their horses, and reaching for rifles. Keso's stallion, Spirit, had half turned so that Wannie saw the scene below in an instant, the cavalry strung out riding along the narrow creek, the officers out in front, the sun reflecting off the shiny brass insignia on their uniforms.

Horses around her neighed and snorted, kicking up dust along the treeless bluff as the Utes dismounted, reaching for rifles.

"They see us, too!" a Ute warrior called in warning.

Below her, the cavalry seemed to pause in split second confusion. She wasn't sure who fired the first shot, the enraged Utes or the surprised soldiers, but abruptly rifle fire cracked and echoed through the hills.

Keso's big stallion whinnied and reared in the uproar. She almost slid off, but Keso reached down, and grabbed her wrist as she clutched his waist. She clung to Keso, feeling the tension in his body as he seemed to be trying to decide what to do. She heard a sound of fear and glanced over at Cleve, whose handsome face was as white as a dead frog's belly. He looked about wildly. In that instant, she almost seemed to smell Cleve's fear along with the scent of dust and sweating horses. Below them, retreating through a few straggly trees, was a major, the light glinting off his brass insignia and the pistol in his hand.

Next to Wannie, a brave cried out and clutched his chest and fell, moaning pitifully.

Keso craned his neck to look back at her. "These poor Utes are in for it now!"

The Utes were firing at the troops. All around them

was confusion, blood, and noise as the Utes scattered to take cover. Below them, the troops tried to retreat, gathering closer to their supply wagons.

She hung onto Keso, knowing he was trying to make a choice of loyalties. Neither group was wrong or right, but some would die today.

Coyote laughed aloud as he cocked his big fifty buffalo gun and took aim. "First the soldiers and then you, son of Ouray!"

Below them, she could see the handsome major, his pistol flashing in the sunlight as he tried to rally his troops. He was out ahead of his men now, urging them into a thin growth of willows that might protect them from the Utes, who had the advantage of the bluffs on both sides.

"No!" Keso shouted a protest, even as Coyote pulled the trigger. The major recoiled from the shot, struggling to stay in his saddle. Even from here, Wannie could see the bright blood in his dark hair.

Keso reached out and with a mighty blow, knocked the gun from Coyote's hand. Taken by surprise, the rifle tumbled from the Ute's grasp and fell down the rocky ledge. With an oath, Coyote scrambled after it.

Along the bluff, almost all the warriors were dismounted now, strung out and firing at the soldiers trapped below them. They were dying, too. In that moment, Wannie heard more screams of agony. Only the three outsiders were still mounted.

"Now, Brewster!" Keso shouted suddenly and dug his heels in Spirit's sides. The big stallion took off like a flash down the embankment, galloping past Coyote and toward the soldiers. Wannie held her breath and clung to his waist. Behind her, Cleve quirted Blue and galloped with them.

The trio was taking a terrible chance, Wannie thought as she buried her face against Keso's back and hung on. They were riding toward the soldiers' lines. Some of them were shooting at anything that moved, and Keso was dressed as a warrior.

"Stop them!" Coyote shouted behind them.

Bullets zinged past the galloping riders and ricocheted off the rocks as the Utes obeyed Coyote. Wannie tensed, expecting to feel a bullet in the back at any moment. Would she feel the bullet that killed her? From the front, she was protected by Keso's body as he rode boldly toward the soldiers' lines, yelling at them to hold their fire.

The distance seemed as long as forever and as short as a heartbeat, Wannie thought as the horses scrambled down the low bluff, sending rocks rolling. Old Blue and Spirit were caught between two opposing forces, both shooting at them as they galloped across barren, rocky ground.

She glanced back at Cleve. He was so terrified, he was crying and cursing, urging his mount on. They galloped past the fallen major, who lay with part of his head blown away, the shiny pistol still in his hand, his eyes open and staring into the blue autumn sky. He was so young and so handsome, Wannie thought as she stared down at him in horror as they galloped past his body.

"Hold your fire!" Keso shouted as they galloped through the scrub brush toward the confused soldiers. "For God's sake, hold your fire!" They rode into the midst of the soldiers with Keso reining in and dismounting, reaching up to lift Wannie down.

"Hold your fire!" he shouted again as Cleve galloped toward them on old Blue. "He's one of ours!"

Keso reached up for Wannie and she slid off into his arms. "You all right, honey?"

"I—I think so." She clung to his neck, shaking as she

suddenly realized the chance they had taken and the horrible sights she had seen.

"Good. Now get behind something and stay low— Coyote will be gunning for us in particular. I'll see what I can do to help."

The wounded captain looked pale enough to faint. "Who—who are you?" he demanded of Keso. "You're dressed like a Ute."

"I am Ute, but I'm also Keso Evans." Keso crouched low.

The other man was bleeding and in shock. " . . . Was there a man dismayed?" he mumbled. "Not though the soldiers knew someone had blundered. Theirs not to reason why, theirs but to do and die, into the Valley of Death—"

"Get hold of yourself, man!" Keso grabbed the dazed Captain and shook him back to reality.

"Who . . . who are you?"

"Keso Evans." He peered into the smudged, dazed face. "Some on the other side want me worse than you."

Cleve made it into the circle of soldiers and slid down the side of old Blue, sweat on his handsome face. He was shaking so badly, he couldn't stand. "Damned Indians! I hope you kill them all."

"It may be the other way around," the wounded officer said as he wiped cold sweat from his pale face. "I—I'm Captain Payne. Did you see Major Thornburgh out there anywhere?"

Keso nodded, his face grim. "He's dead. You're in command now, Captain. I'd suggest you circle your supply wagons—they'll try to take those. Tell your men to pile up the boxes and bales of blankets from those wagons, anything that will stop a bullet, and stack them in the empty spots."

Captain Payne waved his good arm. "You men heard him. We're going to be here awhile. Dig in!"

Wannie huddled closer to Keso. Cleve ignored her, collapsing in sobs behind a wagon. Around them, bullets sang and kicked up dust in the September afternoon. Here and there a man was hit and cried out. Some never knew what hit them.

Abruptly, Keso spotted her. "Wannie, I thought I told you to seek shelter."

"Oh, stop ordering me around!" Wannie answered. "I'm not going to hide like a frightened rabbit—these men need help. Come on, Cleve, you can—"

"No," he whimpered, "why should I risk my neck? Oh God, why is this happening to me? Don't these people know who I am?"

"No, and don't give a damn either," Keso snapped. "For once, act like a man, Brewster, and do something to help if for no other reason than it might save your neck."

That thought alone seemed to galvanize the young heir into action. He didn't stop whimpering, Wannie noted with disgust, but at least he was dragging boxes and bales around, helping to fortify the rough circle the soldiers had built.

They were trapped like rats, Wannie realized in horror as she looked around and saw the Utes were strung out on both sides of the narrow draw along the treeless, arid buttes. Many of the horses and the mules that pulled the wagons had been hit. The Utes were shooting at the horses deliberately, she thought, knowing that without horses, the soldiers could never manage to escape. Keso had led Spirit and Blue to safety partially shielded by a wagon.

On the distant bluff, she could just barely recognize Coyote's ugly face smiling at her as he loaded his rifle. She knew from his expression what he was thinking. In her mind, she saw the soldiers all dead and the Utes riding in. Coyote would claim her as his prize and she would be forced to submit to his lust. Taking her and killing Keso had to be the foremost thoughts on his mind.

Wannie took a deep breath and calmed herself. There were wounded and dying men on both sides of this battle. She couldn't do anything for the warriors, but maybe she could help the wounded around her. She must not think of anything else but what she could do to relieve their suffering. "Is there a doctor?"

The soldier nearest her nodded and pointed to a plump, older man. "Doctor's hurt, too, miss."

She crawled over to him. "How bad are you hurt?"

He paused in bandaging his own arm and smiled at her. "I must have died and gone to heaven. Otherwise, how would an angel appear to me?"

"I'll do what I can to help out, Doc," she shouted over the gunfire, screams, and snorting horses, "but I'm no angel and I don't know much about nursing the wounded." She tried to smile back, but she was quaking inside. She knew how to speak French and Latin, could recite poetry, and knew which fork to use at a formal banquet. At this moment, Wannie would have exchanged all that for the calm, efficient knowledge possessed by Keso, who was bringing order to the barricaded troops and encouraging the injured captain.

"You'll do, miss," Doc said as he finished wrapping his own arm. "Let me get my medical bag and some whiskey—we've got our hands full."

"Whiskey?"

"It's the only disinfectant I've got," he shouted back, "and besides, a dying man should have a little comfort."

"We've got a chance if we can hold out." She didn't know whether she was encouraging him or herself. Only Keso seemed to be calm, piling up boxes to stop bullets, reloading rifles, soothing panic-stricken men.

The old doctor didn't look as if he believed her, but he didn't say it. He took the first drink from the bottle and a little color returned to his face. "You're right, young lady. Can you tear up your petticoat for bandages?"

"Sure," Wannie said and smiled with an assurance she didn't feel. "All we've got to do is hold out—help will come."

"Who says so?" Cleve's voice rose in a hysterical shriek near them as he paused. "Who's going to help and from where? I should have stayed with the Utes, I should have tried to make a run for it, I should—"

"You should shut up and get ahold of yourself," Keso shouted at him. "For God's sake, Brewster, if you're too shaky to shoot, keep the other men supplied with ammunition!"

Instead, Cleve cowered down behind some sturdy boxes, sobbing. How could she ever have thought he was so wonderful because he knew the latest dance steps and what to do with a finger bowl? What a silly little fool she'd been!

Too late, she saw Keso as he was: a man among men. All Keso knew was how to survive in a hostile environment, look after her, provide her with food, save her life. Wannie made a private vow to herself as she tore up her petticoat and watched Keso in action. If she survived this ordeal, she would spend the rest of her life making it up to him!

In the meantime, she and Doc worked in a dirty, smelly hell. Around them, men cried out and slumped to the ground, horses fell as bullets hit them. The noise of gunfire and the acrid odor of gunpowder mingled with the scent of blood and sweat. The reflection of sunlight off the brass buttons and rifles, lance tips and shiny butcher knives almost blinded her. Oh, if she could only wake up and discover this had all been a terrible nightmare!

She helped Doc bind a soldier's wounds. " . . . Water," he muttered, "drink of water."

Wannie crawled across the circle toward a water barrel. Only when she saw the mud around the barrel did she realize a bullet had pierced it. Most of the water had run out. She crawled to another and was relieved to find it full. So many men and horses, she thought, and how few barrels of water?

Her own lips were dry and cracked. She had a sudden vision of herself naked and diving into the cold water of the stream near the Evanses' cabin. She would swim and drink all the cold, clear water she wanted. Keso would be with her and they would laugh and dive like two otters and then make love on the bank.

A shot ricocheted off a wagon wheel near her, jerking her back to hard reality: there might not be enough water to last all these men and horses more than a day. She got a dipperful, swallowed hard, and ignored the temptation to drink it herself.

Keso crawled across the circle, shielding her with his body. "What are you doing?"

"Getting water for a wounded man," she shouted over the gunfire. "Keso, this water isn't going to last very long."

He looked around as if counting men. "You're right. If we don't get reinforcements soon, we could be in big trouble. I'll alert the captain to start some kind of rationing."

Wannie looked out across the dry prairie grass, blowing like a brown sea in the wind. "Isn't there a creek out there?"

"Milk Creek," Keso nodded, "not much more than a trickle and it's a couple of hundred yards away. Any man who tries it will be a sitting duck."

"Oh, Keso, I love you so much and now I'll never get a chance to show you." She was choking back tears.

He reached out and touched her cheek tenderly. "Honey, you don't know how long I've waited to hear you say that. I was afraid you were regretting last night."

"Regret?" Her eyes widened with wonder. "It was the most wonderful night of my life."

"Good. We'll get married and I'm going to build you a house up at Waanibe with a swing for our kids."

"And a yard full of wildflowers?"

"Anything you want, honey."

Cleve joined them just then and jerked the dipper from Wannie, gulping the water down and spilling half of it.

"Cleve, no!" Wannie protested.

Keso grabbed him by the throat. "You bastard! That was for a wounded man!"

"I don't give a damn about common soldiers," Cleve said as he shook Keso's hand off and wiped his wet mouth. "Are you telling me we'll run out of water?"

"We've got enough for a day or two, maybe," Keso muttered. "I'll have Captain Payne set up a rationing system. From now on, only the wounded and Wannie get water."

"I can do without—I'm not wounded." She gave Cleve a sneer. "You're rotten and selfish. Why didn't I see that?"

"Because you're just like me," Cleve snapped.

"Not anymore," Wannie said, "thank God, not any more."

Keso grinned. "You know, brat, you're growing up. You may make me a half-decent wife after all."

"Egad, what fools you two are!" Cleve snorted. "None of us are going to get out of this alive. We're pinned down here."

"Oh, shut up, Cleve," Wannie said and jerked the dipper out of his hand, "I'm sick of your whining." She refilled the dipper, her own mouth so dry it was a terrible temptation to drink it herself, but she dared not. She crawled back to where Doc was working and held the dipper to the wounded man's lips. "Here you are, soldier, water. Pretty soon, there'll be a relief column and you'll be in the infirmary with lots of hot chicken soup and soft pillows."

His grimy hand reached out to steady the dipper. "Thank you, miss. You—you drop out of the sky?"

"Not hardly!" Wannie tried to keep up a cheery front as she bandaged him.

"A lady's petticoat," the soldier said and smiled, "close as I'll ever get to a lady."

She leaned over and kissed his smudged forehead. "I'll bet there's a girl waiting for you somewhere."

"Mary. Her name's Mary." The man smiled weakly, gasping a little as he looked up at Doc. "Help coming?"

Doc hesitated and nodded. "Sure, soldier, now you just lie still and take it easy."

" . . . Need to help my bunkies," he whispered, "where are O'Reilly and Matson, Doc?"

She followed Doc's gaze to where two soldiers lay sprawled and bloody against the barricades.

"Hey, they're doing fine without you, soldier," Doc lied, "they don't need your help now. You close your eyes and rest awhile and this young lady will sit here and hold your hand, won't you, miss?"

"Of course." She looked up at Doc and he sighed and shook his head. This soldier was dying. She wanted to cry, but knew she must not. Doc crawled away and she took the soldier's hand. "Hold on, soldier, there'll be help coming."

He smiled at her, smudges of powder and bright

blood on his pale face. "Wait 'til Mary hears I was bandaged with a lady's petticoat."

Wannie forced herself to laugh and winked at him.
"You think she'll be jealous?"

"We're gettin' married when I get back," he gasped,
"I see you're wearing a weddin' ring."

"Yes." She squeezed his hand, listening to the gunfire
and the shouts and screams and curses around them.
"Think about your girl, soldier, think about your wedding."

His eyes flickered closed and he smiled. She wondered about the girl and what she was doing at this very
minute while her man lay dying in a desolate valley at
a place nobody ever heard of.

"I—I need to go with my bunkies," he murmured
and closed his eyes. "We always did things together,
rode with the Major long time . . ."

"They're waiting for you, soldier," she promised and
ran a gentle hand over his forehead, "I promise they're
waiting for you."

"Good boys," he whispered so softly she had to lean
closer to hear him, "they're comin' to my weddin'."

Wannie held his hand, her vision blurred with tears.

"Mary?" he whispered, "Is that you, Mary?"

"Yes, I—I'm here." She fought to keep her hot tears
from dripping on his face as she leaned over and kissed
his lips. He smiled and then his fingers went limp in
hers.

"Soldier?" she leaned close to his face. "Soldier, can
you hear me?"

The slight smile remained on his lips, but he was gone
to join his buddies.

For just a moment, Wannie buried her face in her
hands and shook. She didn't have time to cry for one
dead soldier when there were so many others who

needed her help. She swallowed hard and pulled the
blanket up over the face that looked so peaceful now.

Wannie got up and hurried to help Doc with the next
one. "It doesn't seem right," she said. "These poor devils came out here under orders and they don't even
know what this is all about."

Doc nodded as he tore away the bloody uniform of
an unconscious man. "There's Utes out there dying,
too, remember, and there'll be Indian women and children wailing in sorrow tonight. A clash of cultures and
a lot of misunderstanding, and men die on both sides."

That was true, Wannie thought. The Utes were only
trying to defend their land and they were dying out
there on those buttes, too, just as soldiers were dying
here.

They finished aiding three more wounded men. She
looked around for Keso, who had led a group of soldiers
to dig a pit out in the middle of the circle of wagons
and barricades. They were moving the wounded into
that pit for protection and also starting to bury the
dead. Cleve had crawled under a wagon for protection
and lay there shaking and cursing.

It was going to be a long day, Wannie thought wearily. She took a deep breath and smelled smoke. Keso
swore suddenly and she crawled to him. "Keso, what
is it?"

He nodded toward the prairie past the wagons. Yellow
and red tongues of flame licked through the dry grass,
aided by a brisk autumn wind. "The Utes have set fire
to the grass—they're going to try to burn us out!"

"Oh, Keso," she cried and put her hand over her
mouth to keep from screaming at the thought of being
burned alive, "what'll we do? We haven't enough water
to—"

"We'll start a backfire. If I can burn off the area
around the wagons and barricades, their fire won't have

anything to feed on. Stay in a safe place, honey." Keso kissed her forehead and ran, crouching low.

"Oh, Keso, be careful!" she called after him, knowing he was intent not on his own safety, but that of all the others.

She watched, her heart in her mouth as Keso and a couple of volunteers crawled out and set backfires, then stood by with wet burlap sacks should the fires blow back toward the wagons. A few embers blew up on the canvas wagon covers, but Wannie and the others grabbed damp burlap bags and climbed up to fight the fires. Some of the wagons were damaged, but they saved most of the supplies. She took a good look at Meeker's threshing machine. It sat there on its wagon like a silent steel monster, a plate on the side claiming Brewster Industries. It all seemed so funny somehow. She began to laugh.

"Egad, Wannie, are you going insane?" Cleve said as he joined her. His handsome face was smudged and there were streaks of soot in his hair. The perfect gentleman.

"No, I'm just tired, Cleve," she replied and leaned back against the wagon wheel and sighed. "It seemed funny, somehow, to see this big threshing machine and think of all these pots and pans from your father's company headed for the agency."

"I'm sure Father collected his money in advance, so we won't take a loss."

She laughed even harder. "I wonder what dear Daddy would say if he knew half those Utes out there trying to kill us are armed with butcher knives from Brewster Industries?"

"I don't see anything funny about that. The damned Indians didn't pay for them."

Wannie wiped her eyes. "Maybe it's not funny, Cleve, just ironic."

He dismissed her with a shrug. "Crazy, that's what you are. Well, I never thought you were worthy of me anyway, not after you told me about your past."

"My past?" She stared at him, thunderstruck. "You'd hold my parentage against me?"

"Why are you surprised?" He rubbed his cleft chin. "After all, I come from generations of aristocrats and you're from common folk, after all."

"You're such a snob, Cleve, I can't imagine why I ever thought you were a good catch."

"Oh, shut up," he snarled, looking around the circle. "Let's figure out how to escape from this death trap."

Wannie shrugged. "Keso will figure out something."

"Keso! Keso! I'm sick and tired of hearing about that damned savage!"

She slapped him then, slapped him so hard, his teeth rattled.

"All right, bitch," he sneered, "I was going to save you, too, so you could replace Maureen as my mistress, but now I see you're not worth it."

"Maureen? You're a bigger cad than I thought, Cleve."

"Every man I know keeps a mistress," he said and dismissed her, "wives expect it."

"I don't think so. Cherokee wouldn't, Keso wouldn't."

"Injuns. They don't even know which fork to use." Cleve turned and walked away, crawling back under the wagon.

Cleve was cowardly, she thought, and only bluffing about a plan. She crept over to Keso. "How goes it?"

He pointed out toward the dying flames slowly moving across the grass. "Our backfire did the trick—their fire won't have enough fuel. In the meantime, we've got an added plus Coyote didn't think of: burning all that brush has done away with protective cover. Their warriors can't sneak up on us by crawling through that tall grass."

"It's nice that something's finally going our way."

He put his arm around her shoulders protectively. "I reckon I haven't done a very good job of looking after you, honey. I'm sorry."

"What are you talking about?" She patted his hand on her shoulder absently. "You've spent your whole life looking after me and I hope you'll spend the rest of our lives doing the same." She paused, biting her lip.

"Honey, what's wrong?"

"Cleve is plotting something. He wants to get away."

Keso laughed. "Don't we all? Even the Utes didn't mean for it to turn into a big fight with the soldiers—it just happened. Poor devils, they've sealed their fate now."

Wannie sighed. "And ours, too, maybe. I'll keep an eye on Cleve—he's liable to do something reckless and he doesn't care what happens to the rest of us."

"He never did, Wannie," Keso said softly. "I don't know why you couldn't see that."

"False values," she said sheepishly. "I hope you'll forgive me."

"Nothing to forgive," he said and hugged her to him a long moment. Then his voice shook, "I love you, brat, and I always have. I'll get you out of here, I promise."

She pulled away from him, wanting to stay in his arms but knowing he was needed to defend this besieged place. "I'd better go help Doc."

"How's Captain Payne?"

"We bandaged him the best we could. He's weak, but still in command. Lieutenant Cherry's helping him."

"Tough luck, the major being about the first one killed." He was looking at the distant creek. "Sooner or later, someone will have to go for water."

"No, Keso!" She put her hands on his shoulders and looked into his eyes. "The Utes burned off all the cover between us and that creek. A bug couldn't crawl across that ground without being seen."

In answer, he turned and looked up at the Utes' position among the rocks along the buttes. Here and there, the sun reflected off a rifle barrel, a lance, or a knife.

"It's not something I'll look forward to," he admitted over the gunfire. "Maybe we'll get some reinforcements before we run out of water—or maybe Ouray will get here and stop this."

"If that old warrior made it to tell him."

Keso frowned suddenly.

"Oh, Keso, what is it?"

He shook his head. "Nothing."

"I know you better than that. You never were a very good liar. By the way, I—I know about Maureen, that maid. Cleve let it slip."

"I'm sorry, Wannie."

"No, *I'm* sorry," she admitted, "I should have known you wouldn't lie to me. I was just so dazzled by him, I didn't want to see him as he really is."

"All right, I might as well tell you," Keso said and rubbed his chin, "there won't be any reinforcements unless we get a messenger out or unless Meeker sends for help."

"Do you suppose he even knows we're under attack here?"

Keso shook his head, his face grim. "The agency is about twenty-five miles from here, so I doubt if they'll hear the gunfire. They're probably going about their daily chores without even realizing the Utes are finally on the warpath. The women and children at the White River Agency are in danger and Meeker won't even know it!"

* * *

The Ute galloped into the agency where Meeker turned and frowned. The Indians came running to meet the rider and gathered around him. More waste of time. Meeker frowned again as he looked out at the half-plowed valley where he had had such big hopes of planting crops. The fine plow from Brewster Industries still lay out there, rusting. If he couldn't get these lazy savages to plow up their racetrack and plant crops, there would be no use for the shiny new threshing machine that should even now be unloaded at the Rawlins depot and on its way to him.

What were those Utes talking about so excitedly? Meeker looked around at the scene. Only white men working, of course. Shadrach Price and Frank Dresser were in a wagon, throwing dirt up on top of the agency roof to stop leaks, while Arthur Thompson was on the roof spreading the dirt.

Nathan Meeker had finally given up hope of teaching these lazy, simple savages to live like white men. It wasn't that *he* had failed; *they* had failed. Why were the Utes so stubborn and determined to cling to their old ways? If they would just let Nathan teach them how to work like white men, this land could be turned into a productive farm and Washington would be so happy with him.

The Indians had stopped talking to the messenger and were staring at him. He had a sudden premonition of danger. There were three white women at the agency—his wife, Arvilla, his twenty-year-old daughter, Josie, and Flora Price and her two small children. All the guns on the place were locked up. If he could only get there before . . .

Josie Meeker had heard the noise and excitement of the rider galloping in, the murmur of excited talk

through the open window. September 29, she thought—
was there some celebration or big happening she was
unaware of?

Curious, she went to the window to look. Daddy had
said he'd sent for troops to protect the agency and cool
things down. Maybe they had been seen. It would be
nice if there were a handsome soldier for her. All Josie
ever saw were Indians and she was uneasy about that
young warrior, Persune, who seemed so smitten with
her.

She wasn't quite sure what happened next. One minute, the Indians were talking among themselves, their
voices fraught with anger; the next minute, she heard
rifle fire. In disbelief, she stared as Arthur Thompson
tumbled from the roof. It had finally happened. Shrieking, she made a frantic dash to find her mother, Flora,
and the children.

The autumn sun stared down as the Utes began chasing down the white men and killing them. A few of the
whites managed to get guns and fight back, but without
success. Others fled like terrified deer.

The women went out a back window, running for the
brush, but the Utes spotted them, chased them down,
and caught them. Then the warriors began to set fire
to the buildings, wanting to wipe out every symbol of
the hated white man and his civilization.

When the agency Utes rode out, they had all three
women and the two small children captives. Behind
them, the flames roared through the agency buildings,
but no white employees ran to fight the fire. All the
white men lay dead sprawled across the despised plowed
field where the Utes loved to race their ponies.

For Nathan Meeker, there was no punishment bad
enough for the indignities they had endured under
this hard taskmaster who never respected or understood them. The Utes killed him, stripped him naked,

and dragged his body up and down that plowed field with a log chain. As a final defiant gesture and to keep his scolding voice still forever, they rammed a wooden stave from an agency flour barrel down his throat.

TWENTY-FIVE

It was late afternoon and the shooting had slacked off. The Utes knew they had the white soldiers trapped, Wannie thought wearily and pushed her dark hair back from her face as she helped Doc tend the wounded.

Keso came over to join her. "How are things going?"

"We've got too many wounded and we're running low on supplies," she said.

Keso chewed his lip. "We can't escape and they know it. If we can just hold out, maybe Ouray will get here."

Wannie glanced up and stared at the horizon to the south. "What's that?"

Keso and Doc both turned to look where she pointed. For a long moment, she almost thought she had imagined it. Then she saw it again—the faint bit of smoke drifting upward into the bright blue sky.

"Smoke," Keso said and his dark face was as grim as his voice, "they must be burning the agency."

An icy hand of fear seemed to clutch her heart. "Maybe it's just a forest fire, maybe it's—"

"There's no mistake, Wannie," Keso said and shook his head, "that's about where it'd be. Nothing else that size."

Wannie put her hand over her mouth for a long moment, watching the smoke grow bigger and darker. "Those people never had a chance."

"They brought it on themselves," Keso said and shrugged. "Meeker was determined to turn Utes into white men and he pushed them too far."

Doc sat back on his haunches and lit his pipe. "Poor devils. Now they all lose, red and white."

"That's right, Doc," Keso nodded and checked his rifle. "This is all the excuse politicians will need for what they've been wanting to do for years—take the Utes' land."

Cleve joined them. "Don't be a silly sentimentalist. The whites will put the land to good use, mine its metals, grow crops, bring in settlers, build towns."

"I suppose," Wannie said, "you'd consider that progress?"

Cleve brightened. "Just think how many plows and tools they're going to need. Why, Brewster Industries will make a fortune!"

She tried to grab Keso's arm but she wasn't fast enough. Keso hit Cleve full in the mouth and they went down in a tangle of arms and legs.

Captain Payne yelled at two privates and they rushed over and separated the pair. "If you two want to fight," the captain shouted, "we've got hundreds of hostiles out there!"

"He's right," Keso said and backed off. "Brewster, we've got to get out of this alive first, then I want the pure pleasure of beating you senseless."

Cleve wiped the blood from his mouth, staring at it in distaste. "You know we aren't going to leave here— the Utes are going to kill us all."

"Shut up, you yellow-bellied coward," Keso snapped. "You'd trade us all for your own safety, wouldn't you? You don't even care about Wannie."

"Wannie?" Cleve said. "You're the one sullying her reputation, staying with her all night—"

"Oh, Cleve, stop it!" Wannie almost screamed at him.

"You're only worried about my precious reputation, what people would say, whether you might get used goods—"

"Now, Wannie," Cleve said and made a soothing gesture, "I know in my heart that nothing happened, that you're still a pure—"

"Well, think again, you shallow, sissy dude!" She got right up in his face, "I made love to Keso—do you hear me? We made love all night!"

"Wannie, no," Keso said and put his hand out to stop her, but she shook him off.

"It's true," Wannie said, "and don't try to protect me. I don't give a damn what Cleve thinks!"

Cleve's face went ashen. Whether it was from hearing a lady use profanity or her bold admission, she couldn't tell and she didn't care. "I—I thought you were a high-born lady, worthy of being the mother of future Brewsters, but you're just a—"

"Watch your mouth, Brewster," Keso warned through clenched teeth, "I'd hate to kill you when we may need you to fight Utes."

"Don't, Keso, he's not worth it," Wannie said softly.

"You're right, honey."

"I'm the one who's had my eyes opened," Cleve almost spat the words out, "you two are just alike—as uncivilized and savage as this damned country you like so well."

Wannie grinned at Keso. "I'd call that a compliment, wouldn't you?"

Keso nodded and Cleve made a gesture as if to wash his hands of them both, then crawled under a wagon and turned his back.

Keso's rugged face turned serious as he looked up at the sun, low on the horizon. "The Utes are resting and waiting. Unless Ouray finally gets here, they've got lots of opportunities to pick us off one at a time. Wannie, how are you and Doc on supplies?"

"As well as can be expected—I'm cooking what I've got now. We'll run out of water before we run out of food."

"It's gonna be a long night," Keso said.

Wannie did the best she could with the food as dusk settled in. Cleve was waiting with a tin plate, but she ignored him and fed the wounded first. Following Keso's suggestions, Captain Payne and Lieutenant Cherry had set up strict rationing. Cleve argued that he hadn't gotten his fair share and threatened to report the officers to the important brass in Washington who knew his father.

Young Lieutenant Cherry spat to one side. "Would you believe, Brewster, that I don't even care? We may not come out of this alive anyhow."

Wannie noted that Keso only took a few sips of his water, then brought it over to her. "Here, brat, I'm not thirsty."

Cleve looked his way. "Since you're helping the captain, you probably got twice as much as the rest of us."

"Brewster," Keso said, his voice cold, "I'd hit you, but then I'd spill the water. Here, Wannie, take this."

Oh, it looked so good. She licked her dry lips. "I—I'm not thirsty."

"Well, if you aren't, I am," Cleve said and reached for it.

She pulled it away. "I'll share it among the wounded, you spoiled bastard."

"Wannie!" His pale eyes went round with shock. "I don't know what's come over you in the last few days unless you're losing your sanity. What would Mother say about a graduate of Miss Priddy's Academy using that word?"

"Would you believe I don't care? I also don't care

what Alexa or any of your social set thinks." She crawled away to share the extra water among several of the most severely wounded, then stopped to talk to the weary doctor. "Doc, is there anything else I can do to help?"

The old man shook his head. "Afraid not. Settle in and get some sleep—it's going to be a long night."

This might be her last night on earth, Wannie thought as she returned to Keso. It was dark now and silence descended over the land and across the treeless, desolate buttes. She could see the faint glow of camp-fires along the horizon as the Utes settled in, too. Time was on their side and they must know it. "Doc says we need to get some rest."

"*You* get some rest, honey." He pulled her against his chest and kissed her forehead. "I've got to stand watch right now, but I'll be back in a couple of hours."

"I'm looking forward to it."

She lay there on a blanket under a wagon, out of the sight of most of the men, staring at her ring and think-ing about marriage and children. What would they name them? Maybe Silver and Cherokee would have some good ideas. Their children could swing in that old swing where Keso used to push her and they'd pick flowers and picnic. In the evenings, they'd sit out on the porch like any old married couple, except they'd have the magnificent view from Waanibe. Every night, they'd go to bed and make love until they were both exhausted and then they'd sleep in each other's arms.

From here, she could see much of the camp. Half the men were on watch around the barricades, rifles at the ready. The other half slept, ready to take the second watch. Her thoughts returned to Keso and she smiled, remembering last night. She wanted him to make love to her again like that. If this were going to be their very last night on earth, she couldn't think of a better way to spend it than in his arms. She dropped off to sleep and was awakened by Keso crawling under the blanket beside her.

"My watch is over," he sighed, "I don't think the Utes are night fighters. A lot of the tribes fear that if they're killed in the darkness, their spirits can't find their way to spirit land."

"I missed you," she murmured and scooted closer to him, laying her head on his broad shoulder.

"I missed you, too," he said and kissed her eyelids. "All the time I was staring up at those bluffs and wondering if Coyote was up there, staring back at me, I thought about last night and how I'd like to be under this blanket with you in my arms."

"So now you are." She snuggled even closer.

"I hope you don't regret that, Wannie," he said as he stroked her hair away from her face. "You've lost your chance at high society and all that goes with it."

"You don't go with it, and that's what I really want." She put her hands behind his head, pulled his face down to her, and kissed him. It was a lingering, warm kiss that made her heart quicken and her pulse race. Yes, it was as good as she remembered it. "And to think, all these years, I've missed this, with you giving me little pecks on the forehead or the tip of my nose," she complained.

"You don't know how many times I've dreamed of doing just what I'm doing now," he whispered, "holding you close and kissing you like this." He kissed her again and again.

His hand went to cover her breast as his tongue slipped between her lips.

She reached up and unbuttoned her bodice so his bare hand was on her naked flesh. "Make love to me. Now that I've had you, I can't get enough."

"I was hoping you'd say that." He tousled her long hair and then covered her breast with his hand, massaging it as her nipple hardened.

He kissed her deeply, gently, as if he wanted to pack all the love he felt for her in one more moment of love-making, knowing that for them, tomorrow might be their last day of life.

She answered his ardor with her own, thinking of how much time they had lost before she realized he was her true love. Knowing this might be the last time they'd be locked in each other's embrace made the lovemaking even sweeter. So little time, she thought, until dawn and probably the final Ute assault. She would not think about tomorrow, she would hold him close to her heart, kiss him, and comfort him. She was afraid to die, but she needn't think of that at this moment. Here in the cool, clear autumn night, time stood still for a moment.

"How long will you love me?" he asked and she kissed him and held up her hand so that the starlight reflected on the ring and no words were needed. *Always. For always.*

Finally, they slept, locked in each other's embrace. She was safe in Keso's arms, she knew, and she dreamed of spending the rest of her life sleeping in her lover's arms while outside their snug cabin, the singing winds made the porch swing creak.

She smiled at the thought and came suddenly awake, realizing it was still the middle of the night. She looked around, wondering what had awakened her.

Keso still slept, exhausted beside her. The camp was quiet, many men asleep at their posts along the barricade. She'd better see about the wounded.

Wannie rolled out from under the wagon, moving quietly as not to awaken her lover. In the moonlight, the harsh worries were gone, his bronze face smooth and handsome and at peace. She wanted to crawl back in next to him, kiss him and hold him close, but tomorrow would be a long day and he would need this rest.

Where was Cleve? She began to look around, then realized he was not manning a barricade. A horse snorted near the water barrel. There were a few horses left besides Blue; so many had been caught in the crossfire and killed. Without horses, they were trapped here. Sooner or later, Captain Payne might try to send out a messenger, but he'd be sending him to almost certain death. Wannie gritted her teeth at the thought, knowing courageous Keso most certainly would be the volunteer. She didn't even want to think about that.

What was that over in the darkness? Someone saddling up the best horse they had left besides Spirit, a bright pinto with unusual markings. In the moonlight, she suddenly recognized the man. "Cleve? Where are you going?"

"Shut up and come with me," he whispered. "This may be our one chance to get away."

"You can't do this," she protested, "they'll need those horses—"

"I'm not going to stay here and die like a cornered rat. I'm a Brewster—let the common men die!"

She realized then that he had two canteens over his shoulder. "You stole water when there's not even enough for all the wounded!"

She grabbed his arm to stop him, but he shook her off and swung up on the horse. The moonlight glinted on the pistol in his belt.

Behind her, she heard running footsteps and then Keso pushed past her, grabbing at Cleve's stirrup as the horse reared and whinnied. "You yellow coward, stop!"

Even as the camp began to come awake, Cleve pulled his pistol and fired. Keso cried out and let go of the stirrup, grabbing at his wounded shoulder.

"Cleve, no!" she screamed, but he paid her no heed

as he put spurs to the horse and took off across the circle. The spotted horse was moving at a full gallop as he reached the barricade. Any other man would have tumbled from the horse, Wannie thought, but the young aristocrat had had all that practice jumping hedges and walls at fox hunts. Cleve leaned into the jump—and the horse cleared the barricade and came down running on the other side.

All the soldiers were awake now, shouting questions. She got one last glimpse of Cleve galloping across the prairie, the moonlight reflecting on the loud paint horse and Cleve's fine yellow hair, and then he was swallowed up by the night.

"Doc, come quick!" She fell down beside Keso, taking him in her arms. His bright blood ran down his shoulder and smeared her dress.

"He got away," Keso muttered as he tried to get up, "the rotten bastard got away!"

"Dearest, lie still, you can't do anything about Cleve." She held him down as the doctor, Captain Payne, and Lieutenant Cherry joined them. Quickly, she explained what had happened as Doc tried to stop the flow of blood.

Captain Payne cursed under his breath. "Damn that spoiled dandy." He looked at Wannie hopefully. "You don't suppose he's gone for help?"

She was embarrassed and ashamed for Cleve. "No," she said and shook her head, "I think the only reason he asked me to go with him was to keep me from raising the alarm."

Captain Payne sighed. I was just about to ask for volunteers to get a message through."

"I—I'll go," Keso muttered and tried to get up.

Doc held him down and poured whiskey on the wound, then began to bind it as Keso moaned despite biting his lip. "You young whippersnapper, you aren't going anyplace. Shot like this, you'd fall out of the saddle."

"Captain," Joe Rankin said and rubbed his grizzled chin, "I'd be willin' to try it, but it's a powerful long way back to Fort Steele."

"Take my horse," Keso whispered, his face pale and beaded with sweat. "Cleve was afraid of him, but Spirit will get you there if you're a good enough rider to stay on."

"I can ride anything on four legs," Joe said.

The captain scratched his head. "Okay, then . . ." He let his voice trail off, but they all knew what he was thinking; the chances of getting through Ute lines were slim, and even if he did, by the time he finally brought help, it might be too late for this doomed garrison.

Lieutenant Cherry said, "Captain Dodge and his black buffalo soldiers are over at Middle Park—that's not so many miles from here. They've been on alert, expecting trouble at the Ute Agency. Maybe we can get a message through to them."

"We don't have another horse except old Blue, and he'd never make it," Keso muttered. "You'd never get there on foot. You might as well stay here and help us man the barricades and hope Rankin gets to Fort Steele. There's a slight possibility that Meeker got a message out to Captain Dodge before the agency burned."

Everyone nodded, their faces grim.

Keso was right, Wannie thought. Unless they got lucky, they were all going to die here, caught like rats in a trap.

Doc was bandaging Keso's arm. "You'll be all right, if you'll take it easy—"

"Easy, hell!" Keso struggled to sit up. "Patch me up the best you can, Doc—we'll have a fight on our hands tomorrow."

Wannie held him close and wiped the sweat from his

dear face. "You'll lie here at least a couple of hours. You'll need your strength once the sun comes up."

Her argument made sense and he relaxed while she held him tight, blinking back tears. They might all die tomorrow, but tonight he was hers to hold.

The captain gave Joe Rankin some encouraging words and a pat on the arm. "Remember we're depending on you to bring help, but for God's sake, don't let the Utes take you alive!" He glanced over at Wannie and didn't continue, but she knew what he was hinting at. As furious and betrayed as the Utes felt, there was no telling what they would do to a prisoner.

Spirit danced around, Joe Rankin hanging on. "You're right, Keso," he called, "this is one helluva horse!"

"I want him back when this is over, you hear?" Keso watched the volunteer, anxiety in his rugged face. No one could ride as well or as fast as Keso, but he was too wounded to go.

A soldier hurried to move a barricade so the black horse could slip out quietly, then put it back behind Spirit as he cantered away. Wannie ran to the barricades to watch as they faded into the night, riding a different direction than the route Cleve had taken. Long after he was gone, she could hear the echo of Spirit's hoofbeats.

Her heart full of fear and hope, she said a little prayer and returned to Keso. "Haven't heard any shots yet, so they may have slipped by the Utes."

Around them, men seemed to be holding their breath, listening. If the Utes got the messenger, this group was doomed. Even if the scout got through, it would be days before help would arrive. Wannie looked around, wondering if there was enough ammunition and able men to keep the Utes at bay that long.

Keso must have read her thoughts. "You go help Doc,

honey," he said, "I'll be all right and ready to handle a rifle after a couple hours rest."

She nodded and went to assist Doc with the wounded men. At least keeping busy kept her mind off what would happen to them if they were taken alive.

Cleve galloped through the night. The bright pinto was soon lathered and blowing. He resisted the urge to take his quirt to the tired horse—not because he was kind, but because he knew the gelding's strength was low and he might need to make a dash for it if he ran across hostiles.

He wasn't sure where he was going, or even what direction; he only knew he wanted to get as far away from the doomed soldiers as possible. The moon came out, lighting up the prairie and almost spotlighting him and the paint horse as they rode, but there was nothing he could do about that except keep riding. There was little cover out here in these dry, rolling buttes.

So far, so good. He smirked at the thought that the soldiers might think he was going for help. He didn't care about common soldiers—why should he bother? For an instant, he thought about Wannie. It was a shame a beauty like that one should finally be used to slake warriors' lust, but it couldn't be helped. She'd chosen Keso rather than Cleve, so let her die with that primitive savage when the Utes overran the camp.

The paint horse was lathered and blowing as Cleve worried about riding through the Utes' lines. In another couple of miles, Cleve would be safely away from the danger and he could rest his horse and take a good long drink of water. He reached to make sure the canteens still hung from his saddlehorn. Wannie had thought it terrible of him to steal from the wounded's rations, but his life was worth more than those common soldiers.

Riding up out of a ravine ahead of him, the Utes seemed to rise out of the ground. In sheer panic, Cleve hauled back on the reins and fired wildly. His second shot took an old man from his horse. Which way to go? What to do? He paused, the pistol in his hand, looking about. The Utes were easy to spot, the moonlight reflecting off the shiny steel butcher knives in their waist bands. Civilization was coming to the savages through Brewster Industries. Daddy would be so proud.

There were too many of them encircling him. Cleve fired again and missed. His next shot hit a younger Ute in the chest. The man moaned and fell. Which way to go? Could he make it through their line? Cleve tried to rein his horse around the growing circle of savages, but at that moment, one of them shot the pistol from his hand and now they closed in around him like wolves ready to make a kill.

His heart pounded so loudly, Cleve was certain they could hear it. He swallowed hard, thinking it would not do to show fear and vomit up his guts before them.

The big ugly one, Coyote, sat his horse, grinning. Cleve panicked and tried to dash between two mounted warriors, but the paint horse balked, weary and confused.

Coyote barked an order and two warriors ran up and jerked Cleve from his horse, fighting and screaming.

He was so terrified he wet himself, but he no longer cared about anything but his life. The Utes seemed to think it was funny; they were laughing, hooting, and jabbing at him with the butts of their lances.

Cleve groveled on the ground. "Please, I'll do anything, only don't hurt me!"

The ugly one dismounted, strode over, and gave him a kick.

"Please," Cleve grabbed him by the ankles, cowering before him. "The girl. You want the girl? She's still in the soldiers' camp. I'll help you get her."

Coyote stood over him. "You ride to bring help for the soldiers?"

"What? No, I ride to save myself," Cleve blubbered, "I don't care about the soldiers. I don't care if you kill them all."

"Much coward!" Coyote sneered. Someone in the crowd translated the exchange and the warriors laughed.

Too late, Cleve remembered that Indians valued bravery. The fact that he cared nothing for his comrades or the girl, cared nothing for anything but his own life, would make them scorn him.

There was one thing that everyone cared about, Cleve thought as he looked up at the hostile ring of faces. Everyone cared about gold, didn't they?

"My—my father is rich—he'll pay!" Cleve saw the reflection on the big knives in their waistbands. "See? My father makes those—he's rich, very rich."

Coyote put his hand on the butt of the knife and grinned, showing ugly teeth. "He make farm machinery, too?"

"Oh, yes! He's much important, makes plows, combines, knives, everything."

A murmur ran through the crowd and Coyote grinned. This encouraged Cleve. Money, he thought, they understood wealth and power. "My father is rich," he said again, "but he'll only pay if you do not harm one hair of my head. Do you understand?"

Coyote nodded and someone in the crowd translated for the others. Coyote took the knife from his belt, turning it over and over in his hands, the moonlight reflecting off it. "We understand. I give you my word, we will not harm one hair on your head."

Cleve let out a great sigh of relief as he stumbled to his feet. He was safe. He was going to be all right, thanks to Daddy. Those trapped back there at Milk Creek were going to die, but what did he care? "I was afraid . . . never mind. I'm going to be fine now."

Coyote said something in his language and abruptly, warriors grabbed Cleve.

He shouted a protest. "You said you wouldn't harm a hair—"

"And we won't," Coyote grinned. "Like white men, we are learning to be clever with words. We did not say what we would do with your body." He looked down at the big knife in his hand as the others drew theirs slowly from their waistbands. "We. are going to see how good your father's knives are and how much we can cut you and yet keep you alive. We promise, we will not harm one hair of your head."

Torture. They were going to torture him. No, not him; didn't they understand that he was Cleveland Brewster, Jr. and he was rich and well-educated? He began to shiver in sheer terror. With a strangled cry, Cleve broke free, turned and ran, but the warriors chased him down, grabbed him, and threw him on the ground.

"Someone build a fire," Coyote said, "I think our captive is cold."

Back at Milk Creek, Wannie worked with Doc to ration out the water. If they didn't get reinforcements soon, they would run out. She'd insisted Keso lie down and rest a moment, telling him he would be needed to man the barricades at dawn when the Utes would certainly attack them again. She looked out toward the darkness. Sound carried a long way out here and it had been very quiet. The scout must have made it through the Ute lines. The Utes would be spread thin and with a little luck and riding a black horse that was strong and fast, the scout might get through and head for Fort Steele.

Abruptly, she heard a long, drawn-out scream. For a moment, as the sound echoed across the valley, she thought it was the most unearthly shriek of sheer horror she'd ever heard. She looked down at Keso. "Do you suppose—?"

The scream came again, long and tortured. "Oh, my God!" She looked down into Keso's eyes, recognition flashing through her brain. "Cleve! They've got Cleve! They're torturing him!"

She jumped up, intending to go over the barricade, run out there, do something, anything to stop that terrible screaming, but Keso caught her hand and pulled her down beside him. "Easy, honey, there isn't anything you can do."

She began to sob, putting her hands over her ears to block out the sound. "This is so terrible!"

"I know it is, Wannie," he said and held her close against his chest with his uninjured arm, "but remember, he brought it on himself. This is one time the poor devil's money isn't going to do him any good."

The screaming went on all night. The Utes had to be keeping him alive to amuse themselves until they were ready to attack the Milk Creek soldiers in the morning. No doubt they had dead warriors and weeping women up on the bluffs and they had to vent the anger that had been building all these years against unjust treatment. Finally, as the dawn turned lavender gray in the east, the screaming weakened and then finally faded away.

Wannie took a deep breath, listening, and breathed a sigh of relief. "Maybe—maybe they let him go."

Keso held her close. "Maybe they did. Now help me

get to the barricades in case they decide to attack again. I wish we had enough water for some coffee."

She let him lean on her, his good arm around her, and helped him over to the piled-up boxes of the barricade. He seemed a lot stronger now, except for the injured shoulder. "Keso, I promise when help gets here, I'll make a big pot of coffee and you can have all you want. Why, I'll bet that scout's almost there and we'll have reinforcements soon."

"Sure we will, honey," he said but his expression was grim and she knew he didn't believe it.

She heard a sound and looked out across the landscape. The sun was just coming up behind a rider as he galloped to the crest of the bluff. She recognized Coyote in his war paint on a fine, unusually marked paint horse—the horse Cleve had been riding, she realized suddenly.

The warrior was out of rifle range and he must know it, poised there against the rising sun, arrogantly shouting a challenge to the weary soldiers. A big knife gleamed in his waistband and he carried a war lance. The first rays of daylight reflected off the object that hung from that lance. The wind increased, blowing and moving Coyote's trophy so that it picked up the light through its silken strands.

Wannie put her hands over her mouth to keep from screaming as she suddenly recognized Cleveland Brewster, Jr.'s magnificent yellow hair.

TWENTY-SIX

Keso stared at the taunting brave in the distance. "Don't look, Wannie," he said. "Anybody got a 'Big Fifty'?"

A soldier put a high-powered buffalo gun in Keso's hands as Wannie buried her face in her skirt and sobbed. Not even that damned Cleve deserved such a fate. And it was awful for Wannie. Now Keso would keep the secret he'd figured out about Cleve's parentage forever; no one else need ever know.

He aimed carefully at the ugly Ute on the butte, still taunting them with Cleve's scalp. Coyote thought he was safely out of range, not counting on someone in this crowd having an old buffalo gun that could shoot such a long distance. Keso took good aim at Coyote's chest as the Ute waved the yellow hair at the soldiers. He seemed to be promising that their hair, too, would hang from his lance once the Utes overran them. Keso aimed very slowly and deliberately. He wouldn't get another chance like this once Coyote realized the range of this powerful rifle.

One thing was certain, Keso thought. He would save his very last bullet for Wannie. Rather than let her be taken by the warriors, he would put a gun behind her ear when she least expected it and put a bullet in her brain. One other thing was certain, Keso vowed. Coyote would never live to enjoy her.

Keso took aim and squeezed the trigger. The shot echoed on the still morning even as Coyote's chest seemed to explode. A look of total surprise was frozen forever on his ugly features as he dropped the lance and tumbled from the pinto horse.

Keso grunted with satisfaction and handed the gun back. "Thanks. There's one who won't give us any more trouble." He took Wannie in his arms, rocking her back and forth to soothe her as he would a terrified child. "It's all right, honey, it's all right."

She clung to him, trembling. All the security she had was in this man's arms. It always had been.

"Reinforcements will come," he told her.

She wasn't sure about that, but she had no more time for the luxury of terror. She took a deep breath, pulled herself together, and returned to caring for the wounded. It was going to be a long day.

It was just barely daylight when Wannie spotted riders coming at a gallop across the prairie. Oh God, the Utes are going to launch a full attack, maybe overrun us, she thought. But even as she opened her mouth to scream, she saw the blue of their uniforms and the brass buttons reflecting the light and their black faces. "Buffalo soldiers! Troopers coming in! Open the barricades quick!"

A cheer went up from the trapped men at the sight of the black cavalry galloping toward them and men ran to open a hole in the barricade. The Utes saw them, too, and laid down a withering barricade of bullets as they came on. Wannie was cheering, urging them on as they galloped through a deadly gauntlet of Ute shells. She hardly dared to hope, as she yelled encouragement. The weary, trapped men were cheering and the Ute fire increased. Suddenly they had made it all the way into the circle, dismounting as the Utes increased their fire and the weary survivors hurried to close the barricade.

The leader dismounted and saluted Captain Payne. "Captain Dodge and Company D of the Ninth Cavalry reporting for duty."

Captain Payne motioned him down behind the shelter of a supply wagon near Wannie and Keso. The other troopers dismounted and tried to put their horses behind protective boxes and bundles. "Glad to see you, Captain Dodge. How'd you know we were trapped here?"

"Didn't." He wiped the sweat from his face. "We'd been alerted that Meeker might need help and were on our way there when we heard all the gunfire." Captain Dodge looked around at the tired, ragged remnants of the command. "Who's in charge here?"

"I am," Captain Payne nodded, "Major Thornburgh's dead."

The other officer's eyes widened with alarm. "What's the situation at the White River Agency?"

"We can only guess," Keso said. "I doubt they need your help anymore. Where's the rest of your men?"

"This is all I've got—sorry."

Like the captain and Keso, Wannie looked around at the grinning black faces and did a mental count. Thirty-five? Thirty-six? That wasn't nearly enough.

Captain Payne's face fell as he realized how few black troopers there were. "Joe Rankin's on his way to Fort Steele for help. We've been pinned down so long, we don't even know how many days it's been."

"Today's October 2, I think," Captain Dodge said.

Could they have been here that long? Wannie tried to think but time had become a blur of death and gunpowder, sunsets and sunrises. "We're glad you came, Captain," she said.

"Hope we can help, miss." He touched the tip of his

hat brim with his fingers in a sort of salute. "My men are mighty brave, even if there aren't many of them. Maybe we can buy you some time."

The men all looked weary and glum. Wannie forced herself to smile, although she, too, was exhausted. Almost mechanically, she helped Doc with the growing number of wounded, handing out hardtack and a little water. They were taking their toll on the Utes, too, she thought. Here and there, up on the bluffs, a man threw up his hands and fell as a soldier's bullet found its mark. Wannie couldn't be glad. In her mind, she saw the sad, dark eyes of thin Ute women and children as they mourned their men. Two cultures in conflict. One had driven the other to reckless attack and now both sides would suffer.

She thought the day would never end and bring with it the cover of darkness. In the sunlight, the Ute marksmen picked off a soldier here and there although the black buffalo soldiers fought as bravely as any.

Once she paused as she passed Keso and gave him a hug. "I want you to know whatever happens, I love you."

He smiled up at her. "Do you realize that when we marry, your name will still be Evans?"

She laughed in spite of herself.

Keso looked up at the setting sun and then at Wannie. "Is there—is there any water at all, Wannie?"

She lowered her voice so that the others wouldn't hear. "No, Keso, I just gave the last of it to a dying man."

She could see by the expression in his dark eyes what he was thinking. Then he turned and looked out at the tiny creek two hundred yards across burned, bare ground from where the soldiers were forted up. "Keso, no! With that injured shoulder—"

"It's better," he assured her. "As soon as it gets dark, honey, someone has to go."

"Let the soldiers do it." She grabbed his arm and put her face against it. "Oh, please!"

"Wannie, honey," he whispered against her hair, "we may have to survive several more days until help gets here . . . if it ever gets here. We can't do it without water."

"I—I can't live if something happens to you."

"Yes, you can," he said and kissed the tip of her nose. "You may be carrying my son, Wannie, and I want that son, want him worse than anything you can imagine except you."

She closed her eyes, imagining that dark, handsome child. He'd be strong and tall like his daddy and then she'd want a little girl, too. "You're right—someone's got to go. I'm strong—I could do it."

"Uh-oh, brat, not you." He shook his head. "Just hold me a minute. When it's dark, someone's got to try for it."

A big black man crawled over to them, yellow stripes shining on his blue sleeve. "Hey, I heard what you're talkin' about. I'm Sergeant Henry Johnson, and I'm game."

"Sergeant," Keso said, "gather up all the canteens you can carry. As soon as it's dark, we'll go for water."

There wasn't any other answer and Wannie knew it. She prayed as she crawled from man to man and dreaded the coming of night.

The time she both welcomed and dreaded finally came; night descended over the desolate valley and the Utes settled in and stopped shooting. At least there would be no more men killed tonight, she thought . . . unless Keso and the black sergeant were spotted.

Her heart almost stopped beating as Keso kissed her

good-bye and gathered up a bunch of canteens. "I'll be back in a few minutes, honey."

"Be careful." It was such a stupid, inane thing to say, but she said it automatically.

He patted her absently, his mind obviously already on the task at hand. "Sergeant, you ready? Got the canteens?"

She heard an affirmative murmur from the soldier and the two crawled through the barricades. Wannie held her breath and leaned forward, willing them to make it. It was two hundred long yards across barren ground through the cold ashes of the brush fire the Utes had set the first day. It might as well be a million miles.

The moon came out and it seemed to light up the barren land bright as day, throwing the pair's distorted shadows across the ground as they crawled, dragging the canteens with them. Keso's wounded shoulder was making it difficult for him to move, but he pulled himself ahead on his elbows. At any moment, she expected a sniper up in the rocks to pick them off. The silence was so loud, she could hear her own tortured breathing as she watched. When a canteen clattered against a rock, it sounded as loud as a locomotive and she winced, thinking at any moment there would be a volley of shots from the buttes. Nothing.

The men had reached the creek now and she could only hope there was enough water in Milk Creek to fill the canteens. She wanted to shout at them to hurry up, but she dared not. Finally, after what seemed like hours, the pair turned and began to crawl back toward the camp in the darkness. Around her, the trapped soldiers watched intently. Like Wannie, she knew they were thinking of water. The soldiers might be able to survive and hold off the Utes until help could arrive, but they couldn't do it without water.

She watched the pair crawling toward the barricade,

expecting deadly rifle fire to shatter the night. There was no sound save the clank of canteens as the men crawled back toward the barricades. About the time Wannie was breathing a sigh of relief, the Utes seemed to discover the pair and opened up with a barrage of rifle fire. It seemed to be echoing around the men, zinging against the rocks.

Keso stumbled to his feet. "Come on, run!"

The sergeant needed no urging. In a half crouch, they ran toward the cheering soldiers, the canteens clanging wildly. Bullets flung up dust in the moonlight as the pair ran, but soldiers scrambled over the barricades, helping the heroes inside. A cheer went up: "Water! We've got water!"

Wannie hugged Keso. "I was so worried about you."

"Here," he said and shoved the canteens at her, "share this water among the wounded, but first have a drink yourself."

It was tempting, so tempting. But around her, wounded men were begging, so instead, she knelt by a wounded man. "Here, soldier, have a drink."

She held the canteen to his lips and he drank thirstily. Not until all the wounded had had a drink did she take a few sips for herself.

In the meantime, Keso was conferring with Captain Payne, Captain Dodge, and the lieutenants. She snuggled in close to Keso to listen.

"All we can do now is wait," Keso said.

Captain Dodge rubbed his mustache. "And maybe pray that the scout got through."

"He's riding my stallion," Keso said. "Spirit will get him there if any horse could."

Captain Payne appeared pale and weak. "It's a long way to Fort Steele and back."

Lieutenant Cherry said, "We've got water now—maybe we can hold out."

Wannie rested her head on Keso's chest, only half-listening to the talk. She would not think about dying, or Cleve's terrible fate. She would concentrate instead on how sweet life was and about spending the rest of her days with Keso and what a wonderful, long life it was going to be. She knew the next several days would be a grueling hell and she was right.

Wannie lost all track of time as she cared for the wounded and tried to organize food for these men. They used up the water and had to make another trip under withering fire. The buffalo soldiers had buried the dead in shallow graves but there was nothing to be done about the dead horses piled around the circle. In fact, the dead horses were providing the soldiers with protection just like the boxes and bales of blankets, but the stench was horrible. This must be what hell is like, she thought in a daze as she worked with Doc. Yet she also knew heaven each night when dusk fell and she settled into Keso's arms to sleep. His shoulder was beginning to heal and there were fewer new wounded each day. The Utes weren't shooting at them as much as they had been; maybe they were running low on ammunition.

Wannie felt dreadfully sorry for Cleve Brewster, but she knew he had brought his terrible fate on himself. One of the officers said he knew the Brewster family and would send a telegram as soon as possible; he promised to go see them when this was over and put Cleve in the best light possible.

Finally, on the morning of October 5, the sentries watching to the north suddenly came alert. "Riders coming! I see blue uniforms!"

Around them, soldiers set up a cheer.

Wannie and Keso ran to the barricades, straining their eyes to look toward the north. Sure enough, a column of cavalry was riding over the hill.

Keso held her against him, tousling her hair. "We made it, honey, we made it." His voice was ragged with emotion.

Wannie wept unashamedly, hugging him as he kissed the tears from her cheeks. "Oh, Keso, I love you!"

Within minutes, a large command rode into the encampment, but there was little rifle fire from the buttes. There had been less and less shooting the last several days.

Keso blinked. "The Utes have been slipping away a few at a time and when they saw the reinforcements coming, the remainder scattered. That old warrior must have made it to Chief Ouray after all!"

The officer led his troops in, dismounted, and saluted the two Captains. "Colonel Merritt and the Fifth Cavalry at your service. Good Lord, what's happened here? It's a miracle anyone's alive."

Wannie stumbled forward, her voice breaking. "Colonel, Doc and I have lots of wounded. Do you have some coffee for them?"

His face seemed to soften as he looked at her. "Young lady, you sit down and my men will make gallons of hot coffee and soup for you and these men. I'd say you've earned it."

Wannie put her face in her hands and wept then; wept for all the dead and wounded on both sides. The army had suffered fourteen dead, forty-four wounded. There would never be any way to know how many dead or wounded Utes had been carried away by grieving relatives.

Keso sat down beside her and hugged her to him as the reinforcements hurried to take charge and provide food and medicine. "So the scout made it through?"

"Sure did," Rankin called out as he rode up, "and look, young fella, I brought your horse back. That's some animal."

"Spirit!" They both ran to greet the weary stallion and old Blue nickered a welcome to his stablemate.

Colonel Merritt took charge, complimenting the survivors on their bravery. "I'll be riding to the White River Agency next. I expect we'll find Meeker and the others dead."

Keso nodded. "Afraid so. The Utes have my sympathy."

"A brave enemy," Merritt agreed. "You two are finished here—get a plate of hot food. Then you can ride along with my column if you wish."

Wannie sipped her coffee and smiled at Keso. "Thanks, Colonel, but we're headed home."

Wearing a fresh bandage, Keso looked stronger as he teased, "You sure about that, Wannie? I still don't know which fork to use—I might embarrass a fancy, educated girl."

"Never," she declared.

Finally, the couple mounted Spirit and Blue and headed east into the Rockies toward home, riding at a leisurely pace because of the tired horses and Keso's shoulder.

They hadn't gone but a few miles when a rider rode out of the woods, blocking their path. It was Ouray.

They reined in, wondering why he came since he rode alone. "I wanted you to know, my son, that I gave orders for my warriors to withdraw."

"Thank you, my father."

Ouray tried to speak, but could not for a long moment. Finally, he swallowed hard. "At least, I have found you. That sweetens what is going to be a bitter time for me as the soldiers use this attack to take action."

"I am sorry," Keso said. "We both tried, but sometimes brave hearts are not enough. I will ask my other father to speak for the Utes to those in Denver and Washington."

Ouray leaned on his saddlehorn and Keso saw that the man was ill. "I envy your other father—he is good. This is your *piwan?*" He looked at Wannie.

Wannie said, "Yes, I'm his woman."

Ouray looked satisfied. "Then my bloodline continues. Do not forget your heritage, my son."

"I will bring your grandsons to see you," Keso said.

The chief shook his head. "No, I am dying, but I must live long enough to help my people. I was too late to stop this attack or what happened at the agency, but I will get the women and children released. The whites finally pushed my peaceful people too far."

"And now they will take your land," Keso said. "Someday, maybe they will realize how great a man you were. Know that I will often think of you." Keso put out his hand and the two shook solemnly.

Then Chief Ouray turned and rode back through the forest and disappeared. They watched him go.

"Oh, Keso," she whispered and wiped her eyes, "do you think the people of this state will ever realize the injustice they have done the Utes?"

"Some of them will and be ashamed. Maybe someday, justice will be done. Until then, Cherokee knows people in government and he and I together will do what we can."

The pair rode on to the Evans cabin.

It was evening at Steel Manor. Cleveland Brewster had just fired "that trashy Maureen," seeing her as a threat to young Cleve's fashionable marriage. He frowned at his wife as they sat in the library, wondering when they would hear from their son. Cleve was the only thing that made his life worth while. Cleveland hoped he outlived Bertha. As she died, it would be his revenge to lean over and whisper in her ear about how much he hated her and how many, many times he'd been unfaithful to her; that he'd only stayed because she had finally given him a son. And such a fine son! Blood will tell.

The doorbell rang and he heard old Jeeves going to answer it. "Now, who could that be this evening?"

Bertha looked at him a long moment, knowing he had never loved her, that he'd married her for her money. Long ago, when she hadn't conceived, she had realized he was going to abandon her.

In desperation, she'd hoped that another man might be able to impregnate her. Bertha had chosen a man who looked enough like Cleveland to pass his child off as a Brewster. She hoped she outlived Cleveland. If she did, she would have her revenge when she leaned over and whispered in the dying man's ear that the son he idolized was not his, but the stable master's, Ian O'Hearn's.

Old Jeeves came into the library, his face grim. "It's a telegram about young Cleve."

She didn't need to ask; she knew. Vengeance is mine, saith the Lord, and it was waiting for them both in that telegram.

Wannie's eyes teared up as she and Keso approached home in the dusk of the crisp October evening. Smoke curled out of the chimney and the dogs began to bark. Over in the pasture, her bay filly raised her head and nickered.

"Look, Keso, it's Dancer. She made it home after all!"

Home, she thought. Yes, this is where I belong and with this man. Oh, it was so good to be here.

Silver ran out onto the porch, calling back over her shoulder, "Cherokee, it's them! It's them!"

Spirit and Blue seemed to sniff the crisp autumn air and know they were home as they nickered and hurried their steps.

Wannie and Keso dismounted and the four of them were hugging and crying, with everyone talking at once.

"You two really had us worried," Silver said as she wiped her eyes, "when Dancer came home without you."

"It's a long story," Wannie said.

"Keso, you're hurt," Cherokee exclaimed.

"I'm okay," Keso said, "and we'll tell you everything that's happened."

"I just pulled a roasted haunch of deer out of the oven," Silver said, "and there's hot berry pie."

The four of them went inside, laughing and talking at the same time.

"Oh, by the way," Wannie said as she held up her left hand so the light gleamed on the silver ring, "Keso and I are getting married and he's going to build us a house up at Waanibe."

"Well, finally!" Cherokee said, obviously relieved. "It's going to be a great winter and a wonderful spring."

They talked about everything and later, Wannie and Keso went out on the porch alone to watch the sun set over the Rockies.

She leaned her head against his shoulder. "I didn't know I could be so happy. *Pour toujours,* my darling."

"I knew you were mine the night Cherokee put you up on that horse behind me and we all rode out of Denver. It just took you awhile to realize it." He took her in his arms and kissed her with a kiss that held a promise: he would love her and only her. Always.

EPILOGUE

True to his word, Chief Ouray forced the hostile Utes to give up their captives. All three women had been raped. Persune, a warrior who claimed Josie Meeker had fallen in love with him, did not want to return her, but Ouray insisted. Josie wrote a book: *Brave Miss Meeker's Captivity!*, and lectured about her ordeal. She and her mother were destitute until Josie was given a job in Washington, D.C. in the Interior Department. Eventually, the government awarded the Meekers damages to be paid out of the Utes' government allotments. Josie died of pneumonia four days after Christmas, 1882. She is buried beside her parents in Linn Grove Cemetery in Greeley, Colorado.

In the final analysis, the Ute outbreak was also a story of three men: Major Thornburgh, Nathan Meeker, and Chief Ouray; all were dedicated to their duty, yet failed in their goals, and died tragically and too soon.

Major Thornburgh received his Medal of Honor posthumously and was given a hero's funeral in Omaha with General Crook and other important people in attendance. It was said there was not a dry eye in the huge crowd as the tiny casket of the Thornburghs' Centennial baby was placed on top of his father's as it was lowered into the grave at Prospect Hill Cemetery.

Nathan Meeker saw himself as a savior and a reformer

of backward savages who should be forced to walk the white man's road. When the Utes reached the breaking point, he died in a most inglorious manner, and is buried in the family plot in the Linn Grove Cemetery.

Chief Ouray, the Arrow, had fought a losing battle to mediate a successful compromise between encroaching civilization and the Utes' ancient ways. He would never leave his beloved mountains, dying less than a year after the Milk Creek tragedy. Some think he held onto life almost by sheer will power against his terminal Bright's disease, so that he might make the best deal possible for his beloved people. At least they would not be sent to faraway Indian Territory. Ouray was approximately 47 years old when he died in August of 1880. His followers buried him in a simple grave at Ignacio. In the dome of the capitol building in Denver, there are sixteen stained glass portraits of those people influential in Colorado's history. The only Native American among them is Ouray.

If this is a tale of three men, it is also a tale of three widows who lived on into the next century, lonely, bereaved, and bitter.

The major's beautiful young widow, Lida Clarke Thornburgh, was only 27 years old at the time of his death. She never remarried and hated Indians all her days. She died in Manhattan, Kansas, in 1930.

Elderly Arvilla Meeker never really recovered from her ordeal and her husband's violent death. She lived with her son, Ralph, and died of senility in 1905.

Chief Ouray's widow, Chipeta, was so bitter at the betrayal of the Utes that she shed all the conveniences and fancy trappings of white civilization and returned to the ancient ways. In her old age she went blind, but lived on until 1924.

And what of all the other players in this drama?

Twelve rank and file military heroes received Medals

of Honor or Certificates of Merit for this battle, although Congress would single out Major Thornburgh, Captain Dodge, and Captain Payne for gallantry.

Captain Payne survived both the Nez Perce and the Ute war, but his health became poor after Milk Creek. He retired from active service in 1886 and died in 1895.

Lieutenant Cherry survived the Ute fight only to be killed by a drunken soldier in a freak shooting incident in Nebraska in 1881.

The black buffalo soldier, Sergeant Henry Johnson, who crawled out under heavy fire to bring water to the wounded, received a Medal of Honor. The great Western artist, Frederic Remington, immortalized the bravery of the black troops at the Milk Creek fight with a sketch for the October, 1891, issue of *Century* Magazine entitled "Captain Dodge's Colored Troopers to the Rescue."

Joe Rankin, the Paul Revere of Carbon County and the Ute War, enjoyed his status as a local hero and was eventually appointed U.S. Marshal for Wyoming by President Benjamin Harrison.

The Utes got the worst of it, as was expected, but only a few people of conscience spoke up to say this peaceful tribe had been pushed and tormented beyond the breaking point, or even mentioned how they had scouted for their white friends against the enemy Sioux. An inquiry was held, but the three white women could not identify which warriors had killed Nathan Meeker and the others, so only one of them, Douglas, served any time in the federal prison at Fort Leavenworth— without benefit of trial. Finally, the government released him to return to the miserable new reservation. No one pressed rape charges because the white women in that Victorian time would not testify; it was too degrading and humiliating.

In September of 1881, the well-known cavalry officer

General MacKenzie and his troops were ordered to force 1500 bewildered Utes off their twelve million acres and across 350 desolate miles at gunpoint to a grim Utah reservation that measured only 270 square miles.

Other soldiers had to hold back eager white settlers and prospectors until the Utes were crossing the border. Then the greedy whites poured across the Utes' land, staking claims and homesteads. *The Utes must go!* had been their battle cry and now the Utes were gone.

Many years later, the Utes finally had their revenge. In the so-called Ute War of 1946-1950, the Utes won a court settlement of $31.7 million for land the government had taken. It was not enough; no amount of money would compensate for the indignities and injustices they had suffered.

In western Colorado, there is a mountain known today as the Sleeping Ute. Seen just at dusk, it appears to be a giant stretched out in slumber, his massive stone arms folded across his great chest, his war bonnet trailing off into granite slopes. When the pale purple shadows of evening touch the mountain's rocky ledges, the outline of the great stone man silhouetted against the sunset seems to come alive, almost seems to breathe.

Local legend says that someday, the Sleeping Ute will awaken from his long, long slumber, stretch his mighty arms and yawn, then rise, the rumble shaking the whole earth. Every time it thunders, small, dark children hold their breath in anticipation and pause to listen, wondering if the moment has arrived.

The Utes say that on the day that the giant ends his slumber, he will lead the downtrodden Native Americans and once again, things will be as they were long, long ago before the white man came. The air will be pure and clean, the land alive with deer and running buffalo, and as far as one can see, there will be no white men; there will be only Indians, rolling prairie, and snow-topped peaks.

The Utes watch their mountain and wait patiently for that day . . .

TO MY READERS

For those of you who are wondering, yes, there really is a mountain called the Sleeping Ute. It's located near the town of Cortez, in southwestern Colorado where there's a tiny Ute reservation. I've been there several times checking to see if the sleeping giant has stirred.

The story about Ouray's kidnapped son is part of Ute legend. Everyone agrees that the child was stolen by the enemy Cheyenne. They disagree on whether he was ever returned. However, even those who say he was say the story had an unhappy ending. The boy thought of himself as Cheyenne and would have nothing to do with what he considered an enemy tribe.

Alferd (no, it's not Alfred) Packer, the "Colorado Cannibal," was first condemned to death and finally had his sentence reduced to serving time in prison for eating five of his fellow hunters near Lake City. Released from prison, he lived quietly until his death in 1907, and is buried in Littleton. It is a legend that the judge who sentenced him said: "Packer, ye man-eatin' son of a bitch, they was seven dimmycrats in Hinsdale County, and ye et five of 'em, God damn ye! I Sentence ye to be hanged by the neck until ye're dead, dead, dead . . . as a warnin' agin' reducin' the dimmycrat population in this state." I'm not sure whether anyone really knew the victims' political parties.

When the students at the University of Colorado were

allowed to choose a name for a new dining hall, the name that won was the Alferd E. Packer Grill.

My characters—Keso, Wannie, Cherokee, Silver, Coyote, Cleve, and all the Brewsters—are fiction. *WARRIOR'S PRIZE* is actually a sequel to *QUICKSILVER PASSION*, Silver and Cherokee's love story. Yes, there really is a mountain in Colorado named Mt. Silver Heels and how it got its name is that state's most beloved legend.

When Mr. Brewster mentioned his nephew, Captain Lexington B. Radley, who went missing during the 1873 Massacre Canyon fight in Nebraska, that was my 1996 book, *TIMELESS WARRIOR*, a time travel Indian romance.

The novel you hold in your hands is #15 of my long, long romantic saga called "The Panorama of the Old West." Each is written to stand alone, but if you want to read them all, some are still available. Check with Zebra Books or your local store to see what can be ordered. No, I'm sorry, but I don't have extra copies.

If you'll send me a #10 stamped, self-addressed envelope, I'll send you a newsletter and an autographed oversized bookmark that lists all fifteen and explains how the stories connect. To those outside the U.S. please ask your post office for postal vouchers that I can exchange for proper postage since I am not allowed to use foreign stamps. Address: Georgina Gentry, P.O. Box 162, Edmond, OK 73083-0162.

In writing this book, I spent many hours in Denver's marvelous Western history collection and several days walking the Milk Creek battle site where Major Thornburgh was killed. This site is still almost as remote and unchanged as it was in 1879. If you'd like to walk the ground yourself, it is in northwestern Colorado, approximately 19 miles northeast of the town of Meeker. For many years, there has been a pyramid-shaped monument at the site dedicated to the fallen soldiers. In 1993, the Utes finally erected their own large monument explaining their side of the story.

While you're in Meeker, you might want to stop at the museum and see the actual plow that destroyed the Utes' racetrack and so began the uprising. The plow is on display there, although the State Historical Society sometimes borrows it to display elsewhere.

You may also drive out to see the valley where the White River Agency once stood and Nathan Meeker and his men were killed. It's approximately two miles south of that town. There's a monument out in the middle of the field where they still grow crops. Tractors were plowing up the soil and it all seemed quite peaceful the day I visited; cars passing by on the highway seemed unaware that anything momentous had ever occurred there.

Western Colorado is one of my favorite areas and I highly recommend it to tourists. The San Juan Mountains were taken away from the Utes years earlier and have produced more than 200 million dollars' worth of precious metals. One of the prospectors who got rich was Tom Walsh. He later bought his daughter, Evalyn, the world's most famous and coveted gem. You may not recognize the Walshes by name, but you have certainly heard of the jewel, the famous Hope diamond. That priceless, giant diamond is on display at the Smithsonian Institution in Washington, D.C.

Although I read dozens of research books before writing this novel, I'll list just a few for those of you who would like to do further reading on the Ute Indian War. Many of these are available at your public library:

THE LAST WAR TRAIL—*The Utes and the Settlement of Colorado*, by Robert Emmitt, University of Oklahoma Press.

MASSACRE: The Tragedy at White River, by Marshall Sprague, University of Nebraska Press.

CHIEF OF THE UTES, by P. David Smith, Wayfinder Press, Ridgway, CO.
PEOPLE OF THE SHINING MOUNTAINS, by Charles S. March, Pruett Publishing Co., Boulder, CO.

So what story will I write next? A number of you have written to ask that I do another romance about a white girl carried off by a handsome Indian brave. I also heard from readers who were intrigued by the tragic Cheyenne dog soldier, Two Arrows, who played a small part in my 1995 novel, *SONG OF THE WARRIOR,* and asked if I would tell his story.

Two Arrows is the hero of my next novel, tentatively scheduled for late 1997 or early 1998. It is based on an 1878 true incident in Cheyenne history that began right here in Oklahoma. The white heroine is Glory Halstead and she's engaged to a cavalry officer. That officer and Two Arrows hate each other. Is it passion or revenge that causes Two Arrows to kidnap the captain's lady? And what will Glory do when she finally has to choose between the pair?

Come along and share the passion and adventure as we ride with the Cheyenne on their last great journey. That handsome warrior will be waiting for you between the pages of my next romance . . .

Pour Toujours,

Georgina Gentry

YOU WON'T WANT TO READ
JUST ONE—KATHERINE STONE

ROOMMATES (0-8217-5206-5, $6.99/$7.99)
No one could have prepared Carrie for the monumental changes she would face when she met her new circle of friends at Stanford University. Once their lives intertwined and became woven into the tapestry of the times, they would never be the same.

TWINS (0-8217-5207-3, $6.99/$7.99)
Brook and Melanie Chandler were so different, it was hard to believe they were sisters. One was a dark, serious, ambitious New York attorney; the other, a golden, glamourous, sophisticated supermodel. But they were more than sisters—they were twins and more alike than even they knew . . .

THE CARLTON CLUB (0-8217-5204-9, $6.99/$7.99)
It was the place to see and be seen, the only place to be. And for those who frequented the playground of the very rich, it was a way of life. Mark, Kathleen, Leslie and Janet—they worked together, played together, and loved together, all behind exclusive gates of the *Carlton Club*.

Available wherever paperbacks are sold, or order direct from the Publisher. Send cover price plus 50¢ per copy for mailing and handling to Penguin USA, P.O. Box 999, c/o Dept. 17109, Bergenfield, NJ 07621. Residents of New York and Tennessee must include sales tax. DO NOT SEND CASH.

WILLIAM W. JOHNSTONE
THE PREACHER SERIES

ABSAROKA AMBUSH   (0-8217-5538-2, $4.99/6.50)

BLACKFOOT MESSIAH (#7)   (0-8217-5232-4, $4.99/$5.99)

THE FIRST MOUNTAIN MAN   (0-8217-5510-2, $4.99/$6.50)

THE FIRST MOUNTAIN MAN: (0-8217-5511-0, $4.99/$6.50)
BLOOD ON THE DIVIDE

Available wherever paperbacks are sold, or order direct from the Publisher. Send cover price plus 50¢ per copy for mailing and handling to Penguin USA, P.O. Box 999, c/o Dept. 17109, Bergenfield, NJ 07621. Residents of New York and Tennessee must include sales tax. DO NOT SEND CASH.

ROMANCE FROM FERN MICHAELS

DEAR EMILY   (0-8217-4952-8, $5.99)

WISH LIST   (0-8217-5228-6, $6.99)

AND IN HARDCOVER:

VEGAS RICH   (1-57566-057-1, $25.00)